PAUL JENNINGS'
WEIRDEST STORIES

ALSO BY PAUL JENNINGS

Unreal!
Unbelievable!
Quirky Tails
Uncanny!
Unbearable!
Unmentionable!
Undone!
Uncovered!
Unseen!

Tongue-Tied!

Paul Jennings' Funniest Stories
Paul Jennings' Spookiest Stories
Paul Jennings' Trickiest Stories
Paul Jennings' Weirdest Stories

The Cabbage Patch series
(illustrated by Craig Smith)

The Gizmo series
(illustrated by Keith McEwan)

The *Singenpoo* series
(illustrated by Keith McEwan)

Wicked! (series) and *Deadly!* (series)
(with Morris Gleitzman)

Duck for Cover
Freeze a Crowd
Spooner or Later
Spit it Out
(with Terry Denton and Ted Greenwood)

Round the Twist
Sucked In . . .
(illustrated by Terry Denton)

For adults

The Reading Bug
    . . . and how you can help your child to catch it.

For beginners

The *Rascal* series

Novel

How Hedley Hopkins Did a Dare . . .
The Nest

More information about Paul and his books can be found at
www.pauljennings.com.au and **puffin.com.au**

PAUL JENNINGS'
WEIRDEST STORIES

VIKING
an imprint of
PENGUIN BOOKS

VIKING

Published by the Penguin Group
Penguin Group (Australia)
707 Collins Street, Melbourne, Victoria 3008, Australia
(a division of Penguin Australia Pty Ltd)
Penguin Group (USA) Inc.
375 Hudson Street, New York, New York 10014, USA
Penguin Group (Canada)
90 Eglinton Avenue East, Suite 700, Toronto ON M4P 2Y3, Canada
(a division of Penguin Canada Books Inc.)
Penguin Books Ltd
80 Strand, London WC2R 0RL, England
Penguin Ireland
25 St Stephen's Green, Dublin 2, Ireland
(a division of Penguin Books Ltd)
Penguin Books India Pvt Ltd
11, Community Centre, Panchsheel Park, New Delhi-110 017, India
Penguin Group (NZ)
67 Apollo Drive, Rosedale, Auckland 0632, New Zealand
(a division of Penguin New Zealand Pty Ltd)
Penguin Books (South Africa) (Pty) Ltd
Rosebank Office Park, Block D, 181 Jan Smuts Avenue, Parktown North, Johannesburg 2196, South Africa
Penguin (Beijing) Ltd
7F, Tower B, Jiaming Center, 27 East Third Ring Road North, Chaoyang District, Beijing 100020, China

Penguin Books Ltd, Registered Offices: 80 Strand, London WC2R 0RL, England

Individual stories Copyright © Lockley Lodge Pty Ltd
First published by Penguin Books Australia Ltd
The Strap-Box Flyer from *Unreal!*, 1985
Snookle, The Busker, Souperman, and *Pink Bow-Tie* from *Unbelievable!*, 1987
Greensleeves, On the Bottom, Frozen Stiff, Mousechap and *Cracking Up* from *Uncanny!*, 1988
Only Gift from *Unbearable*, 1990
The Mouth Organ, Ice Maiden and *Birdman* from *Unmentionable!*, 1991
Noseweed, Thought Full, What a Woman and *Wake Up to Yourself* from *Undone!*, 1991
Round the Bend from *Unseen!*, 1998
Lennie Lighthouse, Spot the Dog and *Hailstone Bugs* from *Tongue Tied!*, 2002

This collection published by Penguin Group (Australia), 2006

18 17 16 15 14 13 12 11 10 9

This collection Copyright © Lockley Lodge Pty Ltd, 2006
Illustrations Copyright © Bob Lea, 2006

The moral right of the author and illustrator has been asserted.

Text and cover design by Adam Laszczuk © Penguin Group (Australia), 2006
Cover illustrations by Bob Lea
Typeset by Midland Typesetters, Australia
Printed in Australia by McPherson's Printing Group, Maryborough, Victoria

National Library of Australia
Cataloguing-in-Publication data:

Jennings, Paul, 1943– .
Paul Jennings' weirdest stories.
ISBN 978 0 67007 064 0.
1. Short stories, Australian. I. Title.

823.3

penguin.com.au

Contents

Lennie Lighthouse 1
Tonsil Eye 'Tis 26
Noseweed 36
The Mouth Organ 54
Greensleeves 74
On the Bottom 92
Snookle 104
Thought Full 111
What a Woman 130
No is Yes 143
The Busker 161
Ice Maiden 183
Only Gilt 192
Frozen Stiff 206
Round the Bend 231
Spot the Dog 244
Mousechap 260
Hailstone Bugs 273
The Strap Box Flyer 290
Souperman 301
Santa Claws 309
Cracking Up 321
Pink Bow-Tie 340
Unhappily Ever After 346
Wake Up to Yourself 353
Birdman 369

Lennie was catching moths.

With his mouth.

Boy it was funny. There he was, standing next to the river in the dark forest, with moths circling around his head. He looked like a little streetlight on a warm summer's night.

'Are you laughing, Ritcho?' he growled.

'No,' I said. 'Of course not. Haven't I kept your secret all these years? Aren't I your best mate? Would I laugh? Would I?'

I tried to choke back my chuckles. Every time he opened his mouth a bright yellow light flickered out from behind his lips.

'I told you to bring a torch,' he said.

'We don't need one when we've got you,' I answered.

Suddenly a moth flew into his mouth and he began to splutter and cough. I just couldn't help letting out a laugh.

'Right,' said Lennie. 'You've had it.' He snapped his mouth closed and shut off the light. The forest was black and quiet. I couldn't see a thing.

'Where are ya, Lighthouse?' I said.

I soon found out. Lennie grabbed me around the neck from behind and pulled me down to the ground. We rolled and struggled and wrestled on the damp grass. It was a sort of half-serious fight. Half meaning it and half fun.

'Don't call me Lighthouse,' he growled from behind his flashing teeth.

I managed to roll him over and shoved his arm up behind his back.

'I've called you Lighthouse for years,' I said.

Lennie spat out some dirt. 'Yeah, but one day someone is going to find out why.'

'Nah,' I said, easing up on my grip. 'Not as long as you keep your mouth shut.'

I started to laugh again. It was a good joke. Quick as a flash Lennie squirmed around and was on top of me. He sat on my chest and pinned my elbows down with his knees.

'Promise,' he said.

'No way, Lighthouse,' I said. 'I can't change. And neither can you. Face it. You're the only person in the world who has teeth that shine in the dark.'

'Right,' said Lennie. 'You asked for it.'

He put his face down close to mine and bared his bright, bright teeth. The strong ray of light glared right into my pupils. I shut my eyes but the beam was so strong I could see it through my eyelids. It was like looking into the sun.

'Torture,' I yelled. 'That's not fair.'

'Promise,' he grunted, 'not to call me Lighthouse ever again.'

'Okay, okay,' I yelled. 'Just let me up.'

We both scrambled to our feet.

'Let's go,' I said. 'The fish have gone off the bite.' We walked over to the river and wound in our fishing lines. I didn't think I should ask Lennie to catch any more moths for bait. Not that night anyway.

We walked silently towards home. Lennie lived with me and my gran. We were more like brothers than mates. He could take a joke so I decided to stir him up a bit more.

'Hey, Lighthouse,' I said. 'I had my fingers crossed when I made that promise. So it doesn't count.'

'You ratbag,' he yelled.

We laughed like crazy devils as he chased me through the inky bush towards home.

2

I should probably start at the beginning. And tell you the whole story about Lennie. Some of it I know because I was there. But the early bit I heard from a nurse many years later. She knew Lennie when he first showed up at the babies' home. This was some time ago. In the days when they still had orphanages.

It was late at night and all was quiet. Ten little babies were fast asleep in their cots. There were only two people looking after them. A nurse with kind eyes and a very wise matron.

'What's that?' said the nurse, peering out into the darkness. 'I can see something down by the gate.'

'And I think I know what it is,' said Matron.

The nurse went outside. A few minutes later she came back pushing a pram.

Matron pulled back the blankets and peered inside. 'Oh,' she said. 'Isn't she beautiful?'

'I think it's a boy,' said the nurse. 'Can't be more than a day old.'

'Look, there's something else,' said Matron. She pulled out the wooden figure of a carved monkey. It was about as big as a milk carton and highly polished. The monkey had a mischievous expression on its face. Matron turned it upside down. On the bottom were written two words, *For Lennie.*

'Well, we know what to call him,' said Matron. 'But I guess we'll never find out who the mother is.'

The nurse took the monkey and felt over it with her fingers. 'I've seen one of these before,' she said. 'I think they have secret drawers to hide things in.' She looked and looked but found nothing. 'No,' she said. 'I must have been mistaken.'

Just then the baby began to whimper.

'He's hungry,' said Matron. She rushed off to warm up a bottle of baby's milk. Lennie opened his eyes.

Matron hurried back and pushed the teat between Lennie's lips. He sucked away happily at the milk. Soon there was none left. Matron began to gently pull the teat out of his mouth.

Chomp.

'Aagh,' screamed Matron. She jumped backwards and fell off her chair.

'What?' yelled the nurse.

'He's bitten off the teat.' She held up the bottle and the nurse gasped. The tip of the rubber teat had been completely sliced off. Little Lennie spat out a chewy bit of rubber and the tip of the teat bounced across the floor.

Lennie began to cry. They both stared at him in amazement.

'It can't be,' said Matron.

'He's only a day old,' said the nurse. 'And he's got . . . he's got . . .'

'Teeth,' yelled Matron. 'Whopping big teeth. In all my years as a nurse I have never seen a newborn baby with teeth that size.'

3

Well, everybody in the babies' home loved Lennie. The nurses thought he was a bit strange with his huge teeth. They seemed to be too big for his mouth. And what with his small baby's head he looked a little bit like a horse when he laughed.

And he laughed a fair bit.

Until adoption time.

People who wanted to adopt new babies would come to the babies' home. And check out all the tiny tots to see if they liked them.

The first people to come pulled up in a really flash car.

'We want a lovely baby,' said the woman with a cold smile.

'All our babies are lovely,' said the nurse.

Little Lennie smiled.

'Oh,' said the woman staring into the bassinet in shock. 'Look at those huge teeth. He'll never do. What else have you got?'

'Nothing,' said Matron. 'I don't think any of our babies would suit you.'

After that Lennie seemed to take a dislike to everyone who came in to adopt a baby. It was like his feelings were hurt.

There was the butcher's wife. She tickled Lennie under the chin.

'Cootchie coo, cootchie coo,' she said.

Suddenly she screamed out.

'Ow.'

Lennie had bitten her finger. Hard. She and her husband moved on without a word.

After that, people were warned to keep their hands out of Lennie's cot.

Time after time people would look at Lennie. Some wanted to take him home. Until he opened his mouth and showed those huge, huge teeth.

One young couple, a pilot and her husband, actually took Lennie home, even though he didn't seem to like them very much. They brought him back the next morning.

'Look,' said the pilot. 'He's totally wrecked it.'

Everyone stared down at the cane bassinet. Lennie had ripped it to pieces with his giant teeth.

'His teeth will seem smaller as his head grows,' said Matron. 'Give him another chance.'

'No way,' said the pilot's husband. 'We don't want Jack the Ripper.'

From then on Lennie rejected every person who wanted to adopt him. He chewed up dummies and spat them out. He chomped on wooden toys until only splinters were left. He bared his teeth and growled. He ripped blankets to shreds. He snapped like a dog at every person who came to look at him. The only toy he didn't bite was the wooden monkey.

He loved Matron. And he loved the nurse. But he could tell when people thought he was strange. And he gave them a hard time.

In the end he was three years old and still in the babies' home. No one had adopted him.

'It will be too late soon,' said Matron. 'Most people want newborn babies.'

Then one day Matron brought Alan and Shirley Dobson to see Lennie. 'I think we might have found the right parents,' she said happily. The nurse looked up and grinned.

She went and fetched Lennie and led him into the room by the hand. He looked at Shirley and gave a low growl, showing his teeth. Then he stared at Alan and gave an enormous grin.

'He's lovely,' said Alan. 'Just what we wanted.' He was peering down at little Lennie with a big smile. And an even bigger set of teeth. They were enormous. They were gigantic. The biggest teeth in the world.

Lennie opened his arms and tottered towards Alan. Then he stared lovingly at Shirley. She had normal teeth. But anyone could see that she loved Lennie already.

'Lubbly Lady,' said little Lennie. He had found some new parents at last.

He was adopted.

4

Lennie came to live on a farm next to me and Gran. It was way up in the mountains, miles from anywhere. There were no other neighbours, just the two farms. Actually, you could hardly call ours a farm. We had one cow and two pet sheep. Which was just as well because Gran had to get around on a walking frame and I had to do all the jobs.

The Dobsons were our neighbours. So Lennie and I grew up together. Sometimes he would stay the night. Or I would go over to his place. We were great mates.

We made tree-huts, chased the sheep and went exploring.

Then, when we were both about five years old and ready to go to school, something happened. Something strange. Shirley and Alan said I wasn't allowed to see Lennie at night. Even worse, they wouldn't let him come and sleep over with me. Lennie had to stay inside after dark.

In the evenings I would sit looking sadly down the hill to his place. I used to love those sleep-overs. Sometimes, when the Dobsons' house was dark, I would see a strange yellow light flickering behind the curtains.

Lennie and I both started school in the same year. Every day at half-past seven we waited for the school bus down by Gran's gate. It was forty kilometres to the school in Bairnsdale.

'Why can't ya come out after dark, Lennie?' I used to ask.

'Not allowed to say,' said Lennie.

That's how it went on for years and years. Until we were both eleven years old. Poor old Lennie. We could muck around all we liked in the day, but at night he always had to be home. He wasn't allowed to have much fun at all. He never went on school camps. For some reason he couldn't even go to the movies in Bairnsdale.

During the day everything was okay. We could run around the bush. Build our tree-huts. Fish. Muck around. But never after dark.

Then it happened. Lennie decided to tell me his secret.

'Leave your window open tonight, Ritcho,' he said. 'I'm coming over.'

I sat up waiting and waiting. No Lennie. Not a sign of him. I lay on the bed reading a book but I couldn't concentrate. Finally, around about midnight, Lennie climbed through the window.

'Well?' I said.

'I'm going to tell you a secret,' he said. 'But you have to promise never to tell anyone. Never.'

'You know me, mate,' I said. 'Would I let you down?'

He looked at me for quite a while. Then he said, 'Get a load of this.'

He walked over to the door and turned off the light.

All was dark.

'So?' I said.

Lennie suddenly opened his mouth. A huge beam of light flared out. His teeth shone like the headlights of a string of cars in a leaking tunnel. My eyes widened with shock. Then I started to laugh. I just couldn't help myself. It was so funny. Teeth that shone in the dark. I fell onto the bed shaking with laughter. I grabbed my sides, trying to stop the ache.

'It's not funny,' said Lennie.

I wiped away the tears and managed to control myself. 'What's happened to ya?' I yelled. 'Luminous toothpaste? Glowing paint? What, what, what?'

'Nah. Nothing like that,' said Lennie.

The room danced with shadows as he spoke. It was like being in a disco where flickering lights spatter the dancers with crazy colours. Weird.

'What then?' I squealed.

'They just grew,' said Lennie. 'When my first teeth fell out, the new ones glowed in the dark. Mum and Dad say I have to keep it a secret. They don't want anyone to know.'

I sat on the bed just thinking for a bit. I had to be careful what I said. Not too serious, not too light-hearted. I wanted to make him feel good.

Finally I said, 'I wish I had them.'

'You're crazy,' he said.

'No,' I said. 'Think about it. You could be famous. You could make big money. Be on TV. In the papers. You could go on the stage. There's big bucks in it. I can just see it. Lennie the Lighthouse, the man with the magic mouth.'

Lennie jumped on me and pinned me to the bed. 'I can just see it too,' he said. 'Ritcho the Rat. The boy with the big black eye.'

He raised a fist in a joking way and shook it in my face.

'Why not?' I asked.

'Mum and Dad say I'll be turned into a freak show.'

Right at that moment Gran's voice came through the door. 'Richard, turn that light off. It's late.'

Lennie shut his trap and jumped off me. The room was plunged into darkness. I could hear a sort of whimpering noise. Was he crying? Oh no, had I said the wrong thing? No. He was laughing. Everything was okay.

We sat there and talked for ages and ages. The room was illuminated by the weird flickering of Lennie's marvellous mouth. In the end Lennie climbed out of the window and headed for home. 'See you, Ritcho,' he said.

'See ya, Lighthouse,' I called after him.

The paddock outside was dark and I could see nothing. All was silent. Suddenly a bright yellow smile appeared, floating eerily and alone in the night air.

And then it was gone.

5

Now the next bit is sad, so I am going to get it over and done with quickly.

Lennie's parents died.

Alan and Shirley Dobson were killed in a car accident. I'm not going to tell you what he went through. It was terrible. It turned out that Alan and Shirley had no relatives in Australia. There was no one who could look after him. So after a lot of mucking around with social workers he was allowed to live with Gran and me.

Lennie was very sad for a long, long time. But he still managed to keep his teeth a secret. He wanted to obey the wishes of his dead parents. Gran found out but she never said a word.

Lennie had always known that he was adopted. It soon turned into the only thing he could think about.

'I like living with you and Gran,' he said sadly. 'But I want to find my first mum.' He was sitting on the top bunk in our room fiddling with his little wooden monkey. 'She left me this,' he said. 'When I was born. The day after tomorrow I'll be thirteen. I bet she would give me a present if she knew where I was.'

He stared down at the monkey. 'This could be a clue,' he said. 'It might help me to find my mum.'

'Show it to Gran,' I said. 'She might know.'

Lennie shook his head. No one was allowed to touch his precious monkey. Gran didn't even know he had it.

'She's very smart,' I said. 'She's been all over the world. She might be able to tell you where it comes from. You never know.'

Gran sat on the sofa and turned the grinning monkey over in her knobbly hands. 'I *have* seen one before,' she said. 'It comes from China.' She handed it back to Lennie. 'It's called a message monkey. But I don't know why.'

The next day Lennie did something unusual. He took the monkey to school. He messed around with it all the way to school on the bus. Then when we got to school he fiddled around with the monkey under the desk. 'Put that away, Lennie,' said the teacher.

'Yes, Mrs Richmond,' he said. Lennie put the monkey away but five minutes later he was at it again.

'Okay,' said Mrs Richmond. 'Once is enough. Give it

to me, Lennie. You can have it back after school.' She grabbed the monkey by the head.

'No,' yelled Lennie. 'You're not getting it.' He hung on to the monkey's legs and wouldn't let go.

'Really, Lennie,' said Mrs Richmond, trying to twist it out of his hands. 'Do as you're . . .'

Pop.

The monkey's head came off. Mrs Richmond went red in the face. 'I'm sorry, Lennie,' she said. 'I didn't mean to break it.'

But Lennie wasn't listening. He was too busy pulling a small roll of paper out of the monkey's insides. He unrolled it and quickly read what was there. His lips trembled. His eyes stared wildly. Suddenly he jumped to his feet and ran out of the class. The body of his precious monkey dropped to the floor – discarded like an unwanted toy.

'Come back,' yelled Mrs Richmond.

She was too late. He was into the school yard, over the fence and out of sight before she could move.

Without stopping to think I jumped to my feet, raced out of the door and belted down the street after him.

We were both going to be in big trouble. But what else could I do? We were mates.

6

I ran around the streets looking for Lennie.

'Lighthouse,' I yelled. 'Where are ya?'

There was no answer from the silent streets.

A little way off I heard the horn of the midday train. It was just about to leave for Melbourne. Something told me Lennie was on it. Don't ask me how I knew. I just did.

I raced down to the station just as the train was about to move. I jumped on and started to walk through the carriages. There he was, crouched down in a seat near the toilets.

I slid into the seat next to him. 'Lennie,' I said. 'What are you doing? Where are you going?'

He handed me the small piece of paper he had found in the monkey. I read it quickly.

My Dear Little Lennie,

I hope you will forgive me for leaving you in the babies' home. But I can't bring you up. I have big problems. I love you very much but I have to let you go. When you are older you will find this note in the monkey. If you want to meet me, go to a place called Donuts in the Basement in Swanston Street, Melbourne. I am going to wait for you on the 1st of May every year. That is your birthday. I will be there at ten in the morning. You will find me next to the donut machine. I will be wearing a black coat. I understand if you don't want to meet me.

Love,

Mum

'It's your birthday tomorrow,' I said.

Before he could say a thing Lennie jumped up. The ticket collector was coming.

'Quick,' he said. 'Into the dunny.'

We both squeezed into the tiny toilet and shut the door. 'Talk softly,' said Lennie. 'It's only meant for one.'

We stayed in there for ages and ages. At least forty minutes. Lennie told me how he had to get to the donut place to meet his mum. If she was still alive. He kept looking at the note as if it was the photo of a long-dead loved one.

'Hurry up in there,' came a loud voice. 'There's five people out here waiting. What are you doing? Hatching an egg?'

We opened the toilet door with red faces and went back to our seat. It was a country train and the conductor kept walking up and down checking tickets.

'How much money have you got?' said Lennie.

'Nothing,' I said. 'What about you?'

'Fifty cents,' he said.

'Tickets, boys,' said a loud voice.

The conductor was tall and tough-looking. I could tell that she was used to handling people trying to sneak a ride without paying. I was right.

'I know you've been hiding in the toilet,' she said. 'The oldest trick in the book.'

We both smiled weakly, trying to think up a good story.

At that very moment the train rushed into a tunnel. The whole carriage fell into darkness. Or should I say the whole carriage did not fall into darkness. Lennie's teeth shone brightly into the gloom. A mouth, all on its own, floating in the air. With a scary-looking grin.

'We haven't got tickets because...' said the row of flashing teeth.

'Aagh,' screamed the conductor. She fled down the aisle and disappeared.

The train sped out of the tunnel and Lennie's teeth returned to normal in the bright daylight. Other passengers turned and stared. They hadn't seen what happened and wanted to know what all the fuss was about.

Thirty seconds later the conductor returned with two railway men in uniform. 'No tickets,' she said loudly. 'And this one put on some sort of mask and scared the living daylights out of me.'

The men pulled us roughly out of our seats.

The train stopped at a tiny country station.

We were tossed out.

'Don't try that again,' yelled the conductor. 'I know your faces.'

7

We stared around as the train disappeared into the distance. The platform had one tiny shed with a verandah. There was no one around. Empty paddocks stretched off into the distance on every side. There was a small car park and an old stone bridge which climbed over the tracks to a dusty road on the other side.

Lennie looked at his watch. 'How will we get to Melbourne in time?' he groaned.

'There might be another train,' I said hopefully.

We were at the back of beyond. The whole world seemed filled with silence. The only sound was a far-off crow calling mournfully into the empty sky. I started to think about Gran. She would be worried.

The conductor had left a box beside the tracks. It was full of engine parts.

Minutes passed. Then hours. It began to grow dark.

'We could try walking,' I said.

'No,' said Lennie. 'We don't know how far it is to a town. Someone is going to come and pick up this box. They might give us a lift.'

He was right about someone coming.

It was well and truly dark when the sound of a motor joined the song of the chirping crickets. After a little while the lights of an old tractor came into view. It crossed the bridge and pulled up with the motor still running. A farmer with a grey beard and a battered hat jumped off and picked up the box.

'Excuse me, mister,' said Lennie's mouth out of the darkness. 'But could you give us a lift?'

'Oh my gawd, oh my gawd,' yelled the farmer.

'Terrible, terrible teeth. Mercy, mercy.' He dropped the box of parts noisily on to the platform.

All you could see of Lennie was his bright teeth. They seemed to be flying alone in the night air like a tiny flying saucer.

The farmer fled back to his tractor and roared up to the bridge. *Crash*. The front wheel hit the bridge wall sending a huge block of sandstone crashing on to the tracks below.

'Stop,' I yelled. 'Come back. Lennie won't hurt you.'

The tractor did a few wobbles and roared into the distance.

Another sound rumbled through the night. Distant – but coming closer. It was a train.

We peered down through the hole in the bridge wall. 'There's a huge block of stone down there,' I said. 'We have to move it. Otherwise the train will . . .'

'. . . crash!' screamed Lennie. He was already scrambling down the track.

'Wait for me,' I yelled.

We jumped on to the tracks and pushed and heaved until our eyes felt as if they were going to pop out of our heads. We just couldn't budge the block of stone. It was too heavy. The train was coming closer and closer. There was only a minute left.

Suddenly Lennie went belting down the track towards the train. He was waving his arms crazily.

And opening and shutting his mouth. Two long

flashes, one short and two more longs. sos. He was spelling out the emergency message with his marvellous mouth.

Lennie tripped. His face smashed down on to one of the iron rails. Quick as a flash he sprang to his feet and looked around with a wild expression. Something was wrong. Something was different. He had blood on his face.

'Oh, Lighthouse,' I shouted.

One of his teeth was missing. There was a big gap in the front.

But he still had plenty of light left. He flashed his message down the track running furiously towards the speeding train. A horn blared its warning.

The wheels of the train locked, sending out a shower of sparks. There was a terrible screech as the train skidded wildly along the tracks. And ground to a halt right in front of Lennie.

He had saved the train.

8

'Amazing,' said the train driver. 'I can hardly believe it. I *don't* believe it. Luminous teeth. Whatever next?'

We sat there in the cabin of the huge locomotive, staring along the tracks. Lennie kept his mouth firmly shut. He hadn't opened it once since the train stopped. The step of opening his mouth at night in public was just too much for him.

'You are heroes,' said the driver as he peered into the

darkness ahead. 'There are over a hundred people on this train. Tell me how you did it.'

I told him how we saved the train. And about the tremendous teeth of the boy sitting next to us. But not about Lennie's mother.

'It's a great story,' said the driver. 'But luminous teeth. Come off it. You sure have a good imagination.'

'No,' I said. 'It's true.'

'No it's not,' said the driver.

'Yes it is,' said Lennie, lighting up the cabin like a wild flashing disco.

Well, the driver just about went through the roof.

'Oh my godmother,' he said.

He didn't stop shaking for about ten minutes. After he'd settled down I told him the story of Lennie's mum and us going to meet her in the morning. Lennie was red in the face. It must have taken a lot of courage to say those first few words.

'I'd love to help you two boys,' said the driver. 'But I've got some bad news, I'm afraid.'

We both looked at him. 'Donuts in the Basement closed down years ago. They pulled it down.'

'What's there now?' said Lennie anxiously.

'A railway station,' he answered. 'An underground railway station.'

9

The train driver's name was Albert. He was a real nice

guy. When we reached Melbourne we rang up Gran from the station. At first she was relieved, then annoyed. But she said we could spend the night with Albert. He took us back to his place and agreed to wake us up well before ten o'clock in the morning.

It was a long night but finally the morning of Lennie's birthday dawned. There were no presents. But it didn't matter because there was only one thing he wanted.

Albert gave us a smile as we headed for Museum Station. 'I'm sorry I can't come with you to look for Lennie's mother, boys,' he said, 'but I have to work today.'

Lennie and I walked slowly along Swanston Street. We had never been to Melbourne before. There were trams and cars and trucks and noise everywhere. Huge buildings.

'I've never seen so many people in my life,' said Lennie slowly. He stared at the crowds rushing by. 'We're never going to find my mother. Not a chance.'

I had to agree with him. But I didn't say it out loud. 'There it is,' I said. 'Museum Station.'

After a bit of nervous mucking around we got up the courage to step onto the escalator. Neither of us had ever been on one. At first I wasn't sure how to do it. But Lennie just walked on as if he had been doing it all his life. He only had one thing on his mind. His mother. I took a teetering step and followed. Down we went, into the brightly lit station. Everything was white and glaring. Except the people's clothes.

'They are *all* wearing black,' groaned Lennie. 'We'd never recognise my mum even if she was here.'

There were hundreds of people milling around. Maybe thousands. We stood beside the escalator, staring down a flight of steps to the main platform below.

I looked at my watch. Two minutes to ten.

'There's not a donut machine anywhere,' I said.

Lennie blinked back the tears. 'She probably gave up years ago,' he said. 'When they pulled the donut shop down.'

A train stopped and another huge crowd spilled out of it. It was hopeless. Even if we had yelled out at the top of our voices or held up a sign, no one would have noticed us up there.

It was ten o'clock. Exactly.

I looked around desperately for help. Nearby was a bloke in overalls. An electrician working on some wires inside a box on the wall. There was a sign saying:

MAINS

STAFF ONLY

'Hey, mister,' I said.

He stood up and grinned. 'Yeah?' he said.

That's when I noticed it. A huge lever with the word POWER next to it. I quickly moved over to the box and shoved the lever up.

'Hey,' shrieked the electrician.

A great roar went up from the huge crowd as the whole station was plunged into darkness.

'Smile, Lennie,' I shouted. 'Smile like you never have in your life.'

Suddenly a brightly lit mouth appeared beside me. A row of shining teeth with one little gap in the front. His smile was floating all on its own in the air. A silence fell over the crowd.

'Look,' I shouted. 'Look down there, Lennie.'

There, far below, was another shining mouth, returning the smile and saying words which could not be heard. But you didn't have to be a lip-reader to see that they were saying, 'Lennie, Lennie. Oh, Lennie.'

Lennie's lips began to make their way down the stairs in little jumps. There was nothing to be seen but two brightly lit mouths rushing towards each other.

For a brief minute Lennie's mouth disappeared as his mother pulled his wet face into her chest.

The station lights came on and there was a wonderful sight. Mother and son together after all these years. A huge cheer went up from the crowd. They thought it was some sort of stunt.

I have to say I wiped away a few tears from my own eyes.

10

Well, everything turned out great. Lennie moved to the city to live with his mum. I miss him, but they both come up and stay with me and Gran in the holidays. We are all the best of friends.

Now you might say that this story is not true. But it is.

And I can prove it.

Every night I go to bed and turn off the light. Then I get out a book and read. I don't need the light on because of a little present that Lennie gave to me. I put it on the pillow and it shines up onto my book.

It is the tooth.

The whole tooth.

And nothing but the tooth.

Tonsil Eye 'tis

Good grief, I am gone. I have had it. That good-looking girl from next door has seen me pulling the hairs out of my nose. She thinks I am grotty. Now I will have to tell her the whole story because I can see by the look on her face that she is disgusted. I have already lost Tara, my girlfriend. I couldn't stand it if Jill got the wrong idea too.

'Listen, Jill. Don't look like that. There is a very good reason why I do it. You don't think I like pulling the hairs out of my nose, do you? It is very painful.'

Jill is not saying anything. She is just staring at me so I go on with the story. 'This little garden gnome business is only here because of my nose-hair pulling. You don't believe me? Well look at this.'

I take my hand off the new garden gnome's head and show her the eye that has grown on the end of my finger. I have never shown anyone this little eye before. I can see with it, which is a fairly unusual thing. When I am not making gnomes, I keep a glove on so that no one can see the eye. Jill's mouth is hanging open with surprise so I decide to tell her about the way the whole thing happened before she thinks I have gone crazy.

2

It all begins when my girlfriend Tara gives me a garden gnome for my fourteenth birthday. It is a horrible-looking garden gnome and it only has one eye. 'It's lovely,' I say to Tara. 'Just what I wanted. A little angry-looking garden gnome.'

It is angry looking, too. Its one and only eye glares at everyone as if its toenails are being pulled out. And its mouth is wide open like someone yelling out swear words at the footy. It is made out of cement but it is very realistic.

'I am so glad you like it,' says Tara in a dangerous voice. 'Because it cost me a lot of money.'

'I can see that,' I answer. 'Anyone can tell that it is a very special garden gnome. I know just the spot for it – down behind the garden shed.'

'Behind the garden shed,' yells Tara. 'You can't put it out in the rain. I don't think you like it.'

'I was only joking,' I say quickly. 'I will put it on the shelf where I can see it all the time.'

So that is how the garden gnome comes to be in my bedroom. Every morning and every night there it is, glaring at me. As the days go by it seems to look grumpier and grumpier.

After a while I find that I can't sleep at night. The

angry gnome gets into my dreams. I wake up at night and find that I can't stop staring at its horrible little face. I keep having a nightmare about being swallowed by it.

I turn the gnome around so that it faces the wall but this does not work either. I keep imagining that it is pulling faces. Finally, I can stand it no more. I grab the gnome by its silly little red hat and am just about to smash it to smithereens when I notice something strange. Inside its mouth, right at the back, is a tiny little face about half the size of a pea. It is stuck on the gnome's tonsils.

I think that whoever made this garden gnome has a strange sense of humour. I decide to remove the little face from the gnome's tonsils. I get a small hammer and a screwdriver and I start chipping away at the little face at the back of the gnome's throat. I feel a bit like a dentist. The gnome's mouth is wide open but I bet he would close it if he could.

After a couple of hits the little face flies off the gnome's tonsils and falls onto its tongue.

The next bit is hard to believe but it really does happen. The little round face rolls along the garden gnome's concrete tongue, onto its lips and flies through the air. It hits me full in the mouth. 'Ouch,' I yell at the top of my voice. 'That hurt.'

It is so painful that my eyes start to water. I am really mad now and I start searching around on the carpet for the little round face. It is nowhere to be seen. I search and search but I can't find it anywhere. My lips are still hurting and I have a funny, tickling feeling somewhere at the back of my throat.

'Right,' I yell at the gnome. 'You have had it.' I pick up the screwdriver and throw it as hard as I can. The point of the screwdriver hits the gnome on his one and only eye and knocks it clean out of his face. Now the gnome has no eyes at all. It is lucky it is only made out of concrete or it would be a very unhappy gnome.

I look around the floor for the eye but I can't find that either. This is when I notice that one of my fingers on my right hand is feeling sore.

3

What happens next is really weird. I find myself looking up at my own face. It is just as if I am lying on the carpet looking up at myself. I am looking down and up at the same time. My head starts to swim. I feel I must be having a nightmare. I hope I am having a nightmare because if not I must be going nuts. There, on the end of one of my fingers, is a little eye. A real eye. It is staring and blinking and I can see with it.

The gnome's eye has somehow grown onto my finger.

I give a scream of rage and fear and then I grab the gnome and run outside with it. I throw it down onto the path and smash it to pieces with the hammer. By the time I am finished all that is left is a small pile of dust and powder.

The gnome is gone for good but the eye is not. No, the eye is still there, blinking and winking on the end of my finger. I shove my hand in my pocket because I can't bear to look at my extra eye. Suddenly I can see what is in my pocket. There is a used tissue, two cents (which is all the money I have in the world) and a half-sucked licorice block. The eye is looking around inside my pocket.

I grin. At first I think that maybe this is not too bad. An extra eye on the end of a finger might be useful. I go back to my bedroom and poke my finger into a little hole in the wall. There is a family of mice nesting there. They get a big fright when they see the finger-eye looking at them and they nick off as fast as they can go.

Next I stick my finger into my earhole to see what is going on in there. My new eye seems to be able to see in the dark, but to be quite honest, there is not really much action inside an ear.

This is when I get the idea to have a peek inside my own mouth. I have always wondered what it is like at the back of my throat and this is my big chance to find out. I poke my finger in and have a look around. It is quite interesting really, I have never seen behind that thing that dangles down at the back before. There are a lot of red, wet mountains back there.

Suddenly I see something terrible. Horrible. A little face is staring back at me. It is the little, round face that I chipped off the gnome's tonsils. It has taken up residence in my throat. It lives behind my tonsils.

I start to cough and splutter. I have to get it out. Fancy having a little round face living in your throat. I try everything I can think of to get it out (including blowing my nose about a thousand times) but it just will not come out.

'Okay,' I say. 'If you will not come out by force I will get you out with brains.' I go down to the kitchen to see what there is to eat. I notice a packet of Hundreds and Thousands that Mum uses to sprinkle on top of cakes.

'Just the right size,' I say to myself. I put three of the Hundreds and Thousands on my tongue and put my finger up to my mouth to see what happens. Sure enough, the little face rolls onto my tongue and eats two of them. It eats the red ones but doesn't seem to like the blue one.

'Right,' I say. I pick out about fifteen red Hundreds and Thousands and put them on my tongue so that they form a little trail. The trail leads onto my lip and down my chin. I open my mouth and watch with the eye on my finger from a distance. The little face rolls out and starts eating. He reaches my lips and still he is not suspicious. A bit later he looks around outside and then moves down to my chin to eat the Hundreds and Thousands I have put there.

As quick as a flash I close my mouth and leave him trapped on the outside. I have won. Or so I think.

The little face tries to burrow back through my closed lips but I have my teeth clenched together. He can't get in.

I raise my hand to grab him, but before I can, he races upwards and disappears into my nose. In about two seconds I can feel him back behind my tonsils. I know that he will not fall for the Hundreds and Thousands trick again.

Just then, there is a knock at the front door. I walk down the hall and put my finger up to the keyhole to see who it is. It is Tara, my girlfriend. I open the door and give her a weak smile. 'G'day,' I say. 'How are you going?'

'I have come to have a look at the garden gnome I gave you,' she says. 'I want to make sure that you haven't put it down the backyard.'

My heart sinks. Tara is standing next to a pile of powder and dust that is the remains of the gnome. She has not seen it yet.

'Come in and sit down,' I say. I try to think of an explanation but I know that I can't tell Tara. She won't like the little face on my tonsils. She certainly won't like my extra eye. Once she wouldn't go out with me just because I had a pimple on my ear. If I tell her the truth she will drop me like a brick.

I can feel the little face moving around at the back of my throat. I have to know what he is up to so I put my finger into my mouth to see what is going on.

'What are you sucking your finger for?' asks Tara.

The little face is right on the end of the dangler thing in my throat. He is swinging on it, having fun.

'Take your finger out of your mouth and answer me, you silly boy,' Tara snaps.

The little face is hanging on to the dangler by his teeth! It hurts like nothing.

'Stop sucking your finger, you idiot,' yells Tara.

Now the face is out of sight. He is hiding up the back somewhere. I shove my finger in further to find out what is going on. This is a big mistake. I touch something that I shouldn't with my finger and it makes me sick. I spew up all over the carpet. Some of it splashes on Tara's shoes.

I get down onto my hands and knees and start sifting through the spew. I hope that the little face has been swept out with the tide. But it hasn't.

'You revolting creep,' yells Tara. 'I am breaking it off. You're dropped. I never want to see you again in my life.' She stands up and charges out of the door.

'Good riddance,' I yell. 'And take your rotten gnome with you. You will find what is left of it on the foot-path.'

I stagger out into the front garden and sit down. I feel terrible. My life is ruined. My girlfriend has dropped me. I have no money (except for two cents). I have an eye on my finger and a little face in my throat. I wish I was dead. I start to cry. Tears fall down my face. And down my finger. The eye on my finger is shedding tears too. Little teardrops fall onto the grass.

Then something amazing starts to happen. Where the tears from my finger are falling, little concrete gnomes start to grow in the grass. I can't believe it. They are sad little gnomes but they are very life-like. They look just as if they are alive.

Ten little gnomes grow, one for each teardrop. The next day I sell the gnomes for ten dollars each. I make a hundred dollars profit.

4

Jill is listening to my story with wide-open eyes. I don't suppose she will believe it.

'Well,' says Jill. 'What a sad tale.'

'Yes,' I answer. I can hardly believe my ears. Jill believes the whole thing. This is when I notice what a spunk she really is.

'What I can't understand,' she goes on, 'is what all this had to do with pulling hairs out of your nose.'

I feel a bit embarrassed but I decide to tell her the truth. 'I am trying to grow more gnomes.' I say. 'But I can't make any tears come. When you pull the hairs in your nose it makes your eyes water.' I hold up my finger and show her my extra eye again.

'Is the little face still there?' she asks.

'Yes.'

'And have you got any more Hundreds and Thousands?'

'Yes,' I answer again, handing over the packet.

'Well,' she says. 'We can't have you pulling hairs out of your nose. It's not a nice habit. Open up your mouth and let me speak to the face.'

I open my mouth and Jill looks inside and speaks to my guest. 'Listen,' she says. 'We don't mind you living in there. But fair's fair. You have to pay the rent. You help us and we will help you.'

So this is how Jill becomes my girlfriend. And we both become very rich from selling garden gnomes. We have got the perfect system. I open up my mouth and Jill calls out instructions to my tenant.

The little face goes up and pulls on a hair in my nose with his teeth. This makes my eye water and drop tears onto the lawn. More concrete gnomes grow out of the grass. Then we give the face his reward – red Hundreds and Thousands.

The gnomes are so realistic that we get five hundred dollars each for them. This means I don't have to have my hairs pulled very often.

You don't believe the story? Well, all I can say is this. If you are ever thinking of buying a garden gnome have a look in its mouth first. If there is a little face on its tonsils – don't buy it.

Noseweed

Think of honey.
Think of rotten, stinking fish.
Put them together and what have you got?
DISGUSTING COD-LIVER OIL.
That's what.

1

The nonsense you have just read was not written by me. My grandson Anthony wrote it. Silly boy.

I love cod-liver oil. I have been eating it for ninety-five years. It is good for you. It is delicious. In fact I would probably have died when I was only eighty if it weren't for my daily dose of cod-liver oil. Wonderful stuff. Full of natural flavour and vitamins.

Just because I am an old man doesn't mean that I don't know anything. But Anthony won't take any notice. He only eats what he likes. Chocolates, hamburgers, ice-cream. Rubbish like that. Bad for you.

We are great mates. We love each other – Anthony and I. We see eye to eye on everything. Except food.

Anthony has been coming to my house every

Christmas since he was born. He loves it. But not at meal times.

I remember when he was only three. Everyone was there at the table. Gran was alive at the time, bless her heart.

I put Anthony's plate of vegetable mush in front of him. He closed his mouth and shook his head. He didn't want vegetable mush. Not even after I had grown the carrots and brussels sprouts in my own backyard. The best carrots in town. I've won prizes for those carrots.

And the little beggar wouldn't eat them. What a nerve. It made my blood boil, I can tell you. He wanted roast beef and plum pudding like the rest of us. And he was only three.

I looked across the table at him. Then I pounced and put him in a headlock. I forced open his jaw. I shoved a spoonful of vegetable mush between his lips and clamped his mouth shut. 'Gotcha,' I yelled.

'Let him go, dear,' said Gran, bless her heart. 'He's only three.'

'Never,' I said. 'Not until he eats his vegetable mush.'

Anthony never said a thing. Not that he could talk, what with me holding him in a headlock. But he didn't fight.

He didn't squirm. He didn't make a sound. He is a stubborn kid. Takes after his Gran, bless her heart.

So that is how it went. I ate my soup with my left

hand and kept Anthony in the headlock with my right one. 'Give in,' I said.

No answer. He didn't even shake his head. Not that he could even if he had wanted to.

Next we had the roast beef. I had to ask Gran (bless her heart) to cut mine up so I could eat with one hand. It took me fifty minutes but I managed it.

'Give in,' I said.

Anthony didn't even blink. He just stared in front of him with a stubborn look in his eyes.

Now I had a problem. Was the vegetable mush still in there? Or had he swallowed it? I dared not let go.

Gran served up the plum pudding, bless her heart. It was delicious. Custard and cream too. Easy to eat with one hand.

I kept the headlock on Anthony. 'Have you swallowed your vegetable mush?' I said. 'If you have I'll let you go.'

No answer. So I didn't let him go.

We had coffee. We had jam tarts. But still Anthony kept his mouth clamped closed. Or I should say I kept it clamped closed.

Everyone left the table except Anthony and me. Hours passed. The afternoon drifted into the evening. But still he wouldn't budge. So we just sat there. Him in his highchair and me putting on the stranglehold.

'He must have swallowed it,' I thought. My arm was getting pins and needles. I couldn't last any longer. So I let go.

Anthony spat the vegetable mush out onto the table. Disgusting.

2

So that is how it is every Christmas when Anthony comes to stay. We have hassles over his food. And now he won't take his cod-liver oil. Even though he is thirteen years old.

Take this year, for example.

I was out in the hothouse when he arrived. I was trying to cross a Granny Smith apple with a Golden Delicious. I wanted to invent a new type of apple. A Golden Gran. Named after Gran. Bless her heart.

Excuse me a minute. A tear is rolling down my cheek. I always start to cry a bit when I think of her. Now she is dead and all. It's lonely without Gran. We were married for sixty years.

Now there is just me. And old Cameo, my horse. I love Cameo but she's not much company. Horses can love you but they can't talk.

She loves apples, does Cameo. She trots across the garden and pinches one out of your hand if you don't watch out.

I was mad about apples, too. If I could name a new type of apple after Gran, her memory would live forever. That's what I wanted to do. I would call it Golden Gran. Just think of it.

But it never worked. I just couldn't manage to develop

a new type no matter how hard I tried.

Anyway, Anthony walked in while I was trying to fertilise my new species. 'Grandpa,' he said. 'I am happy to be here. I am glad to see you again.' He planted a kiss on my wrinkled old face. Then he said, 'But I am not having cod-liver oil this year. I am too old for it. And I hate the stuff. It makes me spew.'

I didn't say anything. I just made my plans. I would get it into him somehow. For his own sake.

Well, the next morning I put some cod-liver oil on a spoon. Lovely, like honey it is. With a smooth fish taste. Then I dipped it in my home-made muesli. Nuts, seeds, fruit, dried vegies. A wonderful mixture.

'Here,' I said. 'I've blended it with my special muesli. Delicious.'

Anthony shook his head. Stubborn boy.

'If you want the money for the movies today,' I said, 'you have to eat your muesli and cod-liver oil.'

'Blackmail,' said Anthony.

'It's for your own good,' I said.

To my great surprise he just nodded and opened his mouth. But I knew what he was up to. I was a kid myself once. He couldn't fool me. He was going to go outside and spit it out. I didn't come down in the last shower.

'Promise me you won't spit it out,' I said.

He looked at me for ages without answering. 'Okay,' he said at last.

I gave him the spoon and he put the muesli and cod-liver oil into his mouth. His eyes started to water. His face went red. He held his hands up to his mouth and rushed over to the sink.

'You promised,' I yelled.

He looked at me with staring eyes. Anyone would think I had pulled his fingernails out. It was only muesli and cod-liver oil, for goodness sake. What a fuss over nothing.

'Swallow,' I said. 'Get it over and done with.'

Anthony grabbed a piece of paper. He scribbled a message.

DISGUSTING. I CAN'T GET IT DOWN. I'LL BE SICK.

I took out my wallet and gave him ten dollars. 'Here's the money for the movies,' I said. 'I've kept my word, now you keep yours. You promised not to spit it out.'

His eyes were still watering. He had the muesli and cod-liver oil in his mouth. He just wouldn't swallow it. Talk about stubborn. He snatched the ten-dollar note and headed for the door. His cheeks were bulging out like two balloons.

'No you don't,' I said. 'You're going to spit it out on the way. I'm coming too. To keep an eye on you.'

I grabbed my walking stick and hat and hobbled after him.

Down the street he went with me following. He stopped at the bus stop. 'Mmnn, mnn, mng, mng,' he said.

I couldn't understand a word. I think he said something like, 'Please go home, Gramps, it's embarrassing.'

Funny that. How kids get embarrassed by adults. I don't think he liked me being with him in my old gardening boots.

'No way,' I said. 'I'm staying until you swallow.'

Lucky I did too. He never would have survived without me.

The bus pulled up and we got on. Of course Anthony couldn't talk. 'Where to?' asked the bus driver.

'Mmm, nn, mng,' said Anthony.

The bus driver looked at him as if he was crazy. 'Knox City Shopping Centre,' I said. 'One and a half, please.'

We sat down and the bus started off. Passengers were staring at us. They were kindly old folk like me. Anthony was going red in the face. Kids get embarrassed about anything these days. He was ashamed of me. His own flesh and blood.

'Won't swallow his cod-liver oil,' I said in a loud voice. 'So I'm making sure he doesn't spit it out.'

The passengers nodded. 'Kids these days are spoiled,' said an elderly lady.

Everyone ooh-ed and ah-ed. They were all on my side. 'My mother couldn't even afford cod-liver oil,' said a bald man up the back.

'Yes,' said a mother with two children on her knee. 'Stick with the little rascal. Don't let him win. Make him swallow it.'

I grinned. I knew I was right. Kids need discipline. There was no way I was going to let him spit out that muesli and cod-liver oil.

And if he was embarrassed having his grandpa around, too bad.

3

Anthony jumped off the bus at Knox City. He tried to lose me in the crowd. Up the escalator, down the elevator. In one door, out of another. But I was too quick for him. He just couldn't shake me off.

Finally he went up to the ticket office at the cinema. 'Which show, love?' said the lady ticket seller.

'Mnn, mmn, mng,' he said.

Fairies in the Dell, I said. 'One and a half, please.'

'Mmnn, mmnng,' Anthony was shaking his head. He didn't want to see *Fairies in the Dell*. He pointed to a sign which said, *Blood of the Devil*.

The ticket seller gave him a ticket and Anthony rushed off. I quickly bought a ticket and followed. *Blood of the Devil*. That was no show for a child.

I hobbled after him into the dark cinema. It was all I could do to find him. I plonked myself down in the next seat. It was so dark that I could hardly see. I had to make sure that he didn't spit the cod-liver oil under the seat.

I didn't look at the screen. I just kept staring at Anthony's lips. My eyes became used to the dark and I could see that his cheeks were still swollen with the muesli and cod-liver oil.

On the screen, worms were coming out of a grave. It was a terrible movie. Disgusting.

Just then something happened. Something that I found hard to believe. Something that you will find hard to believe. A little tubular shape like a worm wriggled out between Anthony's lips.

'Aagh,' I screamed. 'A worm.'

'Shhh,' said someone behind.

'Quiet,' barked another voice. 'If you're frightened, don't go to horror movies.'

'Quick, Anthony,' I whispered fiercely. 'Spit it out. It's okay about the cod-liver oil. Spit it out.'

The worm thing was wriggling further and further out of his mouth. It sort of snaked its way up past Anthony's eye.

He shook his head. Talk about stubborn. It was just like when he was three. Once he made up his mind, that was it.

The worm thing grew longer and longer. It oozed out of his mouth and wrapped itself around his head. What could it be? Terrible, terrible.

'Spit,' I yelled. 'For heaven's sake, Anthony. Spit.'

'Shut up, you old fool,' said a voice behind us in the darkness.

I had to save Anthony. Had to get this wretched thing out of the boy's mouth. I reached up and touched the writhing worm.

It wasn't a worm. It was a plant. A long tendril grew out of his mouth and twirled around his head.

My mind started to spin. What had I done to the poor boy? What was going on?

And then I realised.

The muesli was growing. One of the seeds had sprouted in the cod-liver oil. It was growing so fast that I could see it move. Like a snake stretching itself. Out and around.

Then something else happened. Two more shoots erupted. One out of each nostril. It looked as if he needed to wipe his nose. Badly.

'Spit it out, Anthony,' I shrieked. 'For heaven's sake, boy, you've got a noseweed.'

Growls and loud whispers came from the audience around.

'Shut up, Pops.'

'Get the manager.'

'Chuck the old fool out.'

Anthony just sat there staring at the screen. He didn't even care that the muesli in his mouth was growing. Nothing would make him open his mouth. He was teaching me a lesson. He was as stubborn as Gran, bless her heart. If only she were here. She would know what to do.

'Come on, boy. Let's go,' I said.

Anthony shook his head. I tried to pull him out of his seat but he was too strong.

'Shut up,' came a voice.

'Keep still,' said another.

I let go. If I made any more fuss they would kick me out of the place. I buried my head in my hands and closed my eyes. I just couldn't look at Anthony's sprouting mouth.

The other people settled down for a bit. I kept my eyes closed and sat still. No one complained. Not at first anyway.

Suddenly a voice said, 'Take off that hat.'

'Yes, we can't see.'

'What a nerve, wearing a hat like that at the pictures.'

'I'm getting the manager.'

I opened my eyes and screamed. Anthony's head was covered in branches and leaves. Stems snaked out of his mouth and nose and twisted upwards. Instead of hair, he had a mass of leaves wrapped around his skull. He looked like he was wearing a ridiculous hat made of bushes. The people behind couldn't see the screen.

Just then a man with a torch arrived down the aisle. It was the manager. He grabbed me firmly by the arm. 'Come with me, you two,' he said. 'You can't carry on like that in here.'

He led us both down the dark aisle and out into the bright light of the foyer.

4

The manager glared at Anthony. 'Very funny,' he said. 'Dressing up like that and spoiling the movie for everyone else.'

'He's not dressing up,' I gasped. 'It's growing out of his mouth. Muesli and cod-liver oil.'

The manager shook his head at me angrily. 'Practical jokes. At your age you should know better.' He turned around and stomped off.

'Spit,' I said to Anthony. 'Get rid of it. Quick.'

He just shook his head. He was still trying to teach me a lesson. And it was working.

'We're going home,' I said. I grabbed his hand and pulled him through the crowds. More leaves and twigs were growing in front of my eyes. And Anthony's eyes too. I couldn't even see his face any more.

A crowd of little kids and their mothers started to follow us.

'Look at that, Mum.'

'How do they do it?'

'It's one of those in-store promotions, dear. It's probably advertising a plant nursery.'

I whispered fiercely to Anthony. 'Pull it out, boy. Quickly. This is embarrassing. Everyone is looking at us.'

Anthony nodded his branches at me. 'Mnn, nmng, nn,' he said.

I didn't know what it meant. Probably something like,

'You embarrassed *me*. Now it's your turn.'

I was tempted to pull the whole thing out myself. But what if the roots grew into his tongue? I might damage his mouth.

A huge throng followed us through the shopping mall.

'Cabbage head,' yelled a little kid.

'Treemendous,' said someone else.

This was turning into a nightmare. I was most embarrassed. What if someone from my bowls club was watching? How humiliating.

Finally we struggled out of the shopping centre and climbed onto the bus. 'One and a half,' I said.

The driver looked at Anthony for quite a bit. Then he said, 'Trees are full fare.'

I threw the money at him and we sat at the back of the bus. Anthony's tree head was growing all the time.

'You'll have to move,' shouted the driver. 'I can't see out of the back window.'

Passengers were staring at us. Whispering and pointing.

I was just about to tell Anthony that this had gone far enough when I spotted something. On one of the branches. A small berry thing about the size of a marble. It was gold in colour.

'An apple,' I shrieked. 'You're growing an apple.'

I parted Anthony's branches and looked into his eyes. Then I examined the tiny fruit. 'You've done it,' I yelled. 'You've done it. It's a Golden Gran. My new species.

One of the seeds has sprouted in the cod-liver oil.'

We both had tears in our eyes. Now Gran would be remembered forever, bless her heart. Anthony nodded his tree and the little apple shook about dangerously.

'No,' I yelled. 'Keep still. It's only small. It won't have any seeds yet. Don't move in case it falls off.'

Anthony froze. He knew how important this was to both of us. He had loved his Gran, bless her heart. She was his favourite. 'Mmn, mnng, mnff,' was all he said.

'Now listen,' I whispered. 'The way this thing is growing, the apple should be ripe in about an hour. Then we can weed your mouth and nose. And keep the apple seeds. Then we can plant them and grow more Golden Grans. In memory of Gran, bless her heart.'

'Mmnff,' said Anthony. I knew that he agreed with my plan.

The bus came to a halt outside my front gate. 'Walk carefully,' I said. 'If the apple drops off before it has grown we are finished. It might be the only one.'

Anthony stood and inched along the aisle of the bus.

'Hurry up,' said the driver.

'This is an emergency,' I said. 'We have to save the apple.'

'Get moving,' ordered a woman dressed in a nurse's uniform.

'We haven't got all day,' said someone else.

I looked at Anthony. 'Don't take any notice,' I said. 'Take your time.'

Anthony moved forward at a snail's pace. There was no way he was going to dislodge that apple. Time passed slowly. The passengers grew restless.

In the end the driver couldn't take it any longer. He jumped out of his seat and grabbed Anthony by a lower branch. He dragged him along the bus and threw him onto the street. Then he looked at me angrily. 'I'm going, I'm going,' I said.

I jumped off and examined Anthony. 'Are you hurt?' I yelled.

He shook his branches slowly. 'Mmple,' he said urgently.

'Apple,' I cried. 'Yes, where's the apple?' I began searching through the branches. It was still there. And it was nearly full grown.

Cameo looked on from a distance. Even the horse was interested in the apple tree.

We walked slowly into the front yard. 'Five minutes more,' I said. 'Then we can pick the apple and weed you.'

Anthony crept forward into the garden. He edged his way towards the front door. Five minutes passed. 'The apple is ripe,' I yelled. 'Quick. Inside and I'll get some cutters.'

Neither of us heard the footsteps behind until it was too late. Well, not footsteps. Hoofsteps.

As quick as a flash, Cameo chomped on the apple. Swallowed it in one go. Then she tossed her head and ripped the whole tree out of Anthony's head.

'Ow,' shrieked Anthony.

Cameo trotted to the other side of the garden, still munching on the remains of the tree.

'Are you all right? Are you all right?' I called.

'Yes,' Anthony screamed. 'Quick, grab Cameo.'

We raced across the grass but we were too late. Cameo had eaten every leaf. Every twig. Not one bit of the tree was left.

5

Well, Anthony and I just sat and stared at the floor. After all that. So near and yet so far. We had almost developed a new apple type. A Golden Gran. But Cameo had swallowed it.

'Never mind, Grandpa,' said Anthony. 'You'll crack it one day.'

He was a great kid. He was just trying to cheer me up. But I knew it was no good. I was getting old. I didn't have much time left on earth. I knew that I would never develop the Golden Gran now. My heart was heavy.

Excuse me if I wipe a little tear from my cheek. But I always get so sad when I think of Gran, bless her heart.

Suddenly Anthony jumped up. 'I know,' he said. 'We'll do it again. Mix up muesli and cod-liver oil. And put it in our mouths. Another tree might grow.'

'You'd do that for me?' I said. 'Even though you hate cod-liver oil?'

Anthony nodded. 'We both will,' he yelled. 'One of us is bound to sprout.'

So that is what we did. I mixed up a new lot and we sat there with our cheeks bulging. It was lovely, was that muesli and cod-liver oil mix. Or that's what I thought. Poor Anthony sat there with tears streaming from his eyes. He thought the taste was terrible.

For two days we sat there. Waiting and waiting and waiting. We couldn't talk. We dared not move. The phone rang but neither of us could answer it. We didn't even go outside.

Two days and two nights. Sitting there with our mouths full of muesli and cod-liver oil. But nothing grew. Not a leaf. Not a twig. Nothing.

Finally Anthony got up and spat into the sink. 'It's no good, Grandpa,' he said. 'I can't go on. It's not going to work.'

He was right, of course. I spat my lot into the bin and went off and had a shower. It was the worst day of my life. I had nothing left to look forward to.

I dried myself and dressed. Then I went out into the kitchen. Just then Anthony rushed in. He was carrying something. Something wonderful.

Two golden apples. 'Golden Grans,' he shouted. 'Look.'

He pointed outside. I ran over to the window and stared out. And there it was. I couldn't believe my eyes. A magnificent apple tree growing in the backyard. Covered in Golden Grans.

The tree was sprouting out of a pile of horse manure. Cameo had done a good job.

'Whoopee,' I yelled. I had never been happier in my whole life.

Anthony grinned and held out an apple. 'You be the first to taste one,' he said.

'No,' I told him. 'That honour is yours.'

Anthony took a bite. He pulled a face and spat. 'Ugh,' he yelled. 'Sorry, Grandpa, but it's terrible. Disgusting.'

I grabbed the other apple and munched. 'Delicious,' I shouted. 'Absolutely delicious. The first apple in the world that tastes like cod-liver oil.'

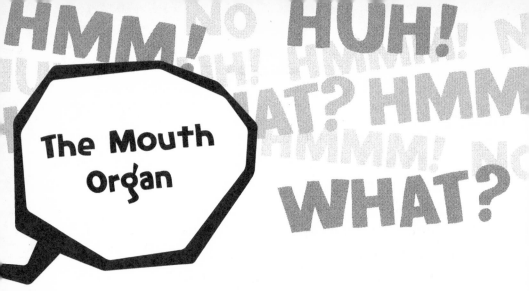

The Mouth Organ

I am not happy standing here in front of the magnolia tree. I play my guitar and peer at my hat on the ground. There's not much money in it. Not much at all. There are only about fifty people in this town and they don't have any spare cash. Still, the buses might be good for a dollar. The tourists have plenty of money. They might throw a cent or two to a poor girl. Until they find out that the tree is dead.

My fingers strum the guitar and I sing a sad song. It's called 'The Ballad of Mrs Hardbristle'.

Now here's something. A young bloke crosses the street. He comes over to listen. He has a ponytail and a headband. He doesn't look like he's worth much. He probably hasn't got twenty cents to his name. Still, I keep on playing. Just in case. He puts his hand in his pocket. Maybe he has a twenty-dollar note for me.

The young bloke pulls out his hand. In it he holds a mouth organ. My heart grows heavy. No money. Not a cent. Just a mouth organ. I stop playing and sit down under the tree with a sigh.

Young Ponytail regards me with a grin. 'I know the

story,' he says. 'I know what you did.'

How does he know? I've never told anybody. I hang my head with shame and my mind goes back seven years.

2

Mrs Hardbristle sniffed. 'We have to get out of here,' she said. 'Fast.'

I was only six at the time but I will never forget it. I was with Mrs Hardbristle and her little Brownie pack. She looked at us all and then at her husband. 'Mr Hardbristle,' she said. 'There is a bushfire. We have to get back to town.'

Mr Hardbristle had come along to 'look after us', but that was a bit of a joke really. He was all bent over and weak and could hardly keep up with us. He was much older than Mrs Hardbristle.

Some of the girls started to cry as wisps of smoke drifted through the dry bush. Even though we were young, we could imagine the cruel flames and blinding smoke that would soon engulf the very spot where we were standing.

We set off as fast as we could. 'Leave me,' yelled Mr Hardbristle. 'Get the girls to safety.' He puffed and wheezed as he followed along behind.

'Nonsense,' said his wife. She put one of his arms over her shoulder and dragged him behind her like a sack. She was strong, was Mrs Hardbristle. A strong woman.

Twigs crackled under our feet. The hot sun scorched our backs. A kangaroo bounded away in fright, desperately trying to escape the flames. Before long the air was filled with smoke. We started to cough and cry. 'Keep going, girls,' ordered Mrs Hardbristle between gasps. 'Keep going.' She was starting to tire. It was too much really, dragging the old man along behind her.

'Don't stop, Brownies,' she shouted.

And we didn't. Somehow or other we all stumbled through the forest until we reached town. I say town, but it only had six shops and a pub and about twenty houses. I was hoping to see my father there waiting with the car. But there was no one. The dusty street was empty. Not a car. Not a person.

Mrs Hardbristle gently put her husband down in the shade. 'The fire is going to take out the town,' she said. 'Girls, into the middle of the square.'

There was a little grassy patch in the middle of the street with a picnic table there. She ran into the general store and came back with a spade and a large blanket. Without a word she started to dig. Mr Hardbristle tried to help but he was too weak.

Smoke swirled in the air. We could hear the flames now. Crackling in the surrounding forest. The sun was blotted out by smoke. The Brownies' faces were black except for the little rivers made by their tears.

On dug Mrs Hardbristle. On and on and on. The hole became deeper. Sweat poured down her forehead. Her uniform was filthy with dry soil and smoke. The heat was terrible. Suddenly the fire was upon us. The general store exploded like a bomb. Flames ate into the walls.

Mrs Hardbristle stopped digging. 'Get in,' she said. She helped her husband into the hole and I climbed in with the other three Brownies. We felt the blanket placed over our heads. Everything went dark. Suddenly we were wet. She was pouring water over the blanket.

Poor old Mr Hardbristle was worried about his wife. 'Get in, get in,' he croaked at her.

'I'll be all right,' we heard Mrs Hardbristle say. 'You look after the girls.'

We felt the fire roar past. Its heat stifled us. Its smoke choked us. But its flames did not claim us. We survived.

When we climbed out the town had gone. Not a building was left. Smoke drifted slowly up from charred timber and twisted tin. Just by the hole we found Mrs Hardbristle. Stretched out. Not burnt but suffocated by the smoke. She had saved us all. And had lost her own life. Mr Hardbristle knelt over the still body of his wife and let the silent tears melt into his beard. His shoulders shook in wordless grief.

Mrs Hardbristle was a heroine. She had saved us from the flames and given up her own life. Our parents were so grateful. They said that they would never forget her.

The town was rebuilt. And in the hole where we had sheltered, our parents planted a little magnolia tree in memory of that brave woman.

Mr Hardbristle was filled with despair and guilt. 'I hid in the hole,' he said. 'And let my wife die. I'm a coward.'

Of course he wasn't a coward. He was bent and weak. And anyway, there's nothing to say that the man has to be the brave one. Why shouldn't it be a woman?

But he wouldn't listen. No matter what we said. He wouldn't leave the little cottage that the people built for him. He just sat there on the porch in his old rocking chair staring at the magnolia tree.

I was only a little girl but I told him something that I heard my mother say to Dad. 'There's no need to feel bad. She would want you to be happy.'

He rocked for a long time and then he said, 'When that magnolia tree flowers, then I will know that she has forgiven me. Then I will be happy. But not until then.'

I ran home and told Mum what he said. Mum smiled sadly. 'Magnolia trees sometimes don't flower for seven years,' she said. 'I don't think Mr Hardbristle has seven years left.'

But she was wrong. Seven years passed. And although the magnolia tree didn't flower, Mr Hardbristle still sat there, watching and waiting. It was a fine tree. Tall, with strong, thin branches.

I was thirteen now. And in the Guides. I wanted that tree to flower more than anything. I wanted Mr Hardbristle to feel forgiven. To know that his wife was smiling upon him.

That's why, in the middle of another hot summer, I decided to water the tree. Our bucket was too small so I filled a big plastic container with water. It once had some sort of powder in it. 'Fertiliser,' I said to myself.

I grasped the wire handle and lugged the water over to the magnolia tree. White powder swirled around in the water. I carefully tipped it out around the roots. Mr Hardbristle sat rocking and watching without saying a word.

In the morning the magnolia tree was dead. Its leaves hung limply, pointing to the ground beneath.

'I can't believe it.' said Dad. He picked up a tiny smudge of white powder on his finger. 'Somebody's poisoned it. They've put blackberry killer on the magnolia.'

I felt like sinking into the ground. I thought it was fertiliser in the bucket. I had killed the tree. I stared over at Mr Hardbristle. His seat was empty. He was in bed and he wouldn't get out. And he would never see the magnolia bloom.

Now there were two guilty people. Mr Hardbristle and me.

No one knew what I had done, except Mr Hardbristle. I just couldn't own up to it. It was too horrible. I felt like going to bed and staying there myself. I could put my head under the blanket and never come out like he was doing.

But I didn't. I decided to make up for what I had done.

I decided to raise money and buy another magnolia tree. A full-grown one. I could even get one that was flowering. Then Mr Hardbristle would feel good again.

'A thousand dollars,' said Mum. 'That's what a full-grown one in a tub would cost. But it wouldn't be the same really, would it?'

I couldn't believe it. A thousand dollars just for a tree. I had no money at all. Not a cent. I picked up my guitar and went down to the magnolia tree. I put my hat on the ground and started to play.

3

Young Ponytail is looking at me with a sort of a smile. He hands over his battered old mouth organ. 'This might help,' he says.

I look at the worn mouth organ and shrug my shoulders. 'I can't play that,' I say. 'Only guitars.' I pat the guitar that my father gave me. Nothing will make me part with it.

The young man puts the mouth organ to his lips and starts to play. Oh, that music. It is beautiful. At times it swells and falls. Then it changes and seems to flitter round inside my head like a flock of bell-birds calling. It is the sound of soft mountain streams. It is the call of the whispering gums. It is the taste of honey on fresh bread. I have never heard music like it. My eyes brim with tears. A burst of sunshine breaks through the clouds.

I take the mouth organ from his outstretched hand.

'Play your own tune,' he says. 'Not other people's. You've got your own melodies, use them.' His smile seems to look into my soul. 'I'll be back for it tomorrow,' he says. 'At twelve o'clock.'

'There's school tomorrow,' I say. 'Meet me at the front gate. I'll be there. Don't worry about that.'

'Make sure you are,' he says. 'Make sure you are. I have to be movin' on.'

I lean my guitar against the tree and watch him disappear down the street towards the river. I guess he is camping out there.

The mouth organ is chipped and worn. It has played many melodies from long-forgotten lives. I can see that. I am just about to hold it to my lips when a tourist bus pulls up.

Ever since the magnolia tree was planted tourists have been coming to look at it. They stop on their way to Sydney. The story of Mr Hardbristle sitting there waiting for the tree to bloom was in the papers. Everyone hopes that they will be there when the tree blooms.

The tourists jump off the bus. A whole mob of them wearing sunglasses and shorts. They have cameras around their necks. They want to take a photo of the tree. They bustle up and fall silent.

'It's dead,' says the bus driver as he stares at the tree. They all look at the limp leaves. They turn around and start to climb back onto the bus. I will never earn any money this way. I put the mouth organ to my lips and try to think of a tune. 'Hang down your head, Tom Dooley. Hang down your head and cry.' It is the only tune I can think of. I start to play it. Mournful, sad notes.

The tourists start to sniff. An American in a big hat takes out his handkerchief and blows his nose. A Japanese lady bursts into tears. The tune is so sad. This mouth organ seems to have a strange power. Soon all the tourists are crying. They are leaning on each other's shoulders and weeping. They are not putting any money into my hat.

Something has gone wrong. The mouth organ is not having the right result. I try to think of a happy song. Something comes into my mind. The cancan. I play a bright, happy dance. The tourists link arms. They start to kick their legs up into the air, first one way and then the other. On they go. On and on. They can't throw money into my hat with their arms linked together. I reach the end of the tune and stop. So do they.

They look at each other with wide open eyes. They don't know what is going on. They rush for the bus. They are leaving without donating anything towards the new magnolia tree. I look over the road at Mr Hardbristle's empty rocking chair. I have to do something quick.

I play another tune. 'Kookaburra sits on the old gum tree.' It is bright and happy. The tourists are bright and happy as they scramble up the re-grown gum trees along the street. They sit on the branches like birds. I try to stop playing but I can't. Once you start a tune you seem to have to keep going until you reach the end.

I get up to the bit that goes 'Laugh kookaburra, laugh kookaburra'. They laugh all right – but not the kookaburras. The tourists sit there in the branches with their heads turned up, laughing like jackasses.

Finally I stop. The tourists start to shriek. They are really scared by all this. They scramble down from their perches and head for the bus again. Still they have not given me one cent. I have a last desperate try.

I start to play 'You can leave your hat on' – a real wild tune. The tourists stop. They start to dance. A sliding, writhing dance. The Japanese man undoes his buttons slowly. He throws his jacket to the ground. The American is flicking off his shoes. Three others are pulling off their jumpers in slow, rhythmic movements. A fat lady is rolling down her stockings. Oh no. I have chosen striptease music.

I try to stop playing but I can't. I have to finish the whole tune. Finally it is over. Thirty tourists stand looking at each other. They have nothing on but their underwear. They scream, they shout, they scramble onto the bus. I decide to let them go. This is not working out at all. The bus takes off down the road in a cloud of dust.

4

What happened? This mouth organ is not solving my problem. I will never get another tree for Mr Hardbristle this way. Then I remember Young Ponytail's words. 'Play your own tune,' he said. 'Not other people's. You've got your own melodies, use them.'

I have never made up a proper tune in my life. What did he mean? I just decide to play about how I feel in my head. I walk over to the shops, throw my hat on the ground and start to blow. From somewhere deep inside me comes the saddest tune. I have never played like this before. I invent it as I go.

The tune is made up of Mr Hardbristle's sorrow. And the tree that I killed. It is mixed with my tears. It is the unspoken story of a girl who made a mistake and a tree that died. The music is so pure that lovers would embrace forever if they heard it.

Mr Windfall comes out of his new general store. He walks like he is in a dream. He stands and watches without moving. His eyes are glass – they see things that no one knows. I stop playing for a moment. 'Don't stop,' he pleads. 'Don't stop.' He takes out twenty dollars from his wallet and throws it into my hat. I smile and play on.

Others gather. They crowd around. There is Mr Ralph, our teacher. He wears a smile that is as soft as the clouds. Sue Rickets and two other tough kids from Year Seven stop and listen. Sue Rickets hates my guts. But not now.

The music has mellowed her. I look around at the people. They are all on a journey. A special journey. The music takes them where usually they cannot go.

In the end I stop playing. I am out of breath. The crowd stands for a bit without moving. Then they suddenly shake themselves. Mr Ralph reminds me of an old dog coming out of a dream. Everyone puts money in the hat. Then they float away on the wings of their memories. I look into my hat. I have taken eighty-four dollars.

If this keeps up I will earn the thousand dollars for a new tree in no time. No time at all. I look at my watch. I have to get home and chop some wood before tea. I run for it.

Tea is over. The dishes are washed. I sit in front of the fire. Mum and Dad like me to play my guitar when the fire is flickering.

But I do not play the guitar. I take out the mouth organ. The tunes I play on the mouth organ have no names. Nor words. Just melodies that speak to the heart. I play a tune about Grandma. It is a jumpy, happy tune. She is tickling me like she used to. I laugh and squirm in my mind as I play. It is almost real. All the pain of loss is gone. There is only happiness.

I look at Mum. Her smile is filled with love. I know that, in her mind, Grandma is holding her in her arms like when she was a baby. In the end we all fall asleep. Me and Mum and Dad. There in front of the fire.

It is morning already. Mum is happier than I have ever seen her. My mouth organ has given her joy. I can't part with this mouth organ. I wonder if Young Ponytail will swap it for my guitar. But I can't part with that either. Dad would never forgive me. He gave it to me for Christmas.

I take the eighty-four dollars and wedge it inside my guitar. I put my mouth organ in a deep pocket. Then I head off for school.

This mouth organ can earn me the thousand dollars for a new tree. But can it do it before twelve o'clock?

5

Our school has only one teacher. And twenty kids. We all learn together in the same room. The big kids help the little kids. Mr Ralph helps everyone. He is a quiet teacher. He never shouts. Everybody likes him.

Mr Ralph looks at me. 'Nicole has hidden talents,' he says. 'She can play the mouth organ.' The kids all look up.

'Play for us,' says Mr Ralph.

I pick up my mouth organ and start to blow. Whatever I think of comes out in the music. The kids all put their heads on the desks. They see what I see. They dream my dreams. The music does it all.

I take them sailing on sparkling oceans. I fly them through the clouds. I show them the bottom of the sea and the highest mountain peaks. Places where the air is so crisp it tinkles when you breathe. I shower them in a waterfall. I dust them with moon powder. I rock them in the arms of loved ones long passed on.

All this I do with my mouth organ. The time blows by as unnoticed as the breeze which comes from the river. Soon it is twelve o'clock. The bell rings. It is lunch time.

The mouth organ trembles in my hand. It wants to return to its owner.

But I only have a mere eighty-four dollars. And I need a thousand. The new magnolia tree has to be seven years old. And they are expensive. I will never be happy until I can look Mr Hardbristle in the eye and see that he is smiling.

I run out of the schoolyard. I hide in the pine plantation nearby.

Young Ponytail arrives at the school gate. I see him from my far-off perch in the branches. I see him looking for me. I see him turn and walk sadly towards the river.

I stay up here in the tree until the bell rings. I feel a bit bad for keeping the mouth organ but it is for a good cause. I am going to use it to get another magnolia tree. Then I will give it back. Maybe.

But something is different. Since I decided to keep the mouth organ things have changed. In class no one looks at me. Mr Ralph doesn't ask me to play any more.

I decide to give it a go without being asked. I pick up my mouth organ to play it. My mouth organ? It is not my mouth organ. It feels cold in my hand. Hostile. It doesn't want to play my tune. A little shiver runs up my spine. I grab the mouth organ in trembling fingers and force it up to my lips. I blow strongly. A horrible, blurting sound explodes into the room.

Everyone in the class groans. The noise hurts their ears. I try again and the mouth organ goes crazy in my hands. It twists and turns as if it is alive. It is trying to get away. I grab it even more tightly and try to blow.

Then it happens. Something terrible. I don't know how. I don't know why. But the mouth organ is inside my mouth. It is stuck in sideways, as if I have a banana jammed in there. My cheeks are stretched out on either side. It hurts something awful. The pain is terrible. My eyes water. The mouth organ is a mouth organ indeed.

I stand up and stagger to my feet. As I breathe, the mouth organ screeches in time. In. Out. In. Out. Horrible bellows. I gasp and the mouth organ gasps with me. A terrible tune. The kids clap their hands over their ears. They try to block out the screeching music. Wheezing discords fill the air.

Looks of pain and fear are thrown at me as I stagger towards the door. I am angry. It's not my fault. I am only trying to make up for killing the tree. I am only trying to get money for a new one. Why does everyone hate me now? I hate them back.

The tune is a tune of pain. My music calls up sights

from the bottom of dark places. It is the sound of broken hearts, of wars and disease. Of murder and theft. Of revenge and unforgiven accidents. I see all this in the eyes of Mr Ralph and the class. I have stirred up demons from deep within myself.

They come for me. The class close around me with outstretched fingers. Their nails are like claws. I break through and run. I burst out of the door, clutching my guitar in my hands.

6

The sun has gone. A chill wind tears at my streaming eyes. Cold rain begins to fall. The mouth organ screams with each panting breath. I stumble out of the school-yard. Mr Ralph and the class follow despite the bellowing shrieks from my mouth. They are after my blood. I have turned them into wild animals. My heart thumps against my ribs. My lungs are screaming for rest. The mouth organ plays the tune of my flight for all to hear.

I stagger through the town. The mouth organ is still lodged inside my mouth. I can't get it out. Shopkeepers and farmers join the chase. My tune of tears irritates everyone. They will do anything to stop it. I stumble and fall at the foot of the magnolia tree. I am exhausted. My breath comes in shrieking howls. The crowd surrounds me.

I hate them. Why have they done this to me? Why won't they leave me in peace? I look at the dead tree.

I wish they were like it. Made of wood. With wooden hearts.

The mouth organ pumps out my terrible tune of hate with each breath. The crowd suddenly freezes – the kids, the shopkeepers, the farmers, Mr Ralph. Every one of them makes my wish come true. They turn to wood in front of my eyes. Wooden faces. Wooden clothes. Wooden hair. Eyes that do not see. I am standing alone. In a street of statues. They no longer thirst for my blood. They stand there like tombstones in the rain. Still. Silent. With raging faces.

For a moment I am numb. I try to pull the mouth organ from my trembling lips but it won't budge. It won't leave its chosen home.

A door bangs open in the street. It is Dr Jenson. He stands for a moment – stunned. Staring at the stiff figures in the street. He is up-wind. He has not heard my tune of terror. He can save me. He is a doctor. He can get this wretched instrument out of my mouth. He runs towards me and then, mid-step, stops. And turns to wood as the first notes reach his ears.

In the silence of the street I suddenly realise what has happened. I can't go home. Mum and Dad will turn to wood too. I can't go anywhere near anyone. There is not a soul who can help me.

Or is there?

7

I wonder if the young man is still down by the river. He is my only hope. It is his mouth organ. If only I can give it back.

I stumble out of town. Past the school. Past Mr Hardbristle's empty porch. Out into the bush. Towards the river. There is no sign of the young man. The cold water of the river flows by uncaring. I follow the bank. Hoping desperately to see the owner of the mouth organ.

In my cheeks I have a mouth organ. And in my hand a guitar.

My feet take me up. And up. The river is far below. I am on a rocky outcrop looking at the chill water lying like dead rope in the valley.

I see him. There he is. His back is towards me. He is heading into the forest. I scream but no scream comes. Just terrible discords bellowing with every breath.

Fear grabs my heart. What if my music turns the young man to wood? Who will help me then? I try not to breathe. I wave my guitar but his back is towards me. Oh, oh, oh. Who will help me? I wave again. But it is no use signalling to the back of a head.

I search around for a stone. A rock. A branch. Anything to throw down and attract his attention. But there is nothing. The rocky cliff face has been swept clean by the wind. A few leaves wedged in crevices are all I can find. I desperately throw them over the edge but the cruel wind steals every one.

The guitar. It's all I have. I throw it high into the air.

My eighty-four dollars fall out and spin towards the water. The money is gone. And the guitar is tumbling down. The wind seems to take it in soft hands. I think I can hear quiet chords plucked by unseen fingers. The guitar spins and twists and plunges onto an outcrop of rocks near the young man. It splinters into a thousand fragments.

The young man looks up. He sees me and smiles. He waits.

8

It takes me an hour to reach him. An hour. And bloody knees and scratched fingers. An hour of painful tunes, gasped out through the false smile of my stretched lips.

At last I reach him. The sounds of my breath have no effect. He does not turn to wood. He puts his hands to my cheeks and then gently plucks the mouth organ from my mouth.

'It does good for those who do good. And bad for those who do bad,' he says.

Tears run down my cheeks. 'I only wanted to get money for a tree,' I cry. 'But everything went wrong.' I remember the silent statues in the town.

The young man hands me the mouth organ. We both know what has to be done. Without speaking we walk back together.

The people are all standing there. Everyone. Still silent. Still made of wood.

I lift the mouth organ to my lips and start to play. It is the sweetest tune. It is the sound of the birth of the world. It is a flower opening. It is a mother's tear plopping on her baby's cheek. It is a foal's first steps. It is the promise of new life.

My wish comes true. Stiff limbs soften. Wooden lips smile. The people are people again. They are caught up by the tune. They are happy. They remember nothing of my hateful melodies. They sway in time to my new tune. All is forgotten.

I look at Mr Hardbristle's window. I can see his face looking out. It disappears. He comes out and stares up at the magnolia tree. The withered leaves are not withered any more. They are green and fresh. My music has brought the magnolia tree back to life.

The young man turns to me and smiles. 'You have one more tune to play,' he says.

I close my eyes and hold the mouth organ to my lips. I just play a tune of love. Nothing more.

When I open my eyes Mr Hardbristle is smiling. Everyone is smiling.

And the magnolia tree is in full bloom.

Greensleeves

My nickname was Greensleeves and I didn't like it. Not one bit. It wasn't what you think though. It had nothing to do with the way I wipe my nose. Nothing at all.

It was because of the watch.

Anyway, let me start at the beginning. You might as well know the whole story.

Dad and I lived in the caravan park in Port Niranda. We were very poor. Always short of cash. Dad used to get paid for digging out tree stumps on people's farms. He would dig a hole under a stump and then shove in a couple of sticks of gelignite. Then he would rush for cover as the whole thing went up with a mighty bang. After that he used to load up the scraps of stump that were left and sell them for firewood.

It didn't pay much. That's why I was so surprised when he gave me the watch. 'Gee thanks Dad,' I yelled. 'What a ripper. A digital watch with an alarm.'

'Try out the alarm,' said Dad with a grin. 'It plays a tune.'

I pressed a couple of buttons and set the alarm. Five minutes later, at exactly four o'clock, off it went.

It played a little tinkling tune called 'Greensleeves'.

I gave Dad a hug. He really was the tops. He could easily have spent the money on himself. He was saving up for the deposit on a house so we didn't have to live in the caravan park any more. Poor old Dad. He only owned work clothes. Old boots, a woollen beanie, grubby jeans and an old battle jacket. He wasn't exactly the best-dressed man in town. But as far as I was concerned he was the best man in town.

'Where did you get the money?' I asked. 'You shouldn't have spent it on me, Dad. You should have bought yourself a new outfit.'

'I've just landed a big job,' he said with a crooked smile. 'A real big job. We'll soon be in the money.'

2

I didn't like the way he said 'real big job.' A nasty thought was trying to find its way into my mind. 'What job?' I asked.

'The whale. I'm going to get rid of the whale.'

'Oh no,' I groaned. 'Not the whale. Not that.' I looked at him in horror. To tell the truth I felt like giving the watch back. Even if it did play 'Greensleeves'.

A whale had stranded itself on the main beach about three weeks ago. It was the biggest sperm whale ever seen. It was longer than three big houses joined together.

And just as high. Before anyone could do anything to save the poor thing it had died.

People came from everywhere to look at this whale. All the motels were full up with rubbernecks. They swarmed down on the beach taking photos. Special buses came up from Melbourne filled with tourists. No one had ever seen such a large whale before.

Then, suddenly, the tourists stopped coming. No one would even go onto the beach or anywhere near it. The whale started to go bad.

What a stink. It was terrible. When the wind blew from the south (which was just about all the time), the whole town was covered in the smell. It was unbearable. People locked themselves in their houses and shut the windows. But it was no good. The terrible fumes snuck under the doors and down the chimneys. They seeped and creeped into every crevice. There was no escape. It was revolting. It was just like living with a bucket of sick under the bed.

Sailors tried to tow the whale out to sea with a tug boat but the cable broke. The whale was too heavy.

Men from the council, dressed in gas masks, tried to move it with bulldozers. It still wouldn't budge. In the end they gave up and refused to go anywhere near it.

And now Dad had offered to take on the job. 'Five thousand dollars,' he said. 'That's what I'm getting for removing the whale. Everyone else has failed. The Mayor is desperate.'

'Five thousand dollars,' I echoed. 'That's enough for – '

'Yes,' interrupted Dad. 'Enough for a deposit on a house.'

I looked around our little caravan. I sure would be glad to move into a house. 'But how are you going to move it?' I asked.

'Not me,' said Dad. *We*. You are going to help.' He was grinning from ear to ear.

'Me,' I gasped. 'What can I do? Tie a rope onto one of its teeth and drag it off? There's nothing I can do.'

'You can scramble into its mouth,' said Dad, 'and get right down deep inside it. Like Jonah. Then you can shove the sticks of gelignite into its guts.'

'What?' I screamed. 'You're going to blow it up? Blow up the whale?'

'Yes,' hooted Dad. 'It'll be a cinch. No one's thought of blowing it up. The gelignite will break it up into small bits and the tide will wash them out to sea. And we will be five thousand dollars richer.'

For a minute I just stood there thinking about the whole thing. I thought about crawling into a whale's gizzards. I thought about the terrible stink. Then I thought about poor old Dad trying to save up for a house. I looked at his worn-out clothes and his faded beanie.

'Okay,' I said with a shiver. 'I'll do it.'

'Shake, Troy,' said Dad, holding out his big brown hand.

I shook his hand. The deal was done. A boy's word is his word. I couldn't get out of it now.

3

The next day Dad and I headed off towards the beach in our old truck. On the back were boxes of gelignite, fuses, ropes, axes and other tackle. As we got closer to the shore the smell became stronger and stronger. What a pong. It was revolting. Dad pulled over to the side of the road and we put on our gas masks. It was a little better with the gas masks on, but it was very hard to talk. We had to shout at each other.

When we reached the beach there were only two people to be seen. I couldn't tell who they were because they had gas masks on too.

'It's Mr Steal, the Mayor,' said Dad. 'And that boy of his.'

I smothered a groan. The Mayor's son Nick was a pain in the bum. And Nick was a good name for him too. He was always nicking things. The only trouble was you could never catch him. He was too quick. If you put your best pen on the desk at school when he was around you could kiss it goodbye. The pen would just vanish. It was no good telling the teachers. If you couldn't prove that Nick stole the pen then you couldn't complain. The teachers would just tell you off instead of him.

'We don't want anyone here while we work,' Dad said to Mr Steal. 'It's too dangerous with all this gelignite around.'

'I'm here to make sure you do a good job,' said Mr Steal. 'I'll take care of Nick. He won't get in your way.'

'Well,' said Dad, 'you both stay here with the truck. I don't want either of you getting any closer to the whale.'

I looked at the rotting whale. Its eyes were like dead white saucers. Seagulls sat on its mountainous back pecking away at the tough hide. Even with the gas mask on I could smell it. The fumes were so thick that you could almost see them.

'Now,' said Dad, peering at me through his gas mask. 'You take two sticks of gelignite at a time into the mouth. Sixteen altogether. I'll drop sixteen sticks down the blow hole. For every stick you take into the whale put a match in this box.' He put a small wooden box down on the back of the truck next to Nick.

We called this the tally box. It helped us to know how many sticks of gelignite had been planted.

'If we don't put in enough,' said Dad, 'it won't blow the whale into small enough pieces. Make sure you put one match in the box for every stick of gelignite. Then we will know we have the right number.'

I nodded at Dad. His voice sounded funny inside the gas mask.

I looked up at Nick. He was staring at the tally box. I could swear that he was sneering at us. Nick was a nasty bit of work. That was for sure.

Dad put a long ladder up against the whale and climbed up onto its back. 'It's slippery,' he yelled, 'but it will be okay.' I watched him drop the first two sticks of gelignite down the whale's blow hole. Then I walked around to the whale's mouth.

My heart sank as I peered into the gaping jaws. It was like a big, wet cave. Every now and then a piece of rotting flesh would break off the roof of its mouth and fall onto its tongue with a wet thunk. I shivered. Then I walked back to the truck to get my first two sticks of gelignite.

I put two matches into the tally box and walked slowly back to the stinking carcass.

4

Dad gave me my instructions. 'Get right down inside her guts. She won't blow properly if you don't. I'd go myself but I'm too big to get right inside. You don't mind do you?'

To be honest I did mind. What if I got stuck? What if I got lost? What if the gizzards collapsed on me and I got buried alive? I stared at Dad's eyes through the gas mask and remembered our handshake. A deal is a deal. With pounding heart I walked into the soggy, wet mouth of the dead whale.

Dad went back to his ladder to finish putting the rest of the sticks down the blow hole. I was alone.

I walked carefully over the sagging, stinking tongue. With every step I sank up to my ankles. My heart was pounding with terror. I shone my torch into the blackness and saw that the roof sloped downwards. On either side were white, glistening shelves of gristle. I forced my legs to take me forward. Soon the roof was so low that I had to go forward on my knees. My jeans were soaked with slime.

Suddenly the whole thing narrowed into a spongy tube like a sausage. I knew that I would have to lie on my stomach and wriggle in. I could hear my breath sucking and squeezing through the gas mask. The goggles were starting to mist up in the damp air. I couldn't do it. I just couldn't do it. I couldn't bury myself inside that giant sausage-shaped bit of guts.

Then I thought of poor Dad and the battered old caravan. I pushed myself forward with a great shove and slithered into the tube. I had the gelignite in one hand and the torch in the other. But I couldn't see anything. I was surrounded by gurgling blackness. I wriggled in further and further. Down, down, down into the darkest depths and all around me the dead whale's decaying dinner.

Suddenly my hand touched something solid. It was like a slimy wall. It seemed to be crawling. It was crawling. It was covered in maggots. I dropped the gelignite and shrieking and screaming pushed myself backwards. Wriggling, choking, scrambling like a fat caterpillar inside the finger of a rubber glove.

I squirted out into the mouth and slithered over the tongue and into the glaring sunshine. Then, before my heart failed me, I staggered over to the truck and grabbed four sticks of gelignite – as much as I could carry. I threw four matches into the tally box and once again entered the unspeakable jaws.

Down I went – into the grizzly gizzards. Then out. Then back down. Then out. How many times I slid down into that filthy throat I couldn't say. Each time I threw matches into the tally box but the pile never seemed to grow. I staggered in and out and in and out. My head swam. My brain pounded. At last I could do no more. I fell onto the ground next to the truck. Nothing would make me go in there again.

Dad counted the matches. 'Fourteen,' he said. 'Two more to go.'

I couldn't believe it. It seemed as if I had taken a million sticks of gelignite in there.

Dad could see that I was beat. 'Don't worry,' he said. 'You've done a great job. I'll just throw the last two sticks of gelignite into the mouth. That should be okay.' He walked over to the whale and threw the last sticks in gently. 'Right,' he yelled at Mr Steal and Nick. 'Get out of the way. We're ready to blow her up.'

Nick and Mr Steal turned to go. And as they did so, I saw Nick shove something into his shirt pocket. It was a little bundle of matches.

My heart jumped up into my throat. He had been taking matches out of the tally box. This meant I had taken too many sticks of gelignite into the whale. I had been into the innards more often than I needed to. I felt faint with fury.

I wanted to run after him and strangle him with my slippery hands. But I didn't. If I told Dad he would make me go back into the whale and count the gelignite sticks. I just couldn't do it.

5

We drove the truck back down the beach to a safe spot. Everyone in the town had gathered at the foreshore to watch the big explosion. They all stood with hand-kerchiefs over their noses to keep out the smell.

Dad lit the long fuse that dangled out of the whale's blow hole and ran back to the truck. I wondered what difference it would make having too many sticks of gelignite inside the whale. It would probably just blow it up into smaller pieces, which would make it wash away easier.

The fuse spluttered and spat. The little orange flame crept up the side of the whale and into the blow hole. I pulled back my sleeve to see what time it was.

My watch was gone. It had fallen off inside the whale.

Oh no. I couldn't bear it. My new watch. I was mixed up. Angry. Crazy. Off my head. I stood up and ran over towards the whale. 'My watch. My watch. My watch,' I yelled.

I could hear Dad's voice behind me. He was shouting and screeching. 'Come back, Troy. Come back. She's about to blow.'

I didn't know what I was doing. I fell into the mouth

and slithered in. Dad's strong hands grabbed my ankles and pulled me out. He dragged me back across the sand. Bumping, jerking, scraping on my stomach. My mouth and eyes filled with sand. Shells and pebbles scratched my face. Tears streamed down my cheeks.

Dad jerked me under the truck. Just in time.

Kerblam. The sky disappeared. The sun blotted out. Sand and whale gizzards filled the air with a black blizzard. It hailed whale. It blew whale. It shrieked whale. It wailed whale.

There must have been fifty sticks of gelignite inside it.

The roar almost burst our eardrums. The truck shook with the shock. Every sliver of paint was sandblasted off its body.

And when the air cleared a great lake had formed in the crater on the beach. Not one tiny piece of whale was left on the sand.

'Whoopee,' yelled Dad. 'We've done it. We've done it.'

'That's not all you've done,' said a cold voice from behind us. It was Mayor Steal and his gloating son Nick. Mayor Steal pointed at the town.

We all turned and stared. The whole town was covered in bits of stinking whale. Pieces of whale gut hung from the lamp posts and the TV aerials. The roofs were littered with horrible bits of red and grey stuff. Windows were broken. The electricity wires were draped with strings of intestines. The streets were filled with lumps and glumps of foul flesh.

If the smell had been bad before it was worse now. It was so bad that it made your eyes water. Every house was smothered in the torn and tattered remains of the whale.

'Don't think you'll get paid for this,' said Mayor Steal in a hard voice. 'It'll take five thousand dollars to clean this mess up. I doubt that anyone in this town is ever going to speak to you again.'

'I can't understand it,' said Dad, shaking his head. 'It shouldn't have gone up with such a big bang. Thirty-two sticks shouldn't have gone up like that.'

'It was him,' I screamed, pointing at the grinning Nick. 'He stole the tally sticks. He took the matches out of the box. They are in his shirt pocket.'

'Don't try to blame my boy,' said the Mayor. 'Don't try to shift the blame onto an innocent bystander.'

'Search him,' said Dad. 'Look in his shirt pocket.'

'No,' said Mayor Steal.

Before Nick could move, Dad grabbed him and searched his pockets.

They were empty.

6

'He's thrown them away,' I shouted. 'He always does that after he nicks something. You can never catch him. I saw him with matches. I saw him. I did, I did, I did.' I was crying but I didn't care. I had gone down into the whale's guts for nothing. We would never get a house now. Never.

'What a low trick,' said Mayor Steal. 'First you blame Nick and now this grubby wrecker searches him. And finds nothing. I want an apology.'

Dad hung his head. Then he looked at Nick. 'Sorry,' he said. 'I shouldn't have done that.'

We turned and walked sadly home through the whale-infested town. The Council workers were already out cleaning up. We both felt miserable. We had missed our chance to earn five thousand dollars. All because of that rotten Nick.

'We will never get a house now,' I said sadly. 'Not unless we win Tatts.'

'Or find a lump of ambergris,' answered Dad slowly.

'What's ambergris?' I asked.

'When a whale is sick,' said Dad, 'it sometimes makes this stuff called ambergris inside its stomach. It's worth a lot of money. But only one whale in a thousand ever has it.'

I brightened up a bit. 'What does it look like?'

'I don't know. I wouldn't have the foggiest,' said Dad, looking around him at the bits of blasted whale that covered the ground.

When we got back to the caravan I could see bits of whale on the roof. One of the caravan windows was broken. I went inside and found a round, grey lump on my pillow. It was about the size of a cricket ball. It was a slippery glob of something from inside the whale. I took it outside and put it on the caravan step.

Then Dad and I went to help the council workers clean up. 'It's the least we can do,' said Dad.

As we went out of the caravan park I saw Nick staring at us from his bedroom window. He was looking at us with binoculars. I pretended not to see him.

Dad and I worked all day helping people clean up their houses. We collected the horrible guts and put it in bins. Then we took it down to the tip on the back of the truck. The people of the town didn't say much. Just about everyone liked Dad and they could see that he was trying to make up for the damage by helping with the cleaning up.

Halfway through the afternoon, while we were sweeping up in the school yard, Mayor Steal pulled up in his Jaguar. He had a little grey-haired man with him. 'This is Mister Proust,' said the Mayor. 'He wants to talk to you.'

Mr Proust spoke with a high, squeaky voice. He looked right at me. 'Are you the boy who went inside the whale?' he asked.

'Yes,' I said wearily.

'Did you see anything that looks like this?' He showed me a coloured photo.

'What is it?' I asked.

'It's ambergris. It comes from inside the sperm whale. We use it to make perfume. The best perfume in the world. But now that whales can't be killed any more it is very hard to get.'

I stared at the photo of a grey slippery glob of something from inside the whale. It was about the size of a cricket ball.

The little man was getting more and more excited. 'One piece that big,' he said, 'is worth ten thousand dollars. That's what I will give you for a bit that size.'

I hadn't seen anything inside the whale. It was too dark. I shook my head. That's when I remembered. 'Back at the caravan,' I yelled. 'I've got a bit back at the caravan and it looks just like that.'

We all piled into the Jaguar and Mayor Steal drove us back towards the caravan park. He seemed to want to please this little man for some reason. As we went past the Steals' house I noticed Nick in the upstairs bedroom. He was throwing something up and down in his hands. It looked like a ball.

When we reached the caravan the ball of ambergris was not on the step. 'Someone's swiped it,' said Dad. He looked downcast and beaten.

'And I know who,' I yelled. 'I saw Nick with it as we went past. It's in his bedroom.'

Mr Proust was jumping up and down excitedly and waving his cheque book around.

Mr Steal narrowed his eyes. 'You are not blaming my son again are you?' He was hissing in a low voice. He was very angry.

Dad looked at me. 'Are you sure? Are you really sure?'

I took a deep breath. 'Yes,' I said.

'We want to search Nick's room,' said Dad. 'Troy doesn't tell lies.'

'And Nick doesn't steal,' said the Mayor.

Both men looked at each other. Finally Mayor Steal said, 'All right. I'll let you search Nick's room. But if you don't find anything you have to agree to one thing.'

'What's that?' asked Dad.

'That if you don't find the ambergris in Nick's room you both leave town tomorrow and never come back.'

Dad and I both blinked. We were thinking the same thing. We didn't want to leave town. We loved Port Niranda. All our friends lived there. My mother was buried in the cemetery there. We didn't want to leave.

There was a long silence. Then Dad said, 'Okay, we search the room, and if we don't find anything we leave Port Niranda tomorrow.' I could see that his eyes were watering.

7

We all trooped up into Nick's room. 'I didn't take nothing,' he yelled at his father. 'You can look where you like.' He was smirking. My stomach felt heavy. He didn't look the least bit worried.

Dad and I searched the room while the others stood and watched. We spent a whole hour at it. Nothing. We searched under the mattress. In the cupboards and drawers. Everywhere.

'I saw you throwing something shaped like a ball,' I said to Nick.

'I don't even have a ball,' he smirked. 'Do I, Dad?'

'No,' said Mr Steal. 'And that's enough searching. There is no ball of ambergris in this room. I expect both of you to be out of town by first thing tomorrow.'

I looked at Dad. He suddenly seemed very old. 'Can't I come back to visit my wife's grave?' he asked.

Mayor Steal shook his head. 'A man's word is his word,' he replied.

Nick was grinning his rotten head off.

I looked up at the clock on the wall. Four o'clock. Time to go.

As we turned to leave I heard a soft noise. Something I had heard once before. A little tinkling tune. A very faint melody. It was 'Greensleeves'.

'There,' I yelled. 'Under the carpet.'

Dad rushed over and pulled back a rug. There was a small trapdoor. He yanked it open and pulled out the ball of ambergris. A little shining piece of watch could be seen poking out of it. It was my watch. The one I had lost in the whale. It must have got jammed in the ambergris when the whale exploded. The alarm was still set for four o'clock and it had just gone off.

Nick ran out of the room yowling. His father ran after him shouting and shaking his fist and calling Nick a thief and a liar.

Mr Proust started writing in his cheque book with a big smile. 'Ten thousand dollars,' he said as he handed the cheque to Dad. 'And you can keep the watch as well.'

We both looked at the sticky watch with big grins on our faces. It was still playing 'Greensleeves'.

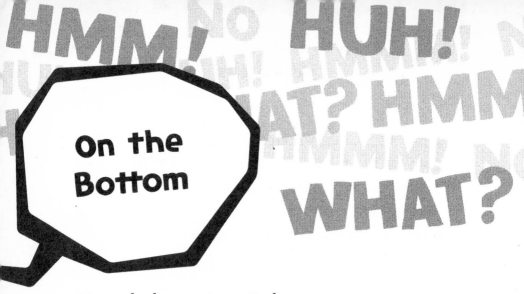

On the Bottom

'It's on the bottom,' says Dad.

'No,' I tell him. 'I've got a fish.'

'It's too big,' says Dad. 'It couldn't be a fish. You're snagged on the bottom.'

He is wrong. I know it is a fish because it is pulling the line out. Snags don't pull on the line.

My rod starts to bend and the line goes whizzing out. Whatever it is, I know I have hooked a whopper.

'You're right, it is a fish,' yells Dad. 'And it's a big one. It's even rocking the boat. Give me the rod, you might lose it.'

Dad always does this. As soon as I hook a fish he wants to pull it in. He thinks that a fourteen-year-old kid can't land his own fish. I shake my head and keep winding on the reel. 'Get the gaff,' I shout. 'I can land it − I know I can.'

For the next hour I play my fish. Sometimes he runs deep and fast and the reel screeches like a cooked cat. Sometimes I get it almost to the edge of our hire boat and then off it goes again. 'I hope it's a snapper,' says Dad. 'Snapper are good eating.'

In the end I win. I get the fish to the edge of the boat and Dad pulls him in with the gaff. I am grinning from ear to ear because I have landed him.

'It's only a shark,' says Dad. 'A small shark. Not much good for eating.' He gives a bit of a grin. 'Well done Lucas. You played him well but you might as well throw him back.'

'No way,' I say. 'You can eat shark. Haven't you ever heard of flake?'

'All right,' says Dad, 'but you have to clean it. You caught it. You clean it.' Dad goes down the steps into the little cabin and leaves me up top to clean my shark. It is about a metre long and it is still kicking around on the deck. I open up a can of Fanta and look at the shark while I am drinking it. After a while the shark stops moving and I know it is dead. I get out my cleaning knife and make a long slit along its belly. I throw the innards and other stuff overboard. Seagulls swoop around fighting for the bits.

Finally I come to the shark's stomach. I decide to look inside and see what it has been eating. This will give me some clues as to what to use for bait. I throw out some fish heads and shells. Then I see something a bit different. I pick up this white, shrivelled thing that looks like a small sausage. For about ten seconds I stare at it. My mind goes numb and I can't quite make sense of what I am seeing. I notice first of all that it has a finger nail. And a ring. Just below the ring is a small tattoo of a bear. An angry bear.

It is a finger. I have just taken a human finger out of the shark's stomach.

2

I give an almighty scream. A terrible, fearful scream. At the same time I throw my hands up and let go of the finger. It spins in the air like a wheel and then splashes into the sea. Quick as a flash a seagull swoops down and swallows it. The finger has gone.

I have to hand it to that seagull. It swallows the whole finger in one go.

Just then Dad comes rushing up from below. 'What's going on?' he yells. 'Did it bite you?' Dad thinks the dead shark has bitten me.

'No,' I croak. 'A finger. In the shark. A man's finger. With a ring and a bear.'

'What are you babbling about, boy?' says Dad. 'What finger?'

'In the shark's stomach. I found a finger. It had a little picture of a bear on it. And a ring. Oooh. Oh. Yuck. It was all shrivelled up and horrible.' As I tell Dad this a little shiver runs down my spine.

Dad goes a bit pale. He has a weak stomach. 'Where is it?' he asks slowly. Dad does not really want to see a human finger but he has to do the right thing and ask to see it.

I point to the empty sky. There is not a seagull in

sight. 'A seagull ate it. I dropped it in the sea and a seagull ate it.'

Dad looks at me for a long time without saying anything. Then he starts up the engine. 'We will have to report it to the police. There goes our day's fishing.'

'How did it get there?' I ask slowly.

'Don't ask,' says Dad. 'It's better not to think about it.' Then he stops talking. He is staring at my hand. He is staring so hard at my hand that I think maybe he has never seen a hand before. His face turns red.

He grabs my wrist and starts shaking my arm around. 'What's this?' he yells. 'What on earth have you done?'

'Nothing,' I say. 'I haven't done anything. What are you talking about?' I can tell that Dad is as mad as a snake. Then I look down at my hand and I can see what the matter is. There on the back of my right hand is a little picture. A tattoo of a bear is on the back of one of my fingers.

3

We both gaze at the drawing of the little bear. 'You fool,' yells Dad. 'You've gone and had yourself tattooed. Don't you know that tattoos don't come off? You're stuck with it for life.' He rushes over to the locker and comes back with a whopping big scrubbing brush. He brushes at my hand so hard that my skin goes red. Tears come to my eyes. Dad stops scrubbing and has another look. The little bear is still there. It has a sad expression on its face. I have a sad expression on my face also.

'It came from the finger,' I tell Dad. 'It must have jumped from the finger onto me. The finger from the shark's stomach.'

Dad looks at me through narrowed eyes. 'Don't make it worse boy,' he says angrily. 'Don't add to your folly by making up a pack of lies about a finger. There was no finger.' He shakes his head. 'This is all the thanks I get for everything I've done for you.' He is really angry about the tattoo.

'There was a finger,' I yell. 'There was, there was, there was.'

Dad turns the boat around and heads for shore. The fishing trip is over. 'Don't you mention one more word about a finger in the shark's stomach,' says Dad. 'You must think that I'm as silly as you. Don't let me hear another word of that cock-and-bull story. Or else.'

It is no good saying anything. He won't listen and I don't really blame him. I can hardly believe it myself. How can a tattoo jump from a dead finger onto a live one? Tattoos don't move. I sit down in the bow and look at my little bear.

This is when I notice something strange. The bear is different. When I first saw my bear he had all four feet on the ground. Now he has one paw pointing. Pointing out to sea. I move my hand around so that the paw is pointing to the shore. The bear turns around. My tattoo moves. It turns around so that its paw once more points out to sea.

The tattoo is alive and it is pointing out to sea.

'It moved,' I say to Dad. He shakes his head. He won't listen. 'The bear can move,' I yell. 'It's pointing out to sea.' Dad revs up the engine and heads for shore even faster than before.

I look at the bear again. It seems to be staring back at me. It wants something. It wants us to go out to sea.

'Go the other way,' I say to Dad. 'The tattoo wants us to head out to sea.'

Dad turns off the engine and the boat stops. He is staring at me with wild eyes. I can tell that he thinks I have gone crazy. Either that or he thinks I am the biggest liar in the world. 'Come here Lucas,' he says. 'We need to have a talk.' He goes down the steps into the cabin.

Quick as a flash I hop up and slam the cabin door. I slide the bolt across and lock Dad inside. He starts to bang and yell but I don't let him out. Instead, I start up the boat and head away from shore. The bear knows best. I decide to follow the bear.

4

I push the throttle forward and the boat surges ahead at full speed. The bear is nodding its little head. It thinks I am doing a good job. It is a nice little bear really. I am quite pleased to have it.

'Let me out,' yells Dad.

The bear shakes its head.

'No,' I say.

'Don't go out of sight of land,' shouts Dad. 'We'll get lost.'

'We have the compass,' I say. 'And the bear. The bear knows where to go.' I am not quite sure but I think I hear a groan come from down in the cabin.

'Look at the petrol,' yells Dad. 'For heavens sake don't use up more than half or we'll never get back.'

He has a point there. I look at the bear on my finger for guidance. It is still waving me on. The sea is becoming rough and the sky is growing dark but on we go. On and on until we can no longer see the land. A wind gets up but still my bear waves me on. The sun is sinking low and clouds are starting to race across the sky. The petrol gauge is showing half full.

And then I see it. A tiny speck on the horizon. 'Is this it?' I say to my tattoo. I am very fond of this little bear. It is nice having a little helper around when you need him.

The bear gives me a paws-up signal. This is it. This is what we have come for.

The speck grows larger and larger until I can see that it is a small rowing boat. There does not seem to be anyone aboard. Dad is still yelling and banging from below but I don't take any notice of him. I slow the boat down and stop next to the dinghy. There is someone in it. A man lying in the bottom. He is lying very still. Very still indeed.

5

I stop the boat and let Dad out. Without a word he rushes over to the edge and looks into the boat. 'See if he's alive,' says Dad. 'I'll get some water.'

I climb down into the little boat and peer at the unconscious figure. He is dressed only in a pair of faded shorts. One hand is wrapped in a bloodstained handkerchief. I can see at a glance that the man has a finger missing. I can also see something else. He is covered, absolutely covered, in tattoos.

There is not one bit of skin that does not have tattoos on it. There are skulls with toothless smiles. There are tigers and forests. There are daggers with snakes twined around them. There is a large heart with 'Sophie' written in it. There are mermaids and eagles. There is even an eye on the bald patch on his head. The tattooed man is terrific. But is he alive?

I put my hand down to see if he has a pulse. I feel just under his neck like they do in the movies. And then it happens. You may not believe this but it really does happen. The tattoos start to move. It is sort of like pulling out the plug in a bath and watching the water run out. The tattoos swirl and slide across his skin. They move in a rush. They pour across his flesh to the same spot. His neck. And from his neck they move on – and out. They swarm up my arm and flow across my chest. Before I can blink the whole lot have completely covered me. I am a tattooed boy. And he has clear, white skin. Not one tattoo is left on him. Not one.

I give a shriek and fall over backwards in the dinghy. I am covered in a zoo of animals, birds, plants and people.

Dad climbs down and holds up water to the non-tattooed man's lips. He swallows. He is alive.

The trip back is a nightmare. The man without the tattoos lies unconscious below. Dad drives the boat flat out for home. I sit staring in the mirror. My whole face is covered in tattoos. They are also on my ears, nose, cheeks and even my eyelids. They cover my chest, my back, my arms and my legs. I sneak a look inside my underpants but thank goodness there are none down there.

We finally get home and the man is taken to hospital. So am I.

There is nothing the doctors can do for me. Tattoos don't come off. No one believes our story about the shark or the tattoos. The doctors all think Dad and I are mad or delirious. They are especially angry with Dad for letting his son get himself tattooed all over his body. There is talk of taking me away from Dad and putting me in a home.

The man without the tattoos does not wake up. He is in a coma.

Finally they let Dad and me go home. I sit in the house feeling very sorry for myself indeed. I scrub and scrub but the tattoos are there to stay. The love heart with 'Sophie' written on it is right in the middle of my forehead. I know what my girlfriend Cheryl will think of that. I'm too worried to leave the house – I don't want anyone to see me.

The little bear is still there on my finger although he is difficult to see among all the tigers and snakes. He seems to smile at me. I wouldn't mind keeping the bear but I do not want the rest. These tattoos have ruined my life. I can't go to school. I won't be able to get a job. I will have to be a tattooed boy in a circus. Sitting there for everyone to gaze at. How embarrassing. I start to cry. Little tears roll across the mermaids on my cheeks.

6

Weeks pass and I do not leave the house. I sit in my room without talking to anyone. Now and then the little bear seems to wave at me. He is my only friend. I would not like to lose the bear but I would give anything to get rid of the other tattoos.

Then, one day, there is a knock on the door. It is the man without the tattoos. He has recovered from his coma. Dad invites him in and tells him to sit down.

The man thanks us for saving his life. He is grateful that we found him in the dinghy. His boat had drifted out to sea and he would have died if my little bear hadn't shown us where he was. After a bit of this polite chat, Tattooless gets down to the point. 'Look, Lucas,' he says, 'you have some things of mine and I want them back.'

He is talking about the tattoos. It turns out that he is a tattooed man from the sideshows. 'They are the best tattoos in the world,' he says. 'They cost me thousands of dollars. And the pain. Oh the pain. It hurts to get them done. I have sat for hundreds of hours while they drilled away at me. And all for nothing. You've got the lot. The tattoos all nicked off and left me. Except the bear. The shark got that when I put my hand over the side of the boat.'

'But why?' I say. 'Why would they leave?'

'Have you ever thought,' says Tattooless, 'what happens to tattoos when you die? They thought I was done for. They were getting out of it like rats deserting a sinking ship. They didn't want to shrivel up with me when I died so they cleared out onto you. But now I want them back.'

'How?' I ask. A nasty thought comes into my mind. I saw a man skin a rabbit once.

'They might come back to me,' says Tattooless. 'After all, it's a bit crowded on you. You're not as big as me and the tattoos are all bunched up.'

I have to admit that he has a point there.

'Hold out your hand,' he orders. I hold out my hand

and we shake like old friends. Nothing happens. We stand there clasping each other for quite a while. Suddenly, with a rush, the tattoos start to move. The whole lot swirl and twirl like slides shining on a moving curtain. They drain off down my arm and back to their owner.

We all grin. I have no tattoos and Tattooless is not tattooless any more. He is covered all over in his drawings again. The tattoos have left me and returned home.

He stands up and heads for the door. 'Wait,' says Dad. Don't go yet. I want to make sure there are none left. You might have missed one.' Dad orders me to take off my clothes. I strip down to my underpants and Dad checks me for tattoos. He does not find any.

'Okay,' says Dad to the tattooed man. 'You can go now.'

The tattooed man holds out his hand but I do not want to shake. Neither does Dad. We decide to give the shaking a miss and make do with a wave.

7

Well that is just about the end of the story. Dad does another check for tattoos but he doesn't find any. I'm glad he doesn't look down the back of my underpants though.

Otherwise he might see my little bear behind.

Snookle

Snookle was delivered one morning with the milk. There were four half-litre bottles; three of them contained milk and the other held Snookle.

He stared sadly at me from his glass prison. I could see he was alive even though he made no sign or movement. He reminded me of a dog on a chain that manages to make its owner feel guilty simply by looking unhappy. Snookle wanted to get out of that milk bottle but he didn't really expect it to happen. He didn't say anything, he just gazed silently into my eyes.

I placed the three full bottles in the fridge and put Snookle and his small home on the table. Then I sat down and looked at him carefully. All I could see was a large pair of gloomy eyes. He must have had a body but it was nowhere to be seen. The eyes simply floated in the air about fifteen centimetres above the bottom of the bottle.

Mum and Dad had already left for work so I wouldn't get any help from them. I gave the bottle a gentle shake and the eyes bounced around like a couple of small rubber balls. The gloomy expression was replaced by one of alarm and the eyes blinked a number of times before settling back to their original position.

'Sorry,' I said. 'I didn't mean to hurt you.' There was no reply, just a long reproachful look.

'Where did you come from?' I asked. 'And how did you get here? What sort of creature are you? What is your name?' I received no reply to my question. In fact, the eyes began to close. He was falling asleep.

A nasty thought entered my mind. What if he was dying? There is not much air in a milk bottle. He might be suffocating if he was an air-breathing creature. I thought about opening the bottle and letting him out. But if I did I could be in for big trouble. He might not go back into the bottle and he could be dangerous. He might bite me or give me some terrible disease that would kill off the whole human race. He might nick off, spreading death and disease wherever he went.

I went over to the window and looked outside. Maybe one of the kids from school would be passing. Two heads would be better than one, especially if the thing in the bottle attacked me. Then I remembered. It was Correction Day and there was no school. The only person in the street was poor old Mrs McKee who was hobbling down her steps to get the milk. She wouldn't be any help. She had arthritis and it was all she could do to pick up one milk bottle at a time. It took her half an hour to shuffle back to the front door from the gate.

Some weekends I used to go and do jobs for Mrs McKee

because her hands were so weak that she couldn't do anything by herself. Her garden was overgrown with weeds and her windows were dirty. All the paint was peeling off the house. I once heard Mum say that Mrs McKee would have to go into an old folks' home soon because her fingers wouldn't move properly. No, Mrs McKee wouldn't be any use if the eyes in the bottle turned nasty.

2

I looked at my visitor again. His eyelids were beginning to droop. At any moment he might be dead. I decided to take the risk. With one swift movement I took the metal cap off the bottle.

The expression in the eyes changed. They looked happy. Then they started to move slowly up to the neck of the bottle. I could tell that the little creature was climbing up the glass even though I couldn't see his body. The eyes emerged from the bottle and floated in the air just above the rim. He sat on the top of the bottle staring at me happily. I couldn't see his mouth or any part of his face but I knew he was smiling.

'What's your name?' I asked. It might seem silly to talk to an unknown creature as if it could answer but I had a feeling that he would understand me. Even so, I got a shock when he did answer. He didn't use words or speech. I could hear him inside my brain.

The word 'Snookle' just sort of drifted into my mind.

'Who are you, Snookle?' I said. 'And what do you want?'

Again he answered without talking. His reply melted into my thoughts. 'I am your servant. Your every thought is my command.' They weren't his exact words because he didn't use words but it is more or less what he meant. Especially the bit about my every thought being his command. That was the next thing I found out – he could read my thoughts. He knew what I wanted without me saying anything.

3

My stomach suddenly rumbled. I was hungry. The eyes floated across the table and over to the pantry. Snookle could fly. The next thing I knew a packet of cornflakes and a bowl flew slowly back with the eyes following close behind. Then the fridge opened and the milk arrived the same way. The cornflakes and milk were tipped into the bowl and sugar added. Just the right amount and just the way I liked it. This was great. He knew I wanted breakfast and he got it for me without even being told. I didn't eat it straight away because I like my cornflakes soggy.

I decided to try Snookle out on something else. I thought about bringing in the papers from the letterbox. Snookle floated over to the front door and opened it. Then he stayed there hovering in the air. 'Go on,' I said. 'Out you go.' The eyes moved from side to side. He was shaking his head. I looked out the door and saw a man riding by on a bike. As soon as the cyclist had passed Snookle flew out and fetched the papers. I knew what had happened. Snookle didn't want anyone to see him except his master. I was his master because I had let him out of the bottle. He would only show himself to me.

I went back to my bedroom followed by Snookle. His preferred altitude was about two metres off the ground. I decided to wear my stretch jeans as there was no school that day. The moment the thought entered my mind Snookle set off for the wardrobe. My jeans, T-shirt and underwear were delivered by air mail and laid out neatly on the bed. The next bit, however, gave me a bit of a surprise. Snookle pulled off my pyjamas and started to dress me. I felt a bit silly. It was just like a little kid being dressed by his mother. I could feel long, thin, cold fingers touching me.

'Cut it out, Snookle,' I said. 'You don't have to dress me.' He didn't take any notice. That was when I found out that Snookle helped you whether you wanted it or not.

My nose was itchy. I could feel a sneeze coming on. As quick as a flash Snookle whipped my handkerchief out of my pocket and held it up to my nose. I sneezed into the handkerchief and said, 'Thanks, but that wasn't necessary.'

I went back to the kitchen for my breakfast. Snookle

beat me to the spoon. I tried to grab it off him but he was too quick for me. He dipped the spoon into the cornflakes and pushed it into my mouth. I tried to stop him by keeping my lips closed but he prised them open with his chilly little invisible fingers and shoved the next spoonful in. He fed me the whole bowl of cornflakes just as if I was a baby.

Now I hope you will understand about the next bit. I am not really a nose picker but I have thought about it now and then. My nose was still a bit itchy and the thought just came into my mind to pick it. I wouldn't have done it any more than you would. Anyway, before I could blink, this cold, invisible finger went up my nose and picked it for me.

Snookle was picking my nose! I nearly freaked out. I screamed and tried to push him off but he was too strong.

After that things just got worse and worse. Snookle wouldn't let me do a thing for myself. Not a single thing.

4

I went back to the kitchen and sat down. This wasn't working out at all well. I could see my future looming in front of me with Snookle doing everything for me. Everything. He had to go. And quick.

I dropped a cornflake into the empty milk bottle and thought hard about getting it out. Snookle floated over and went into the bottle to get it. I moved like greased lightning and put the top back on that bottle before Snookle knew what had hit him. He was trapped. He didn't even try to get out but just looked at me with sad, mournful eyes as if he had expected nothing better.

Now I was in a fix. I didn't want to leave Snookle in the bottle for the rest of his life but I didn't want him hanging around picking my nose for me either. I looked out of the window. Poor old Mrs McKee had managed to get back to the house with one of her bottles of milk. Soon she would make the slow trip back to the letterbox for the next one.

I picked up Snookle and slowly crossed the road. Then I put his bottle down outside Mrs McKee's house. I grabbed her full bottle of milk with one hand and waved goodbye to Snookle with the other. His eyes stared silently and sadly back at me.

That was the last I ever saw of Snookle.

Over the next few days a remarkable change came over Mrs McKee's house. The grass was cut and the flowerbeds were weeded. The windows were cleaned and someone repainted the house. The people in the street thought it was strange because they never saw anyone doing the work.

I went over to see Mrs McKee about a week later. She seemed very happy. Very happy indeed.

Thought
Full

'I am never eating meat again,' I yelled at Dad.

He just smiled at me as if I was crazy.

You might think I'm crazy too. I mean most people who live on farms eat meat. So I'll tell you what. You be me for a while and see how you feel about it at the end.

1

It all starts because of the new steer. We have this cow called Slipped-in-the-Mud and it gives birth down in the bottom paddock. To the sweetest little calf you have ever seen.

The calf has a cute white patch on its face. It sucks away at its mother's udder and gets white froth all around its mouth.

And it likes you. It nuzzles up for a pat. Oh, it is so wonderful. It moos in a real soft way. It looks at you with those big brown eyes. Straight away you decide to call it Moonbeam.

You have never loved anything like you love this little calf.

'Dad,' you say. 'Can Moonbeam be mine? To keep forever? Just mine? Please.'

Dad shakes his head sadly. 'Sorry, Bomber,' he says. 'We can't afford to have it eating grass and not earning its way. Once it's weaned we have to sell it.'

'There's plenty of grass around here,' you yell.

'No there's not,' says Dad. 'We need every blade for the heifers who are going to give us milk. Steers do not grow up into cows. They become bulls. And they eat plenty.'

Tears fill your eyes. You just can't stand it. 'I won't let him go,' you shout. But deep in your heart you know that you are only a kid. You have no power. There is nothing you can do to stop them selling Moonbeam. You run off to your room and bang the door. You are so angry that you don't come out for at least five minutes.

The next day is really the start of all the weird things that happen. You wake up in the morning to find a terrible smell in the room. In the bed in fact. You look at your hands and give a scream. Your hands are all covered in sloppy green slime.

It stinks something terrible. How did it get there? Is someone playing a trick? What is going on here? Where did this horrible stuff come from? It looks like the goo that bubbles in the bog down by the front gate.

You think about it for a while and decide not to tell Mum and Dad about it. But it is too late. Mum is already in your bedroom and she is not rapt in what she sees.

'I told you to have a shower last night,' says Mum

angrily. 'Look, your sheets are all dirty. They're covered in green slime.'

'I did have a shower,' you say. 'Honest.'

You can tell that Mum doesn't believe you. You find it hard to believe yourself. How could your hands have got so dirty when you were asleep in bed all night?

You don't worry too much about it though because you have Moonbeam to think about. You take a walk down to his paddock for a visit. He is the best friend that you have ever had. When he licks your hand it is like being rubbed with soft, wet sandpaper. You put your arms around his neck. 'I will never let them sell you,' you say.

Suddenly you notice Dad standing behind you. 'Don't keep going on about it, Bomber,' he says. 'Every animal on a farm has to earn its keep. Moonbeam has to go. Times are bad and we need every penny we can get.'

Moonbeam sucks your fingers. He is only a calf. It is not his fault that he was born a male. Your heart is breaking because Moonbeam is going to be sold.

You worry about it all day and on into the evening. It is so bad that you find it hard to get to sleep that night. You toss and turn and try to hatch up plans to save your calf. In the end you nod off into dreamland.

2

At seven o'clock you are awakened by a smell. It is not the whiff of eggs and bacon sizzling in the kitchen.

It is not the smell of toast. It is not the scent of a warm, summer morning. It is the stink of slimy mud. You look under the blankets. You are soaked in it. Your pyjama trousers and top. Your feet and hands. A terrible, squelching, green ooze. The sheets are soaked.

Your brain freezes. Someone must have sneaked into the room and dumped sloppy mud on you. But who? Mum and Dad would never do such a thing.

You grab the sheets and try to sneak down to the laundry with them before Mum sees the mess.

But you are too late.

Mum catches you. At first she doesn't say anything. She just stares at you with one of those looks that says, 'How could you, Bomber?'

She calls a family conference.

This is the very worst thing. Family conferences are for times when the three of you have to work through a problem. 'Communicating,' says Mum.

But what it really means is that you get a big lecture.

'I slave away in that laundry,' says Mum. 'And Dad does the ironing. And what do you do, Bomber? You wander around outside in bare feet and make the sheets filthy. Now is that fair? I ask you.'

You start to give your side of the story. 'But I haven't been outside. I don't even remember...'

Dad doesn't wait for you to finish. 'It's that silly calf,' he says. 'The boy is going down the paddock talking to the calf in the middle of the night. It's not good enough, Bomber. As soon as that calf is weaned I'm taking it to the market.'

'But ...' you start to say.

'No buts,' says Dad. 'That calf has to go.'

Nothing will change his mind. Usually Dad is reasonable. He is a great father. But nothing will make him believe that you have not been down with Moonbeam in the middle of the night.

This is ruining your life. What is going on? How are you getting dirty in your own bed? Something has to be done. And quick.

That night you go to bed as usual. Well, not quite as usual. You get your alarm clock and tie it around your neck. Then you set it for one o'clock in the morning. If someone is dumping mud in your bed you are going to be awake to catch them.

Finally you fall asleep.

3

No sooner have your eyes closed than, 'Ding, ding, ding, ding.' What a racket. The alarm makes a terrible noise. Straight away you wake up and find out that it is one o'clock.

But where are you? Everything is dark around you. Overhead there are pinpoints of light. What are they doing there on the ceiling? You look again. There is no ceiling. The lights are stars. You are outside in the cold, still night.

The wind is fresh on your cheek. The water is wet on your arms and legs.

'Water?'

Is this some terrible dream? No, it is not. Worse luck. Your heart sinks. You know where you are.

You are on your hands and knees scratching in the bog down by the front gate. You are covered in green gunk.

Oh no. What is going on here? Why are you outside? You must be sleepwalking. Sleepdigging. This is terrible. Horrible.

You quickly start off towards the house. But you feel uneasy. You keep looking back at the bog. It seems to be calling you. Your feet want to take you back to the disgusting, bubbling slime. It is almost as if a magnet is pulling you back. You have this terrible urge to turn around and dig in the bog.

But you are strong. You don't go. The feeling gets weaker as you move away from the bog. But it is still there all the same. Like a silent voice in your mind calling.

Just as you reach the front door you hear noise from the barn. A moo. Moonbeam.

'What the heck,' you say. 'I might as well go and check on him while I'm here.'

You sneak into the barn and see Moonbeam curled up in the hay. Oh, he is beautiful. You start to stroke his soft, brown coat. You don't think of anything but wonderful Moonbeam. You do not realise that someone else is there too.

A hand falls on your shoulder and you just about jump out of your skin.

'Bomber. What are you doing here?'

It is Dad.

Your mind starts to race. What can you tell him? This looks bad. 'I was sleepdigging,' you say. 'In the bog. That's where all the slime is coming from.'

Dad does not believe you. That is clear. 'Bomber,' he says. 'Don't give me that. You are sneaking out to see Moonbeam. You have used up your last chance. I am definitely taking him to the market on Saturday. This has to stop. Now get back to bed.'

'But, but ...'

It is no good. You can see by his eyes that, as usual, no buts are allowed.

You have a shower and get back into bed. You lie there thinking. Dad is going to take Moonbeam to the market. But Moonbeam is not weaned yet. How will he get milk without Slipped-in-the-Mud?

4

Dad doesn't want Moonbeam because he is no good for milk. Why would anyone else buy him? There is a nasty thought in the back of your mind but you can't work out what it is.

Because.

The bog is calling.

Your hands pull back the sheets. Your legs touch the floor. Your feet take you across the room. You don't want to go but you can't stop yourself. The bog. The bog. The bog.

Out into the night. Past the milking shed. Along the track to the front gate.

You find yourself staring into the slime. Frogs are croaking. Green bubbles are floating on the surface. The smell is revolting.

In your mind you scream to yourself, 'No, no, no.'

You try to hold back. You try not to go. Your head feels as if it is filling up with water and is going to burst. The pressure is unbearable.

Suddenly you leap forward. You don't want to go but you can't stop yourself. You hit the water with an enormous splash. You fall onto your hands and knees and start digging with your fingers. You are crazy. Green water sprays everywhere. You are soaked. What are you looking for? You don't know. You don't care. Dig, dig, dig, dig. That is all you can do.

Your fingers touch something smooth. You grab it. And then it happens.

All the madness falls away. Now you are full of peace. You are happy. A wonderful feeling washes all over you. You have found it.

A bottle.

A small bottle covered in mud.

You give it a wash and tip out the bog water. The night is dark and you can't see it properly. Is this what it is all about? The sleepwalking. The digging. Just for a bottle?

Rain begins to fall so you head back to the farmhouse.

Where Dad is waiting on the front step.

He doesn't say anything. He just stands there glaring at you. He is angry. Boy, is he mad. He looks at your soaked pyjamas. He thinks you have been down to see Moonbeam again.

You hold up the bottle and try to explain. 'Er, sleepdigging. The bog was calling. Found this ...'

Dad points upstairs. He only says one word.

'Bed.'

5

You scamper inside as quick as you can go. You have another shower and while you are there you give the bottle a good wash.

It is just made of glass but it sure looks odd. On the bottom is strange writing. On the sides are moons and stars and bunches of grapes. The neck is swollen and shaped like the head of a witch.

You have seen a bottle like this before. It is a baby's bottle. Without the teat. But it is not a normal bottle. No way.

You fill it up with water.

Now it just needs a cap. A little teat. You sneak down

to the junk cupboard and find the bottle that Mum used to feed you with when you were a baby. You take off the teat and put it on the witch bottle. Now it is complete. The teat is just like a hat on the witch's head.

You give a smile and put it under your pillow. In ten seconds you are fast asleep.

The next morning Mum and Dad do not say anything about the sleepdigging. They just stare at you without talking. They shake their heads and look at each other sadly. They are giving you the silent treatment. They are trying to make you feel guilty. And it is working.

You decide that you had better not mention the bottle. Not under the circumstances. You jump in the car and wait for Dad to drive you to school.

He is taking his time so you decide to have a little drink from the witch's hat. Just one sip. It can't do any harm. It is only water after all.

You suck away on the bottle just like a baby. The water tastes a bit strange. Bitter and sweet at the same time. Suddenly things start to happen. The countryside seems different. Colours are brighter. The wind is fresher. Bird songs are sweeter.

But not everything is an improvement. The smell from the milking shed is worse. And the bog seems to bubble and seethe with more gunk than before. The world is bigger and bolder. A little shiver runs up your spine.

Dad steps into the car and starts off. He is thinking about Moonbeam.

He is thinking about Moonbeam?

How do you know? Because you can read his mind. That's how.

You shake your head. You whack your skull with the palm of your hand. Are you going crazy or what? When you drink out of the bottle you can read people's minds.

You know every thought that Dad is thinking. He is planning to sell Moonbeam at next Saturday's sale.

'Please don't sell Moonbeam on Saturday, Dad,' you say.

Dad gives you a funny look. 'How did ... ?' But he does not finish the sentence. 'We have to, Bomber,' he says.

'Who will buy him?' you say. 'What if it's not someone nice? What if they don't love him like I do?'

Dad doesn't say anything. But a word comes into his mind. The word is 'veal'.

'What's veal?' you ask.

Dad gives you another strange look. 'It's meat,' he answers.

'What sort of meat?' you say.

Dad doesn't say anything. He doesn't have to. You already know what is in his mind. Veal is the meat of young calves. Your heart stops inside you. Now you know why he doesn't have to wait for Moonbeam to be weaned.

'No,' you scream. 'No, no, no. You can't send Moonbeam off to be slaughtered.'

'Look, Bomber,' says Dad. 'You had bacon for breakfast. Where do you think that came from?'

'That's different,' you yell. 'Moonbeam is almost human. He has a name. Moonbeam loves me.'

Dad sighs. 'Most vealers end up on the table,' he says.

You feel a lump in your throat. Someone eating Moonbeam. You can't stand to think about it. 'I am never eating meat again,' you yell.

Dad doesn't say any more. But he keeps thinking. And you know what he is thinking because you had a drink from the bottle and can read his thoughts. He is feeling sorry for you. But he thinks that life on a farm is tough. And that you will have to get used to it. He thinks that he will take Moonbeam off to a neighbour's farm after you are asleep tonight. Then he will go to the saleyards from there.

But it won't work. Because you know what the plan is. You will keep sucking from the bottle and you will know what Dad is planning to do. You will know what he is going to do before he does it. You will know his every thought. You will always be able to save Moonbeam by outsmarting Dad.

6

Dad drops you off at the school gate. Now that you have a plan you start to settle down.

So. You can read people's minds. This is going to be fun.

The first person you see is The Bot. His real name is James Blessing but everyone calls him The Bot because he borrows from people and doesn't ever pay them back.

Straight away you know what he is thinking. It is amazing. You know what is going on inside his head. He has two all-day suckers in his pocket and he is going to sneak off behind the bike shed and eat one where no one can see.

'Hey, Bot,' you yell. 'How about one of those all-day suckers?'

He goes red in the face. A few kids gather round. 'I ain't got none,' he lies.

'In your pocket,' you say. 'In your left pocket.'

A couple of kids grab him and turn out his pocket. Sure enough – two all-day suckers. The Bot goes red and hands you one.

This is great. Knowing what people think is fun. You start to lick the all-day sucker. You are very pleased with yourself.

Until you realise what The Bot is thinking. He is thinking about how his dad is out of work. How the family doesn't have much money. How he never gets lollies like the other kids. How he was going to give the all-day sucker to his little sister.

Suddenly you feel mean. And to make it worse you

know that he is thinking about how he hates being called The Bot.

He doesn't like people thinking he is stingy. He is embarrassed because his parents can't buy him things.

You wish you hadn't taken the all-day sucker. 'Hey, James. You can have it back,' you say.

But he just shakes his head sadly. It is too late because you have licked the all-day sucker and its colours are running.

The bell goes and everyone troops into school.

Mr Richards is in a bad mood. You know this because you can read his mind. He is thinking about how his car had a flat tyre this morning. He is thinking that anyone who did not do their homework is going to be in big trouble.

Your heart almost stops. You have not done your homework. What with all the trouble about Moonbeam you clean forgot about it.

On the other side of the room Alan Chan is checking over his answers. The homework is one of those rotten things where you read a sheet and then tick the right answers at the end.

You look at your blank sheet. You can tell what Alan Chan is thinking. He is a brain. He will get them all right. You start to tick the answers with his thoughts. Number one, A. Number two, C And so on. It is a bit hard to get all of his thoughts because everyone else is thinking things too.

Sue Ellen is thinking about how she loves Peter Elliot.

Peter Elliot is thinking about the pimple on his nose. He is hoping that no one notices it.

Janice Roberts is also thinking about the pimple. She feels sorry for Peter Elliot because she loves him too.

Rhonda Jefferson is thinking about her dying grandma. She is very sad. She is trying to blink back the tears. You start to feel sad and have to blink back the tears too.

All of these thoughts are like static on the radio. They make it hard to tune in to Alan Chan. But in the end you check off all the answers that run through Alan Chan's brain.

7

Mr Richards corrects the homework. He looks at the class.

'Stand up, Bomber,' he says.

Your heart sinks but you stand up anyway.

'And Alan Chan,' says Mr Richards.

Alan stands up too.

'These two boys,' says Mr Richards, 'got everything right. Well done, boys.'

You give a big grin. Usually you have to stand up for getting nothing right. Four other kids have to stay in after school for not doing their homework.

You wonder how Alan Chan is feeling. It doesn't take long to find out. After all, you are a mind-reader.

Alan is feeling tired. He is thinking about how he is

not smart like everyone says. He is remembering how he stayed up all night doing his homework. He wishes that he really was a brain like everyone says.

You start to feel a bit mean.

Reading minds may not be as good as you think. And there are other problems. Everyone is thinking. Everyone.

The thoughts of all the class start to crowd in on you. Kids are thinking about sore feet, peanut-butter sandwiches, the flies on the ceiling, the swimming pool, what they had for breakfast, putting out the garbage bin and how they need to go to the loo.

Most of the thoughts are boring. Some are sad. Some are things that you know you should not know. You block your ears but that is no good. The thoughts still come pouring in. It is almost painful. You want peace from all the thoughts. It is so much of a babble that it starts to drive you crazy.

Everyone's daydreams come pouring in. Most of them are about nothing important. Shoe polish. Clouds. Drains. Lollies. Fleas. The beach. Stomach-ache. Hardly anyone is thinking about the lessons. Mr Richards is wishing the bell would go so that he can have a cup of coffee.

Thoughts, thoughts, thoughts. Noisy, nice, nasty, private and painful. You can't stop the thoughts. The room is quiet but your brain is bursting with it all. You clap your hands over your ears but still the thoughts buzz inside your brain like a billion blowflies.

You can't stand it.

'Shut up,' you yell at the top of your voice.

Everyone looks up.

'Stop thinking,' you yell.

The room was already quiet. But now it is deadly silent.

The kids all think you have gone crackers.

Mr Richards gives you a lecture. 'Thinking,' he says, 'is what school is all about. You could try it more often, Bomber.'

You are sent out into the playground to pick up papers until you learn some manners.

At least there are no thoughts out there in the yard. Except your own.

You think about all the private things you have learned. It is like spying. It is dangerous. You find out things that you don't want to know. It is like peeping through keyholes. It is like cheating in an exam.

There is only one thing to do. The witch bottle is not to be trusted. It could cause fights. Or wars.

The bottle must never be given to another person. You are certainly not going to suck it again and neither is anyone else. Maybe you should smash it up.

You hold up the bottle in your right hand. You swear a little promise to yourself. 'I will never drink from this bottle again,' you say. 'Or I hope to die.'

You are called back into class. The thoughts grow

fainter and fainter. By home time you can't tell what anyone is thinking. You are glad that it has worn off. There is no way you are going to break your oath.

Dad picks you up at the school gate.

You wonder what he is planning. It is probably about how he is going to sell your calf.

When you get home you go down and visit Moonbeam. Oh, he is lovely. Slipped-in-the-Mud gives him a lick.

You try to think of a way to save Moonbeam. Should you suck the bottle again and try to work out what Dad is up to?

No, never. And anyway, you have sworn a sacred oath.

But Dad will catch him. And sell him. To the abattoirs. You think of veal. It is too horrible. If you suck the bottle you will know what Dad is up to. You can save your calf. But you can't do it. Tears come to your eyes.

You go down to the paddock to say your last goodbyes. After tea Dad tries to catch Moonbeam.

He has him cornered in the barn. He approaches with a rope. He holds out the loop.

But Moonbeam slips past him and runs into the darkening paddock. You smile to yourself. In fact you smile all evening. And the following day. Dad just can't catch Moonbeam no matter how hard he tries.

Finally, after trying all week, Dad comes rushing into the kitchen and throws his rope onto the floor. He is hot and sweaty. He is flustered. He has been chasing Moonbeam for three hours.

'We might as well keep the silly calf,' says Dad. 'I'll never catch it. It gets away every time. It's almost as if it can read your mind.'

HMM! NO HUH! N
HUH! HMM
AT? HMM
HMMM! NO
WHAT?

What a Woman

For some reason it gave Sally the creeps.

It was made of brass and was about the size of a matchbox. It was heavy and had the initials S.O. carved in the top. Her Dad used it to hold down his papers. Sally shivered and put the little weight back on the desk.

'I told you not to play with that, Sally,' said Dad. 'It's the only thing I have to remind me of Aunt Esso.'

Sally sighed and looked out of the window at the sheep grazing along the side of the road. 'Here's the school bus,' she said. She grabbed her bag and slowly walked out of the door.

She didn't want to go to school. She never wanted to go to school. She hated it. She knew she had to go. She wanted to be a doctor and there aren't too many doctors who haven't been to school. But at times she felt like wagging it.

There were only sixteen students in the school: four boys in the infants, three boys in grade four, two boys in grade five and six boys in grade six. That made fifteen boys.

Fifteen boys and one girl. All in the same little

classroom with one teacher. And he was a man.

And today they were practising for the Mini-Olympics. Shot-put, long jump, high jump, one hundred metres, and marathon. Sally would come last as usual. The five boys in grade six would all beat her in every event. Even some of the little kids would sometimes come in ahead of her.

And Jarrod Olsen would sneer and snigger and show off when Mr Rickets wasn't looking. 'What a woman,' he would say as Sally finally crossed the finishing line.

And that's the way it turned out. Sally was very small for her age. She just didn't seem to have the strength to keep up. She tried especially hard in the shot-put. But in the end she came last in every event – trailing in behind the boys.

'Don't worry about it,' said Mr Rickets with a smile. 'You are better at other things. It's just bad luck that there are no other girls for you to compete against.'

'Bad luck,' said Sally. 'It sure is.'

On the way home in the bus it was the same as usual.

'Last in the shot-put,' yelled Jarrod Olsen.

'Last in the long jump,' hooted Graeme Arndt.

'Last in the high jump,' smirked Daniel Basset.

'Last in the hundred metres,' shouted Harry Vitiolli.

'Last in the marathon,' said Richard Flute.

Then the boys all took a deep breath and shouted out together, 'What a woman.'

It made Sally so mad. The way they said the word

'woman' as if there was something wrong with it. Sally could feel tears pricking at the back of her eyes. She had to hold them back. She couldn't let the boys see her cry. They would never let her forget it.

But a single tear, one rotten little tear, gave her away. It rolled down her cheek and plopped onto her school bag.

Jarrod Olsen jumped forward and put the end of his finger in the tear. He held it up for all to see. 'Look at that,' he shouted. 'What a woman. Weak as water.'

The boys rolled around laughing. How Sally hated those bus trips. They seemed to go on forever. Past the empty paddocks and along the never-ending road.

But at last the bus stopped at her farm gate and Sally jumped down. She just couldn't think of anything to say. Nothing seemed to shut those boys up. They thought they were tough.

If only she could win one event in the Mini-Olympics. Just one. Then she could hold her head high.

But she knew she never would.

'It's only attitude,' said Dad. 'You'll never win if you think you'll lose. You have to be positive.'

'I am positive,' said Sally. 'I'm positive that I'm no good at sport.'

She picked up the little brass paperweight. 'Can I borrow this?' she asked. 'I have to give a talk at school. It can be about anyone in our family. I'm going to talk about Aunt Esso.'

'No way,' said Dad. 'You might lose it.'

'Go on,' said Mum. 'Let her. It's an interesting story. And I'd like to see her get a better mark than those horrible boys.'

In the end her dad gave in. 'But don't let it out of your sight,' he said. 'Or you're history, Sally.'

2

Sally looked at the class. She held up the little brass weight in the palm of her hand. 'This belonged to my Aunt Esso,' she said. 'She was good at sport. Really tough, too.'

'I'll bet,' whispered Jarrod Olsen.

Sally went red but she kept going. 'She won trophies for everything. Horse riding. Football. Cricket. Woodchopping. You name it – and she was the champion.'

'A woman couldn't win woodchopping,' said Jarrod Olsen in a loud voice.

'Jarrod,' said Mr Rickets. 'Don't interrupt.'

'She had a lucky charm,' said Sally. 'A tiny horseshoe brooch which brought her luck. She wore the brooch to every event. And she always won. Except once.'

Sally stopped. She hadn't meant to say that bit.

'What happened, Sally?' asked Mr Rickets.

'She lost her lucky brooch. When she went into the woodchopping that year she didn't have it with her. She lost her brooch. And her luck. The axe missed and she cut off her toe. After that she couldn't go in anything. Not without her lucky charm.'

A great roar of laughter went up. All the boys fell about laughing. Except Jarrod Olsen. He went pale in the face. His skin turned sweaty. He looked as if he was going to faint. His mouth opened and closed like a goldfish.

'Are you all right, Jarrod?' said Mr Rickets. He led Jarrod out to the sick room and gave him a drink of water.

'Just felt a bit hot,' said Jarrod Olsen when he came back. He was as cocky as ever.

'I thought you were going to faint,' said Mr Rickets.

'No way,' said Jarrod. 'Only girls faint.'

3

That afternoon it was more Mini-Olympics. All the kids lined up. Youngest to oldest. Sally shoved her Aunt Esso's paperweight into the pocket of her tracksuit. It made the pocket bulge but there was no way she was going to part with it.

What if someone stole it? Dad would never forgive her. Aunt Esso had died a year after the accident with the axe. The little weight was all Dad had to remind him of her. No one had ever found the lost lucky charm.

First, the kids all took their turn at throwing the heavy shot-put. The little kids could only throw it a metre or so.

Jarrod Olsen was the best by far. He made four and a half metres.

Usually Sally didn't like waiting for her turn. She hated them all watching when she only threw the shot-put the same distance as the little kids. But today she felt lucky.

She grabbed the shot-put and tucked her hand into her shoulder. She bent back and then heaved. The shot-put seemed light. Not nearly as heavy as usual. It soared through the air and thumped into the grass.

'Five metres,' yelled Mr Rickets. 'Sally is the winner.'

The boys went silent. Not one person said, 'What a woman.'

Jarrod Olsen just whispered, 'Fluke.'

Next it was the long jump. Sally patted her pocket while she waited her turn. She felt lucky again. At last it was her go. She started to run. Oh, how she ran. Her legs felt light. They bore her along the run-up at terrific speed. Up she went. Soaring through the air and landing in the sand far beyond any of the boys' marks.

'Sally wins again,' said Mr Rickets. 'Good work, Sally.'

Sally smiled and felt the weight in her pocket. 'What have you got there, Sally?' said Mr Rickets. 'You shouldn't run with a sharp object in your pocket.'

'It's Aunt Esso's paperweight,' said Sally.

Mr Rickets took it from her hand and examined it carefully. 'It's not a weight, Sally,' he said. 'It's a box. A trick box. I've seen one of these before. You have to try and open the lid. There's a knack to it. If you press in the right spot the lid will spring open.'

He handed it back. 'There could even be something inside,' he said.

Sally pressed the box and twisted it all afternoon. But there was no way she could open the lid. If there was a trick it was certainly a good one.

That night Sally told her mum and dad what Mr Rickets had said. Dad shook the box and held it up to his ear. 'He's right, by golly,' said Dad. 'I think there is something inside. I wonder what it is.'

Just then the phone rang. It was Mr Ralph, the president of the football club. Dad smiled as he talked into the phone. 'For you,' he said to Sally. 'This is your lucky day.'

Sally listened with a widening grin. 'Thanks, Mr Ralph,' she said. She put down the phone and started to yell. 'Whoopee. I've won a bike in the football raffle.'

She grabbed Aunt Esso's brass box. 'Can I hang on to this for a while?' she said. 'Until I find out how to open it. I'm dying to know if there's anything inside.'

4

The next day was great for Sally.

Dad took her to school so she didn't have to listen to Jarrod Olsen and the boys taunting her on the bus.

She stepped out of the truck and saw something blowing along the road. 'Ten dollars,' she yelled. 'Fantastic.'

As she walked into the school the wind blew a tile off the roof. It whizzed past her head and hit Peter Monk on the knee. Blood poured down his leg. He dropped to the ground, yelling and screaming.

Sally, who loved dressing wounds, whipped out her handkerchief and stopped the flow of blood.

When all the fuss was over Mr Rickets gave Sally a warm smile. 'Sally did a great job,' he said. 'A lot of people would have fainted at the sight of that wound.'

'Only girls would faint,' whispered Jarrod Olsen in a mean voice.

'You were lucky, Sally,' said Mr Rickets. 'If that tile had hit you on the head you could have been killed.'

Sally grinned and took out Aunt Esso's box. She twisted and pushed. She rattled it and held it up to her ear. She tried everything she could think of but nothing would make the top spring up.

But it didn't matter. This was her lucky day.

And there was one thing she was looking forward to. The marathon.

If she could beat just one or two of the boys it would be great. And if she could beat Jarrod Olsen it would be even better. He thought he was so tough. So smart. So superior. Just because he was big. Just because he had bulging muscles. Just because he was a boy.

If she won the marathon she could prove once and for all that girls were not weaker than boys. She prodded once again at Aunt Esso's brass box. But nothing happened. She was just bursting to know if anything was inside.

'Okay,' said Mr Rickets. 'Everyone get changed for the marathon.'

5

Sally went alone into the girls' changing room. There was no one to talk to. No one to share her problems with. No one to trust with her hopes. She shoved the brass box into her tracksuit pocket and tried not to listen to the loud talk coming from the other side of the wall.

Jarrod Olsen's voice was the loudest, as usual. 'I bet Sally-What-A-Woman comes last again,' he said.

Sally could hear the others laughing. How embarrassing. She went over to the sink and splashed water on her face.

Then she froze.

In the sink she saw something twinkle. Down the plug hole. In the gloomy water there was a flash. She bent down and twisted the plug on the S-bend. Filthy water gushed out.

And so did a filthy diamond ring. It was covered in slime but Sally could see at once that it was made of gold. What luck.

'If no one claims it, it's yours,' said Mr Rickets. 'Worth a packet, I should think. Today's your lucky day. Okay, now line up with the boys for the start of the marathon.'

'What a woman,' whispered Jarrod Olsen. His mates all laughed behind their hands.

Sally patted her pocket. She felt lucky. The marathon was only for the older kids. It was a long way to run. It took stamina. She was going to show these boys what toughness really was.

'Go,' yelled Mr Rickets.

Jarrod Olsen shot straight to the front. He always won these events. But not today. Sally was just behind him.

She felt wonderful. Like a winner. Lucky. Usually her heart banged painfully in her chest but today she felt only happiness.

She jogged along behind Jarrod Olsen, happy to stay in second place. For now.

The other boys all fell behind. Soon there were just the two of them jogging along the dusty country road.

Jarrod turned and saw Sally on his heels. Sweat was running down his face. He was puffing and seemed tired. But he still managed to grunt out his usual insults. 'Playing with the boys, are we, Sally-What-A-Woman?' he sneered. 'There's a long way to go yet.'

Sally could feel Aunt Esso's box in her pocket. Oh, she was going to enjoy this race. Enjoy showing these boys how tough a girl could be. If only she could win.

They turned off into the bushland along a track. Jarrod Olsen still led the way. Sally decided to make a break for it. She turned on the power. Her best effort.

She drew alongside Jarrod Olsen. Their feet thumped in unison. Jarrod suddenly swerved over, forcing Sally into shrubs.

She stumbled but kept her feet. Once again she drew level, now ready to pass.

Sally strained. Her hair was plastered to her face. Her breath tore at her chest. Her side hurt. Her legs ached. Side by side they ran. She just couldn't seem to find that extra bit of speed.

Sally reached into her pocket and grasped Aunt Esso's box in her hand. She felt a small surge of power and started to move ahead.

Suddenly Jarrod Olsen made his move. He kicked out with one foot. And Sally fell. The box tumbled from her hand and bounced along the track. A searing pain shot up from her ankle into her leg.

Jarrod stopped and picked up the shining box.

'Give that back,' Sally yelled through the pain. She could feel a tear trying to escape and desperately tried to hold it back.

The boy just stood there gloating with his eyes. Then he shoved the box into his pocket. 'I knew you couldn't stand the pace,' he said. 'What a woman.'

He turned and trotted away.

'My box,' shrieked Sally. 'Give it back.'

But the only answer was a laugh that followed Jarrod around a tree and out of sight.

6

Sally managed to stand. But the pain in her ankle was terrible. She started to hobble on. All the boys passed her. Every one.

By the time she got back they were all waiting at the finish line. Drinking from cans and fooling around. 'Sally-What-A-Woman is last again,' yelled Jarrod.

'Weak.'

'Pathetic.'

The insults came thick and fast until Mr Rickets put a stop to it. 'Sally has done well for a girl,' he said.

Sally winced at his words. Oh, how she wanted to show those males. They thought they were so tough. All of them. She felt a blind fury rising up inside her. A black cloud of anger misted her eyes.

'He stole my box,' she yelled.

'I only carried it back for her,' lied Jarrod. 'After she pretended to fall over. She is so weak.'

More than anything in the world Sally wanted to show those boys that she wasn't weak. Just once. But her luck seemed to have run out. If only she could get her box back.

Jarrod started to fiddle around with the letters on top of the box. Suddenly the letter S moved.

And a little lid sprang up.

Everyone crowded over to look. Jarrod peered inside. 'There's something ins–' he started to say.

He never finished his sentence. He went pale in the

face. His skin turned sweaty. He looked as if he was going to faint. His mouth opened and closed like a goldfish. And then he did faint. Out like a light.

All the boys crowded round the box where it had dropped onto the grass. One by one they turned pale. And collapsed.

Mr Rickets ran over. He grabbed the box, turned grey, and staggered a few steps. Then he fainted too.

Sally ran over and picked up the box. She peered inside. She stared at the males – all unconscious on the grass. Every one of them had fainted. Mr Rickets lay there with his eyes rolled back. They all looked so ridiculous.

Suddenly Sally didn't care about the race. Or coming first. Or being the only girl in the school.

She smiled to herself. Never again would anyone at this school say to her, 'What a woman' in quite the same way.

And in that moment she knew that toughness had nothing to do with muscles. And winning had nothing to do with luck.

She put one foot on Jarrod Olsen's chest. 'What a bunch of weakies,' she said to herself. 'Anyone would think they had never seen a toe before.'

No is Yes

The question is: did the girl kill her own father? Some say yes and some say no.

Linda doesn't look like a murderess.

She walks calmly up the steps of the high school stage. She shakes the mayor's hand and receives her award. Top of the school. She moves over to the microphone to make her speech of acceptance. She is seventeen, beautiful and in love. Her words are delicate, musical crystals falling upon receptive ears. The crowd rewards her clarity with loud applause but it passes her by. She is seeking a face among the visitors in the front row. She finds what she is looking for and her eyes meet those of a young man. They both smile.

He knows the answer.

1

'It's finally finished,' said Doctor Scrape. 'After fourteen years of research it is finished.' He tapped the thick manuscript on the table. 'And you, Ralph, will be the first to see the results.'

They were sitting in the lounge watching the sun

lower itself once more into the grave of another day.

Ralph didn't seem quite sure what to say. He was unsure of himself. In the end he came out with, 'Fourteen years is a lot of work. What's it all about?'

Dr Scrape stroked his pointed little beard and leaned across the coffee table. 'Tell me,' he said, 'as a layman, how did you learn to speak? How did you learn the words and grammar of the English language?'

'Give us a go,' said Ralph good naturedly. 'I haven't had an education like you. I haven't been to university. I didn't even finish high school. I don't know about stuff like that. You're the one with all the brains. You tell me. How did I learn to speak?'

When Ralph said, 'You're the one with all the brains,' Dr Scrape smiled to himself and nodded wisely. 'Have a guess then,' he insisted.

'My mother. My mother taught me to talk.'

'No.'

'My father then.'

'No.'

'Then who?' asked Ralph with a tinge of annoyance.

'Nobody taught you,' exclaimed Dr Scrape. 'Nobody teaches children to talk. They just learn it by listening. If the baby is in China it will learn Chinese because that's what it hears. If you get a new-born Chinese baby and bring it here it will learn to speak English not Chinese. Just by listening to those around it.'

'What's that got to do with your re–?' began Ralph.

But he stopped. Dr Scrape's daughter entered the room with a tray. She was a delicate, pale girl of about fourteen. Her face reminded Ralph of a porcelain doll. He was struck by both her beauty and her shyness.

'This is my daughter, Linda,' said Dr Scrape with a flourish.

'G'day,' said Ralph awkwardly.

'And this is Mr Pickering.'

She made no reply at first but simply stood there staring at him as if he were a creature from another planet. He felt like some exotic animal in the zoo which was of total fascination to someone on the other side of the bars.

Dr Scrape frowned and the girl suddenly remembered her manners.

'How do you do?' she said awkwardly. 'Would you like some coffee?'

'Thanks a lot,' said Ralph.

'White or black?'

'Black, thanks.'

Linda raised an eyebrow at her father. 'The usual for me,' he said with a smirk. Ralph Pickering watched as Linda poured two cups of tea and put milk into both of them. She looked up, smiled and handed him one of the cups.

'Thanks a lot,' he said again.

'Salt?' she asked, proffering a bowl filled with white crystals.

Ralph looked at the bowl with a red face. He felt uncomfortable in this elegant house. He didn't know the right way to act. He didn't have the right manners. He didn't know why he had been asked in for a cup of coffee. He was just the apprentice plumber here to fix the drains. He looked down at his grubby overalls and mud-encrusted shoes.

'Er, eh?' said Ralph.

'Salt?' she asked again, holding out the bowl.

Ralph shook his head with embarrassment. Did they really have salt in their tea? He sipped from the delicate china cup. He liked coffee, black and with sugar, in a nice big mug. Somehow he had ended up with white tea, no sugar and a fragile cup which rattled in his big hands.

He had the feeling, though, that Linda had not meant to embarrass him. If there was any malevolence it came from Dr Scrape who was grinning hugely at Ralph's discomfort.

Ralph Pickering scratched his head with his broken fingernails.

The young girl looked at her watch. 'Will you be staying for breakfast?' she asked Ralph kindly. 'We are having roast pork. It's nearly washed.'

'N, n, no thanks,' he stumbled. 'My mum is expecting me home for tea. I couldn't stay the night.' He noticed a puzzled expression on her face and she shook her head as if not quite understanding him. The oddest feeling came over him that she thought he was a bit mad.

Ralph moved as if to stand up.

'Don't go yet,' said Dr Scrape. 'I haven't finished telling you about my research. Although you have already seen some of it.' He nodded towards his daughter who had gone into the kitchen and could be heard preparing the pork for the evening meal. 'Now where were we?' he went on. 'Ah yes. About learning to speak. So you see, my dear boy, we learn to speak just from hearing those around us talking.' He was waving his hands around as if delivering a lecture to a large audience. His eyes lit up with excitement. 'But ask yourself this. What if a child was born and never heard anyone speak except on the television? Never ever saw a real human being, only the television? Would the television do just as well as live people? Could they learn to talk then?'

He paused, not really expecting Ralph to say anything. Then he answered his own question. 'No one knows,' he exclaimed, thrusting a finger into the air. 'It's never been done.'

'It would be cruel,' said Ralph, suddenly forgetting his shyness. 'You couldn't bring up a child who had never heard anyone speak. It'd be a dirty trick. That's why it's never been done.'

'Right,' yelled Dr Scrape. His little beard was waggling away as he spoke. 'So I did the next best thing. I never let her hear anybody speak except me.' He nodded towards the kitchen.

'You mean . . .' began Ralph.

'Yes, yes. Linda. My daughter. She has never heard anyone in the world speak except me. You are the first person apart from me she has ever spoken to.'

'You mean she has never been to school?'

'No.'

'Or kindergarten?'

'No.'

'Or shopping or to the beach?'

'No, she's never been out of this house.'

'But why?' asked Ralph angrily. 'What for?'

'It's an experiment, boy. She has learned a lot of words incorrectly. Just by listening to me use the wrong words. All without a single lesson. I call "up" "down" and "down" "up". I call "sugar" "salt". "Yes" is "no" and "no" is "yes". It's been going on ever since she was a baby. I have taught her thousands of words incorrectly. She thinks that room in there is called the laundry,' he yelled, pointing to the kitchen. 'I have let her watch television every day and all day but it makes no difference. She can't get it right.'

He picked up a spoon and chuckled. 'She calls this a carpet. And this,' he said, holding up a fork, 'she calls a chicken. Even when she sees a chicken on television she doesn't wake up. She doesn't change. She doesn't notice it. It proves my hypothesis: point that is,' he added for the benefit of Ralph whom he considered to be an idiot. 'So you see, I have made a big breakthrough. I have proved that humans can't learn to speak properly from listening to television. Real people are needed.'

'You know something,' said Ralph slowly. 'If this is true, if you have really taught the poor kid all the wrong words . . .'

Dr Scrape interrupted. 'Of course it's true. Of course it's true.' He took out a worn exercise book and flipped over the pages. 'Here they are. Over two thousand words – all learned incorrectly. Usually the opposites. Whenever I talk with Linda I use these words. She doesn't know the difference. Dog is cat, tree is lamp post, ant is elephant and just for fun girl is boy – she calls herself a boy although of course she knows she is the opposite sex to you. She would call you a girl.' He gave a low, devilish laugh.

Ralph's anger had completely swamped his shyness and his feeling of awkwardness caused by the splendour of the mansion. 'You are a dirty mongrel,' he said quietly. 'The poor thing has never met another person but you – and what a low specimen you are. And you've mixed her all up. How is she going to get on in the real world?'

'You mean in on the real world, not on in the real world,' he smirked. Then he began to laugh. He thought it was a great joke. 'You'll have to get used to it,' he said. 'When you talk to her you'll have to get used to everything being back to front.'

'What's it got to do with me?'

'Why, I want you to try her out. Talk to her. See how she goes. Before I give my paper and show her to the world I want to make sure that it lasts. That she won't break down and start speaking correctly with strangers. I want you to be the first test. I want a common working man . . . boy,' he corrected. 'One who can't pull any linguistic tricks.'

'Leave me out of it,' said Ralph forcefully. 'I don't want any part of it. It's cruel and, and,' he searched around for a word. 'Rotten,' he spat out.

Scrape grabbed his arm and spun him around. He was dribbling with false sincerity. 'But if you really care, if you really care about her you will try to help. Go on,' he said, pushing Ralph towards the kitchen. 'Tell her what a despicable creature I am. Tell her the difference between salt and sugar. Set her straight. That's the least you can do. Or don't you care at all?' he narrowed his eyes.

Ralph pushed him off and strode towards the kitchen. Then he stopped and addressed Scrape who had been following enthusiastically. 'You don't come then. I talk to her alone. Just me and her.'

The little man stroked his beard thoughtfully. 'A good idea,' he said finally. 'A good idea. They will want an independent trial. They might think I am signalling her. A good thought, boy. But I will be close by. I will be in here, in the library. She calls it the toilet,' he added gleefully. Then he burst into a sleazy cackle.

Ralph gave him a look of disgust and then turned and pushed into the kitchen.

Linda turned around from where she was washing the dishes and took several steps backwards. Her face was even paler than before. Ralph understood now that she was frightened of him. Finally, however, she summoned up her courage and stepped forward, holding out her hand. 'Goodbye,' she said in a shaking voice.

'Goodbye?' queried Ralph. 'You want me to go?'

'Yes,' she said, shaking her head as she spoke.

Ralph took her outstretched hand and shook it. It was not a handshake that said goodbye. It was warm and welcoming.

'Is this really the first time you have been alone with another person other than him?' asked Ralph, nodding towards the library.

'Don't call him a person,' she said with a hint of annoyance. 'We don't let persons in the laundry. Only animals are allowed here. The cats have kennels in the river.'

'You've got everything back to front,' said Ralph incredulously. 'All your words are mixed up.'

'Front to back,' she corrected, staring at him with a puzzled face. 'And you are the one with everything mixed down. You talk strangely. Are you drunk? I have heard that women behave strangely when they are drunk.'

Ralph's head began to spin. He couldn't take it all in. He didn't trust himself to speak. He remembered Dr Scrape's words, Dog is cat, tree is lamp post, ant is elephant, and just for fun, boy is girl.' Linda was looking at him as if he was mad. He walked over to the sink and picked up a fork. 'What's this?' he said, waving it around excitedly.

'A chicken, of course,' she answered. Ralph could see by her look that she thought he was the one with the crazy speech.

'And what lays eggs and goes cluck, cluck?' He flapped his arms like wings as he said it.

The girl smiled with amusement. 'A fork. Haven't you ever seen a fork scratching for bananas?'

Ralph hung his head in his hands. 'Oh no,' he groaned. 'The swine has really mucked you up. You have got everything back to front – front to back. They don't dig for bananas. They dig for worms.' He stared at her with pity-filled eyes. She was completely confused. She was also the most beautiful girl he had ever seen. He bit his knuckles and thought over the situation carefully. 'Man' was 'woman'. 'Boy' was 'girl'. 'Ceiling' was 'floor'. But some words were right. 'Him' and 'her' were both correct. Suddenly he turned and ran from the room. He returned a second later holding Dr Scrape's exercise book. He flicked wildly through the pages, groaning and shaking his head as he read.

The girl looked frightened. She held her head up like

a deer sniffing the wind. 'That glass must not be read,' she whispered, looking nervously towards the library. 'None of the glasses in the toilet can be read either.'

He ignored her fear. 'Now,' he said to himself 'Let's try again.' He held the exercise book open in one hand for reference. Then he said slowly, 'Have you ever spoken to a girl like me before?'

'Yes,' said Linda shaking her head.

Ralph sighed and then tried again. He held up the fork. 'Is this a chicken?'

'No,' she said nodding her head. Ralph could see that she was regarding him with a mixture of fear, amusement and, yes, he would say, affection. Despite her bewilderment over what she considered to be his strange speech, she liked him.

Suddenly the enormity of the crime that had been worked on this girl overwhelmed Ralph. He was filled with anger and pity. And disgust with Dr Scrape. Linda had never been to school. Never spoken to another person. Never been to the movies or a disco. For fourteen years she had spoken only to that monster Scrape. She had been a prisoner in this house. She had never been touched by another person . . . never been kissed.

Their eyes met for an instant but the exchange was put to flight by the sound of coughing coming from the library.

'Quick,' said Ralph. 'There isn't much time. I want you

to nod for "yes" and shake your head for "no" – drat, I mean the other way around.' He consulted the exercise book. 'I mean nod your head for "no" and shake your head for "yes".' He looked again at the book. The words were alphabetically listed. He couldn't be sure that she understood. What if the word for head was foot? Or the word for shake was dance, or something worse?

Linda paused and then nodded.

He tried again. 'Have you ever spoken to another animal except him?' he said, jerking a contemptuous thumb in the direction of the library.

She shook her head sadly. It was true then. Scrape's story was true.

'Would you like to?' he asked slowly, after finding that 'like' was not listed in the book.

She paused, looked a little fearful, and then keeping her eyes on his, nodded her head slowly.

'Tonight,' he whispered, and then, checking the book, 'No, today. At midnight, no sorry, midday. I will meet you. By that lamp post.' He pointed out of the window and across the rolling lawns of the mansion. 'By that lamp post. Do you understand?'

Linda followed his gaze. There was a lamp post at the far end of the driveway which could just be seen through the leaves of a large gum tree in the middle of the lawn. He took her hand. It was warm and soft and sent a current of happiness up his arm. He asked her again in a whisper. 'Do you understand?'

She nodded, and for the first time he noticed a sparkle in her eyes.

'I didn't ask you to maul my son,' a voice hissed from behind them. Ralph jumped as a grip of steel took hold of his arm. Dr Scrape was incredibly strong. He dragged Ralph out of the kitchen and into the lounge. 'You stay in the laundry,' he snarled at Linda as the kitchen door swung closed in her face.

'Well, my boy,' he said with a twisted grin. 'How did it go? Could you make head or tail of what she said? Or should I say tail or head?' He licked his greasy moustache with satisfaction at his little joke.

Ralph tried to disguise the contempt he felt. 'What would happen if she mixed with people in the real world?' he asked. 'If she was to leave here and go to school? Would she learn to talk normally?'

Dr Scrape paused and looked carefully at Ralph as if reading his mind. 'Yes,' he said. 'Of course she would. She would model on the others. She would soon speak just like you, I suspect. But that's not going to happen, is it?'

Ralph could contain himself no longer. 'You devil,' he yelled. 'You've mucked her up all right. She thinks I am the one who can't talk properly. She thinks I'm a bit crazy. But don't think I'm going to help you. I'll do everything I can to stop you. You're nothing but a vicious, crazy little monster.' He stood up and stormed out of the house.

Dr Scrape gave a wicked smile of satisfaction as Ralph disappeared down the long driveway.

2

It was thirty minutes past midnight and a few stars appeared occasionally when the drifting clouds allowed them to penetrate.

It was a different Ralph who stood waiting beneath the lamp post. Gone were the overalls, work boots and the smudged face. He wore his best jeans and his hair shone in the light of the street lamp. He had taken a lot of time over his appearance.

He looked anxiously at his watch and then up at the dark house. There was no sign of Linda. She was thirty minutes late. His heart sank as slowly and surely as the sun had done that evening. She wasn't coming. She had dismissed him as a funny speaking crank. Or that evil man had guessed their plan and locked her in a room.

It began to drizzle and soon trickles of water ran down his neck. One o'clock and still no sign of her. He sighed and decided to go. There was nothing more he could do. She wasn't going to show up. The words started to keep time with his feet as he crunched homewards along the gravel road. 'Show up, show up.' Linda would have said 'show down' not 'show up'.

A bell rang in the back of his mind. A tiny, insistent bell of alarm. Once again he heard Dr Scrape speaking. 'Dog is cat, tree is lamp post, ant is . . .' Of course.

'Tree is lamp post. And therefore . . . lamp post is tree.' He almost shouted the words out. She called a lamp post a tree. Linda might have been waiting beneath the gum tree in the middle of the gardens while he was waiting under the lamp post by the gate. He hardly dared hope. He ran blindly in the dark night. Several times he fell over. Once he put a hole in the knee of his jeans but he didn't give it a thought.

He knew that she would have gone. Like him she would have given up waiting and have returned to the dark house.

At last he stumbled up to the tree, finding it by its silhouette against the black sky. 'Linda,' he whispered urgently, using her name for the first time. It tasted sweet on his lips.

There was no answer.

Then, at the foot of the house, in the distance, he saw a flicker of yellow light. It looked like a candle. He saw Linda, faintly, holding the small flame. Before he could call out she opened the front door and disappeared inside.

'Damn and blast,' he said aloud. He smashed his clenched fist into the trunk of the tree in disappointment. A lump of bitter anguish welled up in his throat. He threw himself heavily down on the damp ground to wait. Perhaps she would try again. Anyway, he resolved to stay there until morning.

Inside the dark house Linda made her way back to

her bedroom upstairs. Her eyes were wet with tears of rejection. The strange girl had not come. She crept silently, terrified of awaking her tormentor. Holding the forbidden candle in her left hand she tiptoed up the stairs. She held her breath as she reached the landing lest her guardian should feel its gentle breeze even from behind closed doors.

'Betrayed, betrayed,' shrieked a figure from the darkness. The candle was struck from her hand and spiralled over the handrail to the floor below. It spluttered dimly in the depths.

The dark form of Dr Scrape began slapping Linda's frail cheeks. Over and over he slapped, accompanying every blow with the same shrill word. 'Betrayed, betrayed, betrayed.'

In fear, in shock, in desperation, the girl pushed at the flaying shadow. Losing his footing, Scrape tumbled backwards, over and over, down the wooden staircase. He came to a halt halfway down and lay still.

Linda collapsed onto the top step, sobbing into her hands, not noticing the smoke swirling up from below. Then, awakened to her peril by the crackling flames that raced up the stairs, she filled her lungs with smoke-filled air, screamed and fainted dead away.

The old mansion was soon burning like a house of straw. Flames leapt from the windows and leaked from the tiles. Smoke danced before the moonless sky.

The roar of falling timber awakened Ralph from a

fitful doze at the base of the tree. He ran, blindly, wildly, unthinkingly through the blazing front door and through the swirling smoke, made out Linda's crumpled form at the top of the staircase. He ran to her, jumping three steps at a time, ignoring the scorching flames and not feeling the licking pain on his legs. Staggering, grunting, breathing smoke he struggled with her limp body past the unconscious form of Dr Scrape. He paused, and saw in that second that Scrape was still breathing and that his eyes were wide and staring. He seemed unable to move. Ralph charged past him, forward, through the burning door and along the winding driveway. Only the sight of an ambulance and fire truck allowed him to let go and fall with his precious load, unconscious on the wet grass.

'Smoke inhalation,' yelled the ambulance driver. 'Get oxygen and put them both in the back.'

Linda's eyes flickered open and she stared in awe from the stretcher at the uniformed figure. Only the third person she had seen in her life. A mask was lowered over her face, but not before she had time to notice that the unconscious Ralph was breathing quietly on the stretcher next to her.

'I want to speak to her,' yelled the fire chief, striding over from the flashing truck.

'No way, they are both going to hospital,' shouted the ambulance driver in answer.

The fire chief ignored the reply and tore the mask

from Linda's gasping mouth. He bent close to her. 'I can't send men in there,' he yelled, pointing at the blazing house. 'Not unless there is someone inside. Is there anyone inside?'

'Mother,' whispered the girl.

The fireman looked around. 'She said "Mother".'

'She hasn't got a mother,' said a short bald man who had come over from the house next door. 'Her mother died when the girl was born. She only has a father. Dr Scrape.'

The fireman leaned closer. His words were urgent. 'Is your father in there, girl? Is anyone in there? The roof is about to collapse. Is anyone inside the house?'

Linda tried to make sense of his strange speech. Then a look of enlightenment swept across her face. She understood the question – that was clear. But many have wondered if she understood her own answer.

As the ambulance driver shut the door she just had time to say one word.

'No.'

The Busker

'Can you lend me ten dollars, Dad?' I asked.

'No,' he answered without even looking up.

'Aw, go on. Just till pocket money day. I'll pay you back.'

He still didn't look at me but started spreading butter onto a bread roll. He was acting just as if I wasn't there. He ate the whole roll without saying one word. It was very annoying but I had to play it cool. If I made him mad I would never get the money.

'I'll do some jobs,' I pleaded. 'I'll cut the whole lawn. That's worth ten dollars.'

This time he looked up. 'You must be crazy,' he said, 'if you think I'll ever let you near that lawn mower again. The last time you cut the lawn you went straight over about fifteen plants I had just put in. They cost me twenty-five dollars to buy and five hours to plant. You cut every one of them off at the base and now you want me to give you ten dollars.'

I knew straight away I had made a mistake by mentioning the lawn. I had to change the subject. 'It's important,' I told him. 'I need it to take Tania to the movies on Saturday.'

'That's important? Taking Tania to the pictures is important?'

'It is to me,' I said. 'She is the biggest spunk in the whole school. And she's agreed to go with me on Saturday night if . . .' Another mistake. I hadn't meant to tell him that bit.

'If what?' he growled.

'If I take her in a taxi. If I can't afford a taxi she's going to go with Brad Bellamy. He's got pots of money. He gets fifteen dollars a week from his Dad.'

'Good grief, lad. You're only fifteen years old and you want to take a girl out in a taxi. What's the world coming to? When I was your age . . .'

'Never mind,' I said. 'Forget it.' I walked out of the room before he could get started on telling me how he had to walk five miles to school when he was a boy. In bare feet. In the middle of winter. And then walk home again and chop up a tonne of wood with a blunt axe. Every time he told the story it got worse and worse. The first time he told it he had to walk two miles to school. The way it was going it would soon be fifty miles and ten tonnes of wood chopped up with a razor blade.

I walked sadly out into the warm night air. Dad just didn't understand. This wasn't just any old date. This was a date with Tania. She was the best-looking girl I had ever seen. She had long blonde hair, pearly teeth and a great figure. And she had class. Real class. There was no way that Tania was going to walk to the movies or go on a bus. She had already told me it was a taxi or nothing. I had to give her my answer by tomorrow morning or she would go with Brad Bellamy. He could afford ten taxis because his Dad was rich.

'I'm going for a walk down the beach,' I yelled over my shoulder. There was no answer. I might as well be dead for all Dad cared.

I walked along the beach in bare feet, dragging my toes through the water. I tried to think of some way of getting money. I could buy a Tattslotto ticket. You never knew what could happen. Someone had to win. Why not me? Or maybe I could find the mahogany ship. It was buried along the beach there under the sand but it hadn't been seen for over a hundred years. What if the sea had swept the sand away and left it uncovered that very night? And I found it? I could claim the reward of one thousand dollars. Boy, would I be popular then. I could hire a gold-plated taxi to take Tania out.

The beach was deserted and the moon was out. I could see quite clearly. I walked on and on, well away from the town and the houses. It was lonely and late at night but I wasn't scared. I was too busy looking out for the mahogany ship and thinking of how I would spend the reward money. Every now and then I could see something sticking out of the sand and I would run up to it as fast as I could. But each time I was disappointed. All I found were old forty-four-gallon drums and bits of driftwood that had been washed up by the heavy surf. It's funny,

I didn't really expect to find the mahogany ship. Things like that just don't happen, but in the back of my mind I kept thinking I might stumble over it and be lucky.

After a while I decided to climb up to the top of the sand dunes that ran along the beach. I knew I could see for miles from up there. I struggled to the top and sat down under a bent and twisted tree. Just at that moment the moon went in and everything was covered in darkness.

'What are you looking for, boy?' said a deep voice from the shadows.

I must have jumped at least a metre off the sand. I was terrified. There I was, miles away from any help, on an isolated beach in the middle of the night. And an unseen man was talking to me from the depths of the shadows. I wanted to run but my legs wouldn't move.

'What are you looking for, boy?' the voice asked again. I stared into the darkness under the tree and could just make out a shadowy figure sitting on the sand. I couldn't see his face but I could tell from the voice that he was very old.

I finally managed to say something. 'The mahogany ship,' I answered. 'I'm looking for the mahogany ship. Who are you?'

He didn't answer me but asked me another question. 'Why do you want to find the mahogany ship, boy?'

'The reward,' I stammered. 'There's a reward of one thousand dollars.'

'And what would you do with one thousand dollars if you had it?' the voice asked sadly.

I don't know why I didn't turn and run. I was still scared but I felt a little better and thought I could probably run faster than an old man if he tried anything. Also, there was something about him that made me want to stay. He sounded both sad and wise at the same time.

'A girl,' I said. 'There's this girl called Tania. I need the money to take her out. Not a thousand dollars, only ten. But a thousand dollars would be good.'

The old man didn't say anything for a long time. I still couldn't see him properly but I could hear him breathing. Finally he sighed and said, 'You think that money would make this girl like you? You think that a thousand dollars would make you popular?'

He made it sound silly. I didn't know what to say.

'Sit down, boy,' he commanded. 'Sit down and listen.'

I nearly ran off and left him. It was all very spooky and strange but I decided to do what he said. He sounded as if he expected to be obeyed, so I sat down on the sand and peered into the darkness, trying to see who he was.

'I am going to tell you a story, boy. And you are going to listen. When I am finished you can get up and go. But not until I have finished. Understand?'

I nodded at the dark shadow and sat there without moving. This is what he told me.

2

Many years ago there was a busker who worked in Melbourne. He stood by the railway station and played music to the people who went by. He dressed completely in flags. His trousers, coat and vest were made from flags and his bowler hat was covered with a flag. When he pushed a button a small door would open on his hat and flags would pop out.

He played a number of different musical instruments. With his feet he pushed pedals which banged three drums. He had a mouth organ on a wire near his face and he played a guitar with his hands. His music was terrible but people always stopped to watch and listen because of his small dog. The dog, whose name was Tiny, walked around with a hat in her mouth and took up the money people threw into it. Tiny had a coat made out of the Australian flag. Whenever the hat was empty Tiny would stand up on her hind legs and walk around like a person. Everyone would laugh and then throw money into the hat.

The Busker, for that is what everyone called him, was jealous of the dog. He could see that the people really stopped and gave money because of Tiny and not because of the music. But there was nothing he could do about it because he needed the money.

As the months went by The Busker became more and more miserable. He wanted people to like him and not the dog. He started to treat Tiny badly when nobody was looking. Sometimes he would blame her if the takings were poor. Often he would forget to feed Tiny for days at a time. The little dog grew thinner and thinner until at last she was so weak that she couldn't hold the hat up for the money. She had to drag it along the ground with her teeth.

Finally a man from the RSPCA came to see The Busker when he was working outside the station. 'That dog is a disgrace,' he said. 'You are not looking after it properly. It is so hungry its bones are sticking out. It is not to work again until it is healthy. I will give you three weeks to fatten it up. If it isn't healthy by then I will take it away and you will be fined.'

A crowd was standing around listening. 'Yes, it's a shame,' said a man who had been watching. 'Look at the poor little thing.' Other people started to call out and boo at The Busker. He went red in the face. Then he packed up his drums and guitar and put them in his car and drove off with Tiny.

It was a long way to The Busker's house for he lived well out of town. All the way home he thought about what had happened.

'It's all the fault of the rotten dog,' he said to himself. 'If it wasn't for her none of this would have happened.' The further he went, the more angry he became. When he reached home he grabbed Tiny by the scruff of the neck and took her round to the backyard. In the middle of the yard was an empty well. There was no water in the bottom but it was very deep. It was so deep you couldn't see the bottom.

'I'll fix you, Tiny,' said The Busker. 'You're not allowed to work for three weeks. Very well then, you can have a holiday. A very nice holiday.' He went and fetched a bucket and tied a rope to it. Then he put Tiny into the bucket and lowered her into the well. The poor little dog whimpered and barked but soon she was so far down she could hardly be heard. When the bucket reached the bottom Tiny jumped out of the bucket and sniffed around the bottom of the well. It was damp from water that trickled down the wall but there was nothing to eat. The Busker pulled up the bucket and went inside.

Tiny looked up but all she could see was a small circle of light far above. She walked round and round the bottom of the well always gazing up at the patch of light at the top.

The next day The Busker went to work without Tiny. He had no dog to carry the hat around so he just put it on the ground for people to put their money in. But hardly anyone did. The Busker tried his best. He played every tune he could think of and he cracked jokes. But it was no good. In one day he took only fifty cents. Now he knew for sure that it was Tiny that the people liked and not him.

He went home and threw some meat down the well. He could hear the faint sound of Tiny barking far below. 'It's no good, Tiny,' shouted The Busker. 'I'm not letting you out for three weeks. That will teach you a lesson.'

Every day The Busker went to work and the same thing happened. He played his music but hardly anyone put money in the hat. 'No one likes me or my music without Tiny,' said The Busker to himself. He was angry. He wanted people to like him. It wasn't the money so much. He just wanted people to like him. Each night when he reached home The Busker threw meat down the well for poor Tiny. 'Hurry up and get fat, Tiny,' he said. 'Because you're not coming out until you do.'

Tiny walked round and round at the bottom of the well. All day and night she looked up, hoping to be taken out. But no one ever came except The Busker and all he did was throw down meat once a day.

The three weeks went very slowly for The Busker. Each day he stood at the station playing his music to the people who walked by without listening. But the three weeks went much more slowly for the little dog who lay at the bottom of the well, always looking up at the sky for the help that didn't come.

At last the three weeks was up. The Busker decided to get Tiny out. He lowered the bucket down into the well but the little dog didn't know what to do. She walked around the bucket but didn't get into it. The Busker hadn't counted on this. 'Get in, you stupid dog,' he shouted. But it was so far down that Tiny could hardly hear him. In the end he had to go and have a rope ladder made. It cost him a lot of money because it was so long.

And it took a long time to make. Tiny was down the well for another week before it was finished.

3

Then something happened that changed everything. The Busker won Tattslotto. A letter came telling him that he had won over a million dollars. He couldn't believe his luck. It was wonderful. The first thing he did was to take his drums, flags and guitar and throw them down the tip. He went and bought himself a new car and a stereo. Every day he went to the shops and bought himself anything he wanted. Soon the house filled with every luxury you could think of.

All this time Tiny was still at the bottom of the well, barking and walking around and around, looking up at the world that was out of reach so far above. Each night The Busker came and threw down meat. And each night he told himself that he would get Tiny out in the morning. But when the morning came he forgot and did something else.

The truth is, The Busker was still unhappy. He had no more friends than before. When he bought things, the salesmen were nice to him. They patted him on the back and told him how wise he was to buy this or that. But as soon as he had bought their goods they lost interest and didn't want to talk to him.

In the end he realised he had only one friend in the world. Tiny. Tiny was the only one who really liked him.

And he had put her down a well. He felt bad about what he had done to his little friend and he rushed to the well to get her out. The Busker climbed down the well to get Tiny. He was frightened because it was so deep but he knew that he had to go. There was a terrible smell in the well which got worse as The Busker went deeper. When he reached the bottom he put Tiny inside his jumper and started to climb back up the rope. All the way up Tiny licked The Busker's face, even though he had put the poor little dog down a well for all that time.

When he reached the top of the well The Busker put Tiny on the ground. What he saw made tears come into his eyes. Tiny's head was bent back and her eyes stared up at the sky. She couldn't straighten up her neck. It was so stiff she could only walk around looking upwards. 'I'm sorry, I'm sorry,' cried The Busker. 'What have I done? Forgive me, Tiny, forgive me.' Tiny licked The Busker on the face.

From that time on Tiny always walked with her head bent back staring at the sky. No vet and no doctor could do anything about it. She had been down the well too long and her neck was fixed in a bent back position for the rest of her life.

The Busker looked after Tiny well from that time on. He fed her the best food and took her with him everywhere he went. Tiny trotted around after The Busker, wagging her tail, even though her neck was bent back and her head stared up at the sky.

The Busker had all the love of the little dog even though he had treated her so badly. But it still wasn't enough. He wanted people to like him. 'What good am I,' he said to Tiny, 'when my only friend is a dog?' He became more and more miserable until one day he hit upon an idea. A great idea. Or so he thought. He put an advertisement in the newspaper which said:

TO GIVE AWAY

FREE MONEY

$1.00 PER PERSON

COME AND GET IT

2 ROSE ST, MELTON

EVERY DAY 9.00 AM

'Tiny,' said The Busker, 'the crowds will like me now. This time I will give them money instead of them giving it to me. I will give away half of all I have. I don't need a million dollars. Half of that will do. Those who need money can come and get a dollar each whenever they like.'

The next morning The Busker set up a tent in his front yard. Inside he put a table and a chair and a bucket full of one-dollar coins. He hung a notice outside which said:

FREE MONEY

$1.00 EACH

At nine o'clock two scruffy-looking boys came in. 'Where's the free money, Pop?' said one of them. This wasn't what The Busker had expected. He didn't really want children. Especially rude ones. But he had to keep his word so he took a one-dollar coin from the bucket under the table and gave it to the boy. The boy looked at it carefully and said to his friend, 'It's real.' Then he turned around and ran out of the tent. The other boy held out his hand, snatched his coin and disappeared out of the tent before The Busker changed his mind.

Soon the tent was filled with more and more children. The word had spread quickly and every child in the neighbourhood was there. 'Form a line,' yelled The Busker. 'And no pushing.' The children were jostling and shoving and some were trying to push in.

The Busker was upset at the rudeness of the children. The first three simply grabbed the money and ran but the fourth child, a girl with big, brown eyes, said, 'Gee, thanks. Thanks a lot.' She turned round to walk out of the tent but The Busker called her back.

'Here,' he said, handing her another dollar. 'You are a very polite little girl. The only one who has said thanks.'

The next girl in the line heard what was said. After The Busker handed her a one dollar coin she said, 'Thanks a lot, Mister,' and then stood there without moving.

'What are you waiting for?' asked The Busker.

'My other dollar,' said the girl. 'I said thanks too. So I should get two dollars as well.'

The Busker sighed and handed her another dollar. After that all of the children discovered their manners and said, 'Thanks.' The Busker had to give all of them two dollars. He smiled to himself. At least they were grateful.

The line grew longer and longer. Soon it reached all the way down the street. After about fifty children had taken their two dollars an old woman came to the front of the queue. The Busker handed her a dollar. She looked at it and said, 'Thank you, love. You are a very kind man. Very kind indeed.'

The Busker smiled and gave her another five dollars. He was pleased that she liked him so much.

As the morning passed, more and more adults joined the queue. The ones who were very polite received more money. The Busker gave fifty dollars to one young woman who said, 'What a wonderful, generous and good man you are.'

'This is more like it,' he thought to himself. 'People really like me. They can see I am really a good man.' He gave Tiny a pat on the head. He didn't even mind when the people in the line paid attention to Tiny. He wasn't jealous of Tiny now that he had his own admirers.

By lunch time the bucket of money was empty. The Busker put up another sign which said:

CLOSED

GONE TO THE BANK

FOR MORE MONEY

The Busker took out two buckets of coins from the bank. 'You had better give me some notes as well,' he said to the teller. He took out ten thousand dollars' worth of notes. When he reached home he found the queue had grown to over a mile long. It went down the street and round the corner. As he went by people waved and a cheer went up. 'Good old Mister Busker,' someone yelled out.

4

Mister Busker. No one had ever called him that before. He felt wonderful. He went into the tent and started handing out more money. Most people received two dollars but the ones who said especially nice things got more. One old man came in, knelt at The Busker's feet and kissed his shoes. 'Oh Great One,' he said. 'I give thanks to you for your great compassion and generosity.'

The Busker was moved. 'There is no need for that,' he said. Then he gave the old man two hundred dollars. The news soon spread along the line. The more good things you said about The Busker, the more you got. A lot of people left the queue because they couldn't bring themselves to do it. But plenty more took their places. Soon everyone was getting at least twenty dollars.

At five o'clock The Busker put up a notice saying he had closed for the night and would be back in the morning. He went inside and sat down. He was very tired and soon fell asleep in the chair. At midnight he was woken up by a noise outside on the street. He went over to the window and looked out. He got a terrible shock. The people were still there in a long queue. They were sitting on the footpath in sleeping bags and blankets. Some had even put up small tents. A man in a van was selling pies, hot dogs and ice-creams. No one wanted to lose their place in the queue and they were all staying for the night. It was like a crowd waiting to buy tickets to see a pop star. The Busker grinned. He felt like a movie star. All of those people were there because of him.

In the morning a television crew came. They did interviews with The Busker and he was on the evening news. People came from everywhere to see the sight. The police arrived to control the traffic and keep the crowds in order. The queue grew longer and longer. And The Busker gave out larger and larger amounts of money. He had to. The people expected it when they said nice things to him. They went to lots of trouble. Some held up signs with his name on. Others had done drawings of him. One group had formed a band and sang a song saying what a great person The Busker was. Two students had made up a poem. He gave them two hundred dollars each.

On the third day the queue was four miles long. On the fifth day it was six miles long. People had to wait for three days to reach the front and The Busker had given away over half a million dollars. The money was brought every morning from the bank in an armoured car.

Tiny ran up and down the line licking everyone with her little turned-up head.

At the end of the week the armoured car brought a large box of money. 'I will need one hundred thousand dollars to see me over the weekend,' said The Busker.

'I'm sorry,' said the bank manager, 'but there are only ninety thousand dollars left. If I were you I would stop now and keep some for myself.' The Busker knew that this was good advice. But he couldn't keep it. The crowd all expected money. Some of them had been waiting in line for three days and three nights. He tried to cut back and give each person less but he couldn't. They all knew what each compliment was worth. Two hundred dollars for a good song about the busker and fifty dollars for a drawing of him. He tried to give less but they started complaining and yelling that it wasn't fair. They said they were being cheated.

The Busker was sick of it. He realised that they didn't really like him. He was tired of hearing people tell him how good he was. But he had to keep going.

Finally the terrible moment came. He ran out of money. There wasn't one cent left. He wrote a sign which said:

OUT OF MONEY

He hung the sign on the tent door and ran into the house with Tiny. The news spread down the line like wildfire. 'There is no more money,' they yelled. The line broke up and the mob charged up to the house. They started yelling and banging on the door. The Busker was scared out of his mind. Someone threw a rock through the window and glass scattered all over the floor.

'Cheat,' he heard someone yell.

'Robber.'

'I've been waiting in the freezing cold for two nights.'

'Get him. Teach him a lesson.'

Another rock smashed through the window. The door was rattling and shaking. The Busker knew it would soon collapse. He ran out of the back door, followed by Tiny. The yard was empty and there was nowhere to hide. He could hear the mob smashing and crashing around inside the house. He had to hurry. Then he saw the well with the rope ladder still hanging down inside. He ran over to it and climbed down, leaving Tiny at the top. He was only just in time. The angry crowd burst into the backyard yelling and shouting.

When they saw that he had escaped they went crazy. They smashed up the house and stole all The Busker's new purchases. They broke everything they could get their hands on. One group even destroyed the back fence and the top of the well. Someone untied the rope ladder and let it go. They had no idea that far below, the terrified Busker was hiding at the bottom.

After a while the police managed to control the mob and send them home. But it was too late to save the house. When darkness came it was a complete ruin. The Busker looked up and saw the moon. He thought it would be safe to call out for help. He yelled and yelled at the top of his voice but no one answered. Nobody could hear him, for the well was too deep. No one knew he was there. Except Tiny.

5

Days passed and no help came. It was cold and dark and smelly at the bottom of the well. The Busker would have starved to death if it hadn't been for Tiny. The little dog ran off in search of food. It was very difficult, for with her head bent back she had trouble picking anything up in her mouth. She had to lie down on her side, grasp a piece of food in her teeth and then stand up. After this she would trot to the well with an old bone or piece of stale bread and drop it down the well.

The days turned into weeks and still no help came. The Busker stayed alive by eating whatever Tiny dropped down the well. Sometimes it was a piece of rotten meat from a dustbin or a gnarled old bone left by another dog. Once Tiny dropped down a dead cat. Whatever it was, The Busker had to eat it or starve.

In all this time, Tiny gave everything she found to the Busker. She ate practically nothing herself. After a month she was skin and bone and so weak she could hardly drag herself to the well.

The Busker shouted and shouted every day but no

one came. He yelled up at the sun, at the clouds, at the moon so far above. But no one answered. Then, one day, a terrible thing happened. Nothing was dropped down the well. No bone, no scraps, nothing. The next day was the same. And the day after that. The Busker licked the water off the wet wall but he had nothing to eat. He knew that his time had come. He couldn't last much longer. He grew weaker and weaker. And he wondered what had happened to Tiny.

At the end of the fifth week The Busker decided to give one more loud shout. His voice was almost gone. 'Help,' he screamed. 'Help.'

He peered up at the small dot of light above. Was that a head looking down? Was that a voice? He strained to listen.

'Hang on,' said a faint voice. 'We will soon have you out.' He was saved.

A little later a steel cable came down the well. There was a small seat on the end. The Busker sat on it and yelled up the well. 'Take me up. Take me up.'

When he reached the top he blinked. The bright light hurt his eyes but he managed to see four or five men with a tow truck and a winch. They were staring at this wild, smelly, dirty man that had come out of the well. 'We had better get you to hospital,' said one of the men. 'You don't look too good.'

'You're lucky to be alive,' said another. 'I never would have heard you if it wasn't for that poor little dog lying over there. I came over to see if it was still alive and heard you calling out.'

The Busker ran over to where the little dog lay on the ground. She was dead. She had starved to death because she had dropped every piece of food she could find down to The Busker. Tears fell down his tangled beard. He picked Tiny up in his arms. 'You can leave me,' he said to the men. 'I will be all right.'

He buried Tiny in a small grave, there in the backyard. On a piece of wood he wrote:

MY FRIEND TINY

R.I.P.

Then The Busker shuffled off. He was never seen again.

6

'And that is the end of the story,' said the old man.

I had forgotten where I was. Sitting there on a sand dune at the beach in the middle of the night. The story had completely taken me in. I looked at the old man but I still couldn't see this face. I wanted to ask him questions. I wanted to know if the story was true. I wanted to know what happened to The Busker. But I never got the chance.

'Go now, boy,' said the old man. 'That is the end of the story. Go and leave me alone. I am tired.'

I didn't want to go but he sounded as if he meant it.

I stood up and walked away along the top of the sand dune. After I had gone a little way the moon came out. I turned around and looked back at the tree where the old man had told the story. I could see him clearly. He had a white beard and was standing there in the moonlight looking up into the tree. Then he walked away, now looking up at the stars and the moon. With a shock I realised his neck was fixed back. He couldn't move it. He was destined to spend all his days looking up, as he had looked up that well so many years ago.

The story was true. And the old man was The Busker. I watched him shuffle away with his bent neck. Then the moon went in and he was gone.

I ran home as fast as I could and jumped into bed. But I couldn't sleep. I lay there thinking about the sad, strange tale of Tiny and The Busker who had tried to use money to make people like him.

The next morning I met Dad on the stairs. He pushed ten dollars into my hand. 'Here you are, Tony,' he said. 'If Tania won't go out with you unless you take her in a taxi, you might as well have the money.'

'Thanks, Dad,' I said.

I stuffed the ten dollars into my pocket. Then I went round to Tania's house and told her to go jump in the lake.

Ice Maiden

I just wouldn't go anywhere near a redhead.

Now don't get me wrong and start calling me a hairist or something like that. Listen to what I have to say, then make up your mind.

It all started with Mr Mantolini and his sculptures.

They were terrific, were Mr Mantolini's frozen statues. He carved them out of ice and stood them in the window of his fish shop which was over the road from the pier. A new ice carving every month.

Sometimes it would be a beautiful peacock with its tail fanned out. Or maybe a giant fish thrashing itself to death on the end of a line. One of my favourites was a kangaroo with a little joey peering out of her pouch.

It was a bit sad really. On the first day of every month Mr Mantolini would throw the old statue out the back into an alley. Where it would melt and trickle away into a damp patch on the ground.

A new statue would be in the shop window. Sparkling blue and silver as if it had been carved from a solid chunk of the Antarctic shelf.

Every morning on my way to school, I would stop

to stare at his statue. And on the first of the month I would be there after school to see the new one. I couldn't bear to go around the back and watch yesterday's sculpture melt into the mud.

'Why do you throw them out?' I asked one day.

Mr Mantolini shrugged. 'You live. You die,' he said.

Mr Mantolini took a deep breath. Now he was going to ask me something. The same old thing he had asked every day for weeks. 'My cousin Tony come from Italy. Next month. You take to school. You friend. My cousin have red hair. You like?'

I gave him my usual answer. 'Sorry,' I said. 'I won't be able to.' I couldn't tell him that it was because I hated red hair. I didn't want to hurt his feelings.

He just stood there without saying anything. He was disappointed in me because we were friends. He knew how much I liked his ice statues and he always came out to talk to me about them. 'You funny boy,' he said. He shook his head and walked inside.

I thought I saw tears in Mr Mantolini's eyes. I knew I had done the wrong thing again. And I was sorry. But I didn't want a redhead for a mate.

2

I felt guilty and miserable all day. But after school I cheered up a bit. It was the first of September. There would be a new ice statue in the window. It was always something to look forward to.

I hurried up to the fish shop and stared through the glass. I couldn't believe what I saw. The ice statue of a girl. It reminded me of one of those Greek sculptures that you see in museums. It had long tangled hair. And smiling lips. Its eyes sparkled like frozen diamonds. I tell you this. That ice girl was something else. She was fantastic.

'You're beautiful,' I said under my breath. 'Beautiful.'

Of course she was only a statue. She couldn't see or hear me. She was just a life-sized ice maiden, standing among the dead fish in the shop window. She was inside a glass fridge which kept her cold. Her cheeks were covered with frost.

I stood there for ages just gawking at her. I know it was stupid. I would have died if anyone knew what I was thinking. How embarrassing. I had a crush on a piece of ice.

Every day after that, I visited the fish shop. I was late for school because of the ice maiden. I filled every spare minute of my time standing outside the window. It was as if I was hypnotised. The ice maiden's smile seemed to be made just for me. Her outstretched hand beckoned. 'Get real,' I said to myself. 'What are you doing here? You fool.' I knew I was mad but something kept drawing me back to the shop.

Mr Mantolini wouldn't meet my gaze. He was cross with me.

I pretended the ice girl was my friend. I told her my

secrets. Even though she was made of ice, I had this silly feeling that she understood.

Mr Mantolini saw me watching her. But he didn't come outside. And whenever I went inside to buy fish for Mum, he scurried out the back and sent his assistant to serve me.

3

The days passed. Weeks went by. The ice maiden smiled on and on. She never changed. The boys thought I was nuts standing there gawking at a lump of ice. But she had this power over me – really. Kids started to tease me. 'He's in love,' said a girl called Simone. I copped a lot of teasing at school but still I kept gazing in that window.

As the days went by I grew sadder and sadder. I wanted to take the ice girl home. I wanted to keep her forever. But once she was out of her glass cage, in the warm air, her smiling face would melt and drip away.

I dreaded the first of October. When Mr Mantolini would take the ice maiden and dump her in the alley. To be destroyed by the warm rays of the sun.

On the last day of September I waited until Mr Mantolini was serving in the shop. 'You can't throw her out,' I yelled. 'She's too lovely. She's real. You mustn't. You can't.' I was nearly going to say 'I love her' but that would have been stupid.

Mr Mantolini looked at me and shrugged. 'You live.

You die,' he said. 'She ice. She cold. She water.'

I knew it was no good. Tomorrow Mr Mantolini would cast the ice girl out into the alley.

The next day I wagged school. I hid in the alley and waited. The minutes dragged their feet. The hours seemed to crawl. But then, as I knew he would, Mr Mantolini emerged with the ice maiden. He dumped her down by the rubbish bins. Her last resting place was to be among the rotting fish heads in an empty alley.

Mr Mantolini disappeared back into the shop. I rushed over to my ice maiden. She was still covered in frost and had sticky, frozen skin.

My plan was to take her to the butcher. I would pay him to keep the ice maiden in his freezer where I could visit her every day. I hadn't asked him yet. But he couldn't say no, could he?

The sun was rising in the sky. I had to hurry.

The ice maiden still stooped. Still reached out. She seemed to know that her time had come. 'Don't worry,' I said. 'I'll save you.'

I don't know what came over me. I did something crazy. I bent down and gently kissed her on the mouth.

4

It was a long kiss. The longest kiss ever in the history of the world. My lips stuck to hers. My flesh froze onto the ice. Cold needles of pain numbed my lips. I tried to pull away but I couldn't. The pain made my eyes water. Tears streamed down my face and across the ice maiden's cheeks.

On we kissed. And on. And on. I wanted to pull my mouth away but much as I cared for the ice girl, I didn't want my lips to tear away, leaving bleeding skin as a painful reminder of my madness. There I was, kissing ice lips, unable to move.

I tried to yell for help but I couldn't speak. Muffled grunts came out of my nose. Horrible nasal noises. No one came to help me. The alley echoed with the noise.

I grabbed the ice maiden and lifted her up. She was heavy. Her body was still sticky with frost. My fingers stuck fast. She was my prisoner. And I was hers.

The sun warmed my back. Tears of agony filled my eyes. If I waited there she would melt. I would be free but the ice maiden would be gone. Her lovely nose and chin would drip away to nothing.

But the cold touch of the ice girl was terrible. Her smiling lips burnt my flesh. The tip of my nose was frozen. I ran out of the alley into the street. There was a group of people waiting by a bus stop near the end of the pier. 'Help, get me unstuck. But don't hurt the ice maiden,' was what I tried to say.

But what came out was, 'Nmn nnmmm nnnn nng ng ng mn nm.'

The people looked at me as if I was crazy. Some of

them laughed. They thought I was acting the fool. An idiot pretending to kiss a statue.

I ran over to Mr Mantolini's shop and tried to knock on the window with my foot. I had to balance on one leg, while holding the ice girl in my arms and painfully kissing her at the same time. I fell over with a crunch. Oh agony, oh misery, oh pain. My lips, my fingers, my knees.

There was no sign of Mr Mantolini. He must have been in the back room.

5

What could I do? I looked out to sea. If I jumped into the water it would melt the ice. My lips and fingers would come free. But the ice maiden would melt. 'Let me go,' I whispered in my mind. But she made no answer.

My hands were numb. Cold pins pricked me without mercy. I ran towards the pier. I spoke to my ice maiden again, without words. 'I'm sorry. I'm sorry, sorry, sorry.'

I jogged along the pier. Further and further. My feet drummed in time with my thoughts. 'Sorry, sorry, sorry.'

I stopped and stared down at the waves. Then I closed my eyes and jumped, still clutching the ice-cold girl to my chest. Down, I plunged. For a frozen moment I hung above the ocean. And then, with a gurgle and a groan, I took the ice lady to her doom.

The waves tossed above us. The warm water parted

our lips. My fingers slipped from her side. I bobbed up like an empty bottle and saw her floating away. Already her eyes had gone. Her hair was a glassy mat. The smiling maiden smiled no more. She was just a lump of ice melting in the waves.

'No,' I screamed. My mouth filled with salt water and I sank under the sea.

They say that your past life flashes by you when you are drowning. Well, it's true. I re-lived some horrible moments. I remembered the time in a small country school when I was just a little kid. And the only redhead. I saw the school bully Johnson teasing me every day. Once again I sat on the school bench at lunchtime – alone and rejected. Not allowed to hang around with the others. Just because Johnson didn't like red hair. Once again I could hear him calling me 'carrots' and 'ginger'. They were the last thoughts that came to me before the world vanished into salty blackness.

6

But I didn't drown. In a way my hair saved me. It must have been easy for them to spot my curly locks swirling like red seaweed thrown up from the ocean bed.

Mr Mantolini pulled me out. He and his cousin. I could hear him talking even though I was only half conscious. 'You live. But you not die yet.'

I didn't want to open my eyes. I couldn't bear to think about what I had done to the ice maiden. I was alive but she was dead. Gone forever.

In the end I looked up. I stared at my rescuers. Mr Mantolini and his cousin.

She had red tangled hair. And smiling lips. Her eyes sparkled like frozen diamonds. I tell you this. That girl Tony was something else. She was fantastic.

'You're beautiful,' I said under my breath. 'Beautiful.'

Mr Mantolini's ice statue had been good. But not as good as the real thing. After all, it had only been a copy of his cousin Tony. I smiled up at her. And she smiled back. With a real smile.

I guess that's when I discovered that an ice maiden who is dead is not sad. And a nice maiden who is red is not bad.

Not bad at all.

Only Gilt

The bird's perch is swinging to and fro and hitting me on the nose. I can see my eye in its little mirror. Its water dish is sliding around near my chin. The smell of old bird droppings is awful. The world looks different when you are staring at it through bars.

Fool, fool, fool.

What am I doing walking to school with my head in a bird's cage?

Oh no. Here's the school gate. Kids are looking at me. They are pointing. Laughing. Their faces remind me of waves, slapping and slopping at a drowning child.

Strike. Here comes that rotten Philip Noonan. He's grinning. He's poking bits of bread through the bars. 'Pretty Polly,' he says. 'Polly want a biscuit?'

I wish I was an ant so that I could crawl into a crack. Then no one would ever see me.

Teachers are looking out of the staffroom window. I can see Mr Gristle looking. I can see Mr Marsden looking. They are shaking their heads.

I hope Gristle doesn't come. 'Get that thing off your head,' he will shout. 'You idiot. You fool. What do you think you are? A parrot?' Then he will try to rip the cage off my head. He will probably rip the ears off my skull while he is doing it.

Mr Marsden is coming. Thank goodness. He is the best teacher in the school. I don't think he'll yell. Still, you never know with teachers. He hasn't seen a boy come to school with his head in a birdcage before.

'Gary,' he says kindly. 'I think there is something you want to say.'

I shake my head. There is nothing to say. It is too late. I am already a murderer. Nothing can change that.

Mr Marsden takes me inside. We go into the sick bay and sit down on the bed. He looks at me through the bars but he doesn't say anything. He is waiting. He is waiting for me to tell my story.

After a bit I say, 'All right. I'll tell you all about it. But only if you keep it secret.'

Mr Marsden thinks about this for a bit. Then he smiles and nods his head. I start to tell him my story.

2

On Friday I walk over to see Kim Huntingdale. She lives next door. I am in love with her. She is the most beautiful girl in the world. When she smiles it reminds me of strawberries in the springtime. She makes my stomach go all funny. That's how good she is.

My dog Skip goes with me. Skip is a wimp. She runs around in circles whenever anyone visits. She rolls over on her back and begs for a scratch. She would lick a burglar's hand if one came to rob our house. She will not fight or bark. She runs off if Mum growls. Skip is definitely a wimp.

Mind you, when Mum growls I run off myself. When she is mad it reminds me of a ginger-beer bottle bursting in the fridge.

Anyway, when I get to Kim's house she is feeding Beethoven. Beethoven is her budgie. She keeps it in a cage in the backyard. She loves Beethoven very much. Lucky Beethoven.

Beethoven can't fly because he only has one wing. Kim found him in the forest. This enormous, savage dog had the poor bird in its mouth. Kim grabbed the dog without even thinking of herself and saved Beethoven's life. But he was only left with one wing and he can't fly at all.

Now Kim loves Beethoven more than anything.

I love Skip too. Even though she is a wimp.

Kim looks at Skip. 'You shouldn't bring her over here,' she says. 'Beethoven is scared of dogs.'

Skip rolls over on her back and begs with her four little legs. 'Look at her,' I say. 'She wouldn't hurt Beethoven.' When she rolls over like that Skip reminds me of a dying beetle.

Kim walks into Beethoven's aviary. She lets me in and locks Skip out by putting a brick against the door. Kim picks up Beethoven and the little budgie sits on her finger. It starts to sing. Oh, that bird can sing. It is beautiful. It is magic. A shiver runs up my spine. It reminds me of the feeling you get when fizzy lemonade bubbles go up your nose.

Kim puts the bird down on the ground. It is always on the ground because it can't fly. 'Tie up Skip,' says Kim, 'and I'll let Beethoven out for a walk.'

I do what she says. I would do anything for Kim. I would even roll over on my back and beg like Skip. Just for a smile. But Kim hardly knows I am here. I tie up Skip and Kim lets Beethoven out for a walk. He chirps and sings and walks around the backyard. It reminds me of a little yellow penguin walking around on green snow.

Skip is tied up so she just sits and looks at Beethoven and licks her lips.

3

After a while Kim shuts Beethoven back in the aviary and puts the brick in front of the door. Skip sticks one ear up in the air (the other one won't move) and looks cute. Kim gives her a pat and a cuddle. 'She's a lovely dog,' she says. 'But you have to keep her away from Beethoven.'

'Don't worry,' I say. 'I promise.'

Kim smiles at me again. Then she says something that makes my heart jump. 'Next to Beethoven, you are my best friend.'

It is hard to tell you how I feel when I hear this. My stomach goes all wobbly. It reminds me of a bunch of frogs jumping around inside a bag.

I walk back to our place feeling great. Wonderful. Mum isn't home so I can let Skip inside. Mum doesn't like Skip being in the house. Skip is a smart dog. She can open the door with her paw if it is left a little bit ajar.

Mum won't let Skip in because she once did a bit of poop under the dresser. It did not smell very nice and I had to clean it up. Skip's poop reminds me a bit of ...

'I think we can miss that bit,' says Mr Marsden who is listening to my story carefully and looking at me through the bars of the bird cage.

'Okay,' I say. 'I'll move on to the awful bit.'

4

I do not see Kim for two days because I have to visit Grandma with Mum. We leave Skip at the dog kennels all day Friday and Saturday. When we get back we collect her from the kennels. Poor Skip. She can't even put up one ear. She hates the dog kennels. She cries and whimpers whenever she has to stay there. But she is too scared of the other dogs to bark.

We drive home with Skip on my knee. She looks at me with those big brown eyes. They remind me a bit of two pools of gravy spilt on the tablecloth.

'Skip can sleep inside tonight,' I say to Mum.

'No,' says Mum. 'You tie her up in the shed, the same as always.'

Poor Skip. That night I do not tie her up. I sneak her into my bedroom and let her sleep in bed with me. She is a very clean dog. She is always licking and chewing herself.

Mum, however, has a keen sense of smell. She will know that Skip has been in. Even when you burn incense in your room Mum can still smell dog. I open the window to let in the fresh air. Then I fall asleep and have a lovely dream. All about how Kim and I and Beethoven and Skip get married and all live together on a tropical island. It reminds me a bit of one of those pretend stories that always have a lovely ending. I wish real life was like that.

The next day is Sunday. I sleep in until the sun shines on my face and wakes me up. A soft wind is blowing into the room. I get out of bed and shut the window.

Skip has gone.

5

I look out of the window and see Skip running around with a yellow tennis ball.

I think about how Mum doesn't like getting dog spit on the tennis balls. It leaves green marks on her hands.

Green marks. Our tennis balls are green.

What is that yellow thing in Skip's mouth? I jump out of the window and run down the yard. Skip sees me coming. A chase. She loves a chase. She runs off at top speed. She reminds me a bit of a rabbit bobbing up and down as it runs away from a hunter.

My heart is beating very fast. 'Please,' I say to myself. 'Let it be a ball. Let it be Mum's best glove. Let it be my new transistor radio. But don't let it be . . .' It is too awful to even say.

I run after Skip. She loves the fun. She runs under the house. 'Come out,' I yell. 'Come out, you rotten dog.' Skip does not move. 'I'll kill you,' I yell. I am shouting. There are tears in my eyes.

Skip knows that I'm mad. She rolls over on her back and begs. Way under the house where I can't even get her. She drops the yellow thing and nicks off.

Oh, no. I can't bear it. I crawl under the house on my stomach. It is dusty and dirty. There are spiders but I don't even notice them.

I stretch out my hand and I grab the little bundle of feathers. It is Beethoven. Dead. He is smeared with blood and dirt and dog spit. His eyes are white and hard. His little legs are stiff. They remind me of frozen twigs on a bare tree. Beethoven stares at me without seeing. He has sung his last song.

Tears carve tracks down my face. They run into my mouth and I taste salt.

Everything is ruined. My life is over. My dog has killed Beethoven. It is all my fault. If I had tied Skip up this would never have happened. My head swims. When Kim finds out she will cry. She will hate me. She will hate Skip.

Her mum will tell my mum. What will they do to Skip?

6

I crawl out into the backyard. Skip is wagging her tail slowly. She knows something is wrong. I feel funny inside. For a second I feel like kicking Skip hard. I feel like kicking her so hard that she will fly up over the fence.

Then I look into her gravy-pool eyes and I know that she is just a dog. 'Oh, Skip,' I cry. 'Oh, Skip, Skip, Skip. What have you done?' Then I say to myself. 'Gary, Gary, Gary, what have you done?'

I tie Skip up. Then I take Beethoven into my bedroom. He is so small and stiff and shrunken. He reminds me a bit of my own heart.

I think about Kim. She mustn't find out. What if I go and buy another yellow budgie? One that looks the same. She will never know. Kim's car is not there. They are out.

I go down to the garage and get this old golden cage that is covered in dust. When I was a little kid I used to think it was made of real gold. 'No,' Mum told me, 'it is only gilt.'

I wrap up Beethoven in a tissue and put him carefully in my pocket. Then I look in my wallet. Seven dollars.

Just enough. I jump on my bike with the golden cage tied to the back. Where do they sell budgies? At the market. It is late. The market will be closing soon.

I ride like I have never ridden before. The wind whips my hair. I puff. I pant. Sweat runs into my eyes. I ride up Wheeler's Hill without getting off my bike. No one has ever ridden up Wheeler's Hill before. My heart is hurting. My legs are aching. I look at my watch. It's five o'clock. The market will be closed.

It is. The trucks are all leaving. The shoppers have gone. The ground is covered in hot-dog papers and cabbage leaves. The stalls are empty.

I look at the trucks. One or two men are still loading. I drop my bike and run from truck to truck. Car parts – no. Plants – no. Watches – no. Chocolates – no. Fairyfloss – no. I look in each truck. None have pets.

I am done. I hang my head. Beethoven is dead. Kim will hate me. Kim will hate Skip. What will happen?

I walk back slowly. Men are laughing. Children are calling. Cats are meowing.

Cats are meowing? Pets.

There is a lady with a small van and in the back are cats, dogs, guinea pigs and birds. There is a large cage full of birds.

'Please,' I yell. 'Please. Have you got any budgies?'

'They are up the back of the truck,' she says. 'I can't get them out now. Come back next week.'

'I can't,' I sob. 'I need it now.'

The lady shakes her head and starts up her van. I take Beethoven out of my pocket and unwrap him. The lady looks at the little blood-stained body. She turns off the engine with a sigh and starts to unload the van.

At last we get the cage of birds unloaded. There are canaries and finches. The cage is filled with birds. There are about twenty budgies. There are green ones and blue ones.

And there is one yellow one. It looks just like Beethoven. It is a ringer for Beethoven. I will put this bird in Kim's cage and she will never know the difference.

'Ten dollars,' says the lady. 'Yellow ones are hard to get.'

I empty my wallet. 'I only have seven dollars,' I tell her.

The lady takes my money with a smile and gently hands me the bird. 'I was young once myself,' she says.

I put the bird in my golden cage and pedal like crazy. My trip back reminds me a bit of a sailing boat skidding to shore in a storm. I hope I can get there before Kim arrives home. I have to put the new bird in the cage before she knows Beethoven is dead.

7

Finally I get home. There is no car at Kim's house yet. They are still out. I rush into the backyard and down to the aviary where the wire door is flapping in the wind.

The new budgie is sitting on the perch in my golden cage. It flaps its wings.

Wings?

Beethoven only had one wing. Beethoven couldn't fly. Oh no. Kim will know straight away that the new bird is not Beethoven.

My plan has failed. I take out the little bird and stretch out its wings. It has one wing too many. 'Little bird, little bird,' I say. 'You're no good to me like this. What will I do with you?'

There is only one thing to do. I throw the tiny budgie up into the air. 'Goodbye, little bird,' I say. It flies off in a flurry of feathers and disappears forever.

I go home.

All is lost. Kim will know what Skip has done. Kim will know what I have done. I let Skip run free. I didn't chain her up like Mum told me. It is all my fault. I am a murderer. I am responsible for Beethoven's death.

I will never be able to look at Kim. She will never want to look at me.

Then I get an idea. I'll bury Beethoven and say nothing. Kim will think he has escaped and walked off.

No. That's no good. Kim will still think Skip opened the cage. And she'll ask me to help look for Beethoven. I would have to pretend to hunt for the bird knowing it was dead.

I get another idea. It is better. But terrible. I will sneak back to the cage and put Beethoven inside. I will lock up the cage with the brick. Kim will think that Beethoven has died of old age.

But Beethoven is covered in blood and dirt and dried-up dog spit.

I will have to clean him. I take Beethoven's body to the laundry and wash him gently. I hate myself for doing this. The blood starts to rinse out. But not all of it. I soak him for a while. I try detergent. I try soap. At last he is clean.

He is clean. And dead. And wet.

8

I go and fetch Mum's hair dryer and I dry out Beethoven's feathers until they are all fluffy and new. I gently close his staring eyes. Then, I sneak down to Kim's backyard. I remind myself a bit of a robber skulking around a jewellery shop.

I go inside the aviary door and put Beethoven down on the sawdust. No one will ever know my terrible secret. I am safe. Skip is safe. Kim will still like us. I close the door, replace the brick and go home.

That night I cannot sleep. I see Kim's sad face. I dream of myself in jail. Nobody likes me. Nobody wants me. I have caused sorrow and pain.

In the morning I look out of my window. I see Kim and her mum and dad. They are gathered around the cage. I can't hear what they are saying. I don't want to know what they are saying. Kim will be crying. Her tears will be falling. If I could see them they would remind me of a salty waterfall.

I see Kim's father put an arm around her shoulder. I wish it could be my arm. I see her mum pick up Beethoven gently in her hand.

I can't look at them any more. Everything is my fault. Poor Skip is just a dog. I should have tied her up. Murderer. I am a murderer. And no one will ever know. My horrible secret will stay with me forever.

I get the golden cage and rush out to the garage. I cut a hole in the bottom with tin snips. I push my head through the hole. I will wear the golden cage for the rest of my life. It is my punishment. It is what I get for what I did. I will never take it off.

9

Mr Marsden is looking at me sadly. 'You made a mistake,' he says. 'A little mistake that made big things happen. But it wasn't your fault. And even if it was, you can't carry around the burden forever. Like a rock on your shoulders. Or a cage on your head. You have to face up to it. Tell Kim. And then go on living.'

We are still sitting on the sick-room bed. Looking out of the window. A girl is slowly walking into the school grounds. She is late for school. She reminds me of a lonely ghost.

It is Kim.

Mr Marsden walks out and brings her into the room.

Her eyes are red, but still lovely. Her face is sad. It reminds me of a statue of a beautiful princess who has passed away. I cannot look at her. I shrink down in my cage.

'I'm sorry to be late,' she says to Mr Marsden. 'But something happened at home. My budgie Beethoven died on Friday. Dad says he died of old age.'

I hang my head in shame. I can't tell her the truth. I just can't.

Friday?

'Not Friday,' I say. 'Yesterday.'

'No,' says Kim. 'He died on Friday. We buried him in the backyard. But someone dug him up and put him back in the aviary.'

I take the cage off my head and throw it in the bin. After school I walk home with Kim. She holds my hand. It sort of reminds me of, well, flying free, like we are up there in the clouds with Beethoven.

HMM! HUH! WHAT? HMM WHAT?

Frozen Stiff

'Where will I put it?' asked Old Jack Thaw in a creaky voice.

I looked at the mouse. Its frozen tail stuck out straight behind it like an arrow. It was poised with one frozen leg raised as if it was sniffing the air. Its frozen eyes stared ahead without blinking.

Jack Thaw had never been to school and he couldn't read or write too well. That's why he needed me. I always stopped off at Jack's place on the way home from school.

'Well,' I said, 'mouse starts with "M". That comes between "L" and "N". So you have the lizard on one side and the numbat on the other.' I pointed at a space between the little ice blocks.

Jack Thaw gave a wrinkly grin. His bare gums showed because he had forgotten to put in his false teeth. He picked up the lizard's ice block and moved it a little bit to the left. Then he placed the frozen mouse in its place on the shelf. It seemed to glare at us from inside its icy prison.

We both stood and stared at the collection of

tiny animals. Birds, spiders. Bats, rats. Grasshoppers, goannas. Fleas, flies. You name it, if it was small and dead it was there. The walls of the freezing room were lined with shelves. On the shelves were thousands of small ice blocks – each one with a tiny creature frozen inside.

Long ago, this had been an ice factory. And Jack Thaw had been an ice man. He used to take blocks of ice around to people's houses on the back of an old truck. But gradually people stopped needing the ice. They sold their ice chests and bought fridges instead. In the end no one wanted ice at all.

So Jack stopped working and started up his collection. Whenever he found a small, dead creature he brought it back to the ice works and froze it inside an ice block. Then he put it on a shelf inside his huge freezer room. This room was so big that you could drive a truck inside it if you wanted to.

A shiver ran up my spine. 'Let's go outside,' I said. 'I'm cold.'

We walked out of the freezer room into the factory. Jack swung the massive doors closed. Then he pointed to the bandage on my finger. 'Have you hurt yourself?' he asked.

I nodded and took off the stained bandage. My finger was bleeding from a deep cut. 'Barbed wire,' I said. 'I cut it on the barbed wire on Gravel's fence.'

Jack took me over to a huge steel bin on wheels.

It was full of salty water. Jack would never usually let me near this bin of water. It was special. He used tap water to freeze the animals. Once I had seen Jack drink a bit of the salty water when he didn't know I was there.

Jack climbed up the side of the bin and dipped in a glass. He held the glass out to me. 'Put your finger in there,' he said.

Without a word I dipped in my bleeding finger.

When I pulled it out my finger had stopped bleeding.

Jack smiled. 'Wonderful stuff, salt water,' he said. Then he shook a gnarled old hand at me. 'Don't you tell anyone about this,' he croaked. 'Or my collection.'

'Don't worry,' I said with a sigh. 'I've told you a million times. I can keep a secret. No one knows about your frozen zoo. Not even Mum.'

Some of the kids at school said that Jack was 200 years old. They were scared of him. I was the only person he ever let in the ice factory.

I walked towards the outside door.

'Come back tomorrow,' said Jack. 'I'm going to the beach. I might find a dead fish. You will have to show me where to put it.' He sure was a funny bloke. All he ever thought about was his precious collection. But he had a heart of gold. He was a good mate.

I waved goodbye. 'See you,' I said. 'I'd better be going. I haven't said goodbye to Jingle Bells yet. I rushed off without saying goodbye to her when I cut my finger.'

2

Jingle Bells was a cow. You might wonder what a cow was doing in the middle of the city. Well, it was the saddest thing. Poor old Jingle Bells was locked in a shed. In the shadow of the high-rise flats. In between the factories and the freeways. Stuck in the polluted, smelly city. Surrounded by smog. Like us.

Only it was worse for a cow.

Jingle Bells had never grazed in the grass. Never stepped on a flower. Never snatched a glimpse of the sky. She was a prisoner in Gravel's shed. He sure was a mean bloke.

Every day for the last two weeks she had been mooing. Long sad moos. They went on and on without stopping.

Jack had told me it was because it was springtime. 'It's the smell of the country,' he had said. 'In between the fumes and the foul air, a tiny bit of pollen from the country is carried on the wind. It gets through a crack in the dark shed. It creeps across the concrete floor. It snakes into Jingle Bells' nostrils. And then she smells the pollen – the little messenger from the bush. It tells her that far away there are other cows. It speaks of soft winds – and blossoms that bend the branches of trees until they touch the cool clover. She moos for the moon and the stars and the dew of the still, cold nights.'

Jack Thaw might not be able to read. But he sure had a way with words. Every time I thought of Jingle Bells after that a tear would come into my eye.

Something had to be done. It was wrong to keep a cow locked up in a dingy shed.

Jingle Bells was my best friend after Jack Thaw. Not that she had ever seen me. She had only heard my voice. And looked into my eye.

Every night after school I would creep along the alley behind Gravel's house and climb over his back fence. Then I would sneak up to his cow shed and peep through a crack in the palings. Jingle Bells would stare at me through the crack and I would stare back at her. We would stand there for ages – eye to eye. Not moving. Just looking.

You can tell a lot from staring at a cow's eye. I could tell that Jingle Bells wanted to get out. Wanted to escape. I knew that she longed for the sunshine. I knew that she hated Gravel, who kept her in this black hole.

Before I left her each night I would poke a little bit of fresh grass through the crack. All Gravel ever gave her was dry old chaff and hay. When Jingle Bells saw the grass she would give six, short, happy moos. They sounded a bit like the first bars of the song 'Jingle Bells'. That's why I named her after the Christmas carol.

Gravel just called her 'the cow'. Whenever he was around, Jingle Bells' long, sad moos could be heard filtering through the sounds of car horns and screeching brakes.

3

Anyway, on the day that it all started I saw something especially sad. I looked through the crack and saw Jingle Bells straining at her rope. She was pulling and pulling. Trying to reach a tiny little patch of sunshine that had leaked in through a hole in the roof. It was only about the size of a twenty-cent coin but Jingle Bells wanted to stand in it. Imagine that. The poor thing wanted to stand in a tiny little splot of sunshine.

I put back my head and gave a scream of rage. Then I fumed and ran. I clambered over Gravel's back fence. I sped down the alley. I tore across the road to the high-rise flats where we lived. My lungs felt like fire but nothing could stop me.

The lift seemed to take ages but at last I reached the fifteenth floor. Our flat was number twenty. I banged on the door until Mum finally opened it. 'What's the rush?' she asked.

'The hammer,' I panted. 'Where's the hammer?'

'Under the sink,' answered Mum.

Without another word I went into the kitchen and grabbed our claw-hammer. 'Be back soon,' I yelled. I headed back towards the cow shed as fast as I could go.

There was no sign of Gravel back at the shed. Inside, Jingle Bells was still mooing with long, sad moos and straining to reach the little shaft of sunshine. 'Don't worry old girl,' I said. 'You're in for a big treat.'

I clambered up onto the top of the shed and started

pulling out nails with the claw-hammer. It was hard work but after about half an hour I had most of the nails out of one sheet of roofing iron.

There was still no sign of Gravel.

At last it was done. I had freed one large sheet of corrugated iron. I ripped it off the roof and threw it into the small garden. Sunshine poured into the shed. Buckets of it. Bathloads of it. A huge waterfall of light. Pouring, streaming, warming. Flooding down into the shed. It smothered Jingle Bells in its glorious flow. She raised her head and gave six, short happy moos. And then another six, and another and another. For the first time in her life she felt the life-giving gift of a warm sun.

I lay there on the roof for maybe an hour. Maybe two. I couldn't say how long for sure. I gazed down at Jingle Bells as she sunned herself. She settled onto the floor in the sun, chewing her cud. She was probably pretending that she was grazing in a grassy glen. I could see that she was happy.

And then, just as Jingle Bells' patch of sunlight started to climb the walls, I felt an iron grip on my ankle. I felt myself being yanked backwards. My stomach scratched on the hot roof. My nose bumped along the corrugations. 'Help,' I screamed. 'Stop. Stop.' Someone was pulling me off the roof from below. I tried to hang on with my fingers but there was nothing to grab onto.

Suddenly I found myself in mid-air. I seemed to hang

there for a second or two and then I plunged downwards. I crashed painfully onto the gravel beneath. The wind was knocked from my lungs and I couldn't breathe.

But I could see. And I didn't like what I saw. Gravel was staring down at me with a wild look on his face. His big red nose was lumpy. His false teeth seemed to have a life of their own. They clacked and jumped out of time as he shouted at me. 'You vandal. You, you, brat. What do you mean by wrecking my shed?'

'It's Jingle Bells,' I managed to gasp. 'I'm letting in the sun.'

He just stood there for a second or two with his mouth opening and closing like a goldfish. 'You've pulled the roof off my shed for a cow? For a rotten old cow that doesn't even give any milk?'

'It's cruel,' I yelled. 'It's cruel keeping Jingle Bells in the dark.'

'I'll show you what's cruel,' he shrieked. He picked up a piece of old rope and started lashing at my legs with it. I wriggled out of his way and climbed up over the fence before he could grab me again. I started to run down the lane. Behind me I heard Gravel's last mean words. 'The cow won't want sunshine for much longer. Tomorrow it goes to the knackery.' His voice was raised in a high-pitched laugh.

4

The knackery. The glue factory. He was going to have

Jingle Bells killed. And all because of me. It was my fault. I started to cry as I walked home. Salty tears trickled down my face and into my mouth.

I had to save Jingle Bells.

That evening I made my plans. I looked out of my bedroom window at the night lights of the city. The oil refinery was lit up like fairyland. Closer to us I could see the West Gate Bridge arching over the Yarra River. The gate to freedom. The road to the country.

I set my clock radio for midnight. That would give me plenty of time to get Jingle Bells through the city and over the West Gate Bridge. We could get away from the main roads before the traffic started.

I reached out to switch off the light. That's when I noticed that my cut finger was better. There was no sign of the cut at all. It was completely healed.

I was soon asleep. Tossing and turning. And dreaming of a ghostly cow calling, calling, calling to me through the fog.

That night there was a power failure. While I was asleep the lights of the city went out. And my clock radio went off.

Mum woke me at the usual time – seven-thirty. 'Come on,' she said, 'you'll be late for school.'

I looked at the window. Sun was pouring in. 'Oh no,' I yelled. 'The knackery truck might already be on the way.'

'What are you going on about?' said Mum.

'Nothing,' I said. 'Nothing. I don't want any breakfast.' I put on my clothes and rushed off without even saying goodbye.

I crept round the back of Gravel's place. I hoped he was still in bed.

The shed door was locked but I was in luck. My claw-hammer was still lying where it had fallen the day before. I smashed off the lock and went into the gloom. Jingle Bells gave six happy little moos when she saw me.

'Shhh,' I whispered, holding my finger up to my lips. Jingle Bells didn't understand. She was glad to see me and she kept mooing.

'Quiet,' I gasped. 'Gravel will hear you. You don't want to end up in the glue factory do you?' I took the rope that was around Jingle Bells' neck and led her out into the backyard. The only way out was up a path at the side of the house. It led to the front garden and the road. We walked in silence along the path. Just as we reached a low window Jingle Bells let out an enormous bellow. A monstrous, mind-numbing moo.

5

There was no use in being quiet any more. 'Run,' I yelled.

But Jingle Bells didn't want to move. She was blinking in the sunlight. She hadn't been outside before. She was looking at the street and the cars. Then she saw something that did make her run. It was Gravel's bloated, blotchy face. It was like the face of the Devil. Jingle Bells took one look at him and started to run out of the gate and down the road. She was really scared. Her udder swung from side to side as she went. It looked like a swollen rubber glove filled with water.

Cows can run fast when they want to. Jingle Bells was disappearing down the road. Out of the corner of my eye I saw Gravel heading for his car.

Jingle Bells reached a T intersection. 'Turn right,' I shouted. 'Head for the West Gate Bridge.' Jingle Bells turned left and headed down the main road towards the city. I tried to catch her but she was too fast. She lurched down the road and past Jack Thaw's old ice works. Jack was standing outside hosing down the footpath.

'Help,' I yelled to Jack. 'Get your truck.' Jack looked startled but he disappeared inside the factory as quick as he could go. Jingle Bells kept jogging along with her neck rope trailing behind her. She was heading straight for the centre of the city. I just couldn't catch up.

The frightened cow was running down the middle of Flinders Street. Cars and trucks swerved out of her way. Drivers blasted their horns and yelled out. The footpaths were crowded with people making their way to work. They all stopped and stared at the cow running down the middle of town.

At last Jingle Bells reached the middle of the city. She turned and looked at Flinders Street Station. 'Oh no,'

I groaned. 'Don't go up the steps.' But she did. She started to walk up the steps into the station. Waves of people burst out of the gates. A couple of trains must have just arrived. Poor old Jingle Bells just stood there on the steps mooing as the crowd swept past like a mob of sheep dividing around a car on a country road.

I battled through the throng and grabbed her rope. I noticed a policeman coming towards us. He was yelling something about cows on the footpath. I knew that if he caught us he would take my name and address. Then Jingle Bells would be taken back to her owner. And the glue factory.

I looked around for escape. There was only one way to go. 'Come on,' I said. 'Into the station.'

I pulled Jingle Bells up the steps and through one of the ticket gates. The ticket collector jumped up and started yelling. 'Hey,' he shouted. 'Come back here. Where is that cow's ticket?'

We kept running. I turned down a ramp and pulled Jingle Bells through the crowds and onto a platform. A train was about to leave. 'On here,' I said. Jingle Bells followed me onto the train.

The train was packed with people on their way to work. Travellers dressed for work in their best clothes stood or sat in the carriage. Everyone moved over for me and Jingle Bells. Most of the people sitting down just kept reading their papers. The ones standing up just stood there trying not to look at each other the way people do in trains. No one seemed worried that there was a cow in the train.

The train pulled out of the station.

There was a kid in school uniform sitting down in the corner. The bloke next to him suddenly poked this boy in the ribs and pointed at Jingle Bells' udder. 'Can't you see there is a lady standing,' he said. 'Get up and give her your seat.'

Everyone cracked up. The whole carriage burst out laughing. Except me. I was embarrassed. I went red in the face.

'Well I think it is disgusting,' said a woman wearing a white dress. 'You can't bring a cow in here. Not in a first-class carriage.' She was standing right behind Jingle Bells. She poked the poor cow in the side with a sharp umbrella. Jingle Bells only did what any cow does when it is frightened. She lifted up her tail and released a large squirt of cow dung. It splurted out all over the woman's white dress. The woman started screaming and shouting and jumping up and down like nothing on earth.

The train was slowing down. It was Spencer Street Station. Not too far from the West Gate Bridge. 'Come on,' I said to Jingle Bells. 'This is where we get off.'

The people on the platform were so surprised to see a cow in the station that they didn't do a thing. We just sailed out onto the road with no trouble at all.

6

I took Jingle Bells' rope and led her along the freeway. We kept to the side of the road – out of the way of the semi-trailers and trucks that roared past. After ages and ages I caught a glimpse of the West Gate Bridge ahead. It towered up over the factories high into the sky.

The road started to slope upwards. We were on the approaches to the bridge. After a while we came to a large green sign. It said:

NO BICYCLES OR HORSES ON THE BRIDGE

'It's okay,' I said to Jingle Bells. 'You're not a horse. And you sure aren't a bike.'

By now the sun was getting up and it was hot. We started to move up the bridge – higher and higher. Trucks and cars sounded their horns. Drivers waved at us. No one had ever seen a boy and a cow crossing over West Gate before. There was no footpath so we had to walk in the breakdown lane.

Sweat was starting to form around Jingle Bells' neck. Every now and then when a very large truck roared by she would give a nervous shudder. She was scared of the traffic. She wanted green fields and so far she had only found black bitumen. 'Don't worry old girl,' I said. 'It gets better on the other side. Only another couple of hours and we will start to see the paddocks.' I sounded cheerful but I was worried. Cows weren't meant to go on long journeys along hard roads. And Jingle Bells had never walked anywhere before. What if she conked out? What if she bolted and I lost her?

I pulled Jingle Bells up to a stop so that we could rest for a while. That's when I saw something good. My heart gave a little extra beat. A long way off behind us, stopped at a red light, was a truck with a little crane on the back.

It was Jack Thaw.

And then I saw something sad.

Gravel in his Volvo. He drove straight through the red light. He was still a long way off but he was coming after us.

'It's Gravel,' I gasped. Jingle Bells understood. Don't ask me how but she did.

She gave one frightened bellow and started to run. I knew that I wouldn't be able to keep up. I would lose her. That's when I did it. That's when I jumped up onto her back.

Jingle Bells trotted along the side of the bridge with me riding on top. I hung on to her horns like grim death. The air was filled with tooting and shouting. The traffic slowed. Everyone wanted to watch the cowboy.

Boy, was I scared. We were right next to the railings on the edge of the bridge. People on the boats beneath looked like tiny insects. In the distance I could see an ocean liner heading along the river towards the sea.

We were a long way up. Or I should say, the river was a long way down.

Riding a cow isn't easy. I jolted up and down. I slipped from side to side. My behind was sore from banging on Jingle Bells' bones. At any moment I knew I would fall off. On and on ran Jingle Bells. Up towards the very highest part of the bridge. I couldn't look behind us but I knew that Gravel was not far away.

Suddenly a car swerved in front of us and squealed to a stop. It was Gravel. He had cut us off. Jingle Bells put on the brakes. She skidded to a stop and I went flying over her head. I landed on the bitumen road. I grazed my hands and face. My head hurt like crazy.

'Got you,' screamed Gravel. He was so mad that he was dribbling with anger. 'That cow goes to the glue factory,' he managed to get out. 'And you go to the police station.'

7

Jingle Bells looked at me with her soft, brown eyes. She wanted me to help. But she knew, deep in her heart, that there was nothing I could do. I was only a boy. The poor cow gave one long moo and then jumped up at the railings of the bridge. She was trying to jump off. She managed to get her two front feet over the railings. Then she started pushing forwards with her back legs. She started to topple.

'No,' I shrieked. 'No, no, no.' I grabbed her tail and

tried to pull her back. She was too heavy. I couldn't hold her. She was slipping. I clung onto her tail. I couldn't let her go. Over she went. Over the rail and into the air. Tumbling, turning, twisting. Down, down, down.

And with her, still hanging onto the tail, was me.

As we plummeted towards the brown water far below I thought I heard an evil voice from above raised in a cackling laugh.

We seemed airborne for ever. A cow with a boy gripping its tail. Spinning through the smoggy air. I was terrified. And yet in another way I found it peaceful. I saw a snatch of sky. A glimpse of brown river. A toss of tumbling cow. Floating. Falling. Fearing. Like two feathers frozen in time. Down we plunged. Down, down, down.

Crack.

We hit the water. It was the loudest, hardest bang I have ever known. The river was like concrete. It flattened my bones. Squashed my flesh. Blackened my brain.

For a brief second I felt myself gurgling deep in the water. And then nothing. I must have been knocked out.

The next thing I remember is being dragged along through the river. My hand was still gripping Jingle Bells' tail. She was swimming weakly for the shore. Sometimes my head was above water and sometimes it was under. I had water in my lungs. I coughed and spluttered.

I was too tired to swim. All I could do was grip the tail in my tortured fingers.

Jingle Bells saved my life. I would have drowned but for her. She was very weak. Dozens of times her head went under the surface but each time she found new strength. Finally she reached the shore. She staggered up the muddy bank a few steps, dragging me behind her. She turned around and looked at me for a few seconds with those brown eyes. Then she collapsed.

She was dead.

'Jingle Bells,' I sobbed. 'Jingle Bells. Don't leave me.' Her eyes stared forward without blinking. My eyes brimmed with tears.

Now she would never see the green fields and taste the cool grass. After all this. After everything that had happened. I crawled over to her and twisted up her head. I didn't know what to do. I remembered my first aid. I put my mouth down onto hers and blew. Mouth-to-mouth resuscitation.

But it didn't work. She was too big. Air leaked out over the sides of her frothy tongue and out through her milky teeth. I just didn't have enough puff to fill the lungs of a cow.

I heard the sound of a car door. It was Jack Thaw. He looked at Jingle Bells' still body and ran back to his truck. He ripped off the outside mirror from the truck door. Then he held it in front of Jingle Bells' immobile mouth. 'What are you doing?' I sobbed.

'Looking for fog,' he said. 'If the mirror fogs up it means she is breathing. If there is no fog she is dead.'

We both looked at the mirror. There was no fog.

'Come on,' said Jack. 'There is nothing we can do here.'

'What about Jingle Bells?' I shouted. 'What about Jingle Bells?'

'She will wash out with the tide,' said Jack. 'Out to the bay. It will be a sort of burial at sea.'

'No,' I shouted. The tears were still running down my face. 'I'm not letting the sharks get her. Or the crabs. We are taking her with us.'

'How?' said Jack.

I pointed to the crane on the back of Jack's truck. 'Put some ropes around her and lift her on to the truck.'

'And then where?' asked Jack.

'Back to your place.'

So that is what we did. We gently lowered Jingle Bells onto the back of Jack's truck and took her body to the ice factory.

8

When we got there I went straight over to the big steel bin that Jack kept his freezing water in. It was on wheels. I tried to push it but it was too heavy. I climbed up on the little ladder and looked inside. It was full to the top.

'What are you doing?' said Jack.

'Lower Jingle Bells in,' I said. 'We are going to freeze

her. We are going to add her to the collection.'

Jack looked at me for a long time with a funny expression on his face. 'All right,' he said. 'But there is no one else in the world that I would do this for.'

He started up the crane and lowered Jingle Bells' body into the huge bin of water.

'Now,' I told him, 'push the bin into the freezer. Push it in with the truck.' I opened the freezer doors and Jack nudged the steel bin into the freezer. He left the rope hanging out of the bin.

'To get the ice block out with,' said Jack.

We shut the freezer doors. 'How long?' I asked. 'How long till she's frozen?'

'Tomorrow lunchtime. By lunchtime tomorrow Jingle Bells will be frozen inside the biggest man-made ice block in the world.' We grinned at each other. It was better than letting her wash out to sea.

Just then we heard a loud banging coming from the street. Jack went over and opened the door to the street. It was Gravel. He was still as mad as a snake. 'Where's my cow?' he yelled. 'I want my cow.'

'It's dead,' said Jack angrily. 'Are you satisfied now?'

Gravel narrowed his eyes. 'A dead cow's worth eighty dollars for pet food,' he said. 'I want it back.'

Jack opened and closed his fist. For a moment I thought he was going to punch Gravel but he didn't. He slammed the door closed in his face. 'Buzz off,' he shouted. 'Jingle Bells stays here.'

Gravel screamed at us through the door. 'I'll be back. Just you see. I'll be back.'

'Ratbag,' said Jack under his breath.

I went home for the night. But Jack slept at the ice works just in case Gravel came back.

At lunchtime the next day we opened the freezer. Jack backed in the crane and attached it to the rope. The crane groaned and smoked. Nothing happened. It had never lifted anything so heavy before. 'Try again,' I yelled.

This time the ice block started to move. Slowly at first – and then with a 'pop' and a 'slurp' it jumped out of the bin. Jack lowered it to the floor.

And there stood Jingle Bells. Inside the great block of ice. A frozen statue. Her unblinking eyes seemed to stare at us. But I knew they couldn't see anything.

'Where does she go?' asked Jack.

'Well,' I said, 'Jingle Bells starts with "J". "J" comes between "I" and "K". You will have to put her between the ibis and the kookaburra.' Jack started up the truck and pushed Jingle Bells' icy home against the wall in front of the kookaburra. Then he started filling the bin up again with tap water.

'Leave the hose running on its own,' I said to Jack. 'I want to talk to you.'

We went outside and shut the freezer door. 'Look,' I said, 'it's not right to leave poor old Jingle Bells there. She is still locked inside. There are no windows in the freezer. It's just like in the shed. I want her to be under the blue sky. In a paddock of grass. And anyway, Gravel might come back and get her. We have to take Jingle Bells to the country.'

Jack scratched his head. 'You're right,' he said. 'Let's do it now.'

9

We loaded Jingle Bells' ice block onto the back of the truck and drove off. We didn't care what people thought. We drove out over the West Gate Bridge with Jingle Bells standing on the back inside the ice block. We were followed by a great, long, snaking queue of cars. Everyone wanted to catch a glimpse of the cow inside the ice block.

After a couple of hours we turned off a side road and headed for the hills. There was no one following us. I hoped.

We went by streams and stretching farms. We went through gum forests and wattle-lined roads. 'This is more like it,' I said. 'This is where Jingle Bells belongs.'

At last we came to a quiet, shady glen. There was long, cool grass surrounded by a leafy gum forest. There were no fences. 'This is it, Jack,' I said. 'This is what we have been looking for.'

We drove the truck into the middle of the field and stopped. Then we unloaded Jingle Bells onto the grass. The ice had melted a fair bit. Her horns were sticking out into the air. I took a shovel out of the truck.

'What's that for?' asked Jack.

'To bury her,' I said. 'To bury her after the ice melts.'

'Don't start digging yet,' said Jack. 'Let's wait awhile.'

Jack and I sat down and gazed at poor frozen Jingle Bells standing in her ice block in the middle of the field. We were hot and tired. The bees buzzed. The birds called. The golden sun shone in the heavens. A hot north wind was blowing.

We sat and watched the still, silent ice cow for a long time. Then we both fell asleep.

I was awakened by something licking my face. I sat bolt upright. It was night time. There was no moon. 'Jack,' I yelled. 'Jack. Wake up.' I couldn't see anything. The air was still warm but the night was black.

I heard heavy footsteps crashing off into the bush.

'What is it?' said Jack. 'What's going on? Where are you?'

Suddenly the moon came out and we peered at each other in the soft light. Then we looked at the ice block. Or I should say we looked at where the ice block had been. It was gone. Melted. And Jingle Bells was gone too. Jack ran over and felt the wet grass. Then he pointed at something. It was a pat of sloppy cow dung. And footprints, no, not foot prints – cow prints. Leading off into the bush.

'Let's go and find her,' I yelled.

Jack put his hand on my arm. 'No,' he said. 'Our work is done. Let's go home.'

I looked at him for a long time without saying anything. I knew he was right. I nodded slowly. We climbed into the truck. Just before the engine fired I heard something wonderful. Six short, happy moos. They sounded a bit like the first few bars of the Christmas carol 'Jingle Bells'.

Jack and I both smiled as we drove down the road without talking. After a while I said, 'Did you know that was going to happen?'

Jack nodded. 'Well,' I went on, 'why don't you thaw out all the animals in the collection and bring them back to life?'

'Because,' said Jack slowly, 'the tank had different water. And now it's gone. I was saving it up for someone or something special.' He wouldn't talk about it any more after that.

10

When we got back to the ice works Jack went inside the freezer to check his collection. 'Look at this,' he yelled. 'Someone has broken in.'

There was a small hole in the roof of the freezer and a short bit of rope hanging down. There was no one around though. And nothing had been touched. All of the frozen animals sat silently on their shelves.

The big bin of water was directly under the hole in the roof. I climbed up and looked in. 'There's something in there,' I said. 'And it's frozen inside the ice. Something has fallen into the water and couldn't get out. It's been frozen with the water inside the bin.'

Jack brought in his truck and tipped the bin over on its side. A giant ice block crashed out onto the floor.

We both stared and stared. Gravel was frozen inside. He must have broken in through the freezer roof looking for Jingle Bells and fallen into the water. Now he was frozen in a block of ice.

His frozen fingers were clawed as if he was just about to scratch someone. His mouth was snarled back in a silent scream. His eyes stared without seeing.

'What will we do with him?' gasped Jack.

'Well,' I said, 'Gravel starts with "G". That comes between "F" and "H". So we put him over there.'

And as far as I know he is still there. Staring out from the ice. With a frozen fox on one side and a hare on the other.

THUMP.

'Oh, gawd,' said my friend Derek.

'What?'

'We've run over a dog.'

Derek's dad looked in the mirror and pulled the Mercedes over to the side of the road. The three of us jumped out and started walking back to the small, still bundle in the middle of the road.

'Don't worry,' said Derek. 'My dad will take care of things.'

We were on our way to a volleyball game. Derek's dad was taking a shortcut because we were late.

It was dark and hard to see. But the dog seemed to be lying very still. I didn't want to look. What if it was dead and all squashed, with blood and guts hanging out? Or even worse – what if it was squashed and alive? What would we do then?

I could feel my stomach churning. I rushed over to a bush and threw up. The spew splashed all over my shoes. Ugh. I hate being sick. And I hate looking like a wimp.

Derek's dad had already reached the dog. He was bending down, trying to see in the dark. Before he could move, a feeble voice filtered through the trees. 'Tinker, Tinker. Come here, boy. Where are you?'

A little old man with wispy hair stumbled onto the road. 'Have you seen –' he started to say. His gaze fell on the small dog lying on the road. 'Tinker?' he said. He fell to his knees with a sob and started to feel all over the dog. He tried to find a pulse.

'Gone,' he said looking up at us as if we were murderers. 'Our poor little Tinker.'

We all stared guiltily at each other. I didn't know what to say. Derek and I walked over to the dog. It was very dark but I could see a little smear of blood coming out of one nostril. The dog was a bit flat and stiff. But that was all. No bones sticking out or anything awful like that. If it wasn't for the glassy, staring eyes you might have thought it was still alive.

The old man clasped the dog to his chest as if it was a baby. Then he stumbled off towards a nearby farmhouse without another word.

I wanted to get back in the car and drive off. I just wanted to put a big distance between us and what we had done. But not Derek's dad. He was so calm. He always knew what to do. He was a pilot in the airforce. He flew Phantom jets. Once he had to bail out over Bass Strait when an engine caught fire. He was a hero. Strong and handsome and tough.

Just the opposite of my dad. Don't get me wrong. I love my dad. But ... well, let's face it. He's no oil painting. And he drives a beat-up old truck. And he's not a pilot. He's a ...

I just couldn't bring myself to say it. Derek was always asking me what my dad does. I didn't want to tell him. It was too awful.

Derek's dad stared up the track. What was he going to do? Jump in the car and drive off? No way. 'Listen, boys,' he said. 'We have to do the right thing. We have to try and make up for what we've done.'

'Dad always does the right thing,' said Derek proudly.

A light was shining on the porch of the small farmhouse. Derek's dad started to walk towards it. We followed along behind. I had a sinking feeling in my stomach. And it wasn't because I'd just been sick.

The old man might not be very pleased to see us. He might go troppo.

But then I cheered up. After all, Derek's dad had parachuted out of a jet fighter at ten thousand metres. He could handle anything.

2

Derek's dad knocked on the farmhouse door. Not a little timid knock like my dad would have done. A real loud, confident knock. Derek smiled.

There was a bit of shuffling and rustling inside and then the door swung open. I could just make out the shape of the dog covered by a blanket in front of the fire inside. The old man stared at us with tear-filled eyes. His lips started to tremble. For a minute I thought he was going to faint.

'The dog just ran out of nowhere,' said Derek's dad. 'We didn't even see it.'

'Tinker,' said the old man. 'Poor darling Tinker.'

'We'd like to do something,' said Derek's dad.

'I know how you must feel.'

The old man beckoned us inside. Derek's dad gave us a confident nod and led the way. The room was gloomy, lit only by a lamp. The old man collapsed into a chair and sank his head into his hands. He started to sob and rub at his eyes. Then he looked up and spoke.

'Please excuse me,' he said. 'I'm not crying for me. I'm crying for Jason.'

'Jason?' said Derek's dad.

The old man held a finger to his lips. Then he hobbled across the room and silently opened a door. We tiptoed over and peeped in. A small boy with a pale face was sleeping peacefully in a rough wooden bed.

'My grandson, Jason,' said the old man. 'His parents were both killed in a car accident last year. He wouldn't talk to anyone. Not a word. Just sat looking at the wall. Until I bought him that dog. As a puppy. It got him talking again. "Tinker," he said. "I'll call him Tinker."'

A tear started to run down the old man's cheek.

We all fell silent and stared at Jason lying there asleep.

The poor kid. His parents were dead. And now his dog, Tinker, was dead too. What would he say when he woke up? Would he lose his speech again?

Derek's dad pulled out his wallet. 'I'll pay for a new dog,' he said.

'Good on ya, Dad,' said Derek. His dad was so kind. He couldn't bring Tinker back to life but he was going to pay for a replacement. We all stared at the wallet. It was stuffed full of money. That was another good thing about Derek's dad. He was rich.

The old man shook his head. 'He won't take to a new dog,' he said. 'It'll have to be Tinker or nothing.'

Derek's dad shook his head sadly. 'I can't bring Tinker back from the dead,' he said. 'No one can do that. But where did you get the dog?'

The old man brightened up a bit. 'Fish Creek,' he said. 'There's a guy down there who breeds them.'

3

We spent ages driving around country back roads. In the middle of the night. Looking for the kennels at Fish Creek where the dead dog came from. 'We'll never find it,' I groaned.

Derek's dad stopped the car at a dark crossroads. 'Get out, boys,' he said.

We scrambled out of the car and stood there in the silent countryside. Derek and I didn't have a clue what was going on.

'Listen,' said Derek's dad.

We listened. We strained our ears. Nothing but crickets and frogs. But then. Then. Faintly. Far away. The sound of dogs barking. We all grinned. Derek's dad was so smart.

'You're a genius, Dad,' said Derek.

I thought about my own dad. He would be at the volleyball match. He'd gone on ahead. On his own. He knew I wanted to have a ride in the Mercedes. He didn't mind having no one to talk to. My dad was a quiet person.

Derek's dad followed the sound of the dogs until we came to the kennels. It was a ratty old place with cages and dumped cars everywhere. As we drew up to the house dozens of dogs began to snarl and snap and howl. I was glad they were in cages. They sounded like they wanted to tear us to pieces.

A big guy in a blue singlet staggered out and looked into the car. He had a bushy beard. In one hand he held a stubby of beer. Over on the porch I saw a speedboat. A brand new one by the look of it.

'Nick off,' growled the guy in the blue singlet. 'We don't like strangers in the middle of the night.'

Derek's dad opened his wallet. 'We've come to buy a dog,' he said.

'Yeah,' said Derek.

The bloke grinned with big yellow teeth and opened the car door. 'In that case,' he said. 'Come in.'

Derek's dad told him the story of little Jason and the dead dog and how we wanted another one the same before he woke up.

'Only one left from the litter,' said the dog breeder. 'And I can't remember if it looks the same as Tinker.' He led us out to a shed and showed us a dog. We all smiled at each other. It was exactly the same as the dead dog. It even had a little brown patch on its left ear.

'Just the shot,' beamed Derek's dad. 'How much?'

'A thousand dollars.'

Derek's dad turned pale. 'How much?' he said again.

'A thousand bucks,' said the dog breeder. 'This is my breeding bitch. It's the only female in the country. They are very rare dogs. Mongolian Rat Catchers.'

'You can afford it, Dad,' said Derek. 'Go on, buy it.'

Derek's dad looked at us. He looked at the dog breeder. He looked at the dog. Then he handed over the thousand dollars. In cash.

What a man. Fancy paying a thousand dollars. Just to help out a little boy he didn't even know.

'My father doesn't even have a thousand dollars,' I thought to myself. 'Geez, Derek is lucky.'

4

'Let's go,' said Derek's dad. 'We have to get back with this dog before little Jason wakes up and finds out that Tinker is dead.'

We jumped into the Mercedes and tore back to the farmhouse. The little man opened the door before we could even knock. 'He's still asleep,' he whispered. 'Come in quick.'

We all walked into the gloomy room and Derek's dad put the new dog on the table. It immediately started to lick the little man's hand. He peered at it carefully and then wiped tears of joy from his eyes. 'Amazing,' he said. 'It's exactly the same. Jason will never know the difference.'

The new dog wagged its tail happily.

'Where's the dead dog?' asked Derek's dad.

The little man picked up a sack and opened it. We all stared into the gloom at the dead dog. There was no doubt about it. You just couldn't tell the difference between the two animals.

The new dog jumped off the table, ran over to the sack and started barking like crazy. It didn't like what was in there at all. The noise was enough to wake the dead. 'Tinker, Tinker?' came a boy's weak voice. The old man threw a quick look at little Jason's door and quickly pushed the sack aside. Then he grabbed the new dog and took it into the bedroom.

We all followed him into the room. Jason was sitting up in bed, calling to the new dog feebly. He looked at it. He frowned. He looked puzzled. 'Tinker,' he said in a worried voice. 'You've lost your collar.'

The old man shuffled back into the kitchen, put his

hand into the sack and took the collar from the dead dog. 'Here it is,' he said. 'I was just cleaning it.'

Jason threw out his arms and hugged the new dog. 'Oh Tinker,' he said. 'I love you.'

5

The Mercedes wound it way through the mountains. Now we were really late for the volleyball match. 'It was worth a thousand dollars,' said Derek's dad. 'Just to see the look on that poor boy's face.'

Derek and I smiled at each other. What a man he was. Always so calm.

'You're the greatest, Dad,' said Derek. He looked at me to see if I was going to disagree. I didn't.

When we got to the volleyball stadium my own dad was not calm.

'Where have you been?' he growled. 'The game's over. I thought you must have been in an accident. I was just about to call the police.'

'Calm down, old boy,' said Derek's dad. 'We've got quite a story to tell you.'

Dad listened to the whole thing in silence. He didn't seem impressed.

'Mongolian Rat Catcher,' he said grumpily. 'Never heard of them.'

'Know about dogs, do you?' said Derek's dad. 'Work with animals, do you?'

Dad looked annoyed. He opened his mouth to tell

them what he does but I got in first. 'Er, we'd better be going,' I said.

Dad drove back down the mountain. Fast. He asked me a lot of questions about Jason and the dog breeder and the old man. But he didn't say much. He was in a grumpy mood. Why couldn't he be cool? Like Derek's dad.

'It's up here,' I said. 'The place where we hit the dog. Just round the bend.'

Dad dropped down a gear and planted his foot. He roared round the corner really fast. Boy, he was in a bad mood.

THUMP.

'Aaagh,' I screamed.

'What?'

'We've run over a dog.'

Dad looked in the mirror and pulled the truck over to the side of the road. The two of us jumped out and started walking back to the small, still bundle in the middle of the road.

My heart jumped up into my mouth. I felt faint. I felt sick. Dad had run over Jason's new dog. And killed it. I just couldn't believe it. The same thing had happened. Twice. In the same night. But now it was Dad who had killed the dog.

And there was no way he was going to be able to fix things up. He didn't have a thousand dollars. And anyway, there were no more Mongolian Rat Catchers left.

We couldn't pull the same trick again.

Dad bent over and looked at the dead dog carefully.

Before he could move, a trembling voice filtered through the trees. 'Tinker, Tinker. Come here, boy. Where are you?'

The little old man with the wispy hair stumbled onto the road. 'Have you seen – ' he started to say. His gaze fell on the small dog lying on the road. 'Tinker?' He said. He fell to his knees with a sob and started to feel all over the dog. His fingers felt for a pulse.

'Gone,' he said looking up at us as if we were murderers. Then his eyes opened wide as he recognised me. 'You've killed two dogs in the same night,' he gasped.

The old man clasped the dog to his chest as if it was a baby. Then he stumbled off towards the nearby farmhouse without another word. Just like he'd done before.

'Hey,' shouted Dad. 'Come back here.'

Why couldn't my dad be more kind and generous? Like Derek's dad. My dad didn't even seem sorry for what he had done. The little man stopped and Dad went towards him.

'Go back to the truck,' Dad growled at me.

I did. I was glad to go back to the truck. I didn't want to see that look in the old man's eyes. I didn't want to hear Jason start crying when he saw the dead dog.

After about ten minutes Dad came back to the truck. He had the dead dog with him. He threw the body onto the back of the truck and started up the engine. 'Show me how to get to the dog kennels,' he said.

'It's no good,' I yelled. 'There are no more Mongolian Rat Catchers left. It was the last one.'

'Just show me the way,' said Dad.

We drove in silence. Except for when I had to point out which way to turn. Why wouldn't Dad listen to me? Why did he have to go back to the dog breeder's place? It was crazy.

6

Finally, we reached the dog kennels. The dogs started up howling and barking just like before. Dad didn't even wait for the dog breeder to come out. He jumped out of the truck and ran up to the door.

I saw it open and Dad disappeared inside.

There was a lot of yelling and shouting. What was going on? Should I go and help? Just then the door flew open and Dad came out. He angrily shoved his wallet into his pocket and strode across to our old truck.

Dad didn't have a new dog for little Jason. He didn't even have the dead dog. He was dogless. And he wasn't in the mood for talking.

Neither was I. Why couldn't my dad be calm and cool and rich? Why couldn't my dad have a wallet full of money to buy a new dog for Jason? Why did we have to drive around in a beat-up old truck and not a Mercedes? Why, why, why?

After a long drive we got back to town. Dad stopped outside the front gate.

Of Derek's house.

'What are we doing here?' I said. 'They're probably in bed.'

Dad gave me a big smile. He ruffled my hair in a friendly way. 'Come on, Ned,' he said. 'I don't think they'll mind.'

Derek's dad threw open the front door and stared at us. So did Derek.

'Hello, old boy,' said Derek's dad. 'What's up?'

Dad took out his wallet.

'Oh, no,' I thought. 'He's going to ask Derek's dad for money.'

But he didn't. Dad took out a great wad of notes. 'Here's your thousand dollars back,' he said.

I stared. Derek stared. We all stared.

Dad smiled. 'Tinker was dead all right,' he said. 'A stuffed dead dog. With glass eyes. The little man threw it under every car that passed. Then he sent the guilty driver off to buy the other dog. That dog breeder has sold his Mongolian Rat Catcher to at least fifty suckers.'

Derek's dad took his money back and stood there with his jaw hanging open. 'How did you know?' he stammered.

I looked at Derek and decided to answer the question myself. I was so happy.

'He's a taxidermist,' I said proudly.

Spot the Dog

Okay, okay, okay. So you don't believe me. Take a look at the picture then. Can you see Spot, the dog? Yeah. See I told ya.

That proves it. It really happened. Spot is real. Not a vision. Not a dream. Not a nightmare. A real-life, barking, peeing dog. So were all the others.

What do you mean you can't see it? And you don't believe me? Look, I'll go over it again.

1

It is Saturday and I have woken up feeling good. The Sharks are playing in the grand final and I am going to the footy to watch them win.

'No you're not,' says Mum. 'You are sick. Remember?'

'That was yesterday,' I say. 'Now I am better.'

Mum puts a hand on my forehead. 'No,' she says. 'I think you have a temperature. You had better stay in bed to be on the safe side.'

I think Mum is on to me. I think she knows that I faked it yesterday so that I didn't have to go to school. But she can't prove it. If you say you have a stomach-ache no one can prove you don't. So yesterday she let me stay home. But now she is making me suffer by forcing me to stay in bed on Saturday. To teach me not to fake it again.

This is serious. I have to do something to get out of here. I know. I will start whingeing. Sometimes parents get so sick of you grizzling and groaning that they will let you out just to get rid of you for a bit.

'I'm bored,' I say. 'There is nothing to do.'

Mum goes into the lounge and brings back a picture. She puts it into my hand.

'It's quite good, Mum,' I say.

It is too. Mum is an artist. She draws pictures of places in our town, Warrnambool. Then she sells them at the Sunday market. This one is like all the others. She draws all the best bits of the town and puts them in the same picture. There is the town hall and Lake Pertobe. You can see the surf beach and the breakwater. There are Norfolk Island pine trees and the railway station.

'There are no people in the picture,' I say.

'You know I can't draw faces,' says Mum.

'I'm bored,' I say again. 'It is a good picture but I am still bored.'

Mum gives me a big smile. 'Spot the dog,' she says.

'What?'

'Spot the dog,' she says. 'I have hidden four dogs in the drawing. See if you can find them.'

I groan. 'That's for little kids,' I say.

'No,' says Mum. 'Try it. They are hard to find.' She walks out of the room with a laugh.

This is no good. I have to get out of here. I have to get to the footy. I don't want to look for stupid dogs in a picture. And anyway, my head feels funny.

'I can't find any Spot dogs,' I yell.

'Try harder,' says Mum's voice from the kitchen.

I wait for a bit. 'There are no dogs in the picture,' I say. 'You are tricking.'

Mum storms into the room. She is grumpy. I can see I am starting to wear her down.

'Listen, Tony,' she says in a low voice. 'I have drawn Spot the dog in that picture four times. If you can find just one of them I will let you get out of bed.'

I grin. 'And go to the footy?' I say.

'Okay,' says Mum. 'But you don't say one more word about going out until you find a dog.'

'It's a deal,' I yell. This is going to be a cinch.

I start to search through the picture, looking for Spot the dog. I turn the picture upside down. I turn it sideways. I look in the trees. I look in the train. I look under the water. And down the drains.

But there is no Spot. Not one silly dog.

My head starts to ache. I get a pain behind the eyes. Maybe there are no dogs in the picture. Maybe it is a trick. Maybe she is getting me back for faking it yesterday.

I can't say anything. If I start to whinge she will not

let me out. I have to find at least one drawing of stupid Spot the dog.

Where is it, where is it, where is it? Where, where, where?

I look and look and look. I stare into the pine-tree branches. I examine the wheels of the train. I even look inside the public toilets. But no dog.

I start to get mad. Mum has got me fooled. If I say anything she will never let me out. And if I can't find a dog I can't go either.

My head is thumping. I feel hot all over. My eyes are going to pop out if this goes on any longer.

I climb out of bed and get dressed. Quietly. Then I climb out of the window.

For some reason I take the picture with me.

2

It is good to be out in the fresh air. Okay, I will cop it when I get back. I will probably be grounded for about ten years. But I will get to see the Sharks play in the grand final. It will be worth it.

The streets are very quiet. It must be earlier than I think.

I have to say that the whole world seems a little odd. I can't quite work it out. It is sort of like looking at a movie. You see it but it isn't quite the same as normal.

I walk on for a bit and try to cheer myself up. Imagine if the Sharks win. They have never won a final before.

There will be a big celebration. And on Monday I will brag about it at school. I will really give it to the kids who barrack for South Warrnambool.

Everything is quiet. Too quiet. There is no shouting. There is no conversation. There is no squealing of tyres. Nothing.

Except.

What is that? A noise. A sad little noise.

Yip, yip, yip.

A dog. I can hear a dog. It is in trouble. It is sort of half barking, half squealing. Like a rabbit in a trap.

'Where are you, fellah?' I say. 'I'm coming.'

But I can't see the dog anywhere. I can't tell where the whimpering is coming from. I look under a car. And another car. I search in the long grass. I look over a brick wall. I peer along the alley next to Stiffy Jones' Funeral Parlor.

No dog. Nowhere.

I know. It is rubbish bin morning. There are bins all along the street. Maybe some ratbag has put a poor little dog into the bin. I start to search through the bins. Oh yuck. Every bin seems to be full of filthy stuff. Cold spaghetti. Fish heads. Scrapings from plates. Urgh.

I will never find the poor little dog. 'Spot,' I say. 'Where are you?'

Yip, yip, yip. He is here somewhere. I must find him before he suffocates.

Spot? Did I say Spot? I don't know this dog's name. I don't even know what it looks like.

I stare at Mum's picture which is still in my hand. I have got Spot on the brain. I am probably feeling guilty about nicking off. Or pretending to be sick. Or not keeping the deal about finding Spot in Mum's picture. I take a quick look at it again.

That's funny. Mum has drawn rubbish bins. You can see inside them. She draws houses and trains and things so that you can see inside. Sort of like X-rays. You can even see inside the whales in the ocean.

Yes, how weird. I can see into the bins in Mum's painting. And there in the video-shop garbage is a drawing of a little dog. Spot. I have spotted him.

I feel stupid. Crazy. But I rush over to the bin and put my ear to it.

Yip, yip, yip. The yelping is coming from inside. I open the top and look into the bin. There he is. A real, live Jack Russell terrier. He is white with black spots. One ear is white and the other is black. Oh, he is cute. The poor little thing. Who would put a dog like that in the rubbish?

I gently lift him out. He licks my face.

'Hello, Spot,' I say. 'Don't worry, I will look after you.'

But I don't have to look after him. Spot jumps out of my arms with a happy *yap*. Then he scampers off and disappears around the corner. Gone home probably. How weird. The dog in the real world was in the same place as the dog in Mum's picture. I check it out again.

What? There is no dog in the bin in the picture.

It is gone. Just like the real one.

3

To be perfectly honest I am not feeling too good. This is crazy. But I can't go home. I will never get to see the footy finals if I do.

I continue on along the main street past the shops. They are all shut. I look at my watch. Ten thirty a.m. That's funny. The shops should be open by now. Maybe my watch is wrong. Maybe it is six o'clock in the morning. I decide to walk down to the T & G Building and look at their clock. But before I get time to take another step I hear it again.

Yip, yip, yip.

Another dog in trouble. Or is it the same little dog? A poor, pathetic yelping fills the air. Oh, it touches my heart. I hate to hear an animal suffering. Where is it?

'I'm coming, Spot,' I say.

I rush around looking for the dog. I scatter a pile of leaves and search through a heap of boxes. I even peer through the slot in a letterbox.

'Spot,' I say, 'are you in there?'

Spot is not in there. I feel silly talking to a letterbox. I hope no one is watching. They will think I am weird. Maybe I am weird.

I snatch a glance along the street. That's a bit of luck. No one is watching. There is not a soul in sight.

Yip, yip, yip.

Where is he? The yipping is pitiful. It sounds as if Spot is growing weak. I picture him in my mind, slowly dying.

Picture him? That's it. I look at Mum's drawing. Then I stare around me. I am outside Collins bookshop. Yes, it is in the picture. And you can see under the street. There is Spot hidden in the drain. You would never have seen him if you didn't know where to look. In the picture he is swimming. Maybe he is drowning. I'd better hurry.

I rush over to the gutter and put my nose against the steel drain cover. It is dark down there.

Yip, yip, yip.

I can see two small points of light. Spot's eyes. There is the sound of splashing. He is swimming in the drain. Just managing to keep his head above water.

'Hang on, Spot,' I say. 'I'm coming.'

I bend over and put my fingers through the steel bars of the drain cover. Oh boy, it is heavy. I strain and struggle. It is too heavy. I look around for someone to give me a hand.

'Help, help,' I yell. 'There is a dog down the drain.'

But there is no one there. Not a soul.

Yip, yip, yip.

I will have to do it on my own.

'Pull, pull, pull,' I say to myself. Oh, my aching back. Oh, my fingers. They feel as if they are going to fall off. Yes, yes. It's moving. Slowly, slowly, I start to drag the steel grate to one side.

Yip, yip, gurgle. Oh no, he's drowning.

'I'm coming, I'm coming.' I pull back the grate and reach down. Spot is swimming weakly. The water is rushing by. I grab him by the scruff of the neck and start to lift him. Mum told me that it doesn't hurt dogs if you pick them up by the back of the neck. That's how female dogs carry their puppies. I hope it is true because Spot is squealing.

Got him. I put the wet dog on the footpath and he shakes like crazy. Water goes all over me. He is a white dog with black spots. One black ear and one white ear. Exactly the same as before.

'Come here, boy,' I say when he has dried himself off.

But Spot does not come here. He runs happily down the street and vanishes around the corner.

I glance at Mum's painting. Sure enough. Just like before, Spot has disappeared. There is no Spot down the drain in the drawing. His image has vanished just as if someone has rubbed it out. This is weird. I start to feel nervous.

I sit down on the edge of the gutter and wonder about this. Am I going to spend the whole morning rescuing Spot? Will I hear whimpering and yipping everywhere I go?

I think I will go home. Things are not quite right in the world. Why aren't there any people in the streets? What is going on?

But then if I go home Mum will keep me in bed.

I stare at the picture carefully. Where is the next Spot going to pop up?

There were four Spots in the drawing. If I can find them all maybe the world will come back to normal. My eyes search the painting. Yes, there he is. The little devil. Hiding in the public toilets. Upside down behind one of the bowls. He looks as if his neck is stuck. Maybe he is choking. Oh shoot, I have to hurry.

4

I race down the street towards the beach where the toilets are.

Yip, yip, yip.

'I'm coming, Spot,' I yell.

I reach the toilets. Oh no. Wouldn't you know it? Spot is in the wrong one. I look at the picture again. He is in the ladies' toilets. I can't go in there.

Yip, yip, yip.

I have to do it. I look around. There is no one to be seen. But what if there is someone inside? What if a girl is in there? I will get arrested. I will be in deep trouble. I will never live it down. Everyone knows everything in a country town.

I can just hear the kids at school. 'Tony took a tinkle in the ladies' toilets.'

I can hear something else too.

Yip, yip, yip.

I take a deep breath and rush into the ladies' toilets. Phew, no one in sight. I have never been in the wrong side of the loo before. There is nowhere to stand and take a leak against the wall. It feels strange. But then everything feels strange. I don't feel well at all.

There is Spot. He is behind one of the toilet bowls. His head is stuck. I gently hold his body and remove him from where he is lodged under a pipe.

But this time I don't let go.

'You're not going anywhere,' I say. 'I've had enough of this. You are coming to the footy with me.'

But Spot has other ideas. He squirms around in my hands and jumps to the ground. Then he bolts out of the toilet. By the time I get outside there is no sign of him.

Rats.

I know before I even look at the picture that Spot is no longer in the toilets. I am right. He has gone.

I also know that there is one more dog hidden somewhere because Mum told me there were four.

I don't care. I can't take any more. I can't rescue any more dogs. I can't live in a world without people. I don't want to go on playing Spot the Dog any longer. I have had enough.

I start to run for home. It is quite a way back but I don't stop. Not once. I puff and pant and grow hot. My head is spinning. I feel as if my brain is going to burst out of my earholes. But I keep going until I am safely in our own garden.

I climb through the window and jump into bed.

Just in time. I can hear Mum's footsteps.

'Are you okay, Tony?' she says as she walks into the room. She doesn't even know that I have been gone.

I decide to tell the truth. After all, parents are there to help you. That's what they are for. When it is all said and done it is best to tell them if you are in trouble. To be honest, I am scared. Dogs are not supposed to vanish out of pictures.

So I tell Mum all about my hunt for the dogs.

And she doesn't believe me. Not one word.

'I wouldn't tell you a lie,' I yell.

'Wouldn't you?' she says.

'No,' I say. 'I've found three of the Spots in your picture.'

'There are no dogs in my picture,' says Mum. 'And I should know because I painted it.'

I take a deep breath. I can't believe it. She did tell me to look for Spot the dog. Oh, my face is so hot. And I am itchy. Why is Mum lying?

'There was a Spot dog in that rubbish bin,' I yell. I point to the drawing of the bin outside the video shop.

'I can't see it,' says Mum.

'The dogs vanish when you find them,' I say.

'Very convenient,' says Mum.

'No,' I shout. 'Really. I've been seeing Spots everywhere.'

'So have I,' says Mum. She puts her hand on my forehead with a smile.

'Where?' I say eagerly.

'All over your face. You've got the measles. You weren't faking after all. I'm sorry I didn't believe you.'

'The measles?'

'Yes, you've been seeing things. Hallucinating. You haven't been out of this room. I didn't tell you to spot anything. There are no dogs in my painting. You just think there were because you've got a fever.'

I look at the painting carefully. There were four dogs but I only found three. There must be one left. I search and search while Mum sits with me with a worried look. I have to prove that it all really happened. I just have to.

'Yes,' I yell. 'There it is. I have been telling the truth. See Spot.'

'Where?' says Mum. 'I can't see anything.' She leans over and examines the painting carefully. She looks at where I am pointing.

'There,' I say. 'That's a dog.'

Mum shakes her head and walks off to phone the doctor. She doesn't believe me.

5

So that is how it all happened.

The full story. You believe me, don't you?

SPOT THE DOG

Turn the page and take a look at the picture. You can see it. You can spot the dog. Can't you?

Mousechap

'You're not taking that dung beetle with you,' said Mum.

'But Mum, Uncle Sid likes dung beetles. He won't mind.'

'Aunt Scrotch will. She doesn't even like boys. You're lucky that she lets you have a holiday there each year. You leave that dung beetle at home with me.'

'Okay,' I said. I put my dung beetle back in his matchbox and shoved it into my pocket. Aunt Scrotch would never know I had it.

The first night at Aunt Scrotch's house was terrible. There I was, lying in bed in the dark. Aunt Scrotch wouldn't let me have the light on. She was too mean to use the electricity. Inside the room it was almost black. There was just enough light to see shadows on the wall. Just enough light to nearly see the eyes that were watching me.

I didn't know what to do. If I screamed the eyes might get me and finish me off. If I lay still, hardly breathing, they might go away. The night was long. I could measure the crawling time by my silent breathing.

The eyes stared. I was sure they stared even though I

couldn't see them. Something moved. Near the clock on the shelf. A rustle? A whisper? A footstep? My dry mouth screamed silently. I wanted to cry out. I wanted to say, 'Who's that?' I wanted to call out for Uncle Sid but my terrified tonsils refused to talk. Instead they trembled – trapped behind the tombstones of my teeth – quivering under the strains of a choked-off cry.

Two pinpoints of light. I could see them now. Moving silently. Blinking on and off. My hand crawled towards the light switch. I fumbled among the tissues. I found my watch. I clasped some coins. Everything except the switch.

Oh switch. Dear, dear, light switch where are you?

'Click.' I found it. The room blazed. I saw at once who owned the eyes. A mouse. A small, grey mouse. It peered at me without moving. It seemed unafraid. Then, to my amazement, it stood up on its hind legs and walked. It walked along the shelf on its back legs. Then it clasped its little paws together under its chin as if it was praying.

I picked up my slipper and threw it straight at the mouse. It scampered off behind the clock as the slipper thunked into the wall.

With a sigh I turned off the light and lay down in bed. I felt as if I was going nuts. Mice don't walk on two legs. And they certainly don't say their prayers. I told myself I was upset because of Uncle Sid. Aunt Scrotch said that he couldn't be disturbed. She said I wasn't allowed to see him. I had come all the way to their lonely old house for a holiday and now I couldn't see Uncle Sid. It wasn't fair.

Footsteps. Oh no, not again. This time they were real footsteps. Human footsteps in the passage outside. I climbed silently out of bed and pulled the door open a fraction. It was Aunt Scrotch creeping along the passage with a torch. Why hadn't she turned on the light? Why was she creeping? And why was every wall in the house lined with boxes of cheese? There were sausages of cheese hanging from the ceiling. There were cartons of cheese stacked in the lounge. There were cheeses in string bags. Cheeses in red wrappers. Cheeses like plum puddings. They dripped from the light fittings. They staggered across the tables.

Cheese, cheese everywhere.

2

Aunt Scrotch tiptoed down the passage to the cellar stairs. She picked up a carton of Edam cheese from the many that lined the walls and held it in both hands. She balanced the torch on top, making it roll from side to side. It sent creepy shadows flashing against the ceiling.

Aunt Scrotch vanished down the cellar steps, leaving the house in darkness. I put on my thongs and crept towards the steps. With thumping heart I made my way down after her. At the bottom I peeped around the corner.

There was a door that was not there last time I had visited. The door was locked from the outside with a large sliding bolt. It had a small window with bars in it. Aunt Scrotch tore away the cardboard from the carton and began throwing huge lumps of cheese through the bars. A loud scuffling, snuffling noise came from inside. It sounded like a hungry animal feeding at the trough.

'Pig,' said Aunt Scrotch as she turned around to come back. I flattened myself against the wall next to some boxes and held my breath. Aunt Scrotch passed by without looking in my direction. Her footsteps shuffled away upstairs to be finally silenced by the soft thud of her bedroom door. She was gone.

In the blackness the sounds of soft gobbling came from behind the locked door. I switched on the passage light and peered through the bars. I nearly fainted at the sight. It was Uncle Sid. His hair was long and wild. A tangled beard surrounded his dribbling mouth. Stains of cheese covered his torn shirt. His feet were bare. He was kneeling down on all fours and nibbling at the cheese with his mouth.

The last time I saw Uncle Sid he was strong and neat and tidy. He was one of those uncles who is always finding ten cents behind your ear. Or pulling off the end of his thumb and putting it back again before you can see how he does it. He was my favourite uncle. And now horrible Aunt Scrotch had him locked up in the cellar.

'Uncle Sid,' I croaked. 'It's me, Julian.'

He didn't even look up. Uncle Sid just kept gnawing away at his cheese.

I was frantic. What was up with him? Why didn't he answer? Angry tears filled my eyes as I yanked at the bolt and opened the door. This time he did look up. Then he scampered over to the corner and peered at me with bright, wild eyes. Before I could open my mouth to say anything, he made a rush for the door and, still on all fours, bolted out into the passage and up the stairs.

I ran after him. I couldn't believe what I was seeing. Uncle Sid was tearing at a large box. On the side was written BLUE-VEIN CHEESE. He was tearing at it with his fingers and his mouth, trying to get at the cheese inside. At last he succeeded. He pulled out the blue and white cheese and began gobbling it down.

The smell was terrible. I hate the smell of blue-vein cheese. Uncle Sid loved it though. He gnawed and nibbled for all he was worth.

After what seemed ages and ages he stopped eating. He turned up his nose and sniffed. He held up his hands under his chin like a dog begging. Then he headed up the stairs towards the house. Suddenly he froze. He began moving backwards. He was frightened of something.

It was Aunt Scrotch. Her mouth was cruel and twisted. And in her arms she held Tiger, her fat tom cat. 'Get him, Tiger,' hissed Aunt Scrotch.

She put Tiger down on the floor and he crouched low, hissing and spitting. Uncle Sid was terrified. He backed down the stairs slowly, never taking his eyes from the vicious cat.

Tiger flattened himself on the floor and crept slowly forward. His tail quivered. His whiskers twitched. He crouched, ready to spring. Uncle Sid seemed to be hypnotised by the cat. I rubbed my eyes. Poor Uncle Sid was scared of a cat. My head swam. Was I going crazy? Was this some terrible dream?

Suddenly Uncle Sid turned and ran for it. On all fours. He fled back into his little prison cell. He darted in with incredible speed.

Aunt Scrotch was almost as quick. She grabbed Tiger just as he was about to pounce. Then she slammed the door closed and locked it. Uncle Sid was trapped inside again.

'You fool,' snarled Aunt Scrotch as she pulled me out from my hiding place. 'Why did you let him out?'

'He shouldn't be locked up,' I yelled. 'Why is Uncle Sid locked up?'

Her voice was like fingernails on a blackboard. 'Can't you see? Can't you guess? Your precious Uncle Sid thinks he is a mouse.'

3

I tried to take it in. I tried to make sense of it. My head swirled. It was true. Uncle Sid acted like a mouse. He sniffed the air like one. He ate cheese. He moved around on all fours. He was frightened of cats.

My poor, dear Uncle Sid thought he was a mouse.

'He should be in a hospital,' I said slowly. 'Not locked up.'

Aunt Scrotch grabbed me by the collar of my pyjamas and pulled me along to the kitchen. She dumped me in a chair. 'He's been in hospital,' she snapped. 'They can't do anything for him. Now I'm stuck with him. I have to look after him. He acts like an animal so I treat him like an animal.'

'It's cruel,' I yelled. 'You don't have to be cruel. You don't have to put cats onto him.'

'You stay away from him,' ordered Aunt Scrotch. 'Don't you go near him. He tries to escape all the time. It's hard to get him back once he is outside. And another thing. I want your help. I am looking for something. Something that is lost.'

'What is it?' I asked. I knew that whatever it was I wasn't going to help Aunt Scrotch. I was angry. I was real mad at her. She was treating Uncle Sid terribly.

'Your uncle invented a new type of mouse trap,' said Aunt Scrotch. 'It is like a little electric fence. Whenever a mouse steps on the wire, its brain waves run along the wire into a little box. Then they run back to the mouse. The mouse sees visions of the countryside, of fresh air. Of fields. Of corn and blue sky. It runs straight off outside and never comes back. The electric fence makes the mice long for the fresh air. They can't stay in a house. The mice are never hurt by it. This mouse fence would be worth millions. Millions of dollars. But after silly Sid started thinking he was a mouse someone stole it. Or Sid hid it somewhere. Anyway, it's gone. If you find it give it to me. It is mine.'

My mean aunt got up and went to the pantry. She took down a jar of chocolate freckles and tipped them onto a plate. All she ever ate was chocolate freckles – little buttons of chocolate covered in hundreds and thousands. I could never figure out how she stayed so thin. You would think that she would get fat from eating nothing but chocolate. She ate about thirty chocolate freckles and never even offered me one.

'Go to bed,' she ordered. 'And remember. If you see that electric mouse-trap fence – give it to me.'

4

I went to bed and turned off the light. But I couldn't sleep. Little eyes were watching me. Little mouse eyes. It was the same mouse that had been watching me earlier. I just knew it was.

I switched on the light and blinked at the little grey mouse. It was in the corner of the room. And close by was a mouse trap with a piece of cheese set in it. It wasn't Uncle Sid's electric-fence type of mouse trap though. It was an ordinary one. The type that snaps down and kills the mouse by squashing it.

The mouse crept closer to the cruel trap. 'Don't,' I said. The mouse took no notice. It crept forward until it was almost touching the trap. Then it did something I still find hard to believe. It picked up a matchstick and held it in its little paws. Then it poked the cheese in the trap with the matchstick.

Crack. The spring snapped down like lightning. The mouse had set off the trap without getting hurt. It was the smartest mouse in the world.

I put one leg out of the bed onto the floor. The mouse just stood there. It didn't seem afraid. Then it started walking across the floor slowly towards the other side of my bed. It stopped every now and then and looked up at me. At last, seeing that I was following, it walked slowly under the bed.

I knelt down and peered after it. A mousey smell came out from under the bed. I could see mouse droppings on the polished wooden floor. There was something different about them though and at first I couldn't work out what it was. Then I realised. The mouse droppings were all laid out in a pattern. They spelt out a word. The mouse droppings formed the word HELP.

The little grey mouse had written a message the only way it could.

Before I had time to take this in the mouse was off again. This time it ran into a small hole in the wall and disappeared. It came out a minute or two later tugging a piece of paper in its mouth. The mouse dropped it at my feet.

I picked up the paper and looked at it. It was a bit of a page out of a diary. Uncle Sid's diary. I recognised his writing. The scrap of paper had been chewed out of the book by tiny teeth.

This is what it said:

I have just discovered that the mouse-trap electric fence is dangerous. If two creatures touch the wire at the same time their brains will swap over. Yesterday a frog and a mouse touched at the same time. The mouse hopped off and the frog scampered aw ...

I couldn't read the rest of the page as it had been chewed off. My mind started to work overtime. I thought about Uncle Sid who thought he was a mouse. And I looked at the mouse who seemed to think he was a person. Suddenly it clicked. I knew what had happened. Uncle Sid and the mouse had touched the electric mouse fence at the same time. Their minds had swapped over.

This mouse was Uncle Sid.

5

'Don't worry, Uncle,' I said to the mouse. 'We will get you back.'

But how? I didn't have the faintest idea what I could do.

The mouse scampered off into its hole once again. This time it tugged out something different. It was a piece of wire. I pulled out the wire. It was about four metres long with little posts hanging off it. There was a small black box attached to the end of it. It was the electric mouse fence.

Suddenly I knew what to do. I picked up Uncle and put him in my pocket. Then I took the electric mouse fence down to the kitchen. I crept quietly. I didn't want to wake Aunt Scrotch.

I set up the electric mouse fence. It took me quite a while to work it out but in the end I found out how it worked. The wire was stretched in a circle with little fence posts stopping it from touching the ground. Both ends were connected to the black box, which had a switch on the side.

I went to turn on the fence but the mouse, Uncle Sid that is, was shaking its head. It pointed to a place where the wire sagged and touched the floor. One of the fence posts was missing. The electricity would go into the floor.

I reached into my pocket and pulled out a matchbox. I placed it under the sagging wire with a bit of bubble gum for an insulator.

Next I tore open some packets of blue-vein cheese. I tipped heaps of it inside the fence. Then I headed to the cellar. On the way I dropped small pieces of blue-vein cheese in a trail on the floor. I opened the cell door where Uncle Sid (or I should say the mouse in Uncle Sid's body) was hungrily sniffing around.

He came out on all fours. It was sad to see a man moving around like a mouse. He followed the blue-vein trail all the way to the kitchen. He ate every bit as he went.

The mouse stood next to the electric fence. It had one paw on the wire. It had the other paw on the ON switch. Uncle Mouse came forward with a blue-veined mouth. He saw the cheese inside the fence. He sniffed. He shuffled forward. And touched the wire. The mouse threw the switch.

Blue sparks flew along the wire. The mouse turned electric blue. Uncle turned electric blue. They flashed and flared. They crackled like crisps. They lit up like light globes.

And then it was over. Uncle Sid stood up and smiled. The mouse fled out of the door. 'Thanks, Julian,' said Uncle Sid with a grin. 'We did it. We did it.'

He was his old self again. He had his mind back. And so did the mouse.

We looked at the electric mouse fence. 'It's dangerous,' said Uncle Sid. 'We can never use it.'

'It's mine,' screeched another voice. 'After all I've gone through it is mine.'

It was Aunt Scrotch. Her face was screwed up like a wet shirt that had been bunched into a ball and left to dry in the corner. She lunged forward at the electric mouse fence.

That was when I noticed that my matchbox was open. 'Oh no,' I groaned.

Aunt Scrotch grabbed the wire with her hands.

She turned electric blue. She shimmered and shone. She beamed and screamed.

The wire fence was flung up to the ceiling. The black box smashed into smithereens.

It was all over.

6

I went home about a week later. Uncle Sid tried to fix the electric fence but so far he has had no luck. He writes to me quite often so I know what is going on. His last letter was a bit short though. He had to leave it and rush out to find Aunt Scrotch. She had run outside again looking for more cow manure.

In my letter back I told him the little dung beetle was doing well. I still keep it in the matchbox. But at lunch time I let it out and give it as many chocolate freckles as it wants.

HMM! HUH! NO WHAT? HMM! NO HUH! WHAT? HUH! HMM! WHAT?

Hailstone Bugs

If you multiply one by one,' says Dad. 'What do you get?'

I know what he is on about but I decide to play dumb. 'One,' I say. 'Once one is one.'

'No,' says Dad. 'If one mouse multiplies with one other mouse the result is eight mice.'

'It wasn't my fault,' I say.

'Yes, it was,' says Dad. 'You made a deal. You said if I let you have one baby mouse you would never ask for another one. One mouse on its own cannot have babies. Nibbles has just had babies. There has to be a father somewhere.'

'She was lonely,' I say.

'What?' yells Dad.

'Foxy brought his mouse, Flick Face, over for an hour or so,' I say. 'Nibbles was lonely. So was Flick Face. Two lonely mice. So we put Flick Face in Nibbles' cage. Just for an hour. Nothing much can happen in an hour.'

'Plenty can happen in an hour,' says Dad. 'In fact

HUH! WHAT? HMM!

plenty can happen in two minutes. You should know the facts of life by now, Troy. Flick Face made Nibbles pregnant. They mated. Mate.' He says the last word in a very sarcastic voice.

'Sorry, Dad,' I say.

'Sorry is not good enough, Troy,' says Dad. 'I am going to have to punish you severely. You have to learn to keep your side of a bargain.'

I groan to myself. What will the punishment be? Washing up duty for a week? Maybe even two weeks. Raking leaves all day Saturday? Grounded for a month? Dad is capable of many cruel and unusual punishments.

'I am confiscating your head-lopper for two weeks,' he says slowly.

'Oh no,' I shriek. 'Not the head-lopper. Not that.'

'Yes,' says Dad. 'I have already locked it in the shed. And if you say one more word it will be two months and not two weeks.'

I stagger out of the room. This is very serious. This is tragic. The end of my life as I know it. A totally unfair and catastrophic punishment.

In ten days' time there is going to be a school concert. I am going to perform a magic trick. And the main part of it is the head-lopping act. How it works is this: I put a kid inside a black box shaped like a coffin. His feet stick out one end and his head pokes out of the other. Above his head is a fake guillotine blade.

I drop the blade down through his throat. Everyone will think I have chopped him off at the neck. But the kid's head does not fall off.

It is a great trick. I saved up for over a year to buy it. In fact I sold over forty mice at three dollars each to get the money. Three times forty is one hundred and twenty. Dollars. That's how much the head-lopper cost.

Nibbles and Flick Face were very good multipliers. Dad didn't know anything about it. Okay, so I shouldn't have started breeding mice. But it did start the way I said. By accident. And Nibbles *was* lonely. I didn't lie about that. After Flick Face's first visit things just got a bit out of hand, that was all.

Me and my mate Foxy sold the baby mice off. Everyone wanted them. So we produced another batch. And then another. We made heaps of dosh out of it until Dad found the latest lot of babies.

Now I have a tragedy on my hands. The winner of the school concert is going into the grand finale. On television. Yes, on TV. It is my chance to be famous.

The way it works is this:

After every act they turn on the applause meter. It can measure sound. The act that gets the loudest clap from the audience is the winner. And that would have been me for sure. No one but no one could beat the head-lopping act. Now I will have to do a card trick and that will never win.

My life is ruined.

2

Foxy and I trudge our way to school.

'What am I going to do?' I say. 'I have been practising the head-lopping act for months. I would have won for sure.'

'Appeal to a higher court,' says Foxy.

'Mum?' I say. 'That won't work. She will just back Dad up.'

'Buy another magic act,' says Foxy. 'There must be other good ones.'

I think about this for a bit. 'There is an act where you can make a boy float in the air,' I say. 'But levitation tricks are very expensive. Hundreds of dollars.'

'We could sell the baby mice,' says Foxy.

'Nah, that would only be twenty-four dollars. And anyway, every kid in the school has already got one.'

This is true. In fact, mice are banned from our school since one of Nibbles' first batch escaped and ate Mrs Brindle's lunch.

Still and all, Foxy has got my brain working overtime. The levitation act is even better than the head-lopping trick. But where can I get the money?

All day I think and think and think. I could sell my surfboard but that would mean big trouble from Mum and Dad. No, I just have to face it. There is no way out. I will just have to do a card trick.

I wander home slowly and sadly. My head feels as if it is in a fog. In fact it *is* in a fog. It is a cold day. I can see my breath floating out in front of me.

Tonight it will probably hail. Whenever the temperature gets down to zero in The Hills it hails. I give a little shiver and hurry home.

That night I beg Dad to give me my head-lopping box back.

'No way,' he says. 'I have just found out that this is not the first batch of mice. If you would like to discuss this further we can . . .'

'It's okay,' I say. 'I get it.'

I hurry out of the room before Dad decides I need more punishments. I go out to the front porch and stare up into the black sky. It is cold and raining. A distant peal of thunder rolls through the night.

My little finger starts to go numb. It always goes numb when the temperature falls to zero. And when the temperature falls to zero it will hail, as sure as eggs are eggs.

And eggs are what seem to fall out of the sky. Great balls of ice start to bounce across the lawn. I have never seen such big hailstones.

They are like rocks.

I am glad I am safely tucked away under the verandah. Otherwise I could get knocked out.

A particularly big hailstone bounces off the lawn and rolls over to where I am standing.

I pick it up and stare at it.

The hailstone stares back.

3

I can't believe it. There are eyes inside the hailstone. I walk over to the light and look at it carefully. There is something inside the ice. It looks like an insect. Amazing.

How could this have happened?

Probably the insect was flying around and got frozen high up in the clouds. Ice formed around it. Sort of like a pearl forming around a grain of sand in an oyster. I have heard of such things before.

'Hey, Dad,' I go to yell. But I stop myself. He is still in a bad mood. It is better to keep out of his way.

The little creature inside the ice does not move. It is frozen solid. Still and all, it sort of seems as if the eyes are looking back at me. I can't see it properly through the ice but that is how I feel.

'Don't be stupid,' I say to myself.

I take the hailstone inside and put it on a saucer next to my bed. When it melts I will take a good look at it. For the time being I have more important things on my mind.

Like how to get some money.

I get into bed but I can't sleep. I start to count hundred-dollar bills in my mind. This always works and in no time at all I am sound asleep.

The next thing I know it is almost morning. The sun is just starting to peep over the mountains. The air is filled with sunlight filtering through the mist.

Butterflies are fluttering, circling each other and dancing like autumn leaves in a gust of wind. Some of them are in pairs, hanging on to each other's legs and flying at the same time.

There is a movement on my bedside table. It is coming from the hailstone. It has melted and left a small pool of water. And an insect, if you can call it that.

The little creature starts to wriggle like a moth coming out of a cocoon. It is alive. Can you believe that? It was frozen and now it is alive. Amazing. Incredible.

It starts to unfold its wings. And move its legs. It is hard to describe but I will have a go. The nearest thing it looks like is a grasshopper. It has six legs but they are all the same size. And its head – this is the weirdest bit – somehow looks human. It has tiny ears and a nose. And eyes that move around. Finally it unfolds its wings. They are beautiful. Red and green and yellow. Like a butterfly's.

Butterflies?

I race over to the window. Those things dancing in the sun weren't butterflies. They were the same as the hailstone bug. Zillions of them. I race to the window but I am too late. They are gone. Fluttered off into the air. All the hailstones have melted in the morning sun.

I haven't figured it all out yet but a thought is trying to worm its way out of my brain. I should have collected more. They might be rare. Or valuable. And now there is only one left.

Or is there?

The saucer is empty. My hailstone bug is gone. Quick as a flash I slam the door shut.

'Where are you, little fellah?' I say. 'Come to Daddy.'

But it does not come to me. Nothing moves in the room. Maybe it has escaped. No, there was not enough time. The hailstone bug is in here somewhere. I search and search and search. Nothing. It is lying doggo. Think. Think.

I look at the walls. I look at my underpants on the floor. All five pairs. Where could he hide? Butterflies like flowers. Bright colours. I don't have any flowers but I do have bright colours.

My bedspread has a pattern of green and red and gold.

Yes, yes. There it is. Cunning little insect. Lying doggo, trying to hide.

'Gotcha.'

I grab it by the wings and quickly drop it into a jar.

I have got myself a hailstone bug.

4

'Wow,' says Foxy as we walk to school. 'It sure is a weird bug.'

Everyone at school is amazed by it too.

'It's cute.'

'Like a fairy.'

'I wonder if it thinks.'

'Its eyes look alive.'

'Let it go, the poor thing.'

These are the sorts of things that the kids say at lunchtime.

'I'll give you twenty bucks for it,' says Susan Grayson.

'Thirty,' says Elaine Chung.

'Thirty-five, fifty,' says Nick Glare.

'Don't sell,' says Foxy.

'I'm not going to,' I say. 'Sorry, folks, but the hailstone bug is not for sale.'

After school Foxy and I walk home together as usual.

'What's the weather forecast?' I say.

'Why?' says Foxy.

'Because my little finger is starting to go numb,' I say.

5

That night Foxy stays over. He looks into the jar. 'You'd better feed it, mate,' he says. 'It might die.'

I hit my forehead with the palm of my hand. 'You're right,' I say. 'The poor thing.'

I open the lid of the jar a fraction and slip in a bit of raw meat.

'Careful,' says Foxy. 'Don't let it out.'

The hailstone bug does not go near the meat. In fact it flutters away from it.

'It looks cross,' says Foxy.

I slip in other bits of food. A frozen pea. A bit of pizza. A chocolate biscuit. The hailstone bug does not eat any of them. Finally I try a bit of honey. The bug swoops down and starts to eat it.

'Look at that,' says Foxy. 'It is using its front legs to feed itself.'

'Like a person,' I say.

Just at that very moment there is a sound on the tin roof of the house.

'Rain,' yells Foxy.

We race outside into the dark night with some jars. It is pouring. Pelting down.

'How's your little finger?' says Foxy.

'Tingling,' I say. 'But just a little bit.'

We both stare at the rain. It pelts down making rivers across the lawn and down the gutters. It is not going to hail. We are not going to get zillions of hailstone bugs and sell them for thirty bucks each. What a let-down.

Plonk.

'What was that?' I say.

'Someone threw a stone on the roof,' says Foxy.

We look at each other.

'Quick,' I yell. 'Before it melts.'

I scramble up on to the wet verandah roof. It is slippery and freezing cold. I can't see a thing.

'Chuck up the torch,' I yell.

Foxy does as I say and I search around in the feeble light. Yes, yes, there it is. One small hailstone, melting quickly in the rain. I pick it up and throw it down to Foxy. He shoves it straight into one of the jars.

I climb down and we go inside.

Both of us stare into the jar. We gasp.

'Look,' I whisper. 'There's another one.'

6

In no time at all the new hailstone bug has hatched out of his chilly home.

'It looks sad,' says Foxy.

'It's not the only one,' I say. 'I'm sad too.'

'Why?'

'Because we aren't going to get enough money from two. Even if we get thirty bucks each for them we would need at least twenty. Thirty times twenty is six hundred. That would be enough for the levitation trick. But sixty dollars is not nearly enough.'

'Let 'em go,' says Foxy suddenly.

'What?'

'I feel sorry for 'em,' says Foxy. 'They sort of look like they know things.'

They do too. But I can't let them go. Sixty dollars is sixty dollars.

'What if they have names?' says Foxy. 'What if they have grandfathers and children and things like that? How would you like being locked up in a jar?'

The two jars are side by side and the hailstone bugs are staring through the glass at each other.

Something I said earlier starts to buzz around in my mind.

'Thirty times twenty is six hundred,' I say to myself.

'What?' says Foxy.

'And once one is eight,' I yell.

'You're crazy,' says Foxy.

'That's it. That's it!' I scream. I carefully take the lid off the first bug's jar. Then I lift it out and place it in with the other one. I put the lid on tight.

Immediately the two bugs start to fly around. They grab each other's legs and do a little mid-air dance.

'What are they up to?' says Foxy.

'You know,' I say.

Foxy goes red in the face. 'We shouldn't be looking,' he says.

'Why not? They're only insects.'

'Their heads are human,' says Foxy. 'They deserve privacy.' He picks up a pair of my underpants and puts them on top of the jar.

'No peeking, mate,' says Foxy.

7

Foxy and I go and watch television. Finally Dad sends us to bed.

'It's school tomorrow,' he says. 'So off to sleep. Both of you.'

We clean our teeth and do all the usual things. Then we take a gander inside the jar.

'Look,' says Foxy.

I grin. It is not what I expected. But it is just what I need.

'Eggs,' I say.

There on the side of the jar is a row of perfectly formed little round eggs. The sort caterpillars lay. There are about twenty of them. Maybe more.

'They should be on leaves or something,' I say. I scratch my head and think. The hailstone bugs come down in the ice. Then they hatch and mate. Then they come down again and it all starts over.

'Quick, to the kitchen,' I say.

We sneak down so that Mum and Dad don't hear us. I fish around in the bottom cupboard and take out a couple of trays.

'Iceblocks,' says Foxy. 'You're a genius.'

We put both hailstone bugs into the other jar and I use a pair of tweezers to pick out the eggs one at a time. I carefully place one egg in each compartment of the ice-cube tray. Finally I cover them all with water.

'They'll drown,' says Foxy.

'No,' I say. 'It's just like hailstones.'

I put the ice-cube trays into the freezer.

Foxy smiles. 'It might just work,' he says.

We close the fridge door and sneak off back to bed.

8

In the morning my dreams have all come true. Well, almost.

Every single iceblock has a little hailstone bug in it.

'Amazing,' says Foxy. 'They must hatch out in the cold water. Then when the ice melts they come out to play.'

We both laugh. We are very happy.

I stick all of the ice-cubes into a jar with the two bugs we already have. I put them outside in the sun to melt.

By the time we have finished breakfast they have all come to life. There are about twenty little creatures all flying around in the jar.

'Each one is different,' says Foxy.

He is right. Some have bigger ears or oddly shaped noses. There is one thing about them that is the same, though. The look in their eyes. They are sad.

It is nearly time for school. 'We can sell them today,' I say happily. 'Then I can buy the levitation trick.'

'What will happen to them?' says Foxy.

'The kids will keep them in jars,' I say. 'They will be well fed. Like pets.'

'Like jail more like it,' says Foxy.

'They don't know anything,' I say. 'They are just dumb insects.'

I gaze into the jar. And twenty-two pairs of eyes gaze back. And I mean gaze, not look.

'What if they are intelligent?' says Foxy. 'Some kids won't feed them properly. Some won't put breathing holes in the jars. Some will go on holidays and forget about them.'

We both sit there in silence. The jar is filled with

misery. Foxy knows it.

And I know it.

I walk out to the backyard with the jar. Foxy follows in silence.

Slowly I unscrew the top of the jar.

'Off you go,' I say.

The hailstone bugs flutter into the air and fill it with joyous dancing. They pair off and hang on to each other's legs as they twirl around. They are mating. It is a wonderful sight. They are free. They circle our heads for a bit. Suddenly they start to rise higher and higher. Soon they are just a handful of sand thrown at the sun. Then they are gone.

Like my hopes of a levitation trick.

9

It's funny when you do the right thing.

I feel good every time I get out of bed. Even this morning, the day of the concert. Okay, so I have done my chance of winning but I feel sort of warm inside. I am glad I let the hailstone bugs go.

Until the moment comes when I am standing on the stage. The lights are on me. The house is packed. What a crowd. I am the final act. They have probably kept the worst until last. I am shaking all over.

There have been some terrific performances. Little Curly Simons nearly brought the house down by singing 'I Love My Daddy'. How can you compete with that?

And the tap dancers sent the applause meter up to ninety-two.

Toula Pappas recited a poem that scored seventy-four and Tran Chong received eighty-three by playing 'Waltzing Matilda' on the violin.

'I need a volunteer,' I say in a nervous voice.

There is a long silence. No one moves. No one wants to be associated with a weak act like mine. Finally Foxy stands up and walks on to the stage. He is a good mate.

'Rigged,' yells someone in the back row.

'Pick a card,' I say. 'Any card.'

'Not that old trick,' says Mickey Bourke.

Oh, this is terrible. Why don't I back out? I am trembling. I hold out the pack of cards. Oh no. My little finger has gone numb. I am so clumsy. The cards slip from my quivering fingers.

The audience are bored already. They snuggle down into their coats. It is a cold night and they want to go home.

I hang my head. What is the use? I might as well give up.

Suddenly I see Foxy. He is over by the door. He is flapping his arms like wings and pointing out into the night. What is he on about? Could it be the bugs? No. Well, it's worth a try.

'Ladies and Gentlemen,' I shout. 'My latest trick, for your entertainment, is . . .' I take a deep breath and a big risk, 'the dance of the magic midgets.'

Nothing happens. And then there is a gasp from the audience. Hundreds of butterflies have flown in the window. They swoop low over everyone's heads. I know what they are going to do next.

'Pair off and dance,' I command.

The little hailstone bugs do what comes naturally. They grasp each other's legs and spiral and turn in the air.

'Amazing, wonderful, what a sight.' The audience is rapt.

'How does he do it?'

'Fantastic.'

I take a deep breath and shout. I know what is coming next. So I get in quick.

'Vanish,' I yell.

The hailstone bugs do one more twirl and fly out the window.

I bend and bow to the audience. The applause meter goes bananas.

Mickey Bourke is puzzled. 'What were they doing? They looked real,' he says suspiciously.

I tell him.

Sort of.

'Don't you worry about that.

'Mate.'

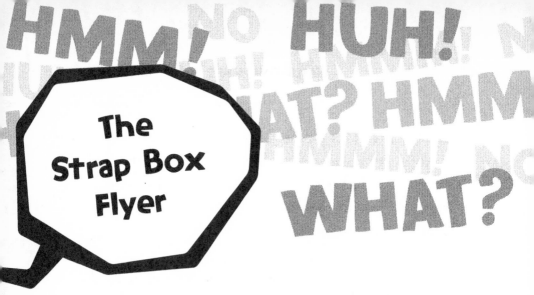

The Strap Box Flyer

Hundreds of people were watching Giffen. They thought he was a bit mad. But they couldn't stop looking. He was very interesting.

Giffen went over to his truck and got out a tube of glue. On the tube it said GIFFEN'S GREAT GLUE. IT WILL STICK ANYTHING. Giffen held the glue over his head. 'This is the best glue in the world,' he said. 'It can mend anything that is broken. Who has something that is broken?'

A small boy came out the front. He held up a bow and arrow. 'My bow is broken,' he said. 'And no one can fix it.' Giffen took the bow out of the boy's hand. He put a bit of glue on the broken ends and joined them together. Then he put the arrow in the bow and shot it into the air. The people were surprised. They all clapped and cheered.

'That's nothing,' Giffen told them. 'You haven't seen anything yet.' He went over to the back of his truck where he had a big crane. It had a rope on the end of it. Giffen grabbed the rope. He put a dab of glue on the end of it. Then he put the rope onto the roof of the car. 'This glue can hold up a car,' he told the crowd. He stepped into his truck and started up the crane. The car was lifted up into the air. The only thing that held the rope onto the car was the glue.

The crowd thought this was great. No one had ever seen glue like this before. 'Now,' said Giffen, 'who wants to buy some of Giffen's Great Glue?'

The crowd rushed forward. Everyone wanted some glue. They couldn't get it quick enough. They thought it was terrific. 'Get it while it lasts,' shouted Giffen. 'Only ten dollars a tube.'

Giffen sold two hundred tubes of glue. He made two thousand dollars in one day. The customers took their glue and went home to try it out.

'You fools,' said Giffen to himself. 'You will soon find out that the glue stops working after four hours.'

2

Miss Tibbs had bought a tube of Giffen's Great Glue. She was a very old lady. She lived all on her own. Most of her friends were dead. There was no one to help her to fix things up when they got broken. So she was very glad to have the glue.

Miss Tibbs collected china. She had spent all of her life saving pieces of china. She had plates and cups and saucers from all over the world. She also had little china dolls and toy animals. She had so many pieces that she didn't know where to put them all. This is why she wanted the glue. She wanted to put up a new shelf.

As soon as she got home Miss Tibbs went and fetched a piece of wood from the shed in her back garden. Then she put some of Giffen's Great Glue along the edge of the wood and stuck it onto the wall. It worked well. The shelf was very strong.

'This is wonderful glue,' she said. 'It dries straight away.' Miss Tibbs started to put her china pieces onto the shelf. She decided to put her favourite piece out first. It was a small china horse. She had owned it for many years. It had been given to her by her father before he died. Miss Tibbs loved this horse. She put it in the best spot, right in the middle of the shelf.

After she had put all of the other pieces out Miss Tibbs sat down and had a rest. She was very tired. She fell asleep in her armchair in front of the fire.

Four hours later Miss Tibbs was woken up by a loud crash. The glue had stopped working. The shelf had fallen off the wall and all of the china pieces were smashed.

Miss Tibbs went down onto her hands and knees. She started to pick up all of the broken pieces. Then she remembered her horse. Her precious horse. She looked for it among the bits. She couldn't find it. Then she found something that made her cry. A leg and a tail and a tiny head. The horse was smashed to pieces.

Miss Tibbs cried and cried. She got her tube of Giffen's

Great Glue and threw it in the fire. Then she decided that she would go and find Giffen. She would tell him that his glue was no good. She would ask him to pay for the broken china.

She hurried back to the place where Giffen had been. But he was gone. There was no sign of him. She knew that he would never come back.

3

Another person who bought the tube of Giffen's Great Glue was Scott Bridges. He had bought it to mend his canoe. It had broken in half.

Scott's father had told him the canoe could not be repaired. He said that its back was broken. He told Scott to take it to the tip. But now that Scott had a tube of Giffen's Great Glue he knew that he could fix it.

The canoe was down at the lake. Scott went down there on his own. He didn't tell his father where he was going. He pulled the two pieces of the canoe together, and put Giffen's Great Glue along the join.

'Great,' yelled Scott. 'It's as good as new. This glue is fantastic.' He pushed the canoe into the water and climbed in. It floated well. It didn't leak at all. Scott began to paddle out into the middle of the lake. He was very happy. And excited. He paddled off as fast as he could go.

Scott was not allowed to go out in the canoe without a life jacket. But on this day he had forgotten. All that he could think about was the canoe and Giffen's Great Glue.

It was a sunny day and the time passed quickly. Soon four hours had passed. Scott noticed that some water was starting to leak into the canoe. He decided to start paddling for home. But it was too late. The glue had come unstuck. The canoe broke in two and sank.

The water was icy cold. Scott was frightened. It was a long way to the shore. 'Help,' he screamed at the top of his voice. But no one heard him. He was the only person on the lake.

Scott started to swim to shore. After a little while he began to get tired. His legs hurt and he had a pain in his stomach. His head went under the water. He tried to get back to the top. But it was no use. His lungs filled with water and he sank to the bottom of the lake.

That night, when Scott did not come home, his father called the police. Divers searched the lake. They found Scott's body. And the broken canoe. In the bottom of the canoe was a tube of Giffen's Great Glue.

4

Giffen was driving away in his truck. Very fast. He knew that he only had four hours to get away. Then the people who had bought the glue would start looking for him. He knew that they would be mad. He did not want them to catch him.

He decided to drive to Horsham. That was a long

way off. They would not know about Giffen's Great Glue in Horsham. He could find some more suckers, and make some more money.

Two days later he arrived in Horsham. He took his truck to the centre of town. Then he put up a sign. The sign said:

TWO HUNDRED DOLLARS PRIZE

FOR ANYONE WHO CAN UNSTICK

GIFFEN'S GREAT GLUE

Soon two men arrived. They were both riding tractors. One of the men got down from his tractor. He walked over to Giffen and gave him two pieces of rope. 'Join these up with your glue,' he said. 'Then we will pull it apart.'

Giffen smiled to himself. 'Okay,' he said. 'I'll do it.' He put a dob of glue on the end of the two pieces of rope. Then he joined them together. The glue stuck fast.

The men took the rope that had been joined. They tied one end to each of the tractors. Then they started the tractors up. There was a lot of smoke and noise. A crowd started to gather. Everyone thought that the glue would break. But it didn't. The wheels on the tractors sent up blue smoke. The engines roared. But still the glue held.

Then there was a loud bang. The engine of one of the tractors had stopped. The other tractor started to drag it along the road. Everyone cheered at the top of their voices.

'Now,' said Giffen, 'who will buy my great glue?'

The crowd pushed forward. Everyone wanted some. The people waved their money. They pushed and shoved. Giffen sold three hundred tubes.

At last everyone went home. Except one man. A short, bald man with a friendly smile. 'Excuse me,' he said to Giffen. 'But I wonder if you would like to buy something from me?'

'What are you selling?' said Giffen in a gruff voice.

'A Strap Box Flyer. It is a small box that will make people fly.'

5

Giffen didn't believe that there was a box that could make someone fly. There was no such thing. This man was trying to fool him. Still, he was interested. It might be a new sort of trick that he could use himself, to make money from the suckers. He looked at his watch. He had to get out of this town before the glue started to come unstuck. He had four hours left. There was plenty of time to talk to the little man.

'Okay,' said Giffen to the little man. 'Show me your Strap Box Flyer.'

'Not here, someone might see us. Come home with me and I will show you how it works.'

Giffen followed the little man home to his house.

It was a small cottage. It was very untidy. The grass was long and some of the windows were broken. Inside there was junk everywhere. There were tools, nuts and bolts, machines and bits of wire all over the floor.

'My name is Mr Flint,' said the little man. 'But everyone calls me Flinty.'

'I'm in a hurry, Flinty,' said Giffen. 'So let me see you do some flying.'

'Very well, very well,' replied Flinty. He went over to a shelf and took down a small box. Then he lifted up the carpet and pulled out a short strap. It looked like a watchband made out of silver.

'I keep the strap in one place, and the box in another,' said Flinty. 'That's to stop anyone stealing my invention. I have to screw the box onto the strap. It won't work unless both pieces are screwed together.'

Flinty fiddled around with the box and the strap. It took a long time. About half an hour. Giffen was getting worried. He did not want to stay much longer. The crowd would be mad when they found out that the glue did not work for long. At last Flinty finished. He had screwed the box onto the strap. He put it onto his arm. It looked just like a wristwatch, only bigger.

'Now,' said Flinty. 'Watch this.' Slowly he rose up off the floor. He went up about ten centimetres.

Giffen could not believe it. His eyes nearly popped out of his head. 'How high can you go?' he asked Flinty.

'As high as I want to.' Flinty floated up to the ceiling.

Then he flew around the room, just like a cloud.

Giffen knew that he had to get the Strap Box Flyer. It was worth a fortune. He could make a lot of money if he had it.

6

'Why are you showing this to me?' Giffen asked Flinty.

'Because you are a great inventor,' said Flinty. 'You have invented Giffen's Great Glue. I am an inventor too. I have invented the Strap Box Flyer. We could be partners. You could help me make the Strap Box Flyer. And I could help you make the glue.'

Giffen did not say anything. He was thinking. He wanted the Strap Box Flyer. But he couldn't stay in Horsham. Once four hours was up his glue would stop working. The things that people had mended would start falling to bits. They would come looking for him. He could even end up in jail.

'Have you got another Strap Box Flyer?' Giffen asked.

'Yes,' said Flinty. 'I have one more. You can try it out if you want to. But first I will have to assemble it. I will have to screw the strap onto the box.'

'That will take half an hour,' said Giffen. 'I will go and get my truck. Then I will be back to try out the Strap Box Flyer myself.' Giffen went off. He had decided to steal the Strap Box Flyer. He wanted to have the truck nearby for a quick getaway.

Giffen could not believe his luck. Once he had the

Strap Box Flyer he would find out how it worked. Then he would make more of them. He could sell them for thousands of dollars each. He would make a fortune. Everyone would want one.

He ran back to his truck. Then he drove to Flinty's house as fast as he could. The Strap Box Flyer was ready. There would just be time for a quick tryout and then he would have to leave town.

Flinty put the Strap Box Flyer onto Giffen's arm. 'Now,' he said. 'All you have to do is to think of where you would like to fly to.'

Giffen thought that he would like to fly over to his truck. It worked. He went gently flying through the air and landed on the roof of his truck. Flinty floated over and joined him. 'Great,' said Giffen. 'Really great. How high can we go with these things?'

'As high as you like,' said Flinty. 'As high as you like.'

7

Giffen forgot about everything except the Strap Box Flyer. He forgot about the time. He forgot about Giffen's Great Glue and he forgot about getting out of town quickly.

'Let's go up to the clouds,' he said to Flinty. And so they flew together. High into the sky. When they looked down the people looked like tiny ants. It was wonderful to fly so high.

Time passed quickly. Hours went by. It started to get

dark. Giffen decided that he would wait until it was night. Then he would be able to get away from Flinty. He would just fly off and lose Flinty in the dark. Then he would drive off in his truck and never come back. He could take the Strap Box Flyer to bits and find out how it worked. Then he could make a lot more of them. And sell them. Then he would be rich.

Flinty flew over to Giffen. 'We are very high,' he said. 'We can't go much higher than this. There will be no air to breathe.'

Giffen looked down. They were so high that he could not see the ground. They were above the clouds.

'I have only made two Strap Box Flyers so far,' said Flinty, 'and yours is the best of the two.'

'Why is that?' asked Giffen.

'Because I joined it together with Giffen's Great Glue.'

Giffen was just in time to see his Strap Box Flyer break into bits. Then he started to fall.

He screamed all the way down.

Souperman

'Look at this school report,' said Dad. 'It's a disgrace. Four D's and two E's. It's the worst report I have ever seen.'

He was starting to go red in the face. I knew I was in big trouble. I had to do something. And fast.

'I did my best,' I said feebly.

'Nonsense,' he yelled. 'Look what it says down the bottom here. Listen to this.'

Robert could do much better. He has not done enough work this term. He spends all his time at school reading Superman comics under the desk.

'That's it,' he raved on. 'That's the end of all this Superman silliness. You can get all those Superman comics, all those posters and all the rest of your Superman junk and take it down to the council rubbish bin.'

'But Dad,' I gasped.

'No buts, I said *now* and I mean *now*.' His voice was getting louder and louder. I decided to do what he wanted before he freaked out altogether. I walked slowly into the bedroom and picked up every one of my sixty Superman comics. Then I trudged out of the front door and into the corridor. We lived on the first floor of the high-rise flats so I took the lift down to the council rubbish bin. It was one of those big, steel bins that can only be lifted up by a special garbage truck. I could only just reach the top of it by standing on tiptoes. I shoved the comics over the edge and then caught the lift back to the first floor.

That was when I first met Superman.

He was making a tremendous racket in flat 132b. It sounded as if someone was rattling the window. It can be very dangerous banging on the windows when you live upstairs. At first I thought it was probably some little kid trying to get outside while his mother was away shopping. I decided to do the right thing and go and save him. I pushed open the door, which wasn't locked, and found myself in the strangest room I had ever seen.

The walls of the flat were completely lined with cans of soup. Thousands and thousands of cans were stacked on bookshelves going right up to the ceiling. It was a bit like a supermarket.

Then I noticed something even stranger. I looked over at the window and saw someone trying to get in. I couldn't believe my eyes. It was him. It was really him. My hero – Superman. In person.

He was clinging to the outside ledge and trying to open the window. He was puffing and blowing and couldn't seem to lift it up. Every now and then he looked down as if he was frightened of falling. I ran over to the window and undid the catch. I pulled up the window and Superman jumped in.

2

He looked just as he did in the comics. He was wearing a red cape and a blue-and-red outfit with a large 'S' on his chest. He had black, curly hair and a handsome face. His body rippled with muscles.

'Thanks,' he said. 'You came just in time. I couldn't hang on much longer.'

My mouth fell open. 'But what about your power?' I asked him. 'Why didn't you just smash the window open?'

He smiled at me. Then he held one finger over his mouth and went over and closed the door I had left open. 'My power only lasts for half an hour,' he said. 'I had to go all the way to Tasmania to rescue a woman lost in the snow. I only just made it back to the window when my power ran out. That's why I couldn't get the window open.'

'Half an hour?' I said. 'Superman's power doesn't last for half an hour. It lasts forever.'

'You've been reading too many comics,' he responded. 'It's S-o-u-p-e-r-m-a-n, not S-u-p-e-r-m-a-n. I get half an hour of power from each can of soup.'

I started to get nervous. This bloke was a nut. He was dressed up in a Superman outfit and he had the story all wrong. He thought Superman's power came from drinking cans of soup. I started to walk towards the door. I had to get out of there.

'Come back, and I'll show you,' he said. He went over to the fridge and tried to lift it up. He couldn't. He strained until drops of sweat appeared on his forehead but the fridge didn't budge. Next he picked up one of the cans of soup and tried to squeeze it. Nothing happened. He couldn't get it open.

'See,' he went on. 'I'm as weak as a kitten. That proves that I have no power.'

'But it doesn't prove that you're Superman,' I said.

He walked over to a drawer and took out a bright blue can-opener. Then he took out a book and flipped over the pages. 'Here it is,' he exclaimed. 'Lifting up refrigerators. Pea and ham soup.'

He took down a can of pea and ham soup from the shelf and opened it up with the bright blue can-opener. Then he drank the lot. Raw. Straight out of the can.

'Urgh.' I yelled. 'Don't drink it raw.'

'I have to,' he said. 'I don't have time to heat it up. Just imagine if I got a call to save someone who had fallen from a building. They would be smashed to bits on the ground before the soup was warm.'

He walked over to the fridge and lifted it up with one hand. He actually did it. He lifted the fridge high above his head with one hand. I couldn't believe it. The soup seemed to give him superhuman strength.

'Fantastic,' I shouted. 'No one except Superman could lift a fridge. Do you really get your power from cans of soup?'

He didn't answer. Instead he did a long, loud burp. Then he held his hand up over his mouth and went red in the face. 'Sorry,' he said. 'I've got a stomach-ache. It always happens after I drink the soup too quickly. I'll just nick into the bathroom and get myself an Alka-Seltzer for this indigestion.'

Indigestion? Superman doesn't get indigestion. He is like the Queen. He just doesn't have those sort of problems and he doesn't burp either. It wouldn't be right. That's when I knew he was a fake. I decided to try the soup out myself while he was in the bathroom and prove that it was all nonsense.

I looked at the book which had the list of soups. There was a different soup named for every emergency. For burst dams it was beef broth. For stopping trains it was cream of tomato. Celery soup was for rescuing people from floods.

I decided to try the chicken soup. It was for smashing down doors. I picked up the bright blue can-opener and used it on a can of chicken soup I found on the top shelf. I drank the whole lot. Cold and raw. It tasted terrible but I managed to get it down. Then I went over to the door and punched it with my fist.

Nothing happened to the door but my poor fingers were skinned to the bone. The pain was awful. My eyes started to water. 'You fake,' I yelled through the bathroom door. 'You rotten fake.' I rushed out of the flat as fast as I could go. I was really mad at that phoney Souperman. He was a big disappointment. I wished I could meet the real Superman. The one in the comics.

3

My comics! I needed them badly. I wanted to read about the proper Superman who didn't eat cans of raw soup and get indigestion. I wondered if the garbage truck had taken the comics yet. There might still be time to get them back. It had taken me three years to save them all. I didn't care what Dad said, I was going to keep those comics. I rushed down to the council bin as fast as I could.

I couldn't see inside the bin because it was too high but I knew by the smell that it hadn't been emptied. I jumped up, grabbed the edge, and pulled myself over the top. What a stink. It was putrid. The bin contained broken eggshells, old bones, hundreds of empty soup tins, a dead cat and other foul muck. I couldn't see my comics anywhere so I started to dig around looking for them. I was so busy looking for the comics that I didn't hear the garbage truck coming until it was too late.

With a sudden lurch the bin was lifted into the air and tipped upside down. I was dumped into the back of the garbage truck with all the filthy rubbish. I was buried under piles of plastic bags, bottles and kitchen scraps.

I couldn't see a thing and I found it difficult to breathe. I knew that if I didn't get to the top I would suffocate.

After what seemed like hours I managed to dig my way up to the surface. I looked up with relief at the flats towering above and at the clouds racing across the sky. Then something happened that made my heart stop. The rubbish started to move. The driver had started up the crusher on the truck and it was pushing all the rubbish up to one end and squashing it. A great steel blade was moving towards me. I was about to be flattened inside a pile of garbage. What a way to die.

'Help,' I screamed. 'Help.' It was no use. The driver couldn't see me. No one could see me. Except Souperman. He was sitting on the window ledge of his room and banging a can of soup on the wall. He was trying to open it.

The great steel blade came closer and closer. My ribs were hurting. A great pile of rubbish was rising around me like a swelling tide and pushing me upwards and squeezing me at the same time. By now I could just see over the edge of the truck. There was no one in sight. I looked up again at Souperman. 'Forget the stupid soup,' I yelled. 'Get me out of here or I will be killed.'

Souperman looked down at me from the first-floor window and shook his head. He looked scared. Then, without warning, and with the unopened can of soup still in his hand, he jumped out of the window.

Did he fly through the air in the manner of a bird? No way. He fell to the ground like a human brick and thudded onto the footpath not far from the truck. He lay there in a crumpled heap.

I tried to scream but I couldn't. The crusher had pushed all the air out of my lungs. It was squeezing me tighter and tighter. I knew I had only seconds to live.

I looked over at Souperman. He was alive. He was groaning and still trying to open the can of soup. From somewhere deep in my lungs I managed to find one more breath. 'Leave the soup,' I gasped, 'and turn off the engine.'

He nodded and started crawling slowly and painfully towards the truck. His face was bleeding and he had a black eye but he kept going. With a soft moan he pulled himself up to the truck door and opened it. 'Switch off the engine,' I heard him tell the driver. Then everything turned black and I heard no more.

The next thing I remember was lying on the footpath with Souperman and the driver bending over me.

'Don't worry,' said Souperman with a grin. 'You'll be all right.'

'Thanks for saving me,' I replied. 'But you're still a phoney. The real Superman can fly.'

'I can fly,' he told me, 'but I couldn't get the can of soup open. When you rushed out of my flat you took something of mine with you. Look in your pocket.'

I felt in my pocket and pulled out a hard object. It was a bright blue can-opener.

Santa Claws

'I've never seen anything like it before,' said the hypnotist. 'You say he had a perfectly normal mouth yesterday?'

'Yes,' said Mrs White, looking at the tiny hole in the middle of her son's face. 'A perfectly ordinary mouth just like anyone else. Now look at it. It's so small there is only just enough room to poke in one pea at a time. The only food he can get into his mouth is soup sucked up through a straw. He can't talk, he can't stick out his tongue and he can't eat.'

A squeaky, gobbling noise came out of Sean's little mouth hole. 'What did he say?' asked the hypnotist.

'He said he can't kiss either. He won't be able to kiss his girlfriend.'

The hypnotist bent over and had another look. 'Incredible,' he said. 'You couldn't even push a pencil through that little opening. I'm surprised a straw fits in. Are you sure you don't know how it happened?'

Sean nodded his head up and down vigorously.

'He has no idea,' said Mrs White. 'He can't remember anything about it at all. He just doesn't know what happened.'

'I don't normally work on Christmas Day,' said the hypnotist. 'But this is different. This is an emergency. What can I do to help?'

'We must find out where Sean's lips have gone,' answered Mrs White anxiously. 'The doctor won't do anything until they find out what happened.'

'But how is he going to tell us? He can't talk.'

Mrs White pulled out a sheaf of paper and a Biro. 'He is very good at writing. I thought he might write it down for us.'

The hypnotist slapped his knee enthusiastically. 'It might work,' he said. 'It just might work. Come and sit at the desk, Sean. We will see what you can remember.'

The hypnotist was very happy. He had never heard of a case of a lost mouth before. He decided he would write this one up. Everyone would be interested in the case of the boy with the smallest mouth in the world.

'Close your eyes,' he said to Sean in a dreamy voice. 'And take five deep breaths. At the end of the fifth breath you will open your eyes . . . You will remember what happened to your mouth . . . You will pick up the pen and write the whole thing down . . . The whole story . . . Right from the beginning . . .'

Sean closed his eyes and took five deep breaths. On the fifth breath he opened his eyes and picked up the pen. This is what he wrote.

1

It all started on Christmas Eve. I had to look after my little brat of a brother. 'Take him into Myer's and show him the Christmas windows,' said Mum. 'Keep him busy for about two hours while Helen and I wrap up his Christmas presents. We don't want him to see us wrapping them up, do we? After all, he still believes in Santa Claus.'

'But Mum, why can't Helen do it?' I said. 'I hate taking him shopping. He's a real pain. He gets lost and he won't do what he's told. It's Christmas Eve and I want to go and see my new girlfriend.'

'Your own brother comes before girlfriends,' she answered. 'And Helen is helping me wrap up the presents. Now off you go and don't give me any more arguments.'

It was no use. I had to go. I took Robert's hand and dragged him out to the tram stop. We lived in Fitzroy and it was only four stops on the tram to Myer's. Robert sat there sucking this dirty big icy pole with loud slurping noises. Everyone in the tram was looking at us. How embarrassing. I tried to pretend I wasn't with him but he kept asking me stupid questions like, 'How come you've got pimples on your chin, Sean?'

After what seemed like ten years we finally got to Myer's. 'I want to go and see Santa Claus,' whined Robert.

'No way,' I told him. 'I'm going to the record bar and that's that.' I grabbed him by the scruff of the neck and pulled him up to the record bar. I wanted to buy a couple of records. My favourite singers are Madonna and Sally Fritz. I have a very sexy poster of Sally Fritz at home on my bedroom wall. Mum doesn't like it. She says it's not very nice.

I didn't have time to buy a Sally Fritz record though. As soon as we got there Robert started up again. 'Santa Claus. I wanna see Santa Claus.'

'No,' I said.

'If you don't take me to Santa I'll pee on the floor,' he yelled.

'You wouldn't,' I said. 'Not in front of all these people.' I looked around. The place was packed out with people doing their last-minute Christmas shopping.

'I will so too,' he shouted at the top of his voice. He started to lift up the leg of one side of his short trousers. People were looking. I went pale. He was going to do it. He was really going to do it with all of Melbourne watching.

'You win,' I said weakly. 'I'll take you to see Santa.' We walked across to the lifts and squeezed in with the rest of the crowd. The lift stopped at the fifth floor and everyone except us got out.

'I think Santa is on the roof garden,' I told Robert.

'He better be,' was all Robert said.

The doors opened and we stepped out into the black night. The whole place had changed. There was no roof garden and no Santa. There weren't even any lights. 'It looks like it's different this year,' I told Robert. 'Santa must be on a different level.'

'You tricked me,' he screamed. 'You tricked me. I'm telling Mum. I'm dobbing on you. You promised to take me to see Santa.'

He really was a brat. I was sick of the whole thing. Why did I always have to get stuck with him? 'There isn't any Santa Claus,' I blurted out. 'It's only an old man dressed up with a cotton-wool beard and a pillow stuffed down his shirt. There's no such person as Santa Claus.'

'There is,' he screamed. 'There is, there is, there is.' He started stamping his foot on the ground. Then he turned and ran back to the lift. He jumped in just as the doors were closing. He was gone.

I rushed over to the closed doors. I had to find him and quick. If he went home alone Mum would murder me. I pushed the button on the wall and waited. That's when I heard the voice. A high, squeaky voice. 'Help,' it said. 'Help me. I can't hold on much longer.'

I looked around but I couldn't see anyone. 'Over here,' squeaked the voice. 'Over on the edge.' I ran over to the edge of the building. A steel rail ran all the way around to stop people falling over. I still couldn't see anything. Then I noticed a hand hanging on to one of the rails. Someone was dangling over the edge of the building. And we were six storeys up. I looked again at the hand – there was something strange about it. It wasn't an ordinary hand. It was a very hairy hand with claws on the end. Long, bent claws like those of a lion.

I peered over the edge and could just make out a dark figure hanging on for grim death. 'Here,' I said. 'Take my hand.' Another clawed hand grasped mine and I heaved the panting figure over the edge. It fell gasping to the floor.

'Thank you,' said the squeaky voice. 'You have just

saved the life of Santa Claws number 16,543.'

I peered at the weird little man who stood before me. He was short with a grubby face and dirty tangled beard that might once have been white. He was wearing a faded Santa Claus outfit which had a big hole in the pants. But the strangest thing about him were the claws on his hands. He held up his hands and extended the claws. They were long and sharp. He could have ripped my ear off with them if he wanted. 'Santa Claws,' he said again. 'Number 16,443.'

I grinned. 'You've got it wrong,' I said. 'It's spelt C-l-a-U-s, not C-l-a-W-s.'

The little man sighed. 'Yes, they've changed it. It should be spelt with a "w" but they thought it frightened the children. Nothing is the same these days.'

I started to laugh. 'Santa with claws. That's a good one. What would Santa want claws for?'

He looked cross. He didn't like me laughing at him. 'How do you think we get up all those chimneys?' he said. 'We have evolved claws just like giraffes have evolved long necks. We need the claws for scrambling up the chimneys.'

'We,' I said. 'What do you mean, "we"? There is only supposed to be one Santa and he certainly doesn't look like you.'

'Rubbish,' he replied. 'How could one Santa possibly get down all those chimneys on one night? There are millions of us.'

'Well, how come you're so grotty then?' I asked. Boy, this bloke was really a nut. I decided to humour him. He might be dangerous.

'You try scrambling up and down chimneys in the middle of the night and see how clean you stay,' he said hotly.

I decided to leave. I didn't want that little brat Robert getting home before me and telling Mum that I said there was no such person as Santa Claus. She wouldn't like that very much at all. I turned round and headed for the lift. Santa Claws came with me. The lift opened and we both stepped in. 'Where are you going?' I asked him.

'Home with you. You saved the life of a Santa Claws and now I have to reward you.'

'Think nothing of it,' I said. 'I don't need a reward.'

I didn't want this grubby, peculiar little clawed person walking around town with me.

'I have to give you your reward. It's the rules,' he insisted. 'You saved my life and now you and all the children in your family get two wishes each. Anything you want.'

This bloke was mad. I looked at his claws again. With one swipe he could rip my hair off. I didn't answer. I was too scared. The lift went straight down to the ground floor and we stepped out into the busy shop. I walked quickly, hoping he would get lost but no such luck. He stuck to me like glue. People were looking at us and whispering to each other but Santa Claws didn't seem to notice.

'Your fly is open,' I told him. 'Do your fly up for heaven's sake.' He bent over and pulled up his zip with one of his claws.

A lady with blue hair came bustling up to us. 'Shameful,' she said angrily. 'Disgusting. How can you walk around in front of all these children with that filthy Santa's outfit? How can they believe in Santa when you look like that?'

Just then the shop Santa came walking along with a sackful of toys over his shoulder. He had a huge woolly beard and shiny vinyl boots. My Santa waved to him. The shop Santa didn't wave back. People were starting to boo and shout at us. 'Let's get out of here,' I said. 'You're making a lot of trouble.'

We ran out of Myer's and jumped onto the tram. Santa Claws sat next to me. Everyone in the tram stared at us the whole way back. Santa was smelly. Even his breath smelled and he had yellow teeth.

'Don't they have toothbrushes at the North Pole?' I asked sarcastically.

Claws looked offended but he didn't say anything. When the conductor came I had to pay Claws' fare. He didn't have any money. 'Left it in the sleigh,' he said. 'When I made that forced landing at Myer's.'

2

Mrs White and the hypnotist snatched at each page as Sean finished writing it. 'Astonishing,' cried the hypnotist. 'Absolutely astonishing.'

Sean continued scribbling away, still in a trance.

3

We finally reached home and I opened the front door. 'Goodbye,' I said to the grubby little Santa. 'You enter by the chimney, I believe.'

To my amazement Claws pushed past me into the lounge room. Mum was out but my big sister Helen and Robert were sitting under the Christmas tree. Robert was crying with large fake tears. 'There he is,' he yelled pointing at me. 'He said there was no Santa. He said Santa was fake.'

Then Helen started in. 'What a mean thing, Sean. Fancy telling a little boy there is no Santa. And on Christmas Eve too. And don't think that bringing that horrible little person here will make things better. Where did you get your outfit?' she said to Claws. 'At the tip?'

'I am in a hurry,' said Claws. 'I have a lot more homes to visit tonight. You have two wishes each. Now quickly, you first, Sean.'

I looked at those claws. They were sharp enough to rip my face off. I decided to humour him. 'Sally Fritz,' I said. 'She is my favourite rock star. Bring Sally Fritz here for a visit.'

In a flash Sally Fritz stood before us. She held a microphone in her hand and was dressed in fishnet stockings, high-heeled shoes, lace panties and a blouse you could almost see through. She must have been in the middle of a concert before Claws produced her in front of us. Her eyes were staring wide. She couldn't work out what had happened. One minute she was on stage in New York and the next she was in an Australian lounge room with three kids and a scruffy little Santa looking at her.

'Repulsive,' said Helen. 'Mum will kill you for bringing someone like that here.'

Sally Fritz put her hands up to her mouth. Then she started to scream at the top of her voice. She was scared out of her wits.

'Quick,' I yelled at Claws. 'Get rid of her.' Sally Fritz vanished without a trace, just as quickly as she had arrived.

'Well, that's your two wishes gone,' said Claws. He looked at Robert. 'What's your first wish, lad? What do you want for Christmas?'

'A machine gun,' yelled Robert. 'A real machine gun.'

A grey, steel machine gun materialised in Robert's hands. It was the most real-looking machine gun I had ever seen. With a cry of joy Robert pulled the trigger. Bullets spat out with a deafening roar. They drilled holes across the floor, up the walls and across the ceiling. We all dived for cover behind the sofa. When the noise stopped the room was filled with bitter blue smoke. And the room was in ruins. There were smashed ornaments and pieces of plaster all over the room.

'Look,' gasped Helen. 'Mum's grandfather clock. It's smashed to smithereens. You're in big trouble, Robert. Mum will skin you alive for this.'

Robert started to cry. He always cried when he thought he was in trouble. 'I don't want it,' he yelled at Claws. 'I wish I never had it.'

The gun disappeared and the room and the clock returned to normal. 'That's your two wishes gone,' he said to Robert. Claws looked at Helen. 'Now it's your turn. What are your two wishes, my girl?'

Helen stamped her foot in temper. 'I don't like you,' she shouted. 'I wish none of us had ever heard of you.'

Suddenly we were alone in the room. Claws was gone. We all looked at each other. None of us could remember what had happened. We had no memories of Claws at all. He had wiped them all out. But for some reason I can remember them now.

4

The hypnotist was reading over Sean's shoulder. He nodded his head smugly. 'The trance,' he said to Mrs White excitedly. 'He remembers because of the trance.'

Sean continued writing furiously without saying a word. Not that he could with a mouth the size of a small marble.

5

Well, that's about the end of the story. I still don't know how I got my small mouth.

Helen was looking around the room. She couldn't even remember that Claws had been there and promised her two wishes. 'I feel as if someone was here,' she said. 'But I can't remember who it was or what happened.'

'Me too,' I said. 'I feel as if someone was talking to us. It had something to do with Santa Claus.'

I wished I hadn't said that. It reminded Robert of what happened at Myer's. He pointed a finger at me and started up again with the phoney tears. 'You said there was no Santa,' he yelled. 'You said he had cotton wool for a beard and a pillow down his shirt.'

Robert started jumping up and down and screaming. Then he ran out of the room and slammed the door.

Helen was mad at me. 'That was mean of you, Sean,' she said. 'You shouldn't have told him there was no Santa. I wish you didn't have such a big mouth.'

Cracking Up

Everybody gets a crabby teacher sometimes. It only stands to reason. Look at it this way: you are going to have lots of teachers in your life. One of them has to be crabby so don't worry about it.

Unless you get one like Mr Snapper.

Oh boy was he mean. He made every school day miserable. Every single one. But May the fifth was one of the worst. I remember it because it was the day we moved into a new house. This is what he did that terrible day.

1. Hit me over the knuckles with a ruler for holding the pen the wrong way.

2. Twisted my ear until it almost came off for asking Mike Dungey how you spell 'urinate'.

3. Made me say the nine times tables in front of the class when he knew I didn't know them.

4. Kept me in after school for putting chewing gum behind my ear.

5. Took me to the office for smiling (when he was telling me off). I can't help smiling. I am just a naturally smiling sort of person. Anyway, it wouldn't have hurt

him to smile a bit. Mr Snapper had never smiled in his life. He had a mean, boy-hating sort of face. You could tell what sort of mood he was in by the number of wrinkles on his face. There were so many that it took me ages to count them all. Two hundred wrinkles was a good day. Five hundred wrinkles was a bad day. They ran across his face like deep rivers of rage.

6.   Forced me to write out 'It is rude to stare' one hundred times.

7.   Made me take his rotten pot plant home for the night.

Snapper had two things in the grade that he liked: Lucy Watkins, who was his pet, and the maidenhair fern which stood in a fancy-looking pot on his desk.

Lucy Watkins was a real snob. She knew she was good-looking and she knew she was smart. She was the only person in the grade that Snapper liked. He nearly smiled at her once. That's how much of a pet she was. He always picked her to take messages to other teachers. He always held up her work for everyone else to look at. And he never told her off. Even when she did the same wrong things as the rest of us.

Anyway, just before home time on the fateful day, Snapper said, 'Lucy, you can choose the person to take the maidenhair fern home for the night.' It was supposed to be a big honour to take the maidenhair fern home and water it. The silly-looking plant couldn't stay at school because of the dust raised by the cleaners when they swept up.

Lucy Watkins went out to the front and looked around slowly. She stared straight at me. I didn't want to take the maidenhair fern home. I knew something would go wrong if I did. I shook my head. 'No,' I whispered under my breath. 'Not me. Please not me.'

She gave a mean sort of a smile and pointed at me. 'Him,' she said. 'Russell Dimsey. It will look nice in his new house.'

2

Snapper didn't look too sure. He didn't trust me to look after the maidenhair fern. 'It's all right Mr Snapper,' I said. 'Give the maidenhair fern to someone else for the night. I'm not too experienced with pot plants.'

Lucy Watkins pouted.

'Dimsey,' Snapper growled at me, 'I keep my word. Lucy has picked you so that is the end of the discussion. You take the maidenhair fern home for the night.' He put his face right up to mine so that I could smell his breath (it was horrible). 'And don't let anything happen to it. If that pot plant dies I will murder you.' He drew his finger across his throat like someone using a knife. 'That pot is an antique. If anything happens to it you are dead meat.' His wrinkles were about one centimetre away from my eyeballs. I could see the hairs in his nose twitching in the breeze when he breathed.

I shuddered.

It took me ages to get home. I missed the bus because I was kept in. And I had to carry the maidenhair fern home in my arms. It was heavy and the delicate fronds kept brushing against my nose and making me sneeze.

When I finally reached home there was someone waiting for me. It was Lucy Watkins. She was sitting on her bike with one foot on the footpath.

She smiled a mean smile. 'Seen the ghost yet?' she said.

'What?' I yelped.

'The ghost. The ghost of the boy who died in there.' She nodded at our new house.

I just looked at her. 'Someone died in our house?'

'Why do you think you got it so cheap?' she sneered. 'No one else would buy it.'

'Who died there?' I asked. I didn't like having to talk to Lucy Watkins but I had to find out.

'Well, two people actually. A boy called Samuel. He died a little before his uncle. His uncle snuffed it later. He was a magician called The Great Minto. He did tricks. And he kept things in bottles.'

'What sort of things?' I tried to stop my voice trembling.

Lucy Watkins smiled a secret sort of smile to herself. 'All sorts of things. Creepy things. Some people said he was a wizard.' The next bit was worst of all. She pointed up to the little attic window on the roof of the house. The window of my new bedroom. 'They both died in that room. And one of them is still there. On moonless nights Samuel's ghostly face looks out. An unhappy little face. The face of Samuel the sad spook.'

'Bulldust,' I said. 'You're making it up. You're just trying to make me scared.'

'You'll see,' said the horrible Lucy Watkins. 'Just you wait until the darkest part of the night. That's when he comes out.' She pointed to the maidenhair fern. Its lace-like fronds were gently waving in the wind. 'You had better not take it into the bedroom. You wouldn't want it to shrivel up from fright. Mr Snapper wouldn't like that.' She started laughing to herself. Cackling away like a chook. Then she rode off without another word.

3

I raced inside as fast as I could go. 'Mum,' I yelled, 'did you know that people died in my room? Two people?'

Mum didn't say anything. Not a word. I knew then that it was true. Now I knew how we could afford such a posh house. It was haunted. No one wanted to buy it so Mum got it cheap.

'I'm not sleeping up there,' I said. 'Not with a ghost hanging around.'

'There's no such thing as ghosts,' said Mum. 'It will be all right after the first night.'

'There isn't going to be any first night,' I yelled.

'Yes there is,' said Mum. 'And it's going to be tonight.'

I took the maidenhair fern up to the bedroom with me.

I put it on my bedside table where it would be safe. I knew that I would have to spend the night in the room. Mum was very strong-minded. She had been like that ever since Dad left home.

I looked at the maidenhair fern. I had to admit that it was a lovely plant. Even if it did belong to Snapper. I poured a little water into the pot. I didn't want the plant carking it in the night. There had already been enough deaths in this room and I didn't want any more.

It was around about midnight when I first saw Sad Samuel. I just sort of knew in my sleep that someone else was in the room. I could feel a presence. I didn't want to look but in the end I forced open my eyes and saw him. By the window. A little wispy ghost with an unhappy mouth. A boy of about my age. He just stood there looking at me sadly.

'Mum,' I screamed. 'A ghost. A ghost. He ... I.'

The ghost didn't look the least bit surprised. He shook his head as if I had done just what he expected.

Mum crashed into the room in her dressing gown. 'What's up Russell?' she yelled. 'Did you have a nightmare?'

I pointed to the ghost.

'What?' she said.

'Him. The ghost.' I managed to gasp.

Mum peered around the room. Then she stared straight at Sad Samuel. 'I can't see anything,' she said. 'It must have been a bad dream.'

'It wasn't a dream. He's still there. Over by the window.'

Mum walked over to the window. She walked right into Sad Samuel. And when I say into him I mean into him. She stood inside the ghost just as if he was a cloud or the end of a rainbow. And she didn't even see him.

I felt sick. My stomach was jumping up and down. My legs were wobbling. l pointed at Sad Samuel with a shaking hand. 'You're on him,' I screamed. 'You're in him. You're standing in him.'

Mum stepped out of Samuel and came over to the bed. 'There, there,' she said, stroking my hair with her hand. 'There's nothing there. It was only a bad dream. Go back to sleep. I'll leave the light on for you.'

Mum closed the door and went back to her room. Sad Samuel just stood there. I now know that you can only see ghosts if they want you to see them. He wanted me to see him. But not Mum.

4

The little ghost beckoned me with his finger. He wanted me to come to him. He drifted over to the door wiggling his finger at me as he went.

I shook my head. 'No fear,' I said in a shaking voice. 'I'm staying here.' There was no way I was going to follow a ghost. He could be heading anywhere.

He seemed upset. He beckoned me again. This time by waving his arm at me furiously. He didn't seem able to speak. Only to wave. 'You're in a dream,' I yelled.

'A nightmare. You aren't really there. I'm going back to sleep.'

I put my head on the pillow and pulled the blanket up over my head. Then I closed my eyes and told myself that there were no such things as ghosts.

The ghost got into bed with me.

No kidding. He snuck down under the covers and started tickling the bottom of my foot with a chilly little finger.

It wasn't like getting tickled by your mum or your dad where they dig their fingers in until it hurts. No. This was different. It was like being tickled by a puff of smoke or the breath of a feather. I tried to brush him off but my hand couldn't find anything to grab. It just passed through him.

I gave a nervous giggle. I was scared but I couldn't help myself. It tickled something terrible. 'Stop it,' I gasped between giggles. 'Please stop it.'

He didn't.

I started to laugh. Louder and louder. I tossed and turned. The bedcovers went up and down. I laughed and lurched. I hooted and heaved. The bed shook as I shrieked with laughter. 'Don't,' I cried. 'Please don't.' But Samuel the Sad Spook had no mercy. He tickled on and on and on. The bedclothes were scattered all across the room. I bucked up and down. Laughing and giggling.

Suddenly there was a terrible crash as I bumped into

the bedside table. The maidenhair pot fell on the floor and broke into a thousand pieces.

Everything stopped. My world froze.

The ghost no longer concerned me. If all it could do was tickle I didn't have much to worry about. But Snapper, he could do much worse than tickle. One look from him could give your warts the wanders. 'It's your fault,' I screamed at Samuel. 'Now look what you've done. You've broken it.' Boy, was I mad. Samuel went back to the window. Now he really looked sad. He was the most miserable ghost in the world. And I was the most miserable boy.

I couldn't mend the pot so I went down to the kitchen to find something else. All I could find was an empty margarine container. I scooped up the dirt from the bedroom floor and pushed the maidenhair fern back into the container. I hoped like mad that it would live.

Sad Samuel followed me around the house while I fixed up the plant. When I had finished he started beckoning to me again. He wanted me to follow him. 'You must be joking,' I yelled. I threw my pillow at him but it just passed straight through his head. His face grew even sadder. A little, broken bracelet of tears spilled down his cheeks.

He wagged his finger at me and shook his head again. He wanted something and he wasn't going to give up until he got it. I buried my head back under the blankets and tried to go to sleep. I hoped that I would wake up in the morning and find that it had all been a terrible dream.

It wasn't. In the morning the ghost was still there. And so was the broken pot. And the dead maidenhair fern. Yes it was dead. Brown and shrivelled. Just like I was going to be when Snapper finished with me.

I took the margarine container and the dirt down the backyard and looked for another plant. I hoped that I could replace the dead maidenhair with something else. All I could find was a stalk of sweet corn. One lonely stick of maize. I pulled it out and shoved it into the margarine container. It looked like a lamp post growing out of a thimble.

The ghost joined us for breakfast. Mum couldn't see it of course. It sat sorrowfully at the end of the table and watched me eat my muesli. I didn't feel sorry for it. Not after what it had done. All I could think about was school. And a slow, lingering death.

Sad Samuel followed me to school. No one except me could see him. 'Nick off,' I yelled. 'Go away, get lost.'

Miss Stevens, the librarian, was right behind me. She thought I was talking to her. 'What a rude boy,' she said. 'I will report this to Mr Snapper.'

My miserable mate followed me into school and sat down in the empty desk next to me. No one could see him except me.

'Dimsey,' growled Snapper, 'where's my maidenhair fern?'

5

I held out the sweet corn in the margarine container. Snapper's nose started to twitch. 'What's that?' he croaked.

'It's your plant,' I said weakly. My stomach was heaving around like a basketball. I felt sick.

Snapper's face resembled a wall that had just been dynamited. One second it was normal. The next it had a million cracks running across it. The wrinkles even ran up under his phoney-looking wig.

'What?' he shrieked. 'Where's my pot?'

'Broken,' I mumbled. 'The ghost broke it. It tickled me in bed.'

'Ghost,' he cried. 'Tickled.' He was spitting and spluttering. He was about to erupt.

I pointed at Sad Samuel. 'Him. He did it.'

Everyone looked at the empty seat. I was the only one who could see the sorrowful spectre. Sad Samuel looked at me gloomily. Then he got out of his seat and came towards me with outstretched hands. 'No,' I yelled. 'No. Not that. Not now.'

Snapper looked down at me with his boiling red face.

Sad Samuel's little fingers began to tickle under my armpits.

I bit my tongue. I did everything I could not to laugh. A little snort burst out. Only a little one but to me it sounded like a thousand bulls bellowing. No one knew why I was laughing.

Snapper grabbed me by my shirt front and sent me

spinning across the room. 'You think it's funny do you? You, you ...' He didn't finish the sentence. A large fish net hung beneath the classroom ceiling. It had shells and things inside it. A short length of fishing line with a hook on it hung down from one edge. I had never noticed the hook before.

The enraged teacher jumped up and down. The hook grabbed his wig and sent it swinging in the air as if it was on a piece of elastic. Snapper's bald head shone nakedly like a cracked duck's egg.

There was dead silence. Snapper glared. His icicle eyes swept the room. Anyone who so much as hinted at a smile was dead. Gone. History. Every eye looked down. Every knee trembled.

The feathery fingers of Sad Sam went to work. I choked a chuckle. I smothered a smile. I grappled with a grin. 'No,' I screamed. Then I began to laugh. Great shuddering, gasping laughs. 'Oh, ooh. Ha. Haaa. Har Har. HaaaaaaHaaaaaaa. Ahhhhhh.'

Snapper snapped. He came towards me with outstretched hands. A madman. A monster.

The laughter spread like measles. The whole grade broke up. They hooted and howled. Lucy Watkins was the only one who didn't laugh. She jumped up and grabbed at the wig. The hook caught on her sleeve. She pulled and pulled. The whole net came crashing down and buried everyone. A squirming, cackling catch of kids.

I crawled out from under the net and nicked off. I raced out of that school as fast as I could go. The laughter followed me all the way up the street.

I couldn't believe it. I was running off from school. I had never wagged it before. I was alone (if you don't count the dejected ghost who tagged behind). I knew I was in big trouble. And all because of that miserable little ghost.

6

We trudged across the park. I couldn't go home yet. It was too early and Mum might catch me. I suddenly spied a hose pipe. I grabbed it and squirted Sam. 'Buzz off,' I yelled. 'Go and make someone else unhappy.' The water went straight through him. He just stood there with his little downturned mouth and beckoned me to follow him.

I didn't. Across the road was the cemetery. I had an idea. Maybe if I walked through there the little ghoul would disappear into a grave. It was worth a try.

We wandered among the graves for a while. You would think a ghost would smile in a graveyard but no luck. He was worse than ever. A real sad sack.

A little way off a burial was in progress. Mourners dressed in black were lowering a coffin into a grave. I walked up quietly. I didn't want to disturb them. The priest was saying a few words. 'Friends,' he said, 'this is a sad occasion for all of us.'

Cold little fingers began working away under my armpits. 'Oh no,' I groaned. 'Not again. Not here.' I fell to the ground. It was agony. It was murder. The ghost was tickling me in the middle of a burial ceremony. I rolled about laughing and screaming. Tears ran down my face. I rolled right up to the edge of the grave laughing and chuckling. The legs of the mourners surrounded me like a forest.

Suddenly it stopped. He stopped tickling. It was like a rainstorm passing as quickly as it had come. The people in black all looked down at me. They were mad. They were furious. You aren't supposed to laugh at funerals.

'The fiend,' said the priest.

'The little savage,' said someone else.

'Get him.'

'Let him have it.'

A large man grabbed me and pulled me up by my collar. I squirmed and wriggled and broke free. I ran for it. I went like the dickens. A few of the mourners came pelting after me but in the end they gave up. How embarrassing.

I puffed down the street with Sad Samuel following. Then I stopped. He was beckoning at me with his wiggling finger. 'I get it,' I said. 'You are going to keep tickling me until I come. That's it isn't it?' He nodded.

'Okay,' I told him. 'You win. Lead on. I'll follow.' I couldn't take any more of it. This little ghost was wrecking my life.

I followed him along the street. He went home and into the back shed. He pointed to a spade. 'You want me to bring the spade?' I asked. He nodded. I guessed that his feathery fingers were weak. They could tickle but they couldn't lift anything heavy.

I picked up the spade and followed the floating spirit. Through the back fence he went. Over the back fence I scrambled. Into the forest. Along a track and into a little clearing. Sad Samuel pointed to the ground in the middle of the clearing. I started to dig. After about an hour of digging my spade hit something. I pulled it out. A black leather case.

Sam was nodding but not smiling. It seemed as if he couldn't even manage a grin. He put his fingers in his mouth and blew. At least I think that's what he did. It looked as if he was whistling. A silent spook whistle.

We sat down and waited. After a bit two more ghosts arrived. Miserable little fellows. By now I was used to sad spectres. They didn't bother me at all.

Sam pointed to the case. I opened it. Inside the lid was written:

THE

GREAT MINTO

MASTER MAGICIAN

The case was filled with cotton wool. I felt around inside the cotton wool and pulled out four small blue bottles. Three of them had one word written on the label.

GRIN

on one.

SMILE

on the next. And

CHUCKLE

on the next.

The last bottle had no label at all. Not a word.

7

I pulled the stopper off the first bottle. Nothing happened. Then: a whisper, a sigh, a puff of cloud. It twisted and hummed. And headed for the nearest ghost. It disappeared into his open mouth. His sorrowful face was transformed. He grinned a ghostly grin.

I opened the second bottle. A whisper, a sigh, a puff of cloud. It twisted and hummed. And went straight to the next ghost. It went in his right ear and vanished. The look of misery left his face. The second ghost gave the biggest smile I have ever seen.

The third bottle, the one with the chuckle, was the same. As soon as I opened it: a whisper, a sigh, a puff of cloud. It twisted and hummed. And sped straight into

Sam's left ear. He wasn't Sad Sam any more. He chuckled silently to himself.

I looked at them for a while. They were all so happy. So glad to be dead (if you know what I mean). 'I get it,' I said at last. 'Minto The Magician somehow stole your happiness. Your smiles and grins. He put them in bottles and left you miserable. Now you've got them back.'

The three grinning ghosts nodded. I held out the last bottle. The one with no label. 'Here,' I said, 'take this as well.' They shook their heads. 'Whose is it?' I asked.

Sam put his hands together and rested his head on them like someone sleeping. 'A dead person?' I said.

He shook his head.

'A dead ghost?'

He nodded.

'Can ghosts die?' I asked.

They all nodded.

'But then you would have the ghost of a ghost.'

By this time they were not listening. They started to spin. Faster and faster. And then, like propeller blades, they became invisible. They spun themselves into nothingness. They were gone.

I never saw them again.

My feet dragged along the ground as I walked home. I had got rid of Sad Sam. But there was big trouble ahead. Tomorrow I would have to go back to school. I was really in for it.

When I reached home Mum was waiting. She looked

at me for a long time without saying anything. She always did that when she wanted me to feel guilty about something. In the end she said, 'The school rang. They told me all about the things you have done. Terrible things. You needn't think that I'm going to get you out of it. You will just have to front up to the school in the morning and take your punishment. And you can go up to your room now and have no tea.'

I went up to my room. It was no good telling Mum about the ghosts. She would never believe me. I thought about running away. But in the end I decided to face the music. Face Snapper that is.

8

It was worse than I thought. The whole school was assembled. I was called to the front. Two hundred pairs of eyes stared at me. Snapper snarled. 'This boy,' he said in a loud voice, 'has disgraced us all. He ran away from school. He laughed at a funeral. He broke my antique vase. He told Miss Stevens to nick off. He talks to himself. And worst of all ... he tells terrible lies.'

Everyone was staring at me. All the kids. All the teachers. My head swam. It wasn't fair. I was innocent. Something came over me. I don't know what. I started yelling. 'It was the ghost. The tickling ghost.' I pulled out the blue bottle and waved it around. 'His smile was stolen. Put in a bottle. I gave it back to him.'

The lines on Snapper's face united in the biggest frown

the world has ever seen. His wrinkles looked like a thousand upside down horseshoes. 'Stop. Enough,' he shrieked. He snatched the bottle from my hand and threw it to the ground. It smashed into a thousand pieces.

There was a whisper, a sigh. A puff of cloud. It twisted and hummed. And headed straight up Snapper's nostrils. It had gone to the nearest miserable person.

'Your punishment ...' he said. And then he stopped, like a startled rabbit. Something was happening to his wrinkles. They were starting to twitch. To move. Like rheumatic sticks they began to bend upwards. You could almost hear them crack. For years and years they had drooped meanly down his chin. Now they were curving upwards. His wrinkles turned to crinkles.

Snapper was smiling. The bottled smile had found a new home.

He beamed at me. 'There will be no punishment,' he said generously. 'Not for a nice boy like you.'

I went and sat down.

Mr Snapper was a terrific teacher. The best I ever had. The class even gave him a nickname.

Smiley.

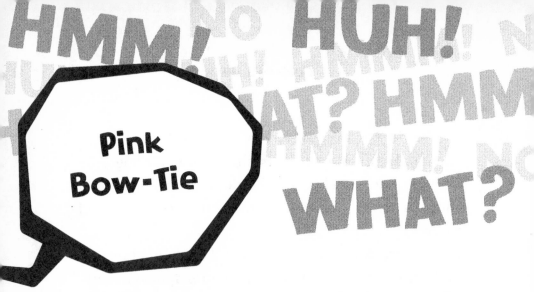

Pink Bow-Tie

Well, here I am again, sitting outside the Principal's office. And I've only been at school for two days. Two lots of trouble in two days! Yesterday I got the strap for nothing. Nothing at all.

I see this bloke walking along the street wearing a pink bow-tie. It looks like a great pink butterfly attacking his neck. It is the silliest bow-tie I have ever seen. 'What are you staring at, lad?' says the bloke. He is in a bad mood.

'Your bow-tie,' I tell him. 'It is ridiculous. It looks like a pink vampire.' It is so funny that I start to laugh my head off.

Nobody tells me that this bloke is Old Splodge, the Principal of the school. He doesn't see the joke and he gives me the strap. Life is very unfair.

Now I am in trouble again. I am sitting here outside Old Splodge's office waiting for him to call me in.

Well, at least I've got something good to look at. Old Splodge's secretary is sitting there typing some letters.

She is called Miss Newham and she is a real knockout. Every boy in the school is in love with her. I wish she was my girlfriend, but as she is seventeen and I am only fourteen there is not much hope. Still, she doesn't have a boyfriend so there is always a chance.

She is looking at me and smiling. I can feel my face going red. 'Why have you dyed your hair blond?' she asks sweetly. 'Didn't you know it is against the school rules for boys to dye their hair?'

I try to think of a very impressive answer but before I can say anything Old Splodge sticks his head around the office door. 'Come in, boy,' he says.

I go in and sit down. 'Well, lad,' says Old Splodge. 'Why have you dyed your hair? Trying to be a surfie, eh?' He is a grumpy old boy. He is due to retire next year and he does not want to go.

I notice that he is still wearing the pink bow-tie. He always wears this bow-tie. He cannot seem to live without it. I try not to look at it as I answer him. 'I did not dye my hair, sir,' I say.

'Yesterday,' says Splodge, 'when I gave you six of the best, I noticed that you had black hair. Am I correct?'

'Yes, sir,' I answer.

'Then tell me, lad,' he says. 'How is it that your hair is white today?' I notice that little purple veins are standing out on his bald head. This is a bad sign.

'It's a long story,' I tell him.

'Tell me the long story,' he says. 'And it had better be good.'

I look him straight in the eye and this is what I tell him.

2

I am a very nervous person. Very sensitive. I get scared easily. I am scared of the dark. I am scared of ghost stories. I am even scared of the Cookie Monster on *Sesame Street*. Yesterday I am going home on the train after getting the strap and I am in a carriage with some very strange people. There is an old lady with a walking stick, grey hair and gold wire-rim glasses. She is bent right over and can hardly walk. There is also a mean, skinny-looking guy sitting next to me. He looks like he would slit your throat for two bob. Next to him is a kid of about my age and he is smoking. You are not allowed to smoke when you are fourteen. This is why I am not smoking at the time.

After about five minutes a ticket collector puts his head in the door. He looks straight at the kid who is smoking. 'Put that cigarette out,' he says. 'You are too young to smoke.'

The kid does not stop smoking. He picks up this thing that looks like a transistor and twiddles a knob. Then he starts to grow older in front of our eyes. He just slowly changes until he looks about twenty-five. 'How's that?' he says to the ticket collector. 'Am I old enough now?'

The ticket collector gives an almighty scream and runs down the corridor as fast as his legs can take him. The rest of us just sit there looking at the kid (who is now a man) with our mouths hanging open.

'How did you do that?' trembles the old lady. She is very interested indeed.

'Easy,' says the kid-man as he stands up. The train is stopping at a station. 'Here,' he says throwing the transistor thing onto her lap. 'You can have it if you want.' He goes out of the compartment, down the corridor and gets off the train.

We all stare at the box-looking thing. It has a sliding knob on it. Along the right-hand side it says OLDER and at the left end it says YOUNGER. On the top is a label saying AGE RAGER.

The mean-looking bloke sitting next to me makes a sudden lunge forward and tries to grab the Age Rager but the old lady is too quick for him. 'No you don't,' she says and shoves him off. Quick as a flash she pushes the knob a couple of centimetres down towards the YOUNGER end.

Straight away she starts to grow younger. In about one minute she looks as if she is sixteen. She is sixteen. She looks kind of pretty in the old lady's glasses and old-fashioned clobber. It makes her look like a hippy. 'Whacko,' she shouts, throwing off her shawl. She throws the Age Rager over to me, runs down the corridor and jumps off the train just as it is pulling out of the station.

As the train speeds past I hear her say, 'John McEnroe, look out!'

'Give that to me,' says the mean-looking guy. Like I told you before, I am no hero. I am scared of my own shadow. I do not like violence or scary things so I hand over the Age Rager to Mean Face.

He grabs the Age Rager from me and pushes the knob nearly up to the end where it says YOUNGER. Straight away he starts to grow younger but he does not stop at sixteen. In no time at all there is a baby sitting next to me in a puddle of adult clothes. He is only about one year old. He looks at me with a wicked smile. He sure is a mean-looking baby. 'Bad Dad Dad,' he says.

'I am not your Dad Dad,' I say. 'Give me that before you hurt yourself.' The baby shakes his head and puts the Age Rager behind his back. I can see that he is not going to hand it over. He thinks it is a toy.

Then, before I can move, he pushes the knob right up to the OLDER end. A terrible sight meets my eyes. He starts to get older and older. First he is about sixteen, then thirty, then sixty, then eighty, then one hundred and then he is dead. But it does not stop there. His body starts to rot away until all that is left is a skeleton.

I give a terrible scream and run to the door but I cannot get out because it is jammed. I kick and shout but I cannot get out. I open the window but the train is going too fast for me to escape.

And that is how my hair gets white. I have to sit in that carriage with a dead skeleton for fifteen minutes. I am terrified. I am shaking with fear. It is the most horrible thing that has ever happened to me. My hair goes white in just fifteen minutes. I am frightened into being a blonde. When the train stops I get out of the window and walk all the rest of the way home.

'And that,' I say to Splodge, 'is the truth.'

3

Splodge is fiddling with his pink bow-tie. His face is turning the same colour. I can see that he is about to freak out. 'What utter rubbish,' he yells. 'Do you take me for a fool? Do you expect me to believe that yarn?'

'I can prove it,' I say. I get the Age Rager out of my bag and put it on his desk.

Splodge picks it up and looks at it carefully. 'You can go now, lad,' he says in a funny voice. 'I will send a letter home to your parents telling them that you are suspended from school for telling lies.'

I walk sadly back to class. My parents will kill me if I am suspended from school.

For the next two weeks I worry about the letter showing up in the letter box. But nothing happens. I am saved.

Well, it is not quite true that nothing happens. Two things happen: one good and one bad. The good thing is that Splodge disappears and is never seen again.

The bad thing is that Miss Newham gets a boyfriend. He is about eighteen and is good-looking.

It is funny, though. Why would she go out with a kid who wears pink bow-ties?

Unhappily Ever After

Albert pulled up his socks and wiped his sweaty hands on the seat of his pants. He did up the top button of his shirt and adjusted his school tie. Then he trudged slowly up the stairs.

He was going to get the strap.

He knew it, he just knew it. He couldn't think of one thing he had done wrong but he knew Mr Brown was going to give him the strap anyway. He would find some excuse to whack Albert – he always did.

Albert's stomach leapt up and down as if it was filled with jumping frogs. Something in his throat stopped him from swallowing properly. He didn't want to go. He wished he could faint or be terribly sick so he would have to be rushed off to hospital in an ambulance. But nothing happened. He felt his own feet taking him up to his doom.

He stood outside the big brown door and trembled. He was afraid but he made his usual resolution. He would not cry. He would not ask for mercy. He would not even wince. There was no way he was going to give Mr Brown that pleasure.

He took a deep breath and knocked softly.

Inside the room Brown heard the knock. He said nothing. Let the little beggar suffer. Let the little smart alec think he was in luck. Let him think no one was in.

Brown heard Albert's soft footsteps going away from the door. 'Come in, Jenkins,' he boomed.

The small figure entered the room. He wore the school uniform of short pants, blue shirt and tie. His socks had fallen down again.

Albert looked over to the cupboard where the long black strap hung on a nail.

Brown towered over Albert. He wore a three-piece suit with a natty little vest. He frowned. The wretched child showed no fear. He didn't beg, he didn't cry. He just stood there.

In the corner a grandfather clock loudly ticked away the time that lay between Albert and his painful fate. The soft 'clicks' of a cricket match filtered through the open window. Albert pretended he was out there playing with the others.

Brown suddenly thrust his hand into his vest pocket and pulled out a piece of paper. He pushed it into Albert's face. Somehow Albert managed to focus his eyes on it and see the words:

BALD HEAD BROWN WENT TO TOWN,

RIDING ON A PONY

Underneath was a drawing of a bald-headed person riding a horse.

'I didn't do it, sir,' said Albert truthfully.

Brown looked at Albert's thick black hair and wiped his hand over his own bald head. The room started to swirl, his forehead throbbed. Jenkins was lying. And he was unafraid. He should be whimpering and crawling like the others.

Brown rushed over to the cupboard and grabbed the strap. 'Hold out your hand,' he shrieked.

Then he rained blow after blow on the helpless, shaking child.

2

Brown sprawled in his leather chair. He was out of breath. He knew he had overdone it this time. He had lost his temper. He wondered if Jenkins would have any bruises. Some of the other teachers might kick up a fuss if Jenkins showed them bruises. Fortunately this was a boarding school and there were no parents around to complain. Brown suddenly wished he had hit Jenkins even harder. He looked out of the window at the sparkling sea nearby. It was the perfect day to be on the water. He decided to go out in his rowing boat. It might help him to forget Jenkins and all the other little horrors in the school.

The sea was flat and mirrored the glassy clouds that beckoned from the horizon. Brown pushed out the small boat and it knifed a furrow through the inky water. He put his back to the oars and soon he was far out to sea with the shore only a thin line in the distance.

Brown was glad to be out of reach of the children he hated, but something was wrong. The sea didn't feel the same, or smell the same. He thought he heard voices – watery, giggling voices. He looked around but there was not another craft to be seen. He was alone on an enamelled ocean.

The boat began to rock gently and Brown felt it gripped in a strong current. It was carrying him away from the land. He tried to turn the boat around and pull for the shore but the current was too strong. The boat sped faster and faster and then began to rock wildly. Brown felt the oars snatched from his hands by the speeding tide. He fell with a crash to the bottom of the boat and clung to the edges as it bucketed through the swirling water.

Laughter filled the still air and echoed in his head. Brown plucked up his courage and peeped over the side of the boat. It was cutting a large circle through the foam, getting neither closer nor further away from the shore.

Suddenly a piercing pain shot through Brown's head. He just had time to notice that the sea had opened up into a large funnel. The water was twirling as if it was going down a plughole. Brown collapsed into blackness as the boat slipped over the rim of the abyss.

3

When he awoke the pain had gone. Brown found himself still in the boat. It was speeding around the inside of the funnel at an enormous rate. He looked up at the rim and beyond that to the clouds which spun like patterns on a drunken dinner plate.

The boat maintained its position, neither falling lower in the funnel nor rising to the surface high above. Brown peered cautiously over the edge and looked down. He gasped as he saw the spiralling funnel twist down and end in jagged claws of rock which clutched hungrily upwards from the bed of the sea.

Brown found his gaze drawn into the shining black wall of the vortex. With a shock he saw a scene unfold within the sea. Two enormous lobsters were holding a struggling, naked man over a pot of boiling water. As they dropped the figure to his death, Brown was sure he heard one of them say, 'I've heard they scream as they hit the water. I don't believe it myself.'

This scene repeated itself every time the boat circled. It was like a record stuck in a groove. Brown saw it a hundred times, a thousand times. It was horrible. He didn't want to watch but his eyes were held by an unseen force. Finally he grabbed the side of the boat, closed his eyes and rocked with all his strength.

The boat slipped down a few notches. When he opened his eyes another scene unfolded. A fat man sat peering through a window at a table laden with food. Trifles, jellies, cakes, peaches and strawberries. Around the table thin, ghostly children sat stuffing themselves and laughing happily. The fat man banged on the window. He was hungry. He wanted to get in. But the children couldn't see him, couldn't hear him and the man banged in vain. He was starving – never to be satisfied.

Brown watched, horrified as the same drama played again and again. Where was this place? Was it hell? Were these people having done to them what they had done to others? For ever? Over and over again?

Brown knew every groove would contain a similar horror. He could stand it no longer. He wanted to see no more. He decided to get it over and done with. He grabbed the sides of the boat and rocked and rocked and rocked. The boat plummeted to the waiting rocks below.

There was a tearing, crushing, splintering as Brown's last scream fled his tortured body.

4

Brown awoke and looked around. With relief he saw he was still in his study. The grandfather clock ticked away loudly in the corner and the soft 'clicks' of a game of cricket filtered through the open window. His leather chair rested in its usual place.

He must have had a nightmare. For a second, but only a second, he wondered if there had been some message in his terrible dream. Then he dismissed the thought and tried to think of another excuse to give Jenkins a belting. He wasn't the least bit sorry for what he had done.

It was then he noticed the room seemed different. The grandfather clock looked taller than usual and the window appeared further from the floor. Everything was bigger. He looked down and saw he was wearing short pants. And his socks were hanging down around his shoes. He was dressed in the school uniform.

And worse – oh – much worse. Albert Jenkins was in the room. A huge Jenkins. He wore a three-piece suit with a natty little vest.

Jenkins shoved a piece of paper into Brown's face. Then he rushed over to the cupboard and grabbed the strap.

Wake Up to Yourself

Look around you.

What do you see?

Maybe your bedroom with games and posters and socks on the floor?

Come on – put down the book and have a look. Right now.

Are you in the back seat of the car with your little brother next to you? Or maybe in school wishing it was home time? You might be outside reading under a tree. Wherever it is – have a good look.

How real is it?

What if it is a dream? Yes, really. What if you are going to wake up somewhere else and it is all gone? Mum, Dad, your pesky little brother. Teachers, school, friends. All gone and you are somewhere else.

In the real world.

What about that, eh?

1

They are picking teams for a football match. Oh no.

It is not one of those games run by the teachers where

everyone gets a fair go. Nothing like that. No, it is a match organised at lunchtime by the kids. There are twenty-one of us lined up.

Out the front are the captains – Keeble and Fitzy. They are the best footballers in the school. They are big and tough and mean. If they crack a joke everyone laughs. Even when it is not funny.

Now they are picking their teams.

'Henderson,' yells Fitzy. Henderson is a fantastic runner. His team will probably win. He walks out and stands next to Fitzy. He knew that he would be the first to be picked.

'Black,' calls out Keeble. Robert Black is also a good footballer. He is small but he is a great kick. He grins and walks over to Keeble.

They keep calling out names.

'Swan.'

'Tootle.'

'Rogers.'

'Tang.'

Each kid walks forward when his name is called and stands next to his captain.

There are twenty-one kids. Ten per side not counting the captains. One boy will be left out. Some poor kid will not be picked. He will be left standing there and everyone will know that he is the worst footballer in the school.

'Please, God, don't let it be me. Please.'

There is a horrible feeling in my stomach. It feels heavy.

'Peters.'

Alan Peters steps out and stands behind Keeble. 'What about Simon Duck? Please call Simon Duck,' I think to myself. But no one calls me.

There are only a few kids in line now. We all look at each other hoping we will not be left at the end.

Now there are only two left. Me and John Hopkins.

'Hopkins,' yells Fitzy. Hopkins gives a big sigh of relief and runs out the front.

Everyone looks at me standing there all alone.

'You can have plucked Duck,' says Fitzy.

The kids all laugh.

'No thanks,' says Keeble. 'We're not that desperate.'

I can feel a hot blush crawling over my face as the boys run off to start the match. I am left on my own with the little kids. Oh, the shame of it. I wish I was an ant so that I could crawl down a hole and never be seen again.

But I am not an ant so I go into the toilets instead. I sit down in a cubicle where no one can see me. I stay there all lunchtime. The minutes drag by. No one knows where I am. No one cares. Finally the bell rings and I am saved. I can go into class.

2

After school I make my lonely way home. The other kids are in twos and threes but no one ever wants to walk home with me.

I think about my little brother. The one I don't have. But will soon. Mum is having a baby and I am sure it will be a boy. He will be my friend. My mate. I will look after him. Show him a thing or two. We will be the best friends in the world.

What is it about me, I wonder? Why don't I have any friends? I ask kids home but they don't come. Is it because I am no good at football? I just don't know.

I would give anything to have a friend.

I reach the front gate of our house. The grass is long and weedy. It is the worst garden in the street. I would cut the lawn for Mum but the lawn mower conked out and we can't afford to get it fixed.

To be perfectly honest, we are broke.

The phone was cut off the other day because Mum couldn't pay the bill. This is a bit of a worry.

'What if the baby comes in the middle of the night?' I say. 'What then?'

Mum pats her swollen tummy. 'You run down to the phone box and ring for a taxi,' she says.

'What if I'm not here?' I say.

Mum gives me a big, warm smile. 'But you will be, won't you, darling?'

She is right, of course. Where else would I be? No one

is going to ask me to sleep round at their place, are they? Not me. No way. To tell you the truth my heart is breaking.

We have chips for tea. I smother mine in tomato sauce and sit down on my mattress to watch TV. We only have one bedroom so I sleep in the lounge on a mattress.

Mum is really tired. It has been a hot day and she is worn out, what with carrying the baby inside her and doing all the housework.

She is the best Mum in the world. She has a great big grin when she talks. She always makes me feel that I am a sort of superhero. She wears beads and long dresses with fringes and has a little diamond stud in her nose. Sometimes she goes down the street with a flower in her hair. In bare feet too.

I would do anything for her. I don't mind not having a father. Mum will do. And the baby. When the baby comes I will have a mate.

But I just hope that he doesn't decide to arrive in the middle of the night.

'Go and lie down,' I say to Mum. 'And I will make you a nice cuppa.'

Mum drinks her cuppa and falls asleep. After a while I decide to go to bed. I jump onto my mattress and pull up the checked blanket. My eyelids begin to droop.

I start to fall asleep. Or am I falling awake? That is the question.

3

When I open my eyes I am back in the schoolyard and the kids are picking sides for the football match.

My mattress is on the asphalt in the schoolyard. I am dressed in my school clothes, not my pyjamas.

'Hey, Duck,' yells Fitzy. 'Get up and stand in line.'

I jump up, embarrassed.

Fitzy does not seem to see my mattress. No one does. Straight away I know that this is a dream. Or maybe a nightmare. I am back at school and they are picking teams again.

Well, I am not going to do it. There is no way that I am going to get back in that line. And not be picked. And sit on the toilet all lunchtime. And walk home on my own all over again. This is just a bad dream and I will get out of it as quick as I can.

I decide to wake myself up. I pinch my arm. Hard. And it hurts. I do not wake up. This does not seem like a dream. It seems real. I shake my head. I pull my hair. The kids all look at me as if I am mad.

'Duck is pulling out his feathers,' shouts Keeble.

A big laugh goes up. How can I get out of this? How did I get into it? On the mattress, that's how. Well, that's how I will get home.

But the mattress is fading. And so is my ticket back. I feel as if I am standing at the station and the train is going without me. Before I can move, the mattress vanishes completely. I know straight away that I am stuck in this dream. Or was the other world a dream? And is this the real one? I really can't tell.

All the kids are looking at me. They want to start choosing the teams. Oh no. Now I have to get in the line again. And not be picked.

But wait, what is this? There is another kid in the group who wasn't there last time. He has a cheeky grin. And on his arm is a little birthmark. It looks like a small map of Australia.

'Come on, Simon,' he says with a wink. 'Who wants to play footy anyway?'

'Yeah,' I say. 'I sure don't.'

'Me neither,' says Tootle. He comes over with Tang, who also does not want to play.

We all grin at each other. Fitzy and Keeble are not too pleased but they don't say anything. I hope they are not going to make trouble for me after school.

I spend all lunch time hanging out with the boy with the birthmark. It turns out that he is my best friend. His name is Matthew but I call him Possum. We have always done everything together – me and Possum.

After school Possum and I walk home together. We reach the front gate of a house. The grass is long and weedy. It is the worst garden in the street. It seems familiar. I feel as if I know this place. As if I should be going inside.

I open the gate.

'Where are you going?' says Possum.

I blink and scratch my head. There is an image in my head. A pretty woman with a flower in her hair. And beads. It is like a far-off dream.

I look at Possum. 'To see er . . . Mum,' I say.

Possum stares at me as if I have gone mad. 'Simon,' he says. 'Your mum died when you were born.'

I try to hold on to the image of a lovely lady who has a big grin whenever she talks. And a diamond stud in her nose. But the vision fades away, just like the mattress. And I am left staring at Possum with my eyes filled with tears.

'Where do I live?' I say.

Possum puts his arm around my shoulders. 'Don't be a donkey,' he smiles. 'You know that you live with us.'

4

We walk past the house with the weedy garden and go out into the countryside. As Possum talks I remember things. How we live in a big house out of town. How his dad is a real great guy. His mum is terrific too. I call them Mum and Dad even though they aren't my real parents.

Possum and I have a room each. And our own TV. We have always been the best of mates. We are like brothers.

We take the short cut across Crazy Mac's paddock when we suddenly hear something. Voices. My heart starts to pump fast and my legs feel like lead.

I know those voices. They belong to Fitzy and Keeble. Every night after school they wait for us. They are bullies. They like to scare us. 'Get them,' yells Fitzy.

I look at Possum. We are not fast runners. We are skinny kids. Fitzy and Keeble will catch us for sure. Then they will . . . I can't bear to think about it. I hate pain.

But Possum is not too worried. He winks at me. 'The river,' he whispers.

We turn and run for it. We bolt towards the river. Across the dry grass, slipping on cow pats. Stumbling, falling, scrambling up and racing on. My chest hurts because I am running so fast. I look behind and see that Fitzy and Keeble are catching up. Oh no. We are gone. Who will save us?

Possum, that's who. By the river is a huge gum tree. It has a rope hanging from a branch. The rope is hooked up on our side of the river. We can use it to swing across to the other side. Possum winks again and I know that he is the one who has put the rope there.

I do not wink back. This is no time for winking. Keeble and Fitzy are nearly up to us. There is no time for two to swing across the river. One can swing and the other will be caught.

'You go,' I yell.

'No, you,' says Possum.

I look down at the water. It is deep and flowing fast. I look at the safety of the other side. Fitzy and Keeble are running and shouting and waving sticks. I am scared stiff. I would love to swing away but I can't leave Possum on his own.

'Together,' shouts Possum.

Fitzy throws himself towards me in a dive for my legs.

'Jump,' I yell.

We grab the rope and launch ourselves over the muddy river. Fitzy crashes onto the bank with a grunt.

Down we swing, down, down, down towards the murky river. We skim across the surface and our feet trail in the water. Then up, up, up towards the opposite side. I let go and tumble onto the bank. Possum touches ground too but he is smart enough to hang onto the rope so that it doesn't swing back to Fitzy and Keeble.

They are angry. Furious. Crazy. Like two baboons. They jump up and down, spitting with rage on the other side of the river.

Possum makes a rude sign with his fingers. It makes Fitzy and Keeble even worse. Possum is really game. He is a great kid. He has saved us. Oh, I would do anything for Possum. He is the best mate in the world.

We walk off towards home. 'What about tomorrow?' I say. 'They will be waiting at the rope.'

Possum walks along with a bit of a swagger. 'But we won't be going that way,' he says. 'Will we?'

5

When we get home there is no one there. We search around for a bit and finally find the place where the chocolate biscuits are hidden. We take them up to my room and start munching on them.

'That river is deep,' I say. 'What if we had fallen in?'

'Yeah,' says Possum. 'We could have drowned.'

'What would it be like to be dead?' I say.

Possum thinks for a bit. 'I don't know,' he says. 'Sometimes I think that if I wasn't here no one else would be either. I can't imagine the world without me in it too.'

'Yeah,' I say. 'Sometimes I think that it is all a dream. And that if I woke up you would be gone. Just as if you were never there.'

We both stop talking and think about this for a bit. All that can be heard is the thoughtful munching of chocolate biscuits.

After about four biscuits each we are still silent. I know that we are both thinking about the same thing. We are thinking how horrible it would be to not have each other. To be in a world without our best mate.

At that exact moment something starts to happen. Over in the corner a shape starts to shimmer and wobble. A sort of ghostly platform on the floor.

'Look at that,' I yell.

'What?' says Possum.

'Something's there,' I whisper. 'A sort of ghost thing.'

'I can't see anything,' says Possum.

My mouth falls open as it takes shape. The image in the corner. It is a mattress. With a checked blanket. I know that I have seen it before.

'A mattress,' I gasp.

Possum is staring at me and shaking his head.

'You sure are a funny guy, Simon,' he says. 'There is no mattress there.'

I look at him and I look at the mattress. It seems to be calling me. But I don't want to go.

'If I get on that mattress,' I say. 'I will not be coming back. You will be gone. I will never see you again.'

Possum is not sure whether to believe me or not. He can tell that I really think there is a mattress there. Even if he can't see it.

I feel a sort of longing. A sadness. And the picture of a face comes into my mind. A woman with a quick smile. And beads. She is padding around in bare feet.

A voice seems to call. Like a call from way down a long drainpipe. 'Simon, Simon,' it says.

The picture in my mind grows stronger. The lovely lady is fat. Much fatter than normal.

'Simon,' she calls in her far-off voice. 'Simon, the baby is coming.'

I look at Possum in panic. 'The baby is coming,' I say. 'The baby is coming. And the phone has been cut off.'

The mattress in the corner is starting to fade. Will I go or will I stay? I know that there is only one chance.

I can choose. Stay in the dream with Possum. Or go back.

But then which is the dream? Maybe the other world with Mum and the baby is a dream. And this is the real one. Possum is real, I know that. Possum is my mate. He starts to scratch at the little birthmark that is like a map of Australia. His eyes grow round. He realises that something scary is happening but he doesn't know what. 'Don't go,' he says. 'Don't leave me, mate.'

'Simon,' calls the far-off voice. 'Oh, Simon, quick. The baby is coming.'

I can't choose. I don't know what to do. The mattress is fading fast. It will not be coming back – I know that for sure. Already the voice has sunk to a whisper. Like someone calling from a boat that is drifting out into a sea of fog.

One word fills my mind. 'Mum.' Suddenly I run over to the mattress and jump onto it. It is warm. And real. I see Possum and the chocolate biscuits start to fade.

'Don't …' says Possum. He never finishes. Like a tear falling into the sea he drops away and is gone.

6

And I am there in the other world. The first thing I see is the plate from last night. With a few cold chips and dried tomato sauce. The room is small and I am on a mattress in the lounge because we only have one bedroom.

Possum is gone for ever. I chose this world and let his one die. A terrible sadness sweeps over me. I feel like a murderer.

But there is no time for this.

The baby is coming.

Mum collapses onto my mattress with a groan. Her nightdress is all wet. 'I'll run down to the phone box,' I shout.

'Too late,' says Mum. 'My water has broken. It's coming.'

Aw, shoot. Aw, gees. It's coming and I am the only one here. What will I do?

I try to remember what they do on TV when babies are coming. 'Push,' I say. I am not sure what she is supposed to push but that is what they always seem to say.

'I am pushing,' groans Mum. She is lying on her back with her knees pointing up to the ceiling.

Then I see something that I have never expected to see. Never in a million years. The top of the baby's head. It is coming out. It is covered in blood and slime and has wet hair stuck down. Oh, oh, what am I going to do?

Suddenly there is a slurping noise. More of the baby is coming out. Mum is groaning. 'Push,' I say.

With a sudden rush the baby is born. It is followed out by wet bloody stuff. The baby has a long cord stuck onto its stomach. Mum has tears in her eyes. What will I do?

I lift up the baby and put it on her panting chest. Straight away it starts to cry. It is alive. It is covered in blood and gunk. But it is alive and screaming. Oh, it is terrible. Oh, it is wonderful.

'Get scissors,' says Mum panting. 'And a clothes peg.'

I rush off and quickly come back with the peg and the scissors. 'Cut the cord,' says Mum. I cut the cord about ten centimetres away from the baby's belly button. Then I clip it off with the peg.

Mum smiles. There is a terrible mess everywhere. 'I'll go for help,' I say.

'No,' says Mum with her big grin. 'In a minute. This is our special moment. Everything is all right. I have done this before, remember.'

'I haven't,' I say.

'Maybe not,' says Mum. 'But you were there the last time too. Now go and get a warm towel and we will clean down the baby.'

Well, everything turns out just right. I am a hero. My picture is in the paper. And on television. At school I have to give talks about how babies are born. All the kids want to be my friend. I am famous.

When they pick teams for football I am always the first one they choose. Even though I am not very good at it.

Life is wonderful. I have friends everywhere.

But now and then I feel sad. Especially when I am down by the river. I think of a mate who tied a rope to the tree so that we could escape from the bullies. A mate who loved chocolate biscuits.

I can see his face when he said, 'Don't go.' I know that I could have stayed and kept his world alive. But I didn't and my heart is heavy.

There is only one way to cheer myself up when this happens. I remember how I delivered the baby. I remember how I wiped him down with the warm towel. And I remember what Mum said as she watched me cleaning him.

'Look at the little possum,' she laughed. 'He's got a birthmark on his arm. It looks like a tiny map of Australia.'

Birdman

Li Foo walked into the water pushing the little raft in front of him. He wiped a tear from his eye and sadly tied a vase to the mast. Then he pushed the raft out to sea and walked back towards the rocky shore. The raft drifted slowly out into the vast Indian Ocean. Li Foo knew that he would never see it again.

1

Sean flapped his wings nervously. It was a long way down to the beach. Everything was set. The feathers were glued on really well. The wooden struts were strong. But would he fly? 'Go on,' said Spider. 'There's only one way to find out.' Deefa barked loudly and ran around their legs, waiting for the fun.

'It's all right for you,' said Sean. 'You're not going in the competition.' Suddenly he ran towards the edge of the sand dune and jumped. He plunged into mid-air and flapped his arms furiously. Panic filled his face. He flapped harder. 'No,' he yelled. 'No.' He plunged down, rolled over in the sand and lay still.

Spider ran down to meet him. 'Are you okay?' he shouted. Sean lifted up a sandy face and nodded. He undid his wings and left them on the sand.

'It'll never work,' said Spider. 'You'll never win the Birdman Competition like that. You can't jump off the end of a pier in those.'

'It doesn't matter,' said Sean. 'I'm going to pick up Uncle Jeremy's hang-glider this afternoon. A real one. You watch me fly over the waves when I get that. This year Buggins isn't going to win for once.'

The two boys walked along the edge of the water. Neither of them noticed the raft at first.

Sean suddenly did six cartwheels along the beach. 'Beat that,' he said.

'That's nothing,' said Spider. 'Watch this.' He tried to stand on his hands but he collapsed onto his face. He stood up and spat out sand. 'That one didn't count,' he grinned. He tried again and the same thing happened. His whole face was covered in sand. It didn't matter how often he tried, Spider just couldn't do cartwheels. Not to save his life.

'Weak,' said a loud voice.

They both looked up. It was Buggins. Big fat Buggins sitting up there on Devil, his big fat horse. He walked Devil past Sean and Spider and then backed up into them. The horse's legs stumbled and spat up sand. Sean and Spider fell back into the waves.

Buggins stared down at them with a smug smile. Then he nodded towards Sean's wings on the beach. 'You'll never win with those,' he scoffed. 'You just watch me tomorrow. I'll take the trophy off again for sure.'

He kicked his horse and galloped along the beach. 'Oh, look,' yelled Sean. 'The dirty ratbag.'

Buggins galloped straight towards Sean's wings. Devil's hoofs pounded into the feathers and plastic. The wings were smashed to pieces.

Sean and Spider stared in dismay. The wings were completely ruined. And to make matters worse, there on top of them was a pile of steaming horse manure. Dropped there by Devil.

Deefa loved horse manure. He barked twice and shoved his face right in it. He pushed his nose into the putrid pile. He rubbed his ears in too. It was a dog's heaven.

Buggins stopped a little way off. He felt safe sitting up there on Devil.

'You wait,' yelled Sean. 'You just wait.' It was a weak thing to say and he knew it. He was so angry that he just couldn't think of anything else.

Buggins laughed horribly and galloped away along the beach. With a weary heart Sean watched him disappear.

'Don't worry,' said Spider. 'You've still got your uncle's hang-glider. These wings didn't work anyway.'

Suddenly Sean saw something. 'Look,' he screamed. 'Over there.' He pointed to where the edge of a little raft poked out of the sand.

2

Spider started to scratch away at the sand with his hands. Sean ran over and helped. 'Wow,' said Spider. 'I wonder where this came from.' The raft had been washed in by the tide. After a bit of tugging and digging they finally pulled it out. They stared at the strange vase tied to the mast.

'There could be anything in there,' said Spider. 'Open it up, Sean.'

Sean brushed at the sand on the vase. There was weird writing on the outside. And a skull and crossbones.

They looked at each other and shrugged. Neither wanted to be the one to open the vase. In the end Sean grabbed the lid and pulled. It came off with a pop. A whiff of grey smoke puffed out. Spider moved back up the beach to safety. Sean looked at his mate. Spider was a good kid but he could be a bit of a wimp at times.

Sean carefully untied the vase and tipped it up. An animal slipped out. A stiff, hard animal like a cat.

They stared at the rigid body. Its eyes were closed. Its fur was matted and wiry. Its legs hung down like open arms.

'Wow,' Sean whistled. 'I've never seen anything like that before.' He turned it upside down. It was hollow in the middle.

'It's a hat,' said Spider. 'A cat hat. Give me a go.' He snatched the cat hat from Sean's arms.

'Don't wreck it,' said Sean. 'It could be valuable.'

Spider put the cat hat on his head. The legs reached down under his chin. It looked as if the cat was hanging onto his face. It seemed weird, perched up there on Spider's hair.

'Give me a shot,' said Sean. Spider shook his head. He was very attached to the hat.

Sean smiled to himself. 'Okay,' he said. 'Suit yourself.' He walked towards the wings and pretended he wasn't interested in the cat hat. He did another five cartwheels – right past Spider.

THE CAT HAT'S EYES CLICKED OPEN.

IT SAW A BOY TURNING

CARTWHEELS ON THE SAND.

THE EYES CLICKED CLOSED AGAIN.

Spider, who was still wearing the cat hat, stared at Sean with a funny sort of look on his face. Then he did five perfect cartwheels on the sand. They were terrific.

'Wow,' Sean yelled. 'Good one, Spider. Fantastic.' Sean really was impressed. Spider could do fantastic cartwheels. And just a minute before, he couldn't even stand on his hands.

Spider looked pretty surprised himself. He shook his head wisely. 'You can learn a lot from me, Sean,' he said. He brushed down the cat hat.

'Maybe it brings good luck,' said Sean.

'Yeah,' said Spider. 'Like a lucky rabbit's foot.'

They walked up the track towards home. On the edge of the cliff a fat man was standing looking out to sea.

He suddenly opened his mouth and burped loudly.

THE CAT HAT'S EYES CLICKED OPEN.

IT SAW A MAN BURPING.

THE EYES CLICKED CLOSED AGAIN.

Spider suddenly felt ill. As if he had eaten about fifty meat pies for breakfast. He tried to swallow but couldn't. He tried to hold everything down. But it was no use. Spider opened his mouth and let out an enormous burp.

'Beauty,' yelled Sean. 'What a ripper.' He was filled with admiration. Spider was pleased with himself. Usually he couldn't do very good burps at all.

3

That afternoon Spider and Sean went down to the railway station to pick up Uncle Jeremy's hang-glider. Spider still had the cat hat perched on his head.

The bloke in the railway station pretended that the boys weren't there, like railway workers often do. 'Excuse me,' Sean said. 'We've come for a hang-glider.' The bloke didn't take any notice. He just went on reading a magazine. Sean tapped on the window-sill with a coin. The porter looked up savagely.

'Can't you see I'm busy,' he growled in a deep voice. 'Wait your turn.' Sean and Spider looked around. There wasn't another person in sight.

After ages and ages the porter came to the window. 'Where's your receipt?' he asked.

'I lost it,' Sean said. 'But the hang-glider's addressed to Sean Tuttle.'

This is when Sean heard the terrible words. 'It's not here. Sean Tuttle picked it up this morning. He was with two other kids.'

'What,' Sean yelled. 'Which kids?'

'I don't know. Just kids.'

'Buggins,' Sean shouted.

'And Thistle and Wolf,' added Spider. 'They've nicked it.'

'You're responsible,' Sean said to the porter. 'The railways have to get it back. Buggins didn't have a receipt.'

The porter glared at them. 'And neither do you,' he said. 'You kids buzz off and don't tell me how to do my job.' He was starting to get angry.

THE CAT HAT'S EYES CLICKED OPEN.

IT SAW A PORTER TALKING.

THE EYES CLICKED CLOSED AGAIN.

Spider spoke in a deep, man's voice. He sounded exactly like the porter. A great big booming voice, coming out of a boy's mouth. 'You kids buzz off,' he said. 'And don't tell me how to do my job.'

'Right,' yelled the porter. Man, was he mad. He headed for the door. Spider and Sean turned and ran for it.

'You shouldn't have done that, Spider,' Sean said when they finally stopped running.

'It was this hat,' Spider said. 'It made me do it. And its

eyes open. I'm sure I heard its eyes click that time I burped.' He took the cat hat off his head. 'Here, you have it.'

4

When they reached home, Sean's father was looking a bit sheepish. 'Is she talking to you yet?' asked Sean. His father shook his head.

Sean smiled to himself. Poor Dad. He was in big trouble. He had agreed to let Sean fly in the Birdman Competition without telling Mum and she was mad at him. She thought it was too dangerous. Dad tried to kid her and joke about it but she wouldn't even crack a smile.

'Buggins has pinched the hang-glider,' said Sean.

Mr Tuttle didn't hear him. He was peering anxiously out of the window. His wife was heading for the door. He held a finger up to his lips. 'Shh ...' he said. 'Not a word about it in front of your mother.' He suddenly saw the cat hat. 'What on earth is that?'

'A cat hat,' Sean told him. 'It brings good luck if you put it on your head.'

Mr Tuttle took the cat hat and put it on his own head. 'I can do with a bit of good luck today,' he said with a grin. 'This might cheer Mum up a bit.'

Just then a number of things happened.

The door opened and Mum walked in. She said exactly the same thing. 'What on earth is that?'

Mr Tuttle sure did look stupid with a dead cat perched on his head.

Sean's mum wasn't alone. Deefa had come in after her. A very hungry Deefa. He gave two woofs and trotted over to the food bowl which was still on the floor. It was full of that horrible canned food that dogs love. A sort of wobbling mound of brown jelly. Deefa trotted over and started to gobble away noisily.

THE CAT HAT'S EYES CLICKED OPEN.

IT SAW A DOG EATING A PLATE OF DOG FOOD.

THE EYES CLICKED CLOSED AGAIN.

A strange look came into Mr Tuttle's eyes. He dropped down onto his hands and knees. 'Woof, woof,' he said. He trotted over to the food bowl and started gobbling at the dog food with Deefa. They licked their lips and swallowed the stuff down like crazy.

The kids' eyes nearly popped out of their heads. So did Sean's mum's. No one could believe what they were seeing. Mr Tuttle was eating yucky, cold dog food. From the same bowl as the dog. Deefa growled. Mr Tuttle barked back. They were fighting over the dog food.

Mr Tuttle suddenly stood up with a wild look in his eyes. He didn't know what was going on. He was confused. And his face was smeared with gravy and bits of horrible meat stuff. 'Ruth,' he gasped, 'I didn't mean to do that. It wasn't what ...' His voice trailed off. He didn't know what to say. Then he grinned.

Mrs Tuttle was trying hard not to smile but she just

couldn't stop herself. 'What's for dessert?' she said with a chuckle. The row was over. They were talking again.

Still and all, Sean thought it was better not to mention the stolen hang-glider. He and Spider were on their own.

Sean looked at the hat. He suddenly had an idea but he pushed it out of his mind. His glider was gone. Buggins and his mates had stolen it. Life just wasn't fair sometimes.

5

'We'll have to use our own plane like all the other kids,' Sean said to Spider. They were walking along the cliff, looking for Buggins.

'What about the cat hat?' said Spider. 'It copies things. It opens its eyes and copies what it sees. I know it does.'

'It's dangerous,' Sean told him. 'You never know what it's going to stare at. Look what happened to Dad.'

'We could figure something out,' said Spider. If you wore the cat and it opened its eyes and saw something...' His voice was drowned out by a roar. They both looked up as a jumbo jet streaked across the sky.

Before he could think any more about it, Sean saw what he had been looking for. It was Buggins and his mates.

Buggins took a short run along the top of a sand dune and launched out into the air. He clung on to a wonderful red and blue hang-glider. Sean's hang-glider. Buggins swooped about three metres above the sand

and then did a wobbly landing on the beach.

Wolf and Thistle pelted down after him. 'Fantastic,' yelled Thistle.

'We're onto a winner,' said Wolf.

'My winner,' Sean said in a tough voice. 'You stole my hang-glider.'

Buggins looked up. 'Get real,' he sneered. 'I've been saving up for this for months. Ask my dad if you like.'

'Hand it over,' Sean said.

Buggins bunched up his fist. 'Come and get it,' he jeered. He walked towards Sean with heavy steps. His two mates were next to him.

'We're not scared of you,' yelled Spider. 'Flatten him, Sean.'

Buggins took another couple of steps forward. There was only one thing to do. So Sean did it. He turned and ran for his life. Spider pelted after him. How humiliating. Sean could hear Wolf, Thistle and Buggins jeering as he ran.

Sean spent the rest of the day trying to mend his bird wings. He used brand new materials. Plastic, wood and wire as well as the feathers. After a couple of hours he put down his tools. He didn't think he could finish in time. There was only one more day left and it was a school day.

'That'll never fly,' said Spider. 'The ones the kids make always crash. We need something else. A bit of help.' He held up the cat hat and winked.

6

'No way,' said Sean. 'Not without testing it first anyway.'

Spider looked at the broken wings. 'But they're busted,' he said.

Sean nodded. 'So, we'll try it out on something else.'

The next day Sean took the cat hat to school.

His plan was to muck around down near the oval while the athletes were practising for the school sports.

There was this kid named Innes who was in Year Twelve. He was a champion high jumper. Sean decided to hang around near him with the hat on. The cat hat would open its eyes and see Innes. Sean would immediately do a wonderful high jump in front of all the kids.

Of course Sean didn't know whether or not the silly thing would open its eyes. That was the only weakness with the plan.

As it happened, the cat hat did open its eyes.

Just as a group of girls jogged up in their tracksuits. At that very moment Innes was running up for a jump. Sean slipped the cat hat over his head. He had to be quick. The jump would be over in a flash. Sean quite liked the idea of doing a great leap in front of the girls.

But they didn't even look at him once. They headed into the girls' changing room.

THE CAT HAT'S EYES CLICKED OPEN.

IT SAW GIRLS GOING INTO THE CHANGING ROOM.

THE EYES CLICKED CLOSED AGAIN.

Sean tried to stop his legs going. He hung onto the fence. But it was no good. Some inner force made him go. Made him follow the girls into their changing room. It was as if he was in a trance. He jogged straight in after them.

The next thing Sean knew – there he was. Surrounded by girls – in their changing room. He opened his mouth to cry out in horror but nothing came out. The girls screamed and yelled. They threw shoes. 'Nerd. Weirdo,' screamed a girl called Esmeralda. Talk about terrible.

Spider just shook his head and grinned while the screaming mob of girls chased Sean clear out of the school.

Buggins and Thistle and Wolf saw the whole thing. They thought it was a great joke.

It was the worst moment of Sean's life. He walked home with a heart full of pain. Talk about embarrassing. Before long everyone in the school would know about it. That cat hat was not to be trusted.

7

All that he could do now was fix up his birdman wings so that they would fly. Sean worked nearly all night. He glued and cut and nailed. Until finally the wings were finished. He didn't even have time to try them out. The competition started first thing in the morning. He would just have to jump off the end of the pier and hope for the best.

'You'll never beat Buggins,' said Spider as they walked towards the pier. 'He's got a proper hang-glider.'

'My hang-glider,' Sean said.

'Use the cat hat,' said Spider. 'We wait until a plane goes over, the cat hat opens its eyes and we're off. Up, up and away.'

'What do you mean, *we're* off. It's me that will be off. Not you. No way. That cat hat is not to be trusted. It stays in my bag out of harm's way.'

And that's how Sean came to be standing there on the end of the pier with his bird wings. With all the others. There were kids everywhere. About two hundred looking on and a mob of competitors.

The planes were fantastic. There were biplanes and triplanes. There were rockets and rickety old things built on top of prams. Mostly they were made out of plastic and wood and paper. Some were like parachutes. Others like helicopters.

None of them had engines. The planes had to glide or be powered by human energy. You could pedal. You could flap. And you could jump. But no other form of power was allowed.

The winner was the one who could get furthest away from the pier.

'Okay, okay, okay, fans,' yelled Wolf. He shouted at everyone through a megaphone. 'The first entry in this year's Birdman Competition is ... me.'

A cheer went up. Wolf's plane was in the shape of

a giant beer can. His legs stuck out at the bottom. His arms poked out of the side like skinny wings. His head was like a marble on the top. Everyone, including Wolf, knew what was going to happen when he jumped off the end of the pier.

'This model,' he yelled, 'runs on brain power and force of will. It's shaped to have minimum wind resistance.' He waddled over to the side of the pier. And jumped.

It was a very high pier. Wolf flew through the air with the greatest of ease. Like a brick. Straight down. He hit the water with an enormous 'thunk'. The beer can broke up and Wolf swam to the ladder on the side of the pier. Everyone cheered and laughed. Kids patted him on the back. If ever there was a showman it was Wolf.

Next it was the turn of a kid called Egan. He had a slide rigged up on the end of the pier. He sat up on the top inside a huge Batplane. Wolf called for silence. The crowd knew that Egan had a good chance of winning. He was a serious competitor. Wolf climbed up the slide. 'What are the specifications of this aircraft?' he asked.

Egan sat in the cockpit dressed in a black wetsuit. He wore black goggles to match his plane. 'It has a five-metre wing span,' he said. 'The construction is canvas stretched on a wooden frame. At the bottom of the ramp it reaches a speed of fifteen knots – enough to carry me forty metres from the edge of the pier.'

The crowd clapped. Everyone was impressed.

Egan's helpers pushed him off. The Batplane gathered speed. It raced down the slide and launched into the air. It swooped upwards for a second or two. Then it hung in the air and plunged down into the sea. The Bat-pilot swam sadly back to the cheers and claps of a disappointed crowd.

8

'The next competitor,' shouted Wolf, 'is Thistle.' There were cheers, and some boos.

Thistle had a huge triplane made out of clear plastic. The three layers of wings were so wide that everyone had to be moved back. The wings hung over both sides of the pier. Thistle's legs stuck out through the bottom of the fuselage.

Thistle held his arms up in a boxer's victory wave. Then he ran towards the water and hurtled over the edge of the pier.

The wings of the plane broke off in mid-air and Thistle torpedoed down into the water. The wings fluttered down after him.

This is how it went on for ages and ages. Plane after plane plunged over the edge. None of them got very far at all. So far, the Batplane had flown furthest from the pier.

Sean's stomach felt all wobbly inside. 'At least if I win the competition it will make up for me going into the girls' changing room,' he thought to himself. But his heart sank. He knew he couldn't win. He felt terrible. Deefa yapped and ran around his feet.

The competition was almost over. There were only two entries left.

'And now,' announced Wolf, 'we have an entry from that dashing young man – Jack Buggins.' Buggins gave the crowd a mock bow. Then he looked at the girls and smiled. Sean's heart sank when he saw a lot of them smiling back.

Buggins pushed through the crowd and came out holding his hang-glider above his head. Or more correctly, Sean's hang-glider. There was a gasp from the mob. It was a beautiful craft. There was no doubt at all about who was going to win.

Buggins ran to the edge of the pier and launched himself off. A gentle breeze took the hang-glider and lifted it into the air. Buggins sailed and swooped above the water. He circled around and even let go with one hand and waved to the crowd.

Then he sailed out to sea and made a graceful landing about fifty metres away. The crowd went crazy. Buggins had won by a mile. No one had ever gone that far before.

Buggins swam back to the pier with the glider. Everyone patted him on the back. He gave a victory wave and leered at Sean.

'Ladies and gentlemen,' said Wolf. 'There is one more contestant – if you can call him that. The feathered freak, Sean Tuttle.'

Sean was ready. And he felt ridiculous with the two feathered wings strapped onto his arms. He flapped them up and down feebly. Everyone laughed. The whole lot of them. Sean looked like a plucked chook.

In the distance and high above, a crop-dusting plane circled the coast. 'Put this on,' whispered Spider urgently. He reached into a bag and pulled out the cat hat.

Sean shook his head. Spider nodded towards the plane. 'This is your only chance,' he said.

Sean stared at the girls who were hanging around Buggins, looking at the hang-glider in admiration. 'What the heck,' he said to himself. 'It's worth the risk.' He put the cat hat on his head and tottered over to the edge of the pier.

'Tuttle is wearing a new form of life jacket,' said Wolf. 'When he crashes his dead cat swims back with him.' Everyone laughed. Except Sean and Spider.

The crop-dusting plane approached the pier. 'Now,' said Spider. The plane flew into a bank of clouds and disappeared.

THE CAT HAT'S EYES CLICKED OPEN.

IT SAW NOTHING BUT EMPTY SKY.

THE EYES CLICKED CLOSED AGAIN.

Nothing happened. Sean still stood there shivering on the end of the pier. Dressed in his foolish, feathered wings. With the cat hat perched up on his head. The noise of the plane disappeared into the distance.

'Well, come on,' said Wolf. 'Get going.'

'He's scared,' sneered Buggins.

'What a chicken,' said Thistle.

'It opened its eyes,' said Spider. 'But too late. The plane's gone.'

'I'm done for,' said Sean. He looked down into the water. It was a long way. His legs were knocking. He couldn't bring himself to jump. 'Ten seconds,' yelled Wolf. 'Jump or you're disqualified.'

9

Sean took a deep breath and stared along the pier. A seagull sat on a post.

THE CAT HAT'S EYES CLICKED OPEN.

IT SAW A SEAGULL FLAP ITS WINGS FURIOUSLY

AND FLY UP INTO THE SKY.

THE EYES CLICKED CLOSED AGAIN.

Sean's wings started to whir. They flapped so fast that he couldn't see them. He thought his arms were going to fall off. Up he went, buzzing like a fantastic dragonfly.

The water fell far below. At first Sean's head swam. The kids looked like ants on the pier. Birds fluttered around. What if he fell?

But then, for some reason, he knew he was safe. He felt like a bird. He was flying as if he had been born with wings. He looped the loop. He plunged down and skimmed the waves and then soared up again above the crowd. He flew sideways and upside down. He twirled and twisted. He flapped like a feathery fiend.

Everyone gasped. Their mouths fell open. Their eyes bugged out. A sigh swept the pier. Sean plunged down and buzzed just above their heads like a dive-bomber. The kids threw themselves down as he hurtled overhead.

It was wonderful. It was weird. Sean had no control over what happened. He just did everything the gull did.

'Yahoo,' yelled Spider. 'Go, Sean, go.' He was so excited that he nearly fell off the pier.

Finally Sean and the bird settled on the waves. Sean let the wings sink and swam back to the waiting crowd.

10

You should have heard the cheering. And shouting. No one had ever seen anything like it before. One of the girls gave him a little peck on the cheek.

Buggins was as mad as a snake. He pushed to the front.

'Tuttle cheated,' he yelled. 'That cat thing did it. It was a powered flight.'

Buggins pulled the cat hat off Sean's head. And put it on his own. 'It's alive,' he said. 'It opened its eyes. I saw it.' Buggins looked kind of pathetic with the cat hat perched on his skull.

He peered along the pier to where Devil was tied up. He saw Sean's dog trotting along towards the horse.

THE CAT HAT'S EYES CLICKED OPEN.

IT SAW A DOG RUNNING TOWARDS THE HORSE.

IT SAW HIM PUSHING HIS HEAD INTO A

PILE OF HORSE MANURE.

THE EYES CLICKED CLOSED AGAIN.

Buggins felt his legs starting to carry him along the pier. 'No,' he screamed. 'No, no, no.'

But nothing ...

could stop him ...

rushing towards the manure.

About the author

The Paul Jennings phenomenon began with the publication of *Unreal!* in 1985. Since then over 7.5 million books have been sold to readers all over the world.

Paul has written over one hundred stories and has been voted 'favourite author' by children in Australia over forty times, winning every children's choice award. The top rating TV series *Round the Twist* and *Driven Crazy* are based on a selection of his enormously popular short-story collections such as *Unseen!*, which was awarded the 1999 Queensland Premier's Literary Award for Best Children's Book.

In 1995, Paul was made a Member of the Order of Australia for services to children's literature, and in 2001 he was awarded the prestigious Dromkeen Medal.

His most recent titles include *Paul Jennings' Trickiest Stories*, his *Rascal* storybooks for early readers and his full-length novels, *How Hedley Hopkins Did a Dare . . .* (shortlisted for the Children's Book Council of Australia Book of the Year Award: Younger Readers) and *The Nest*.

This collection of twenty-six stories has been hand-picked by Paul from the *UnCollected* series and contains some of his weirdest and most wonderful tales.

This collection of twenty-five hilarious stories has been hand-picked by Paul from the *UnCollected* series and is sure to have readers laughing out loud.

This special edition anthology boasts twenty of Paul's spookiest fun-filled yarns, hand picked by the author for a spine-tingling reading experience.

ALSO FROM PAUL JENNINGS

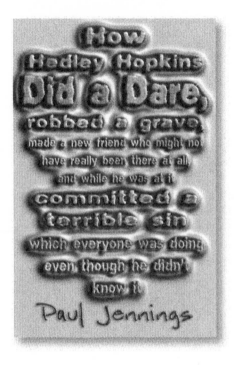

They say there is something awful in the sand dunes . . .

Hedley Hopkins has a few problems; he is the new kid at school, straight off the boat from England. The only friends he has made are the kids at the Loony Bin, especially bald-headed, long-armed Victor. But if he could just fulfil a dare and dig out the hideous skull hidden in the grave in the sand dunes, he could impress the bullies at school and become their friend.

Readers of all ages will love this coming-of-age tale by Paul Jennings at his very best!